Legends f

THRE

豫
漢
荊

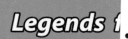

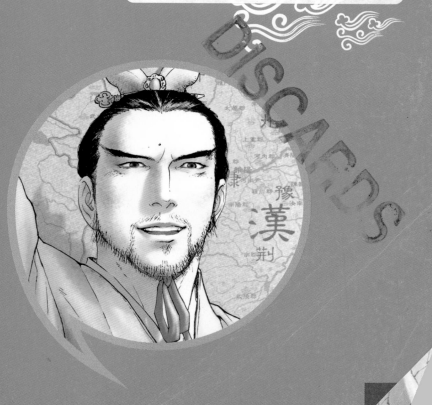

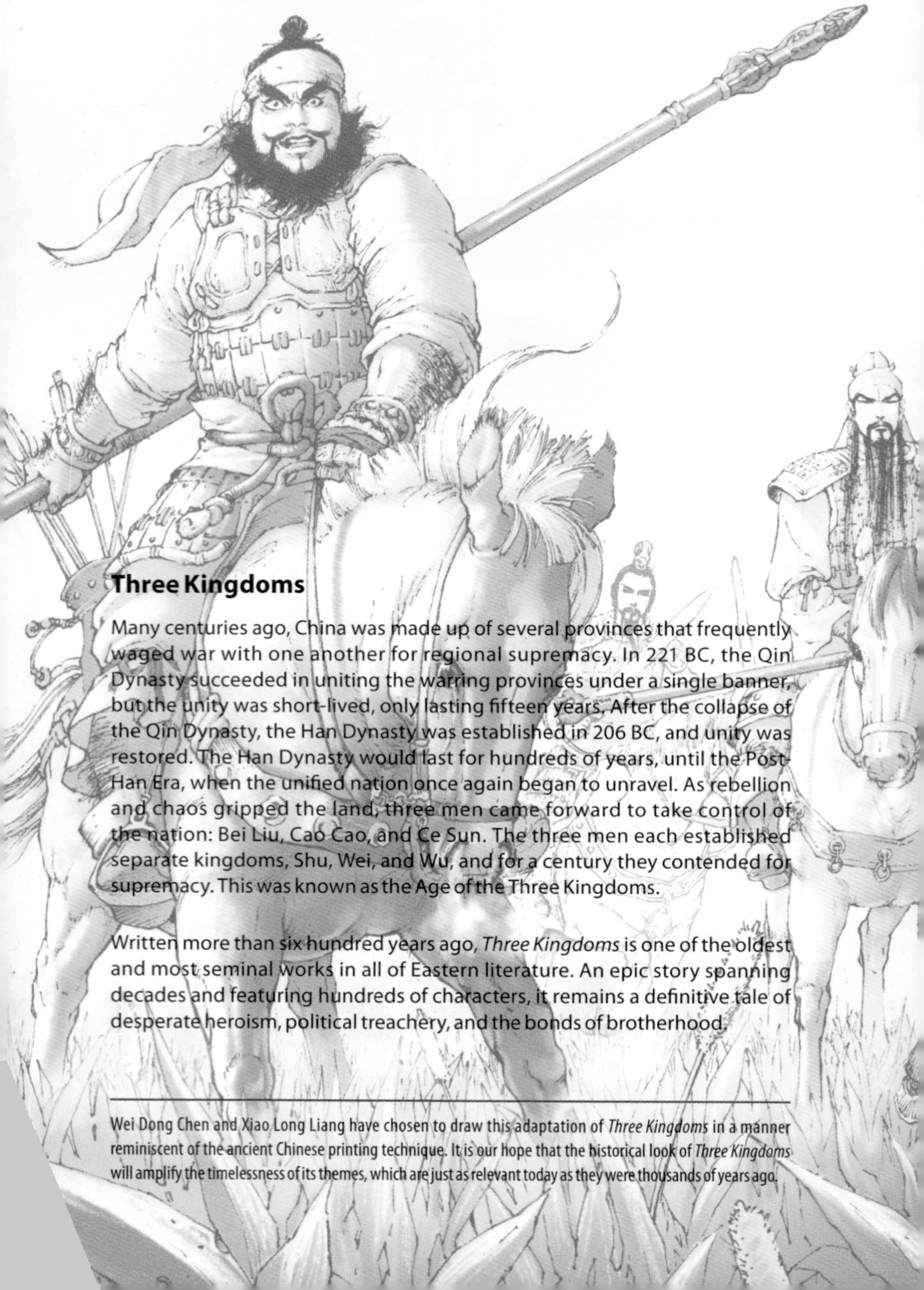

Three Kingdoms

Many centuries ago, China was made up of several provinces that frequently waged war with one another for regional supremacy. In 221 BC, the Qin Dynasty succeeded in uniting the warring provinces under a single banner, but the unity was short-lived, only lasting fifteen years. After the collapse of the Qin Dynasty, the Han Dynasty was established in 206 BC, and unity was restored. The Han Dynasty would last for hundreds of years, until the Post-Han Era, when the unified nation once again began to unravel. As rebellion and chaos gripped the land, three men came forward to take control of the nation: Bei Liu, Cao Cao, and Ce Sun. The three men each established separate kingdoms, Shu, Wei, and Wu, and for a century they contended for supremacy. This was known as the Age of the Three Kingdoms.

Written more than six hundred years ago, *Three Kingdoms* is one of the oldest and most seminal works in all of Eastern literature. An epic story spanning decades and featuring hundreds of characters, it remains a definitive tale of desperate heroism, political treachery, and the bonds of brotherhood.

Wei Dong Chen and Xiao Long Liang have chosen to draw this adaptation of *Three Kingdoms* in a manner reminiscent of the ancient Chinese printing technique. It is our hope that the historical look of *Three Kingdoms* will amplify the timelessness of its themes, which are just as relevant today as they were thousands of years ago.

THREE KINGDOMS
Vol. 03

To Pledge Allegiance

Created by WEI DONG CHEN

Wei Dong Chen, a highly acclaimed and beloved artist, and an influential leader in the "New Chinese Cartoon" trend, is the founder of Creator World in Tianjin, the largest comics studio in China. Recently the Chinese government entrusted him with the role of general manager of the Beijing Book Fair, and his reputation as a pillar of Chinese comics has brought him many students. He has published more than three hundred cartoons, which have been recognized for their strong literary value not only in Korea, but in Europe and Japan, as well. Free spirited and energetic, Wei Dong Chen's positivist philosophy is reflected in the wisdom of his work. He is published serially in numerous publications while continuing to conceive projects that explore new dimensions of the form.

Illustrated by XIAO LONG LIANG

XiaoLong Liang is considered one of Wei Dong Chen's greatest students. One of the most highly regarded cartoonists in China today, XiaoLong's fantastic technique and expression of Chinese culture have won him the acclaim of cartoon lovers throughout China. His other works include "Outlaws of the Marsh" and "A Story on the Motorbike".

Original Story
"The Romance of the Three Kingdoms" *by Luo, GuanZhong*

Editing & Designing
Design Hongs, Jonathan Evans, KH Lee, YK Kim,
HJ Lee, JS Kim, Lampin, Qing Shao, Xiao Nan Li, Ke Hu

Original Chinese edition published by Anhui Fine Arts Publishing House.

CAO CAO

Following Zhuo Dong's death, Cao Cao takes control of Yan Province and consolidates his power by enlisting the services of several accomplished military commanders and strategists. He then leads a campaign against the Yellow Scarves, emerging victorious. The remaining Yellow Scarves join his army, which swells by 300,000 men, making only Shao Yuan his equal. Cao Cao uses his new power to attack Xu Province, where his father was killed years earlier. However, Bei Liu comes to the aid of Xu and drives out Cao Cao's forces. Meanwhile, Bu Lu invades Yan Province, forcing Cao Cao's forces to pull back and fight a new threat. After underestimating Bu Lu and losing a series of battles, Cao Cao finally drives the warlord from his land, all the way to Bei Liu in Xu Province. Back in control of his territory, Cao Cao schemes to ally himself with Emperor Xian, which will couple his power with royal influence.

JIA GUO

Jia Guo is Cao Cao's most trusted advisor. It is Jia Guo who advises Cao Cao to ally himself with Emperor Xian. Because he understands the power of royal edict, Jia Guo is able to offer counsel that is both shrewd and wise.

BEI LIU AND HIS SWORN BROTHERS

Bei Liu, Yu Guan, and Fei Zhang are three men from the countryside who swore a blood oath to protect one another and the land they call home. They have been called upon many times by multiple lords and governors to assist in battles waged across the nation.

In the events of *To Pledge Allegiance*, Bei Liu and his brothers are summoned to Xu Province to help Governor Qian Tao fight off the forces of Cao Cao. By a stroke of fortune, Cao Cao is forced to withdraw his troops from Xu and return to his home province, Yan, when he learns that Bu Lu and his forces have launched an attack in his absence. Despite the fortunate timing, Bei Liu is credited with saving Xu Province, and Governor Qian Tao insists that he and his brothers assume control of the territory. Bei Liu steadfastly refuses the offer at first, but ultimately relents.

Once he assumes control of Xu Province, Bei Liu accepts a defeated Bu Lu's request to dwell in his lands, despite the objections of Yu Guan and Fei Zhang. Bei Liu's faith in Bu Lu is soon betrayed, though, when Cao Cao conspires to summon Bei Liu's forces into battle and convince Bu Lu to take over Xu Province in their absence. Of course, Bei Liu is not easily fooled, and he just may have seen what's coming...

BU LU

After killing Zhuo Dong, Bu Lu was driven out of the capital city of ChangAn by Zhuo Dong's allies, Jue Li and Si Guo. While the legendary general searches for a place to establish his rule, he learns that Cao Cao has invaded Xu. Sensing an opportunity, Bu Lu invades Cao Cao's home province of Yan. However, all does not go according to plan: despite numerous protests by his chief advisor, Gong Chen, Bu Lu refuses to launch an attack on Cao Cao's forces while they are on the defensive, allowing the enemy forces precious time to regroup and launch their own attack. The ensuing battles go mostly in Bu Lu's favor, but ultimately Cao Cao's forces prevail when Bu Lu once again refuses Gong Chen's counsel. Soon Bu Lu is driven out of Yan and again is in search of a home.

Bu Lu enters Xu Province, which has just been entrusted to Bei Liu and his two blood brothers. Despite his pledge of allegiance to Bei Liu, Bu Lu is soon persuaded by Cao Cao to take over the province while Bei Liu's forces have been called away to battle. Though Bei Liu has left Fei Zhang in charge of defending the province, Bu Lu assumes control almost without incident. He then allows Bei Liu to remain in the province, and avoids the bloodshed that would have otherwise occurred.

GONG CHEN

Gong Chen is Bu Lu's wisest advisor, a cunning and ruthless strategist who specializes in the arts of forgery and deception. Gong Chen's counsel is responsible for Bu Lu's victories in many battles, and when the proud general refuses his advisor's input, defeat is never far away.

SHAO YUAN

After Zhuo Dong's death, Shao Yuan and his advisors debate the pros and cons of forming an allegiance with the weakened, but still powerful Emperor Xian. His advisors are unable to offer a consensus, and when Shao Yuan can't commit to a course of action he loses one of his best advisors, Jia Guo, and perhaps his best chance at the throne.

QIAN TAO

Qian Tao was the ruler of Xu Province when one of his soldiers killed Cao Cao's father. Now the son seeks revenge, and the frail governor turns to Bei Liu and his sworn brothers to save both his life and the future of his province.

Chapter 1

A Son's Revenge and the Battle of Xu Province AD 193

Summary

After the death of Zhuo Dong, Emperor Xian escapes from the capital of ChangAn, and the city falls under the control of Zhuo Dong's allies Jue Li and Si Guo. A power vacuum is thus created, and Cao Cao and Shao Yuan emerge as the most powerful men aiming to inherit the throne.

While Shao Yuan and his advisors debate their next move, Cao Cao's forces do battle with the remnants of the Yellow Scarves. When he wins the battle, Cao Cao gains 300,000 troops. He then uses this enormous force to invade Xu Province, ruled by Governor Qian Tao, where years before his father was killed by one of the governor's soldiers. Qian Tao then turns to Bei Liu for help in fighting off the invading army.

Meanwhile Bu Lu launches an attack on Cao Cao's home province of Yan. When word of the attack reaches Cao Cao, he withdraws his troops and returns to fight for his homeland. Although saved by a coincidence of timing, the governor of Xu and his people credit Bei Liu with the victory, and he is asked to assume control of the province. Qian Tao soon dies and Bei Liu is installed as governor of Xu.

XiLiang
Zhuo
ChangShan
BeiHai
PuYang
C
A
B
XiaoPei
LuoYang
HuLuo
GuanDu
XiaPi
XuZhou
ChangAn
XuDu
HanZhong
NanYang
ShouChun
HeFei
XiangYang
ChengDu

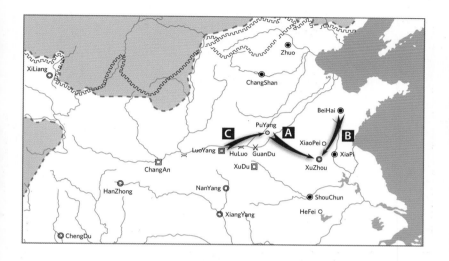

A Cao Cao's victory against the Yellow Scarves increases the size of his army, and he launches an attack against Xu Province to avenge his murdered father.

B Bei Liu comes to Xu's defense at the request of Governor Qian Tao.

C Bu Lu mounts an attack on Yan Province in Cao Cao's absence. Cao Cao receives word of the attack and withdraws his forces from Xu to return to Yan.

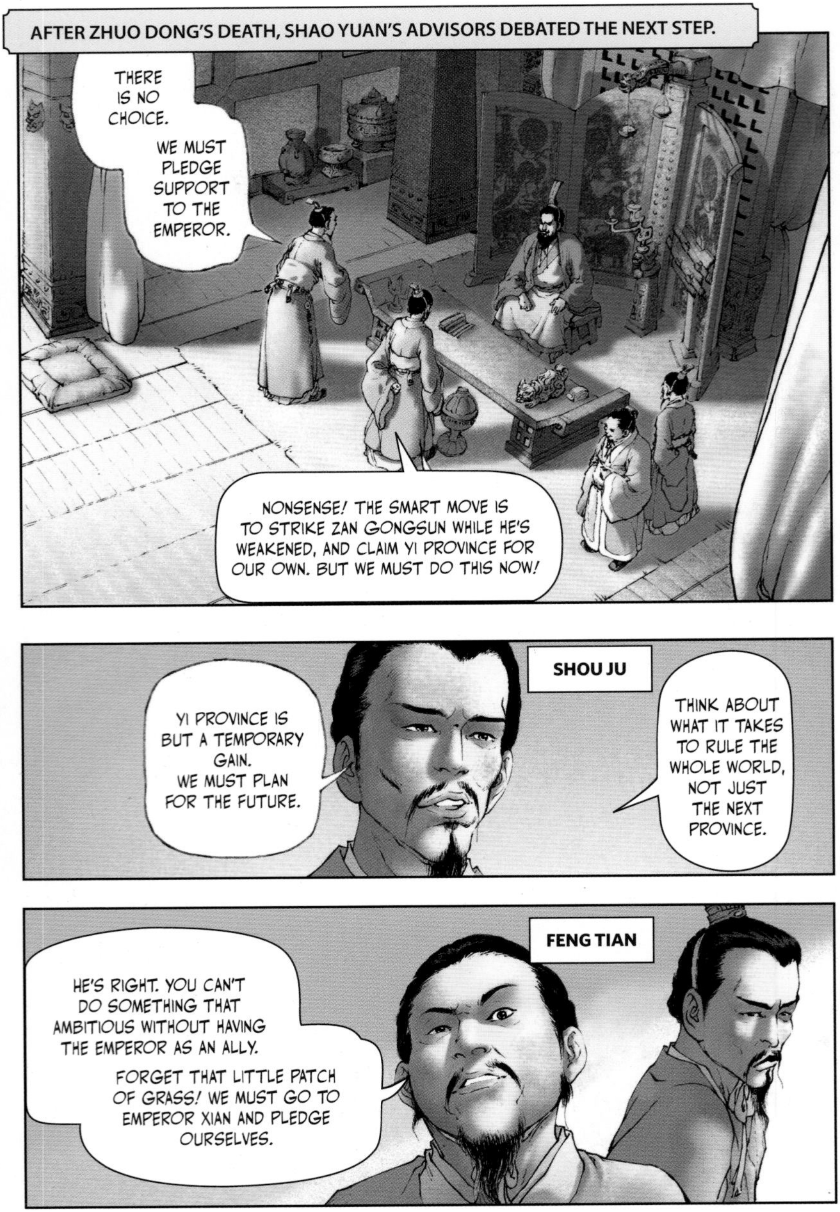
AFTER ZHUO DONG'S DEATH, SHAO YUAN'S ADVISORS DEBATED THE NEXT STEP.
THERE IS NO CHOICE.
WE MUST PLEDGE SUPPORT TO THE EMPEROR.
NONSENSE! THE SMART MOVE IS TO STRIKE ZAN GONGSUN WHILE HE'S WEAKENED, AND CLAIM YI PROVINCE FOR OUR OWN. BUT WE MUST DO THIS NOW!
SHOU JU
YI PROVINCE IS BUT A TEMPORARY GAIN.
WE MUST PLAN FOR THE FUTURE.
THINK ABOUT WHAT IT TAKES TO RULE THE WHOLE WORLD, NOT JUST THE NEXT PROVINCE.
FENG TIAN
HE'S RIGHT. YOU CAN'T DO SOMETHING THAT AMBITIOUS WITHOUT HAVING THE EMPEROR AS AN ALLY.
FORGET THAT LITTLE PATCH OF GRASS! WE MUST GO TO EMPEROR XIAN AND PLEDGE OURSELVES.

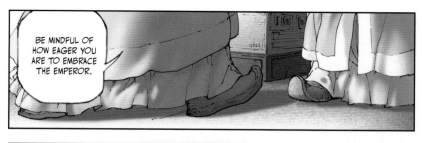

BE MINDFUL OF HOW EAGER YOU ARE TO EMBRACE THE EMPEROR.

ZHUO DONG'S UNDERLINGS MANAGED TO DRIVE OUT BU LU. WE COULD END UP WITH A KNIFE IN OUR BACK.

PEI SHEN

THAT'S TRUE. EMPEROR XIAN IS A HAPLESS PUPPET WHO IS ONLY ON THE THRONE BECAUSE ZHUO DONG PUT HIM THERE.

JI FENG

MIND YOUR TONGUE! TO SPEAK ABOUT OUR RULER THAT WAY IS AN ACT OF TREASON!

OH, WAKE UP, WILL YOU? THE DYNASTY IS OVER, HISTORY! OBSESSING ABOUT IT WILL ONLY GET YOU LEFT BEHIND.

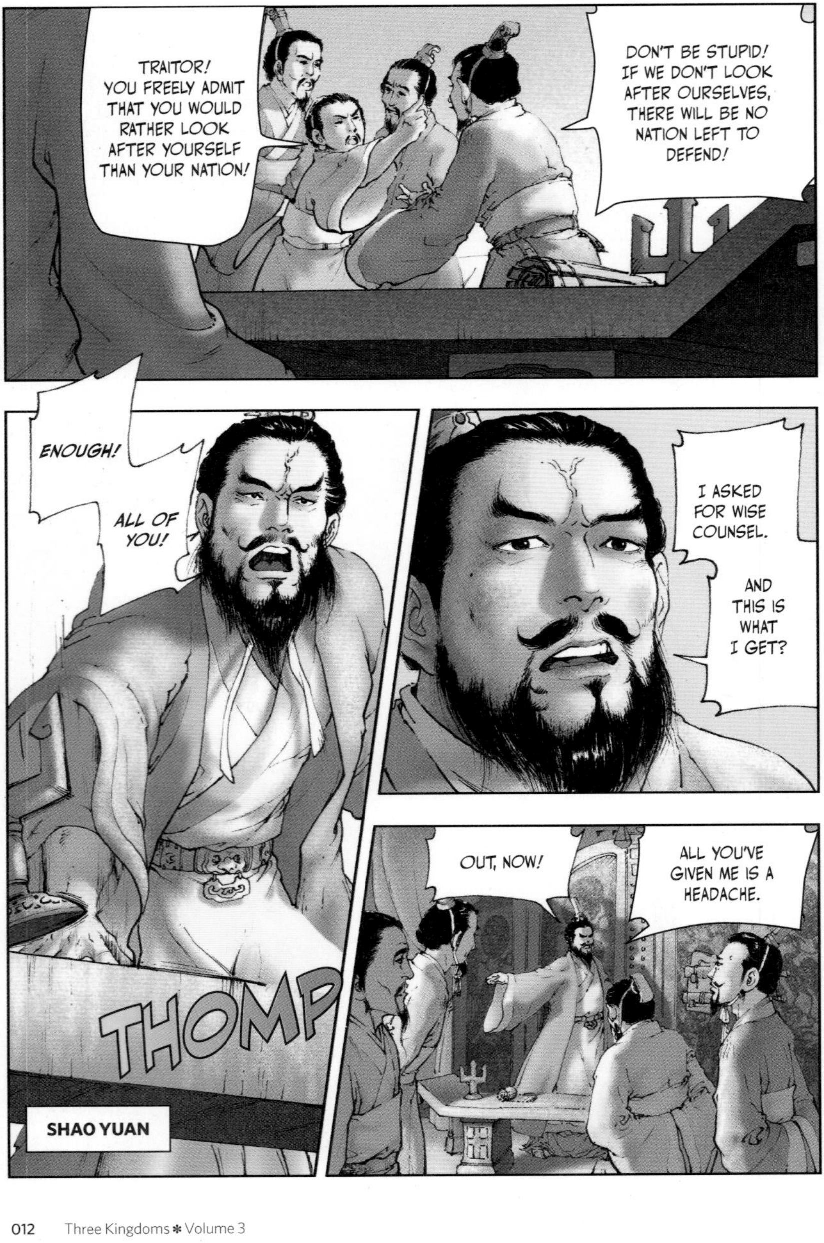
TRAITOR! YOU FREELY ADMIT THAT YOU WOULD RATHER LOOK AFTER YOURSELF THAN YOUR NATION!
DON'T BE STUPID! IF WE DON'T LOOK AFTER OURSELVES, THERE WILL BE NO NATION LEFT TO DEFEND!
ENOUGH!
ALL OF YOU!
THOMP
SHAO YUAN
I ASKED FOR WISE COUNSEL.
AND THIS IS WHAT I GET?
ALL YOU'VE GIVEN ME IS A HEADACHE.
OUT, NOW!

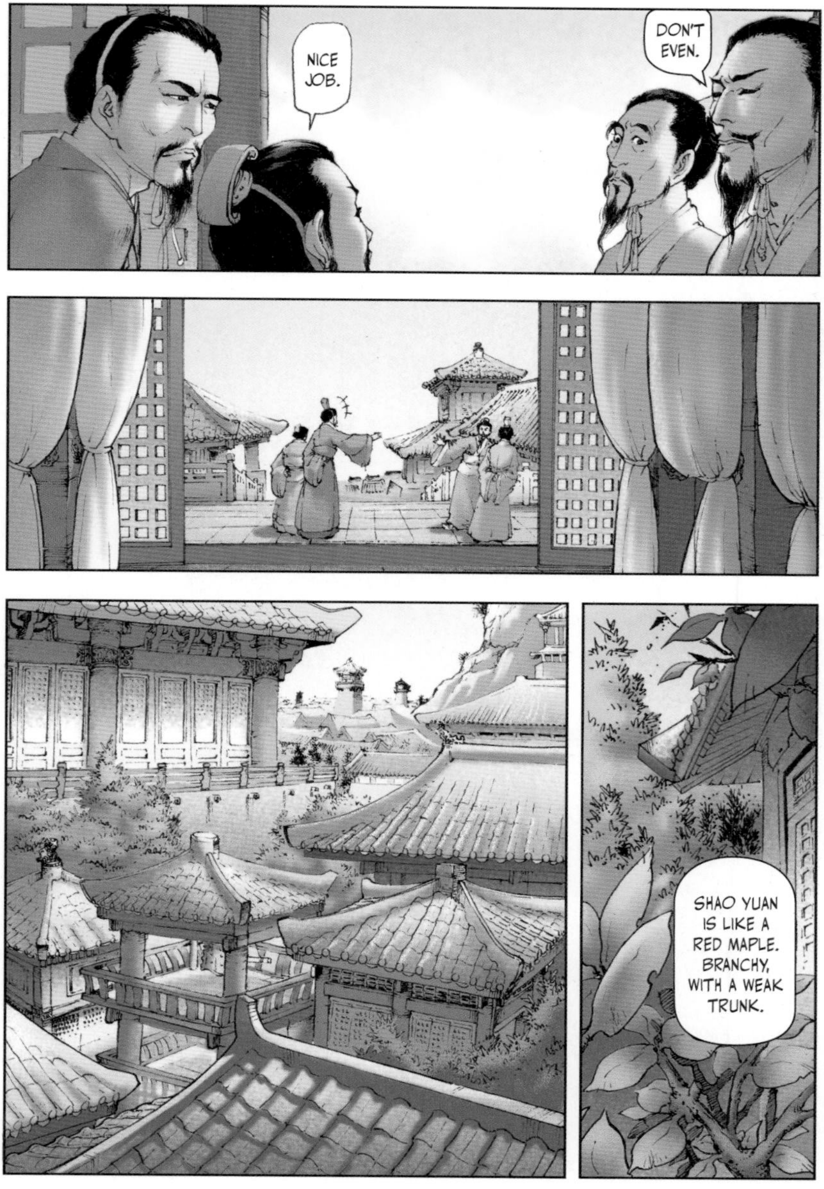
NICE JOB.
DON'T EVEN.
SHAO YUAN IS LIKE A RED MAPLE. BRANCHY, WITH A WEAK TRUNK.

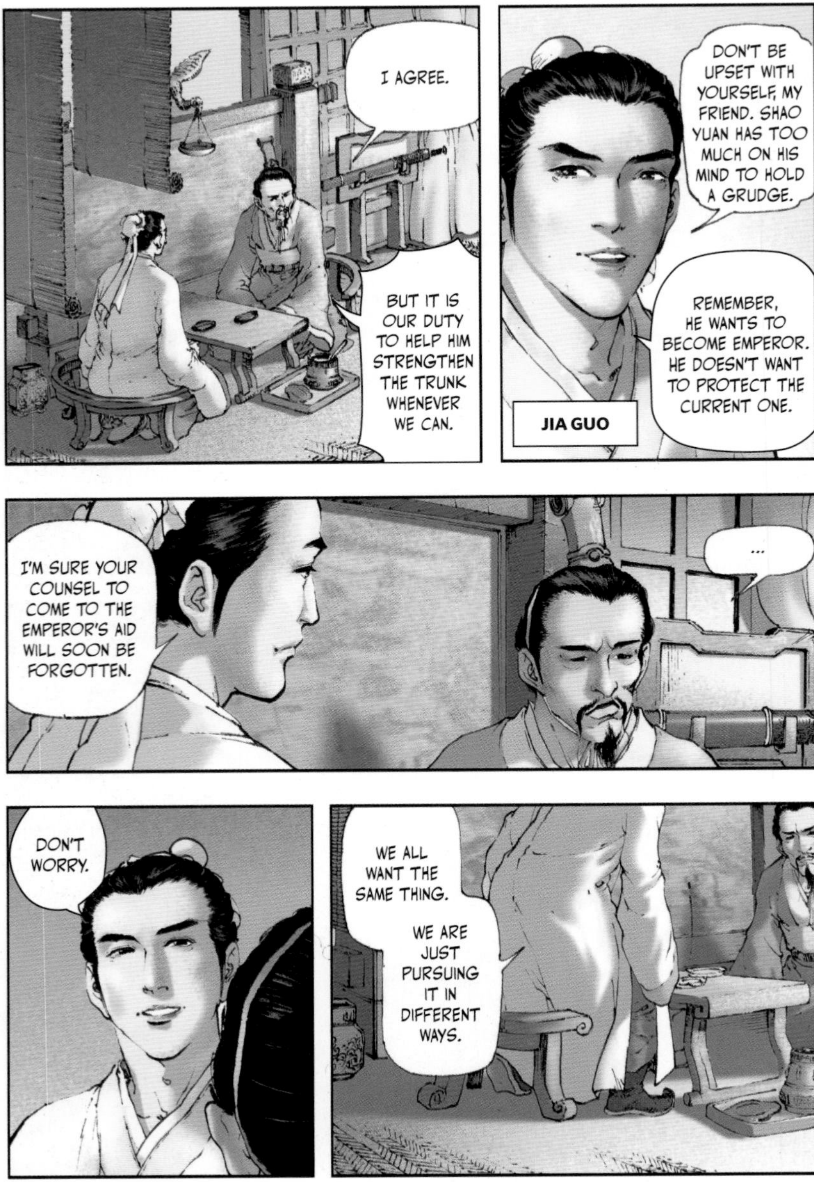
I AGREE.
BUT IT IS OUR DUTY TO HELP HIM STRENGTHEN THE TRUNK WHENEVER WE CAN.
DON'T BE UPSET WITH YOURSELF, MY FRIEND. SHAO YUAN HAS TOO MUCH ON HIS MIND TO HOLD A GRUDGE.
REMEMBER, HE WANTS TO BECOME EMPEROR. HE DOESN'T WANT TO PROTECT THE CURRENT ONE.
JIA GUO
I'M SURE YOUR COUNSEL TO COME TO THE EMPEROR'S AID WILL SOON BE FORGOTTEN.
...
DON'T WORRY.
WE ALL WANT THE SAME THING.
WE ARE JUST PURSUING IT IN DIFFERENT WAYS.

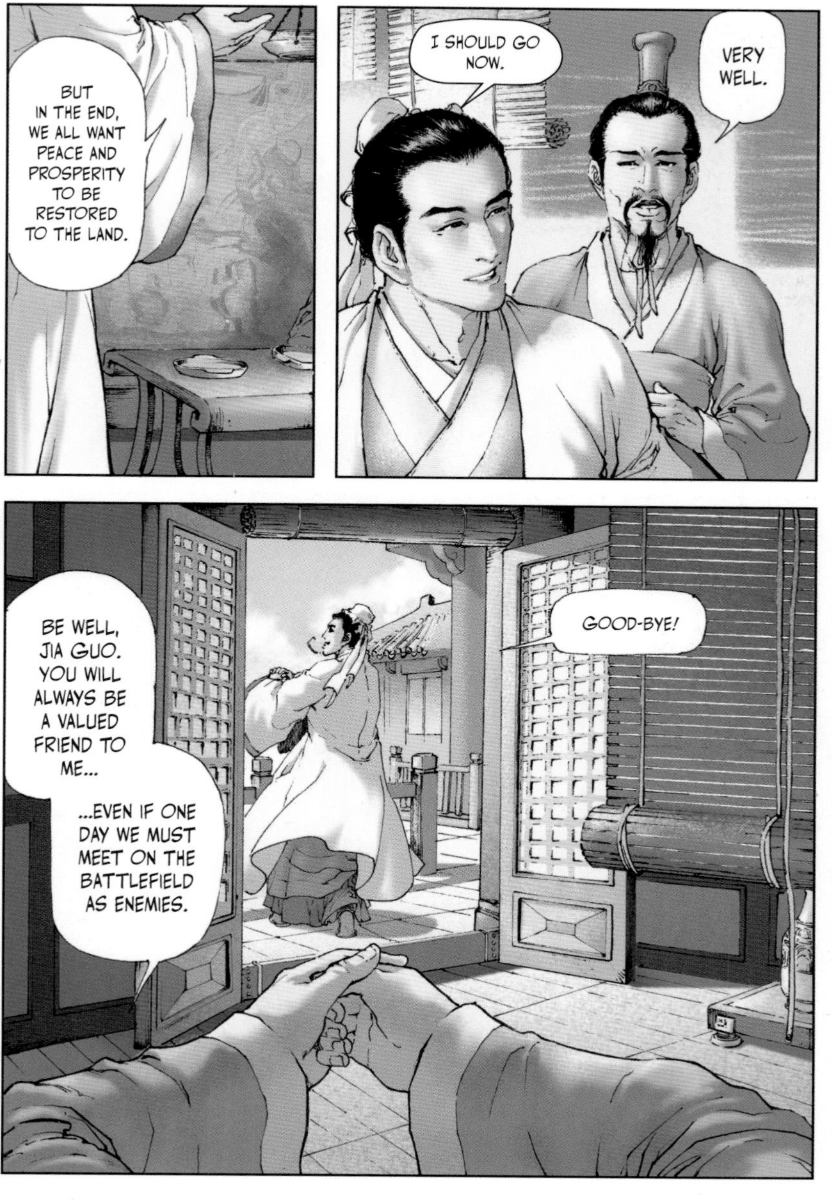
BUT IN THE END, WE ALL WANT PEACE AND PROSPERITY TO BE RESTORED TO THE LAND.
I SHOULD GO NOW.
VERY WELL.
BE WELL, JIA GUO. YOU WILL ALWAYS BE A VALUED FRIEND TO ME...
...EVEN IF ONE DAY WE MUST MEET ON THE BATTLEFIELD AS ENEMIES.
GOOD-BYE!

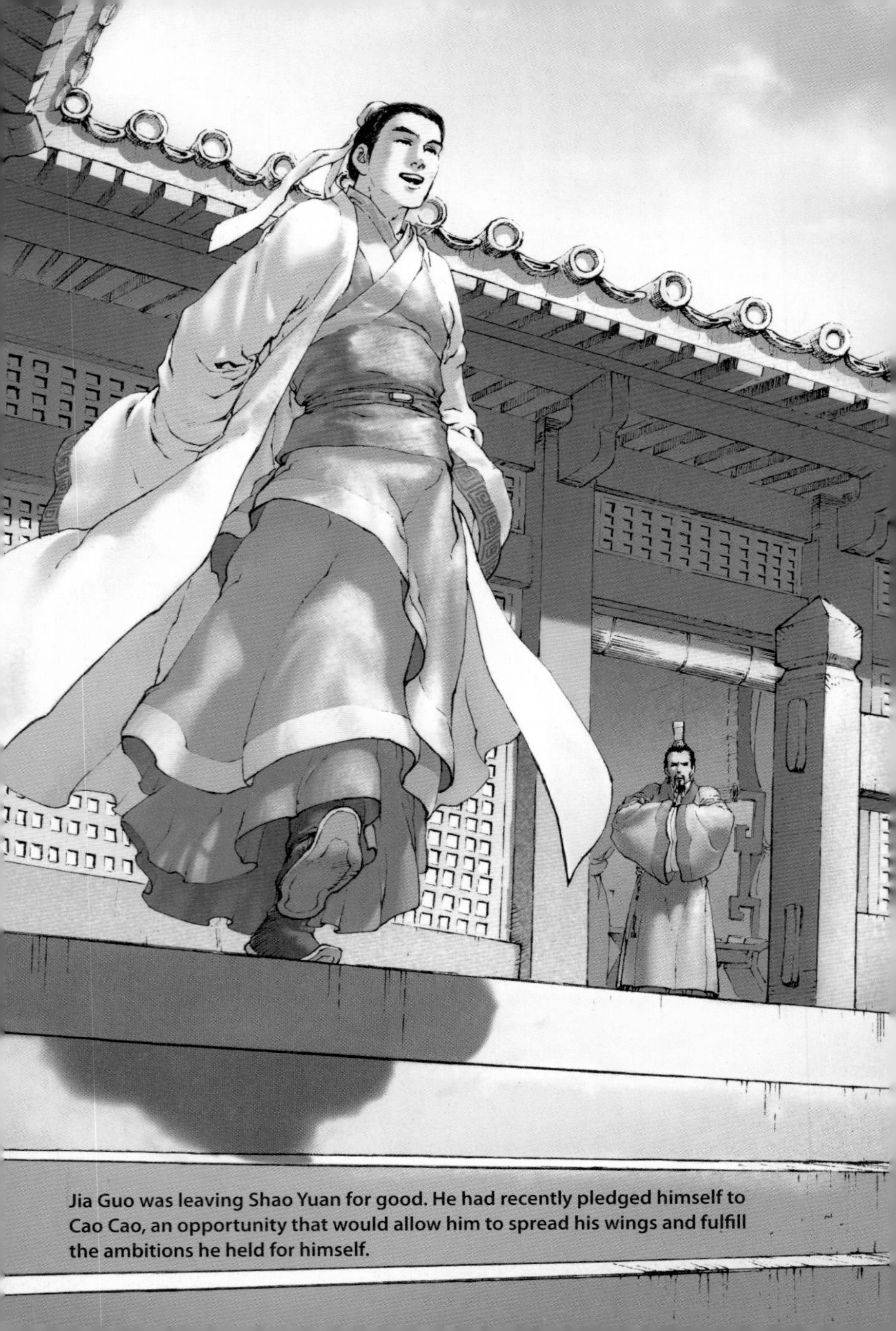
Jia Guo was leaving Shao Yuan for good. He had recently pledged himself to Cao Cao, an opportunity that would allow him to spread his wings and fulfill the ambitions he held for himself.

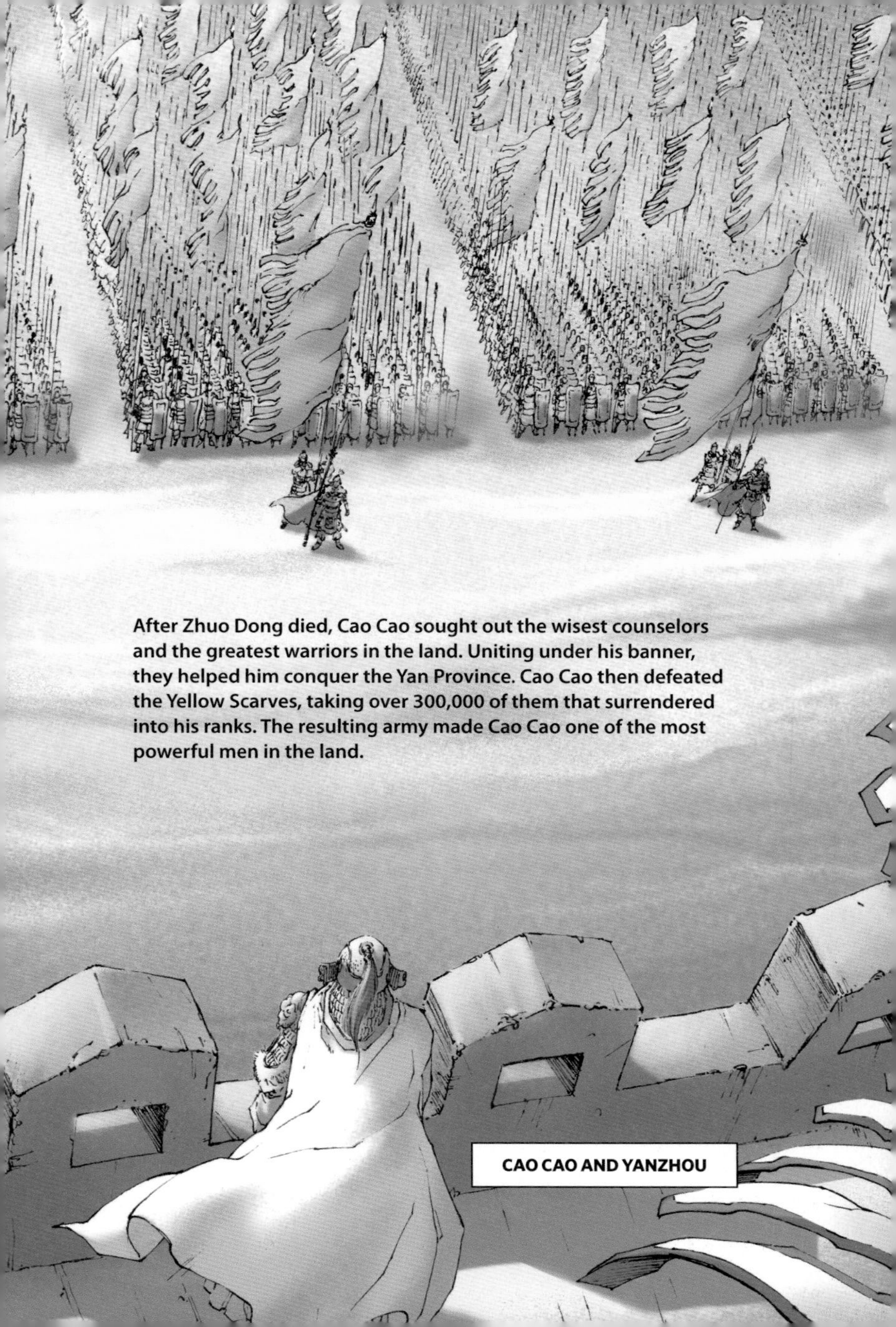
After Zhuo Dong died, Cao Cao sought out the wisest counselors and the greatest warriors in the land. Uniting under his banner, they helped him conquer the Yan Province. Cao Cao then defeated the Yellow Scarves, taking over 300,000 of them that surrendered into his ranks. The resulting army made Cao Cao one of the most powerful men in the land.
CAO CAO AND YANZHOU

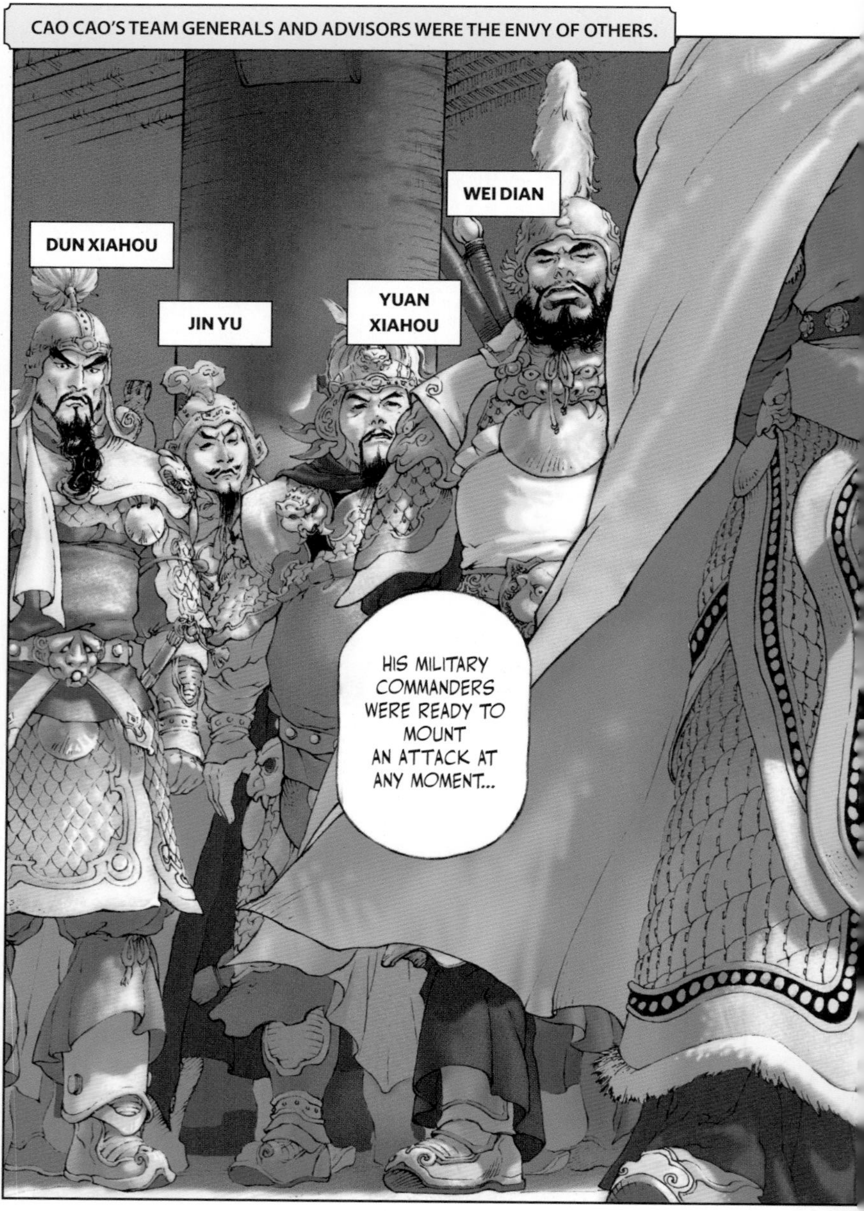
CAO CAO'S TEAM GENERALS AND ADVISORS WERE THE ENVY OF OTHERS.
DUN XIAHOU
JIN YU
YUAN XIAHOU
WEI DIAN
HIS MILITARY COMMANDERS WERE READY TO MOUNT AN ATTACK AT ANY MOMENT...

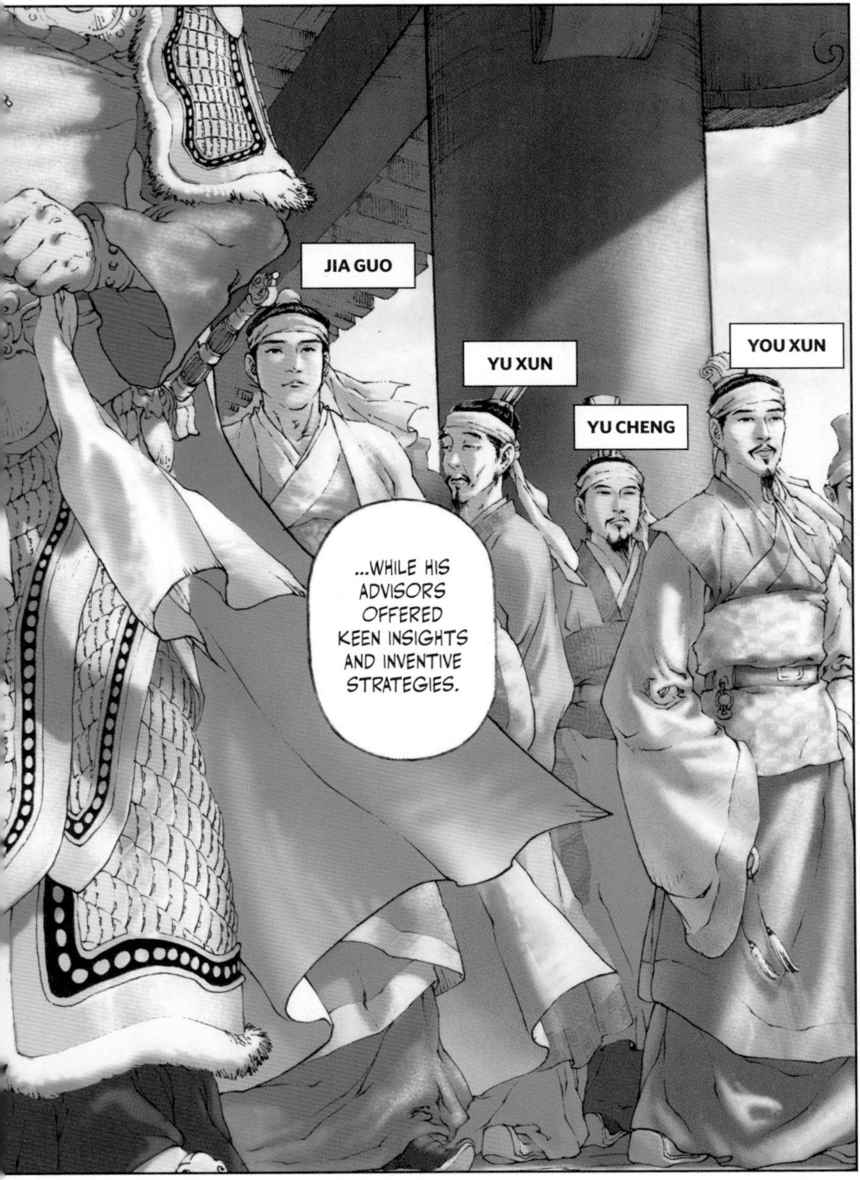
JIA GUO
YU XUN
YU CHENG
YOU XUN
...WHILE HIS ADVISORS OFFERED KEEN INSIGHTS AND INVENTIVE STRATEGIES.

GENTLEMEN, WE HAVE BUT ONE OBJECTIVE TODAY.

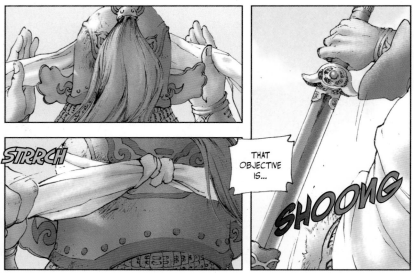

STRRCH

THAT OBJECTIVE IS...

SHOONG

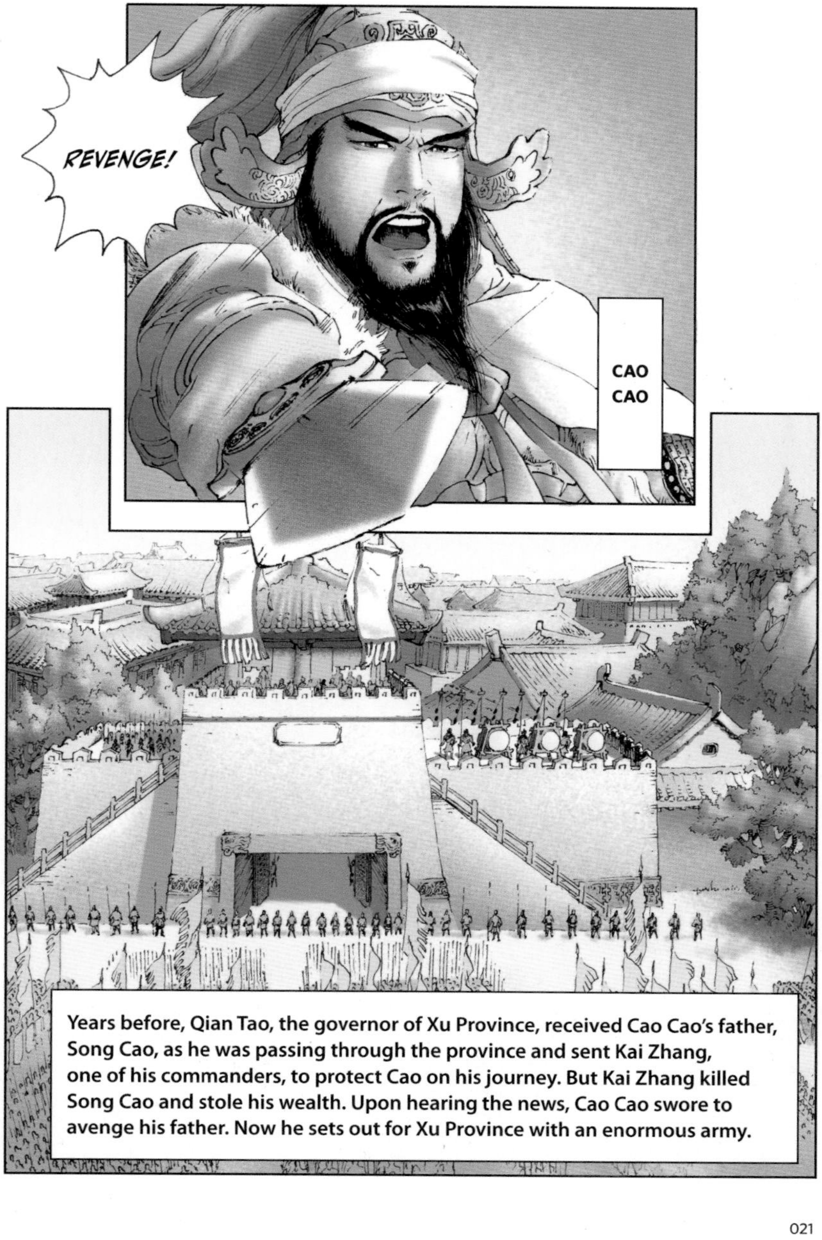
REVENGE!
CAO CAO
Years before, Qian Tao, the governor of Xu Province, received Cao Cao's father, Song Cao, as he was passing through the province and sent Kai Zhang, one of his commanders, to protect Cao on his journey. But Kai Zhang killed Song Cao and stole his wealth. Upon hearing the news, Cao Cao swore to avenge his father. Now he sets out for Xu Province with an enormous army.

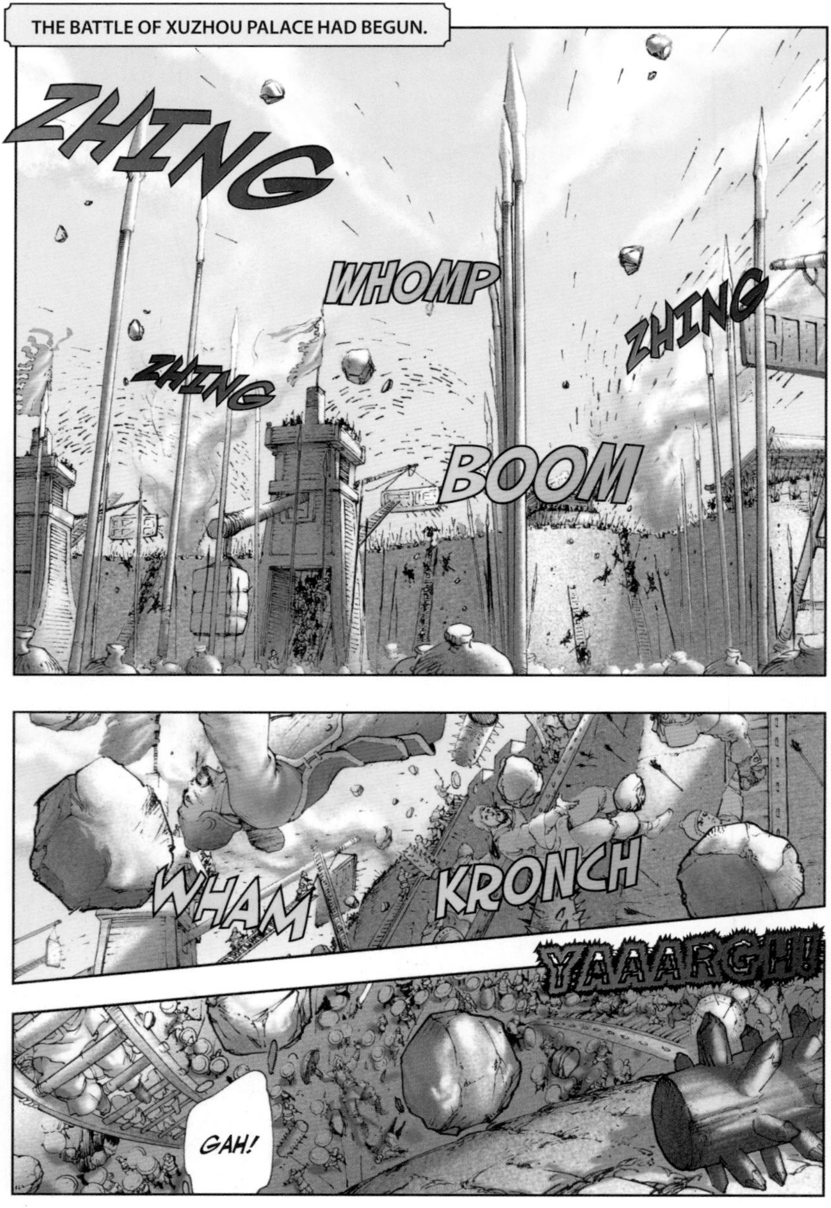
THE BATTLE OF XUZHOU PALACE HAD BEGUN.
ZHING
WHOMP
ZHING
ZHING
BOOM
WHAM
KRONCH
YAAARGH!
GAH!

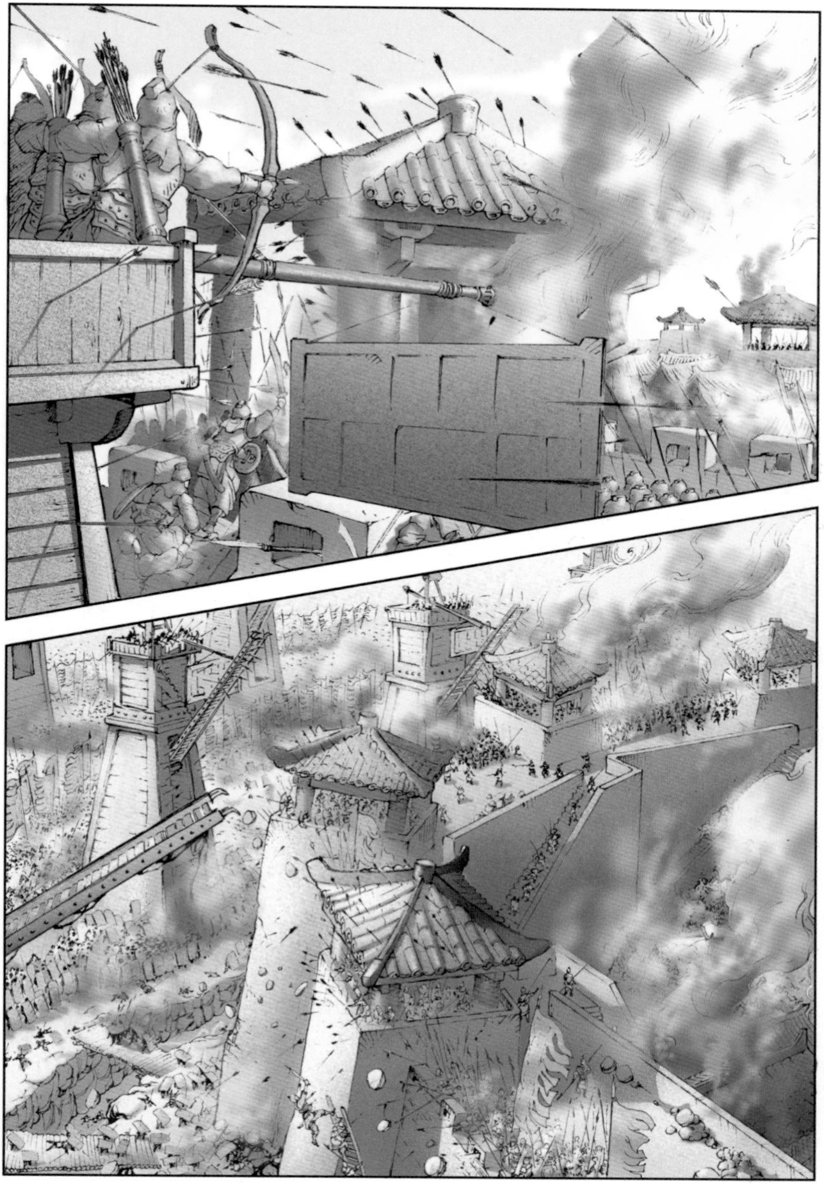

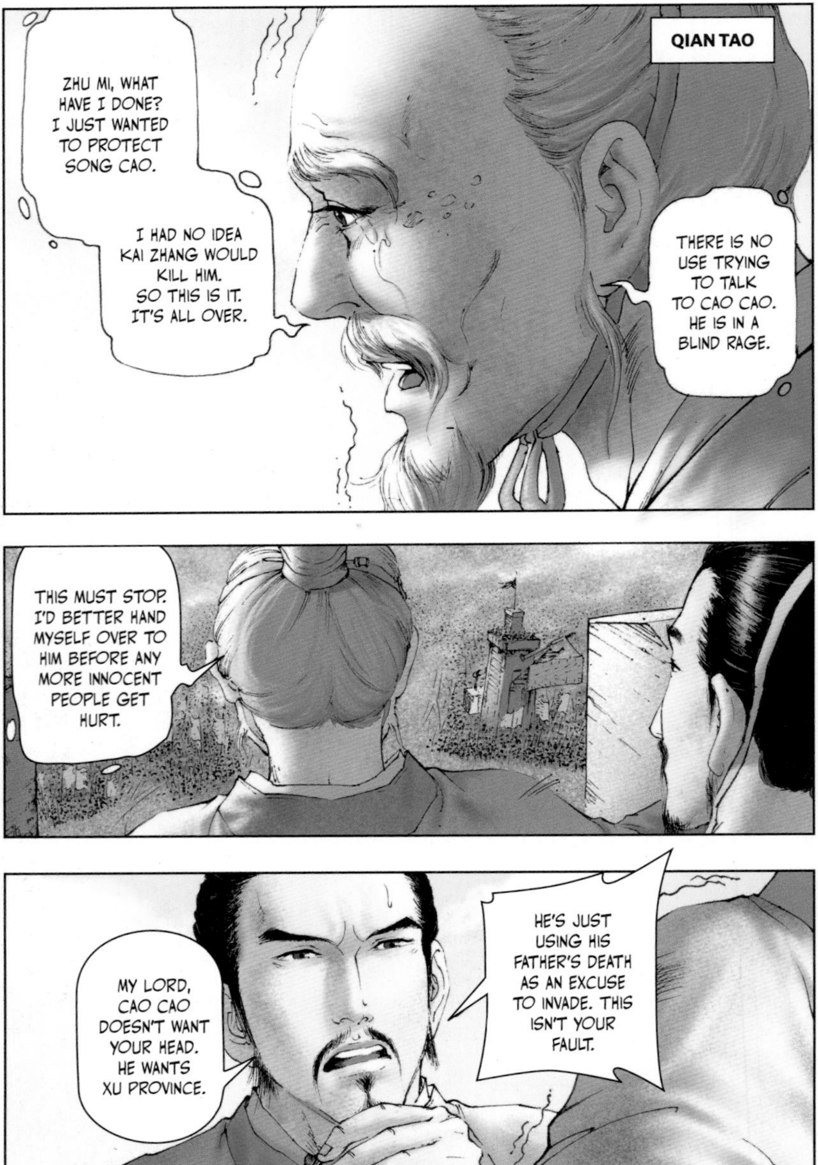
QIAN TAO
ZHU MI, WHAT HAVE I DONE? I JUST WANTED TO PROTECT SONG CAO.
I HAD NO IDEA KAI ZHANG WOULD KILL HIM. SO THIS IS IT. IT'S ALL OVER.
THERE IS NO USE TRYING TO TALK TO CAO CAO. HE IS IN A BLIND RAGE.
THIS MUST STOP. I'D BETTER HAND MYSELF OVER TO HIM BEFORE ANY MORE INNOCENT PEOPLE GET HURT.
HE'S JUST USING HIS FATHER'S DEATH AS AN EXCUSE TO INVADE. THIS ISN'T YOUR FAULT.
MY LORD, CAO CAO DOESN'T WANT YOUR HEAD. HE WANTS XU PROVINCE.

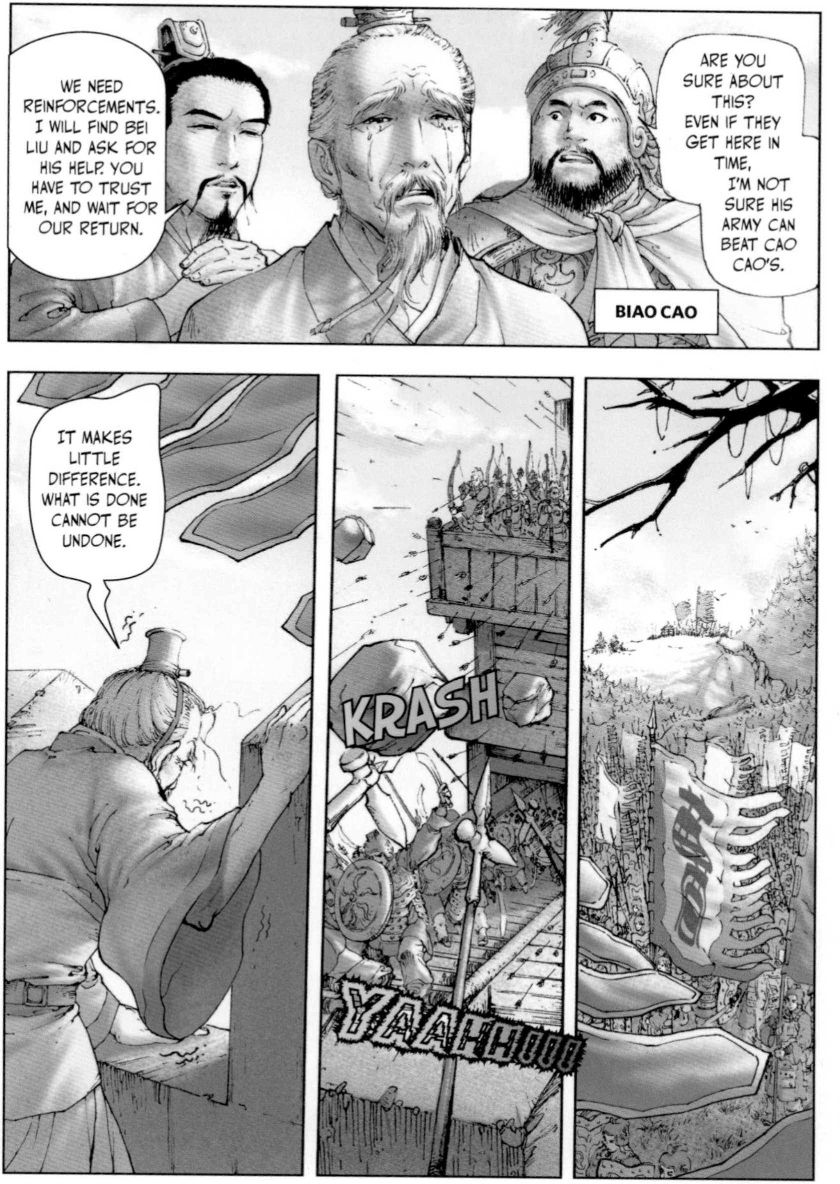
WE NEED REINFORCEMENTS. I WILL FIND BEI LIU AND ASK FOR HIS HELP. YOU HAVE TO TRUST ME, AND WAIT FOR OUR RETURN.
ARE YOU SURE ABOUT THIS? EVEN IF THEY GET HERE IN TIME, I'M NOT SURE HIS ARMY CAN BEAT CAO CAO'S.
BIAO CAO
IT MAKES LITTLE DIFFERENCE. WHAT IS DONE CANNOT BE UNDONE.
KRASH
YAAHH!!!!

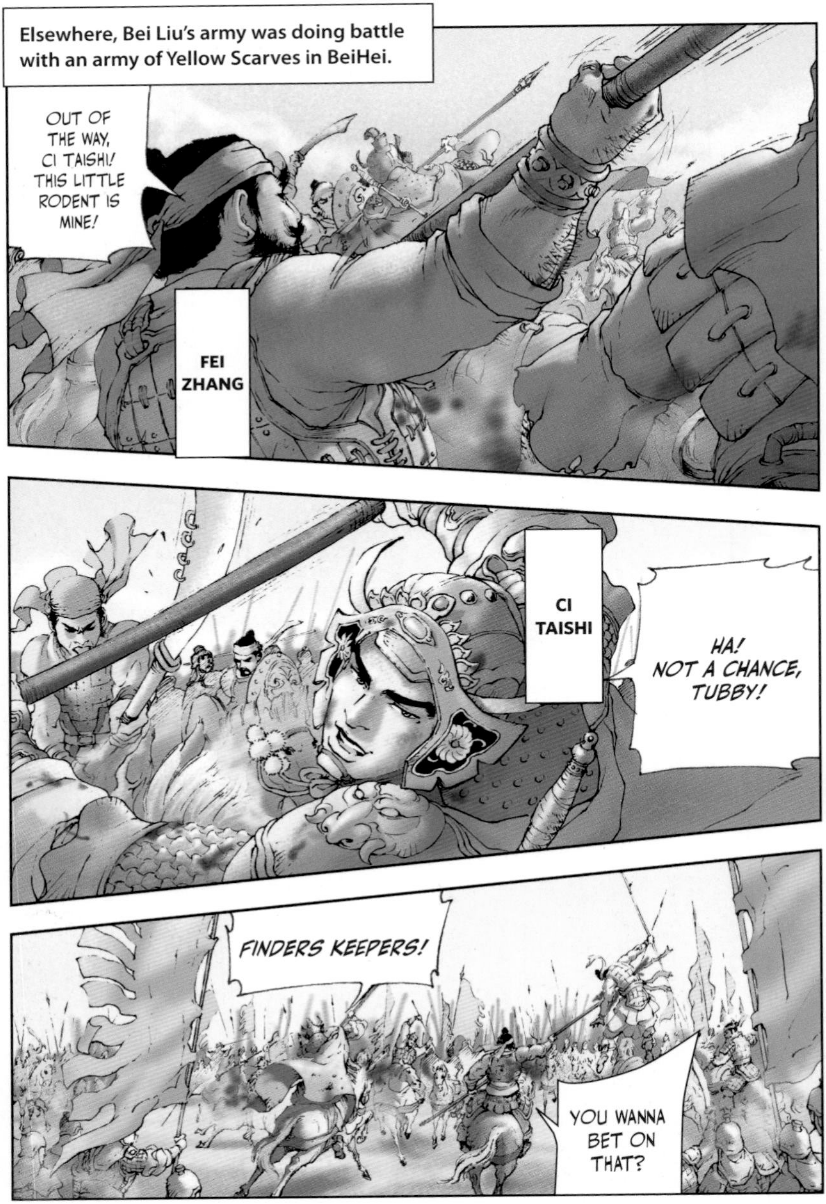
Elsewhere, Bei Liu's army was doing battle with an army of Yellow Scarves in BeiHei.
OUT OF THE WAY, CI TAISHI! THIS LITTLE RODENT IS MINE!
FEI ZHANG
CI TAISHI
HA! NOT A CHANCE, TUBBY!
FINDERS KEEPERS!
YOU WANNA BET ON THAT?

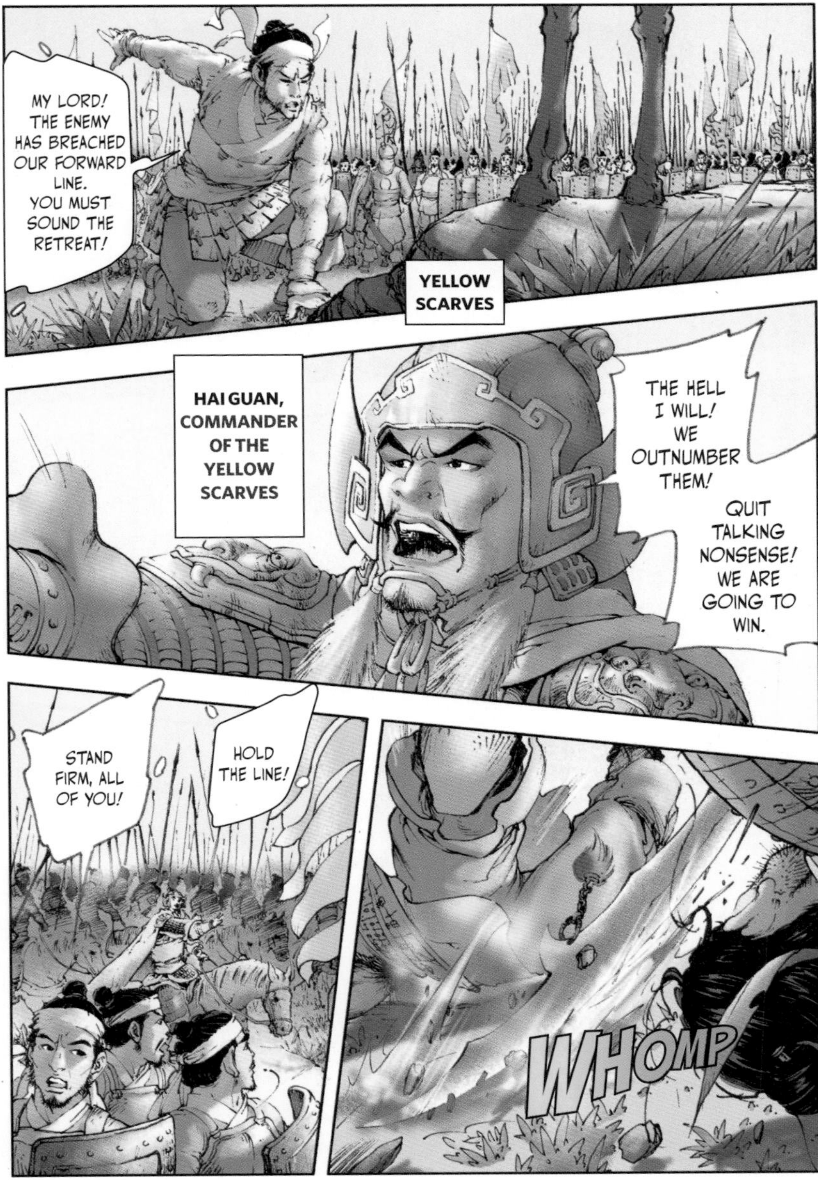

MY LORD! THE ENEMY HAS BREACHED OUR FORWARD LINE. YOU MUST SOUND THE RETREAT!
YELLOW SCARVES
HAI GUAN, COMMANDER OF THE YELLOW SCARVES
THE HELL I WILL! WE OUTNUMBER THEM!
QUIT TALKING NONSENSE! WE ARE GOING TO WIN.
STAND FIRM, ALL OF YOU!
HOLD THE LINE!
WHOMP

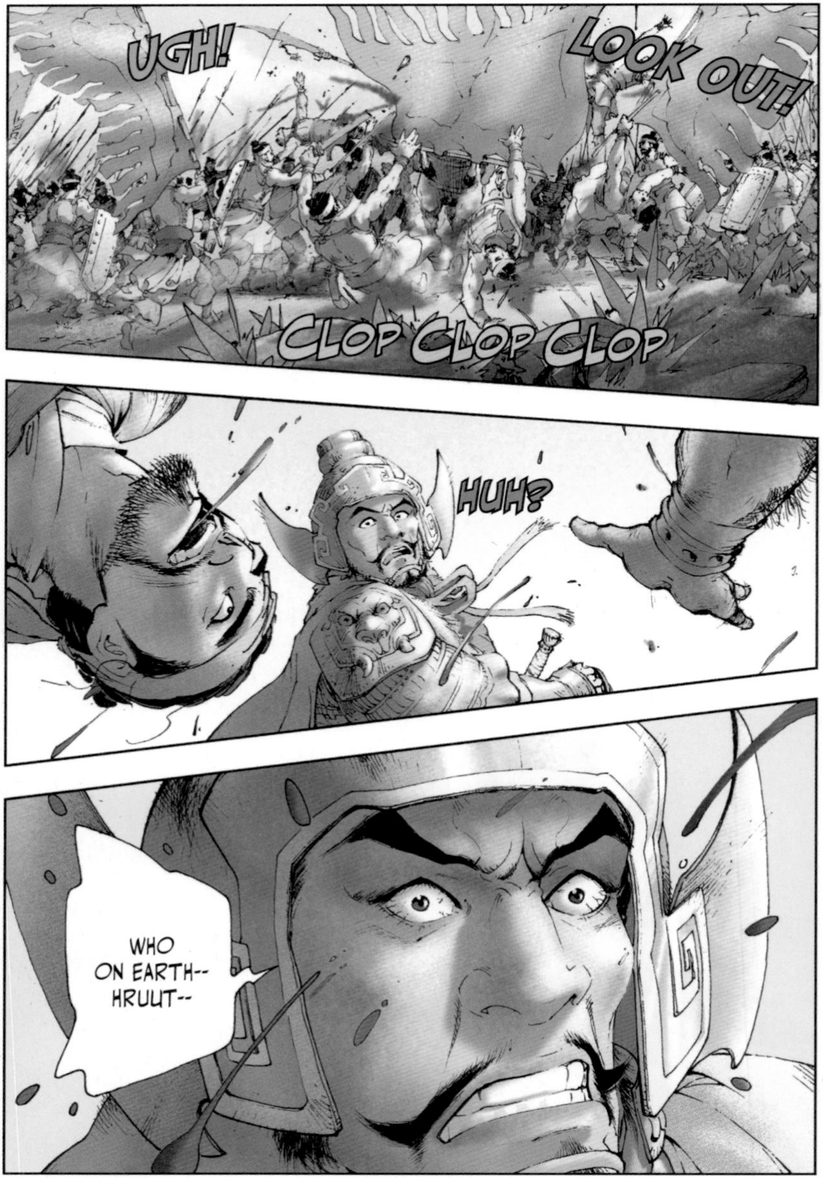
UGH!
LOOK OUT!
CLOP CLOP CLOP
HUH?
WHO ON EARTH-- HRUUT--

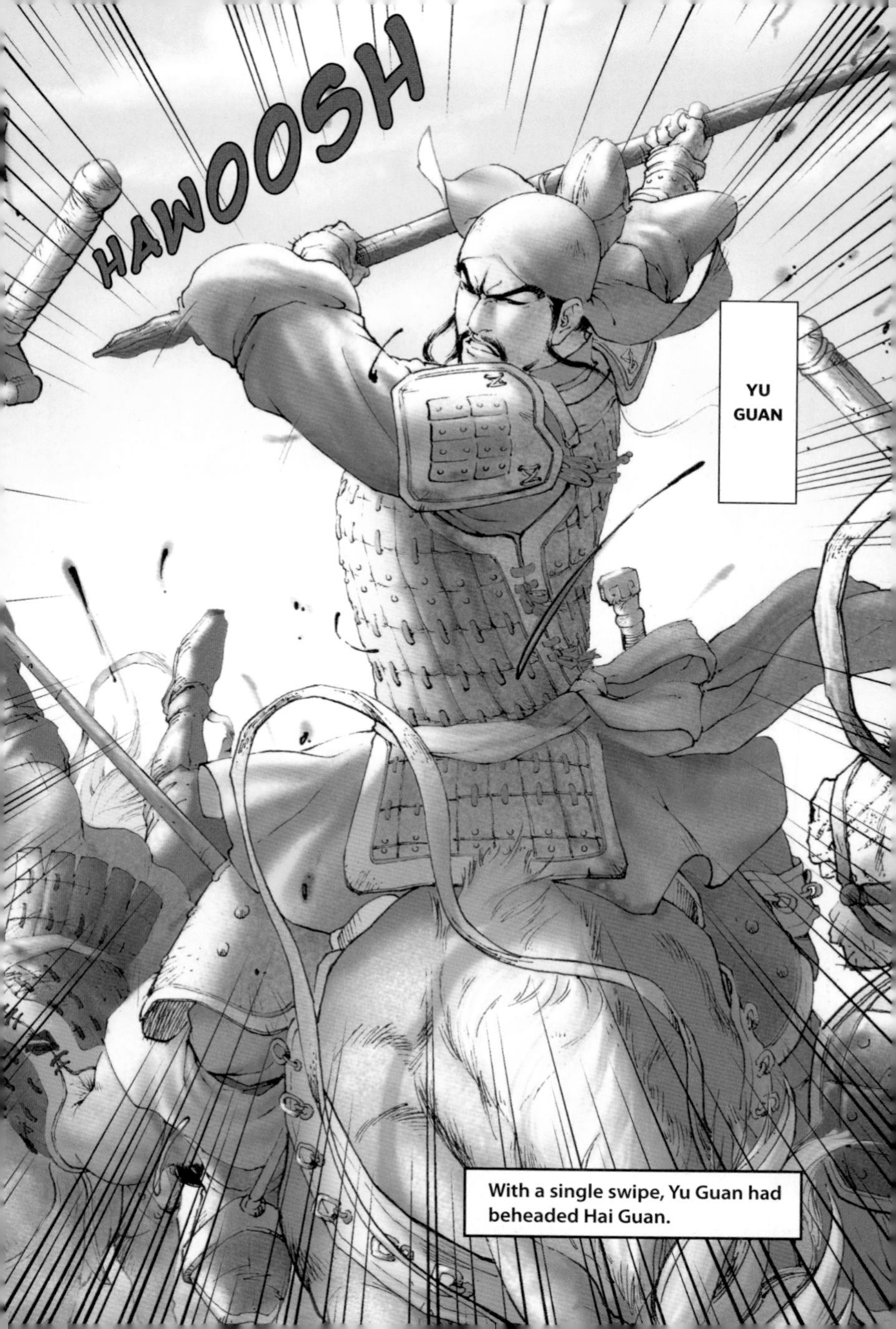
HAWOOSH
YU GUAN
With a single swipe, Yu Guan had beheaded Hai Guan.

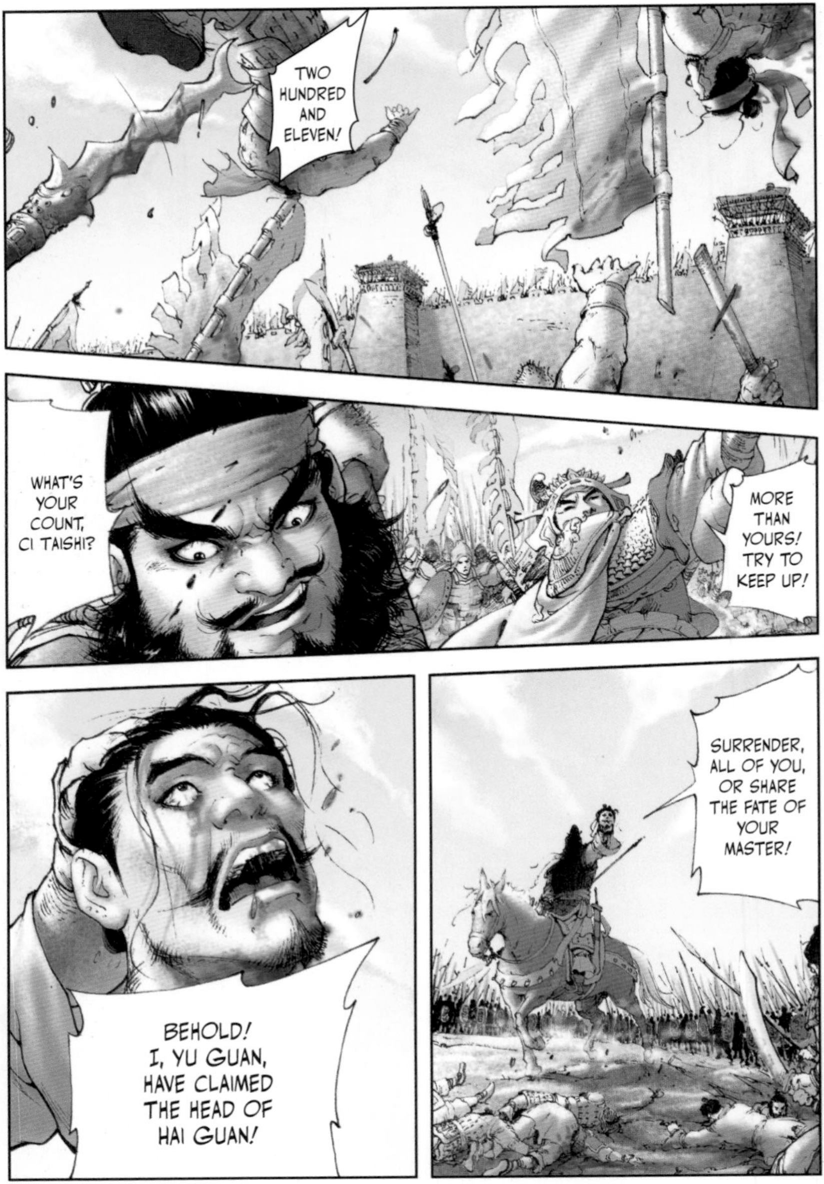
TWO HUNDRED AND ELEVEN!
WHAT'S YOUR COUNT, CI TAISHI?
MORE THAN YOURS! TRY TO KEEP UP!
BEHOLD! I, YU GUAN, HAVE CLAIMED THE HEAD OF HAI GUAN!
SURRENDER, ALL OF YOU, OR SHARE THE FATE OF YOUR MASTER!

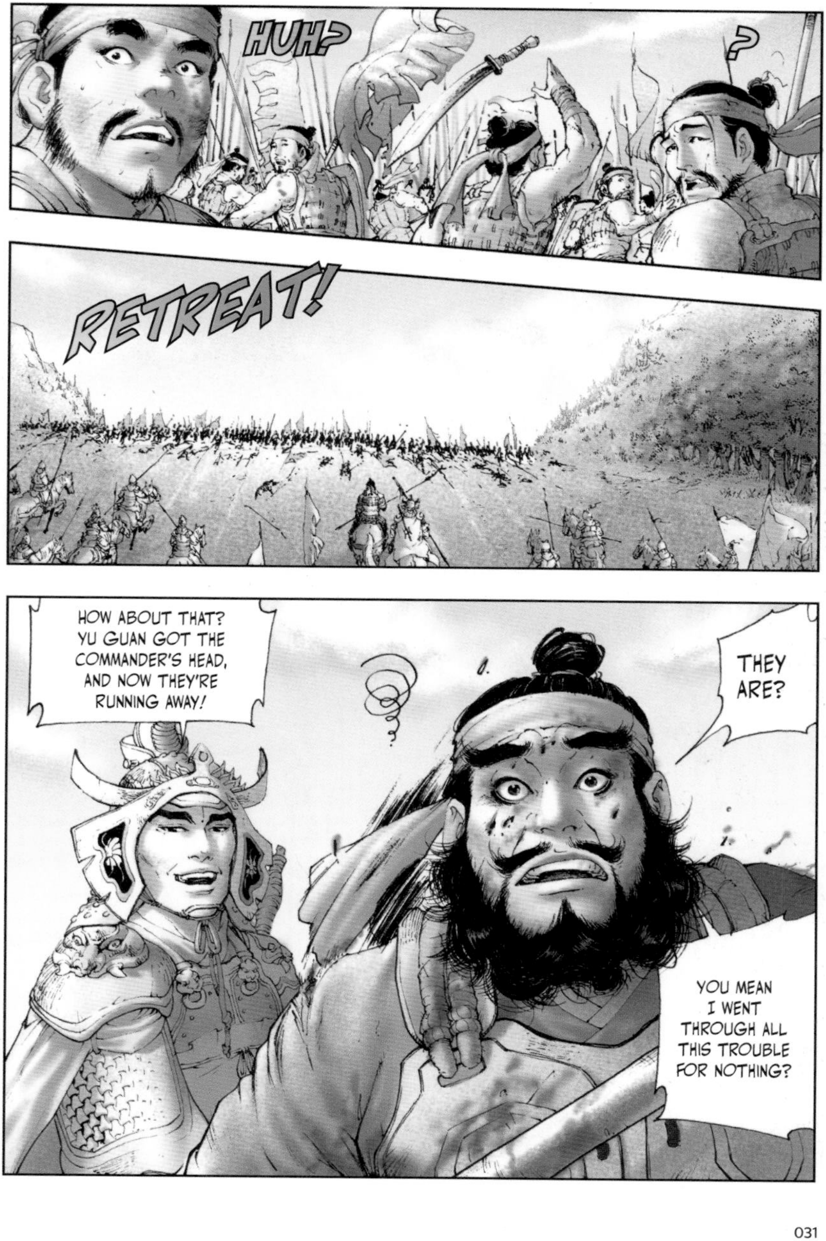
HUH?
?
RETREAT!
HOW ABOUT THAT? YU GUAN GOT THE COMMANDER'S HEAD, AND NOW THEY'RE RUNNING AWAY!
THEY ARE?
YOU MEAN I WENT THROUGH ALL THIS TROUBLE FOR NOTHING?

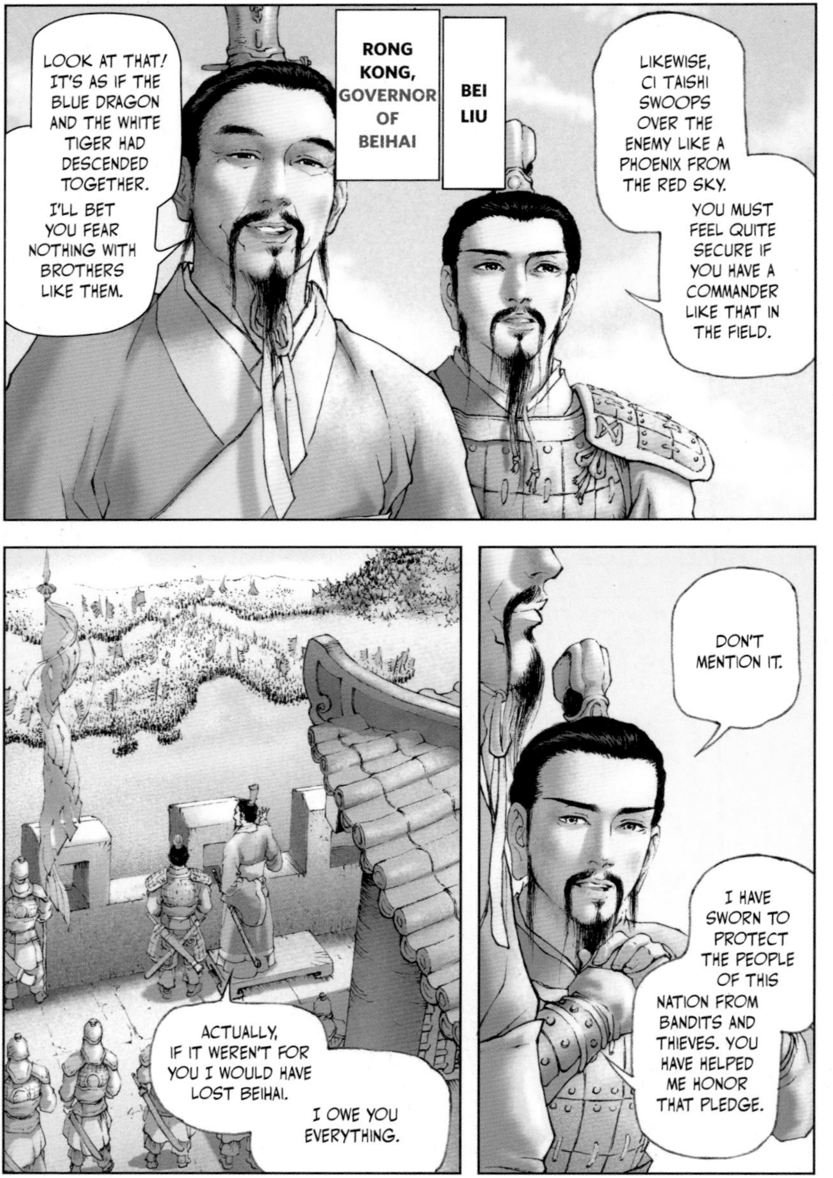
LOOK AT THAT! IT'S AS IF THE BLUE DRAGON AND THE WHITE TIGER HAD DESCENDED TOGETHER.
I'LL BET YOU FEAR NOTHING WITH BROTHERS LIKE THEM.
RONG KONG, GOVERNOR OF BEIHAI
BEI LIU
LIKEWISE, CI TAISHI SWOOPS OVER THE ENEMY LIKE A PHOENIX FROM THE RED SKY.
YOU MUST FEEL QUITE SECURE IF YOU HAVE A COMMANDER LIKE THAT IN THE FIELD.
ACTUALLY, IF IT WEREN'T FOR YOU I WOULD HAVE LOST BEIHAI.
I OWE YOU EVERYTHING.
DON'T MENTION IT.
I HAVE SWORN TO PROTECT THE PEOPLE OF THIS NATION FROM BANDITS AND THIEVES. YOU HAVE HELPED ME HONOR THAT PLEDGE.

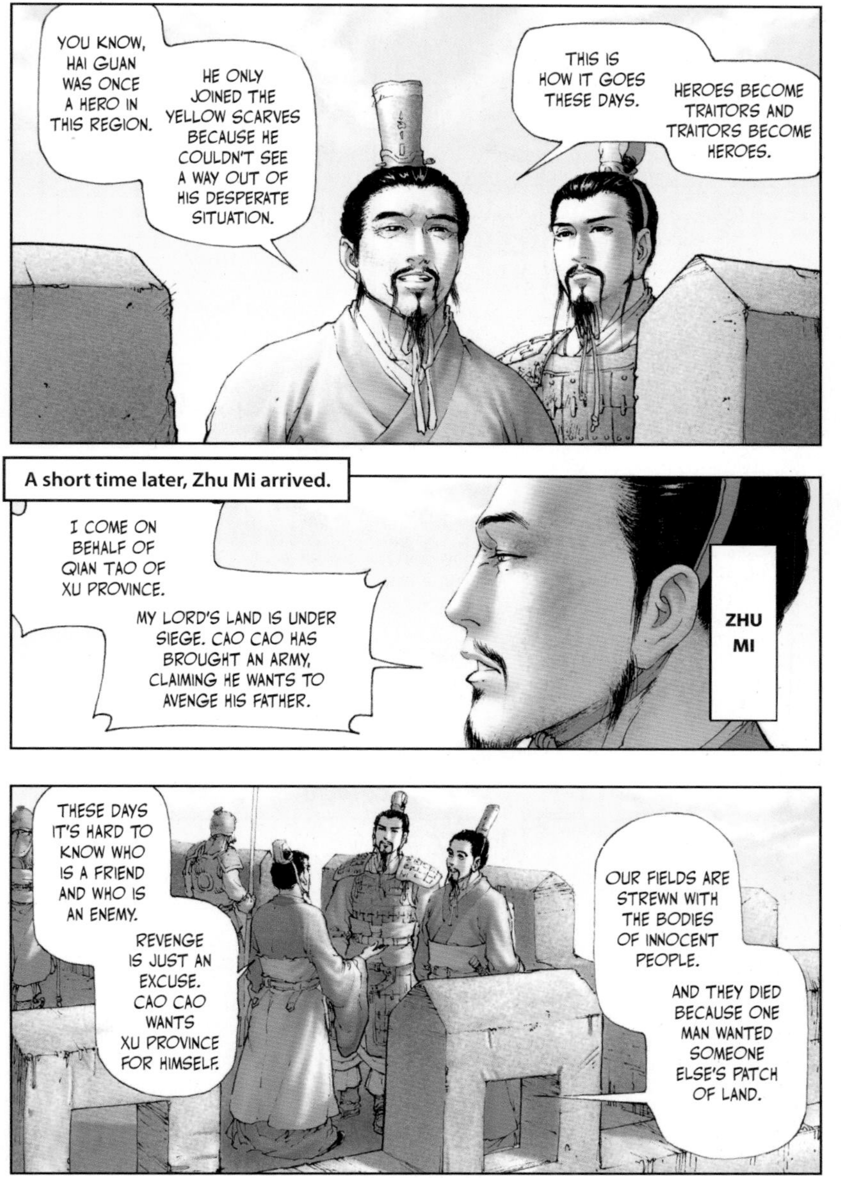
YOU KNOW, HAI GUAN WAS ONCE A HERO IN THIS REGION.
HE ONLY JOINED THE YELLOW SCARVES BECAUSE HE COULDN'T SEE A WAY OUT OF HIS DESPERATE SITUATION.
THIS IS HOW IT GOES THESE DAYS.
HEROES BECOME TRAITORS AND TRAITORS BECOME HEROES.
A short time later, Zhu Mi arrived.
I COME ON BEHALF OF QIAN TAO OF XU PROVINCE.
MY LORD'S LAND IS UNDER SIEGE. CAO CAO HAS BROUGHT AN ARMY, CLAIMING HE WANTS TO AVENGE HIS FATHER.
ZHU MI
THESE DAYS IT'S HARD TO KNOW WHO IS A FRIEND AND WHO IS AN ENEMY.
REVENGE IS JUST AN EXCUSE. CAO CAO WANTS XU PROVINCE FOR HIMSELF.
OUR FIELDS ARE STREWN WITH THE BODIES OF INNOCENT PEOPLE.
AND THEY DIED BECAUSE ONE MAN WANTED SOMEONE ELSE'S PATCH OF LAND.

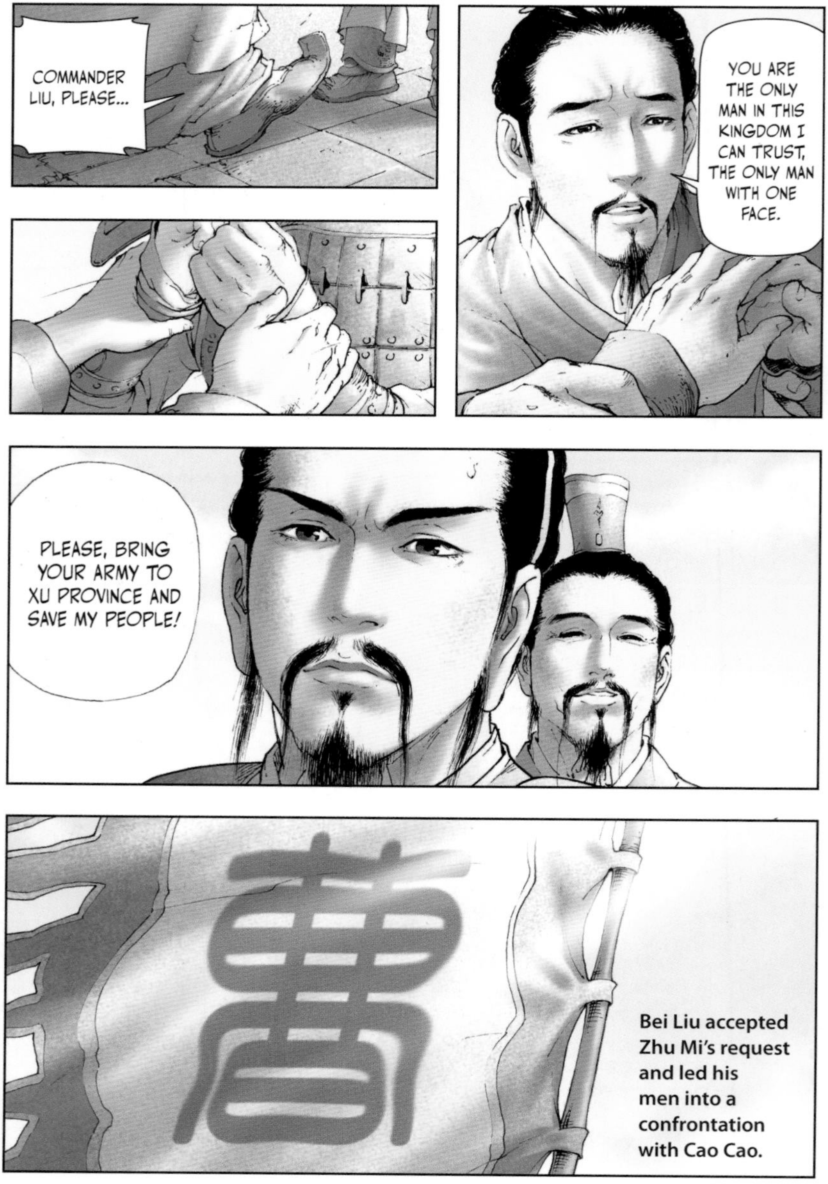
COMMANDER LIU, PLEASE...
YOU ARE THE ONLY MAN IN THIS KINGDOM I CAN TRUST, THE ONLY MAN WITH ONE FACE.
PLEASE, BRING YOUR ARMY TO XU PROVINCE AND SAVE MY PEOPLE!
Bei Liu accepted Zhu Mi's request and led his men into a confrontation with Cao Cao.

CAO CAO

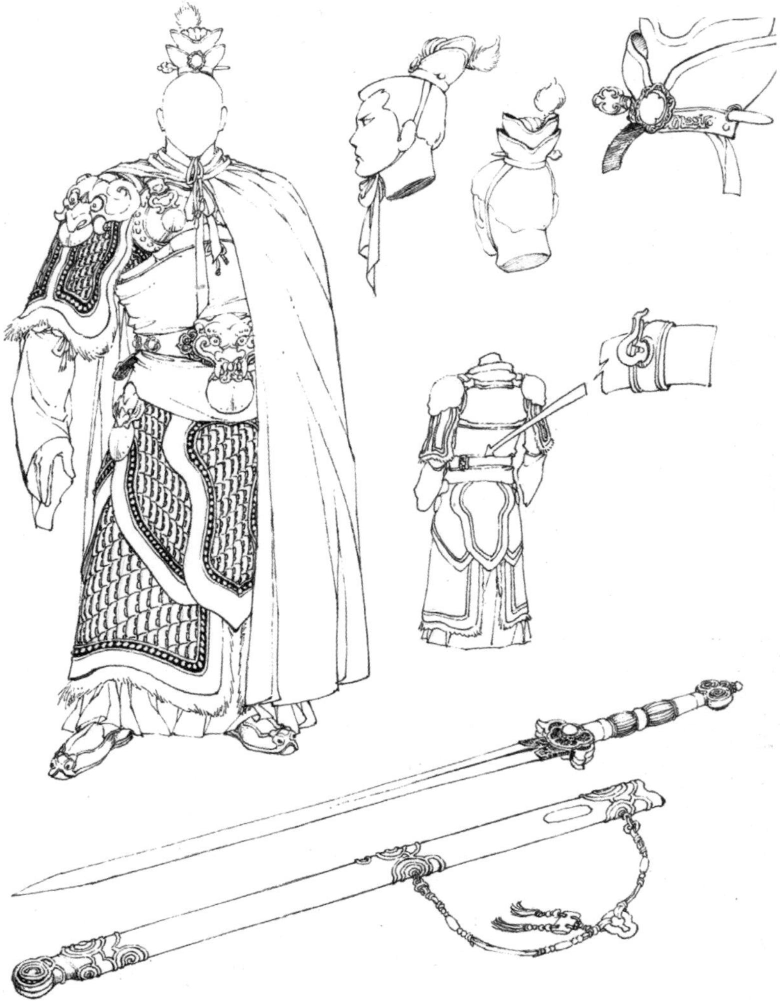

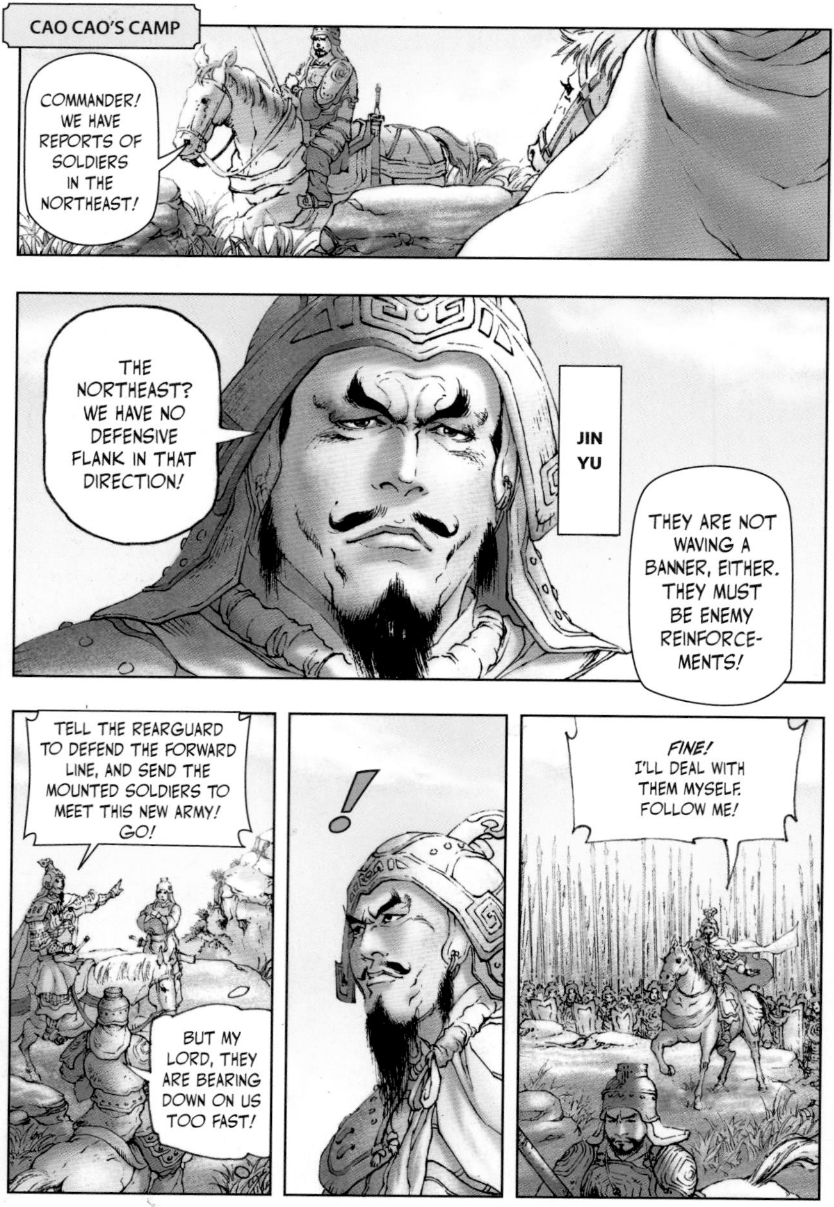
CAO CAO'S CAMP
COMMANDER! WE HAVE REPORTS OF SOLDIERS IN THE NORTHEAST!
THE NORTHEAST? WE HAVE NO DEFENSIVE FLANK IN THAT DIRECTION!
JIN YU
THEY ARE NOT WAVING A BANNER, EITHER. THEY MUST BE ENEMY REINFORCE-MENTS!
TELL THE REARGUARD TO DEFEND THE FORWARD LINE, AND SEND THE MOUNTED SOLDIERS TO MEET THIS NEW ARMY! GO!
BUT MY LORD, THEY ARE BEARING DOWN ON US TOO FAST!
!
FINE! I'LL DEAL WITH THEM MYSELF. FOLLOW ME!

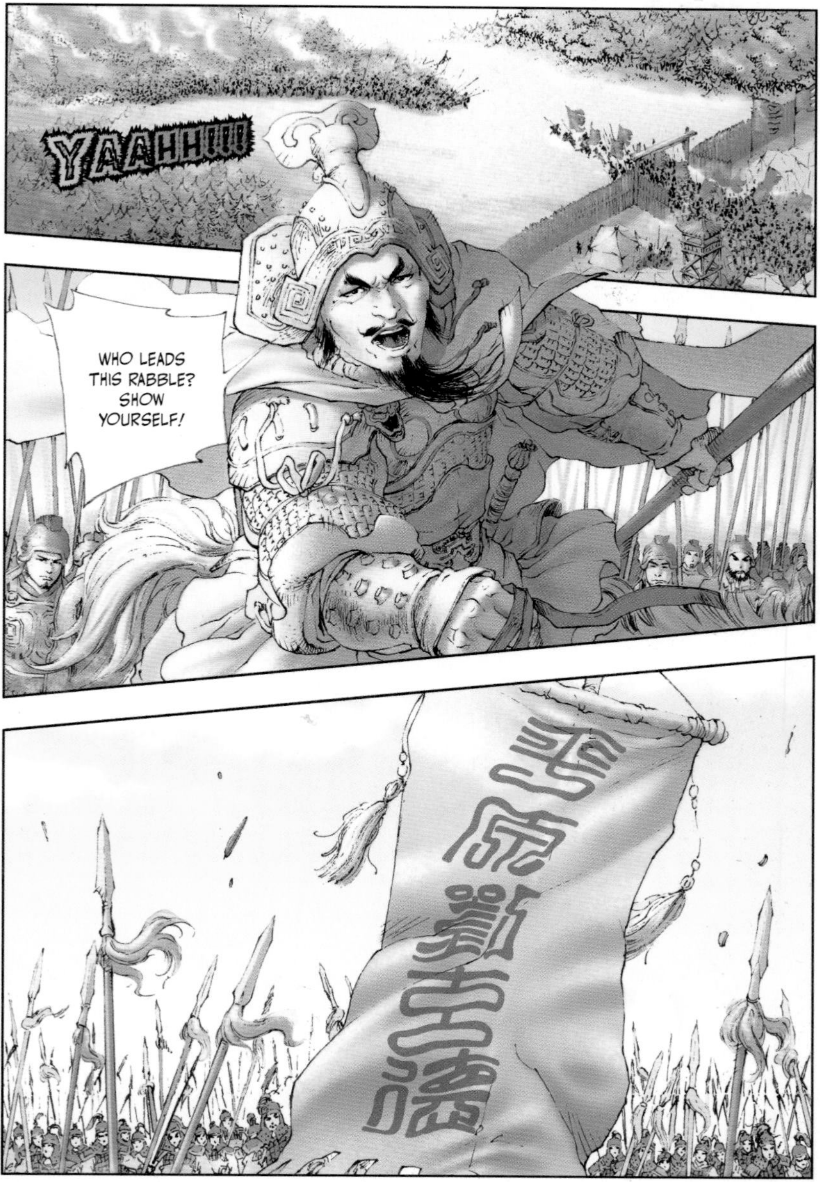
YAAHH!!!
WHO LEADS THIS RABBLE? SHOW YOURSELF!

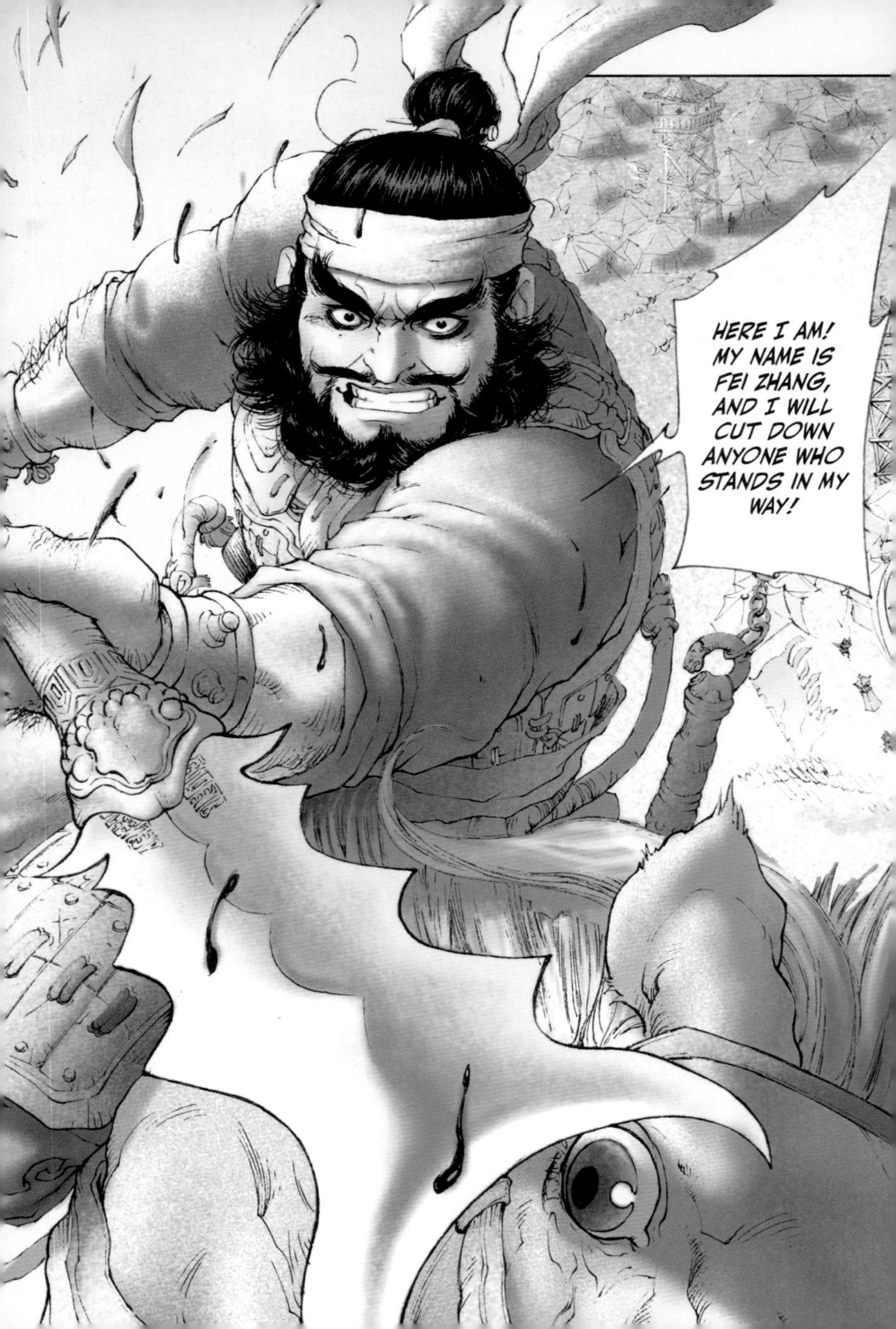
HERE I AM! MY NAME IS FEI ZHANG, AND I WILL CUT DOWN ANYONE WHO STANDS IN MY WAY!

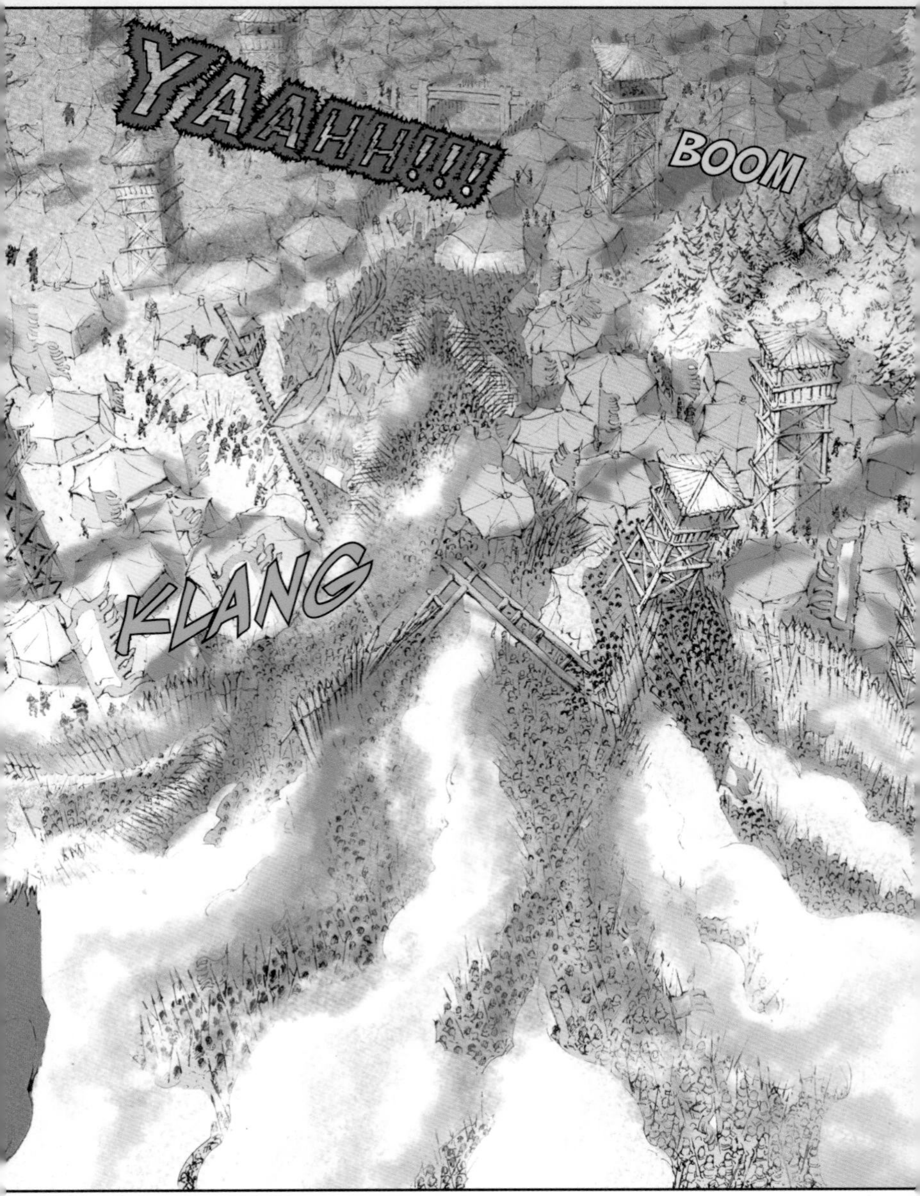
YAAHH!!!
BOOM
KLANG

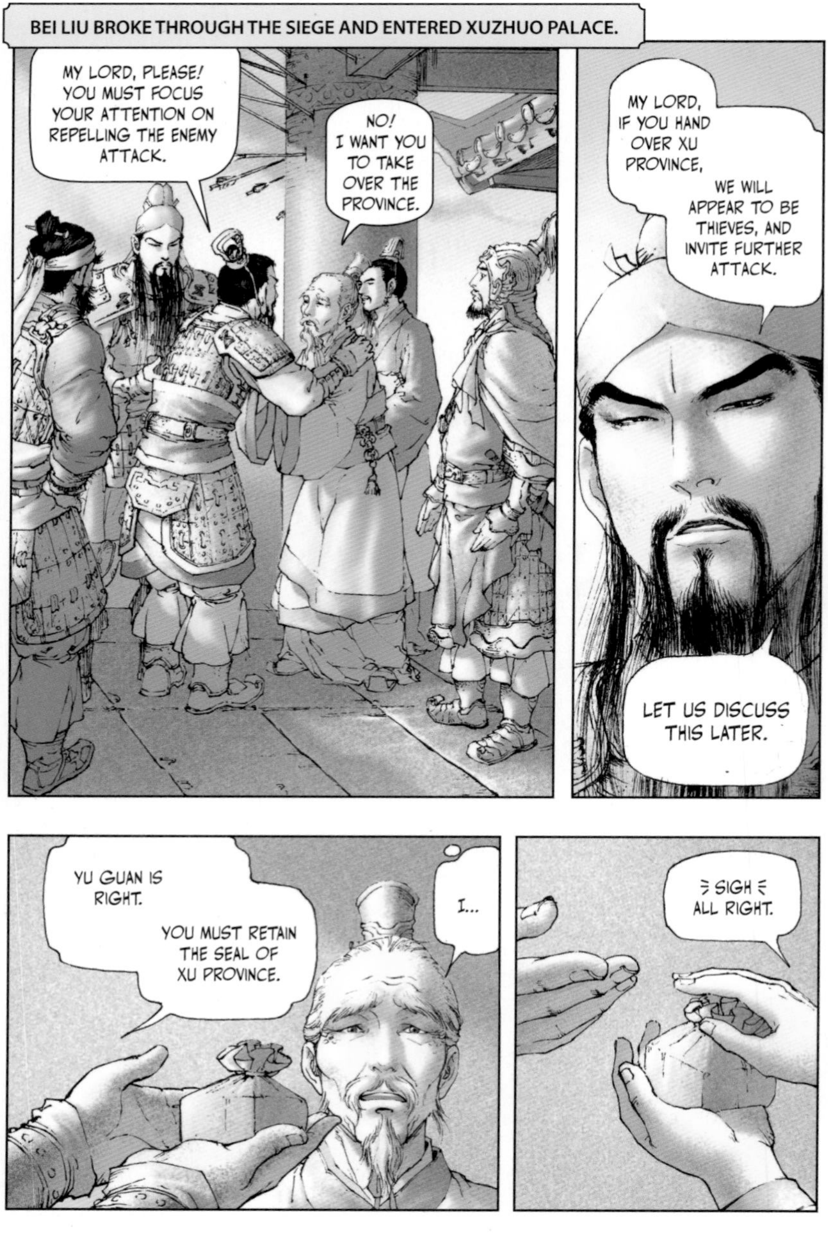
BEI LIU BROKE THROUGH THE SIEGE AND ENTERED XUZHUO PALACE.
MY LORD, PLEASE! YOU MUST FOCUS YOUR ATTENTION ON REPELLING THE ENEMY ATTACK.
NO! I WANT YOU TO TAKE OVER THE PROVINCE.
MY LORD, IF YOU HAND OVER XU PROVINCE,
WE WILL APPEAR TO BE THIEVES, AND INVITE FURTHER ATTACK.
LET US DISCUSS THIS LATER.
YU GUAN IS RIGHT.
YOU MUST RETAIN THE SEAL OF XU PROVINCE.
I...
≡ SIGH ≡ ALL RIGHT.

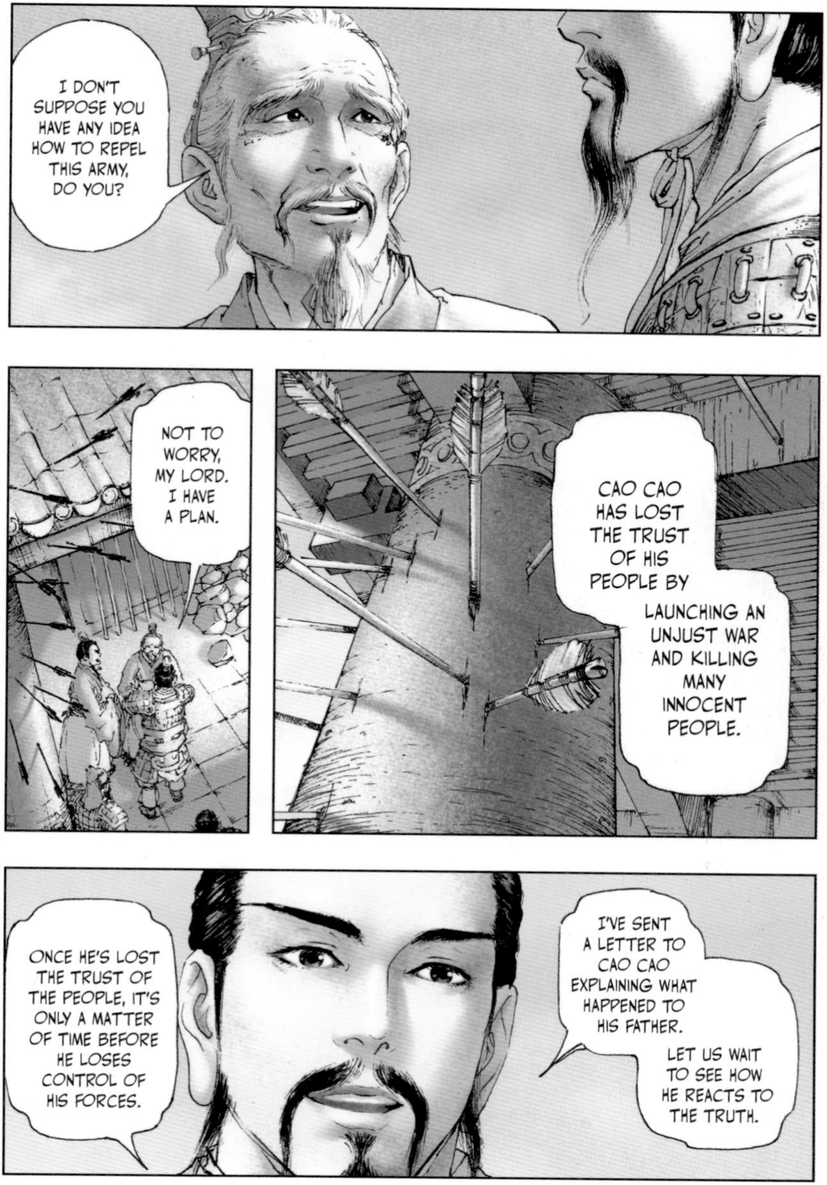
I DON'T SUPPOSE YOU HAVE ANY IDEA HOW TO REPEL THIS ARMY, DO YOU?
NOT TO WORRY, MY LORD. I HAVE A PLAN.
CAO CAO HAS LOST THE TRUST OF HIS PEOPLE BY
LAUNCHING AN UNJUST WAR AND KILLING MANY INNOCENT PEOPLE.
ONCE HE'S LOST THE TRUST OF THE PEOPLE, IT'S ONLY A MATTER OF TIME BEFORE HE LOSES CONTROL OF HIS FORCES.
I'VE SENT A LETTER TO CAO CAO EXPLAINING WHAT HAPPENED TO HIS FATHER.
LET US WAIT TO SEE HOW HE REACTS TO THE TRUTH.

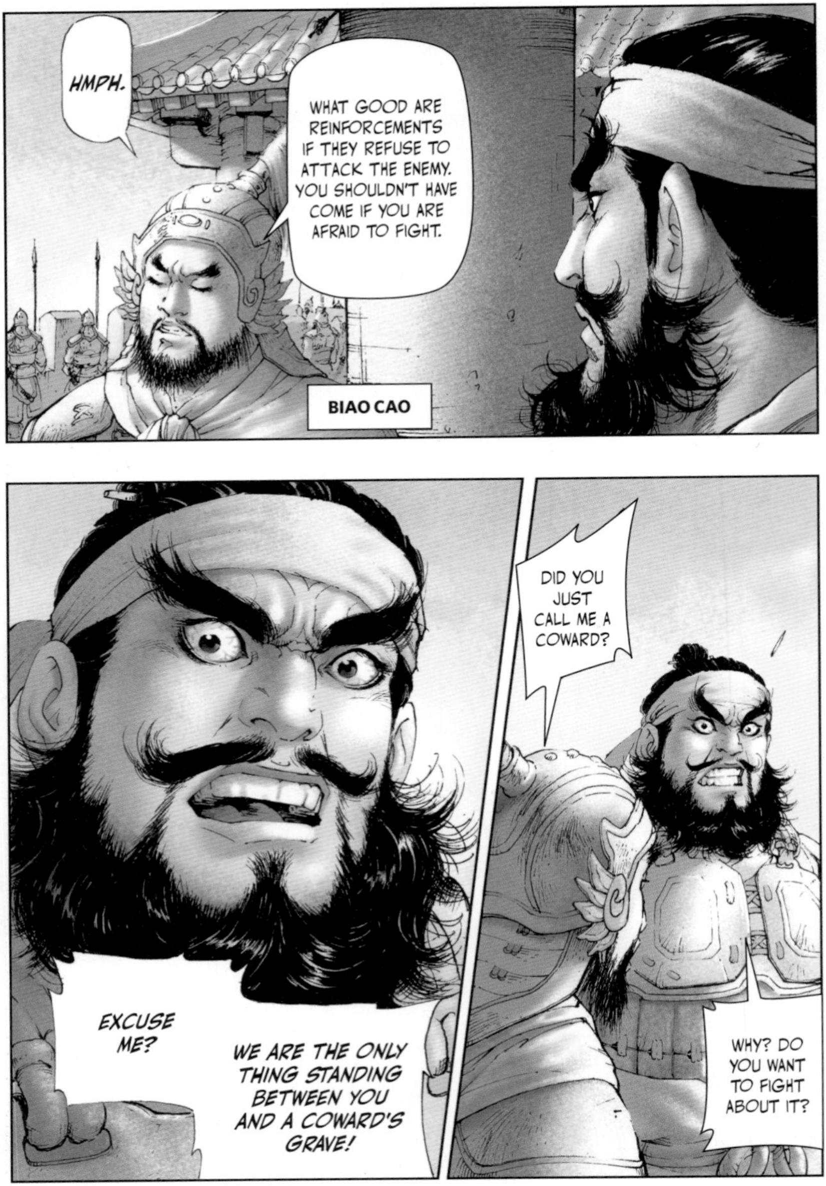
HMPH.
WHAT GOOD ARE REINFORCEMENTS IF THEY REFUSE TO ATTACK THE ENEMY. YOU SHOULDN'T HAVE COME IF YOU ARE AFRAID TO FIGHT.
BIAO CAO
DID YOU JUST CALL ME A COWARD?
WHY? DO YOU WANT TO FIGHT ABOUT IT?
EXCUSE ME?
WE ARE THE ONLY THING STANDING BETWEEN YOU AND A COWARD'S GRAVE!

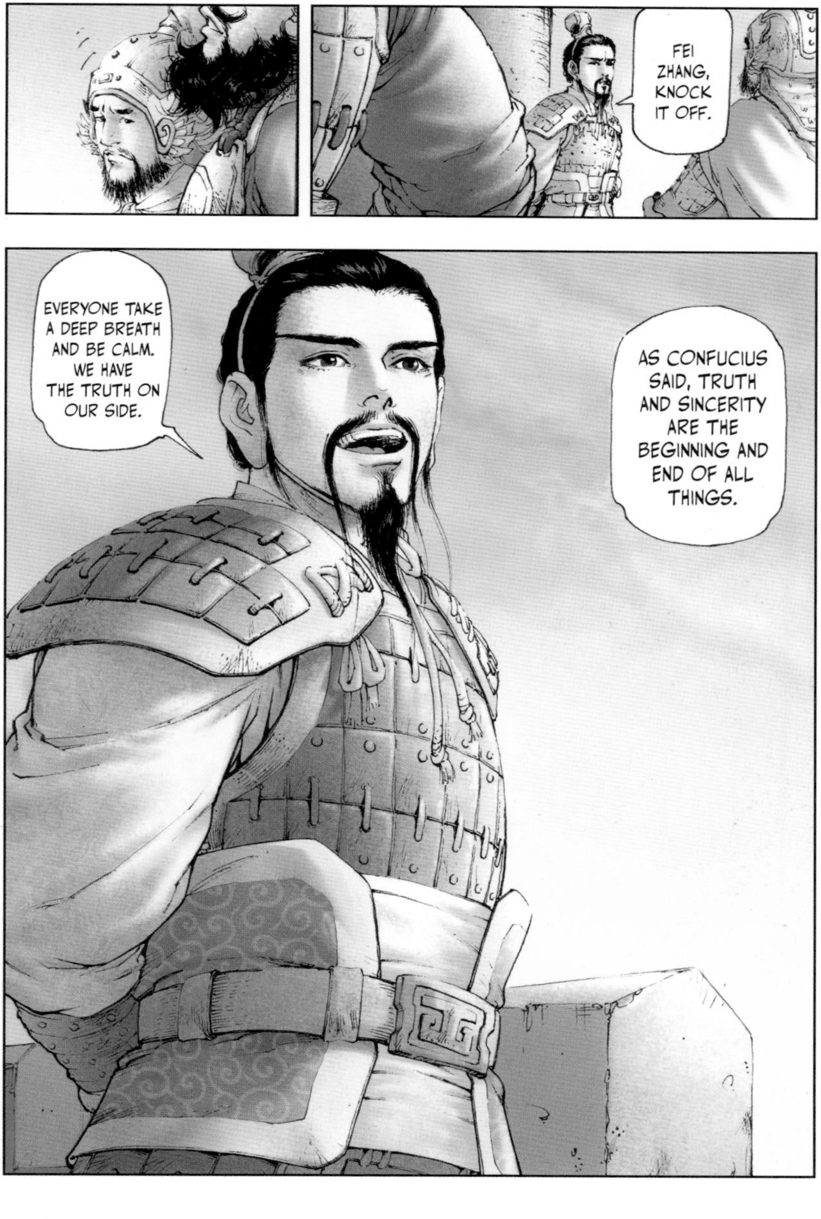
FEI ZHANG, KNOCK IT OFF.
EVERYONE TAKE A DEEP BREATH AND BE CALM. WE HAVE THE TRUTH ON OUR SIDE.
AS CONFUCIUS SAID, TRUTH AND SINCERITY ARE THE BEGINNING AND END OF ALL THINGS.

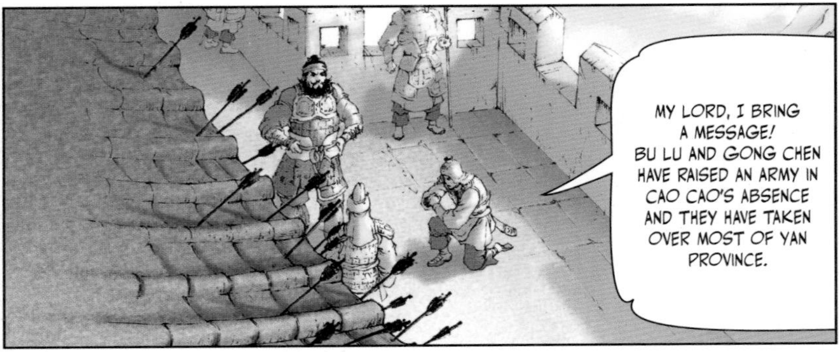
MY LORD, I BRING A MESSAGE! BU LU AND GONG CHEN HAVE RAISED AN ARMY IN CAO CAO'S ABSENCE AND THEY HAVE TAKEN OVER MOST OF YAN PROVINCE.

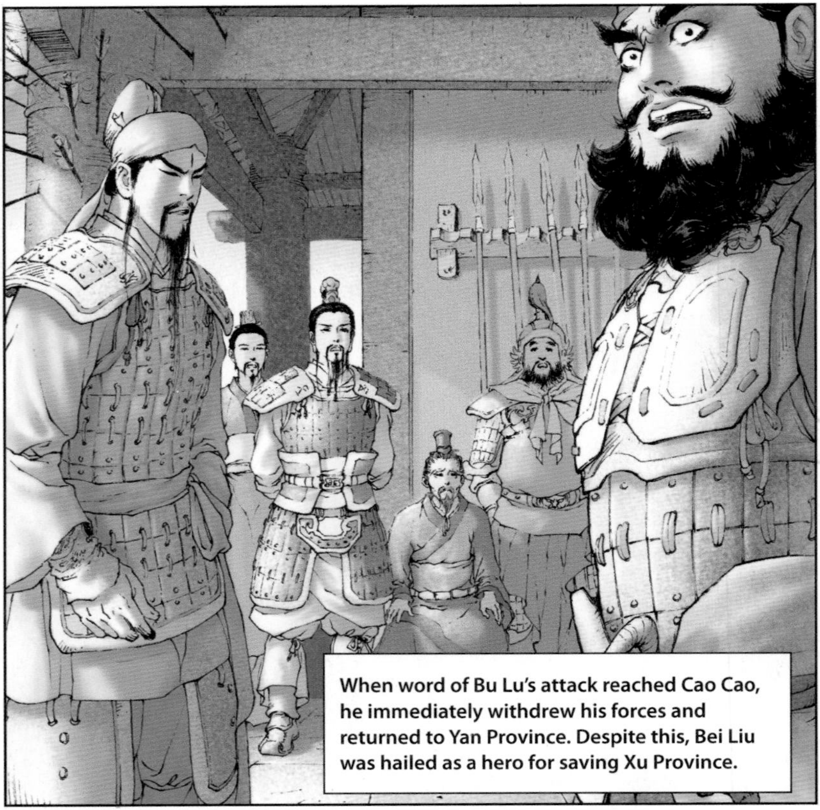
When word of Bu Lu's attack reached Cao Cao, he immediately withdrew his forces and returned to Yan Province. Despite this, Bei Liu was hailed as a hero for saving Xu Province.

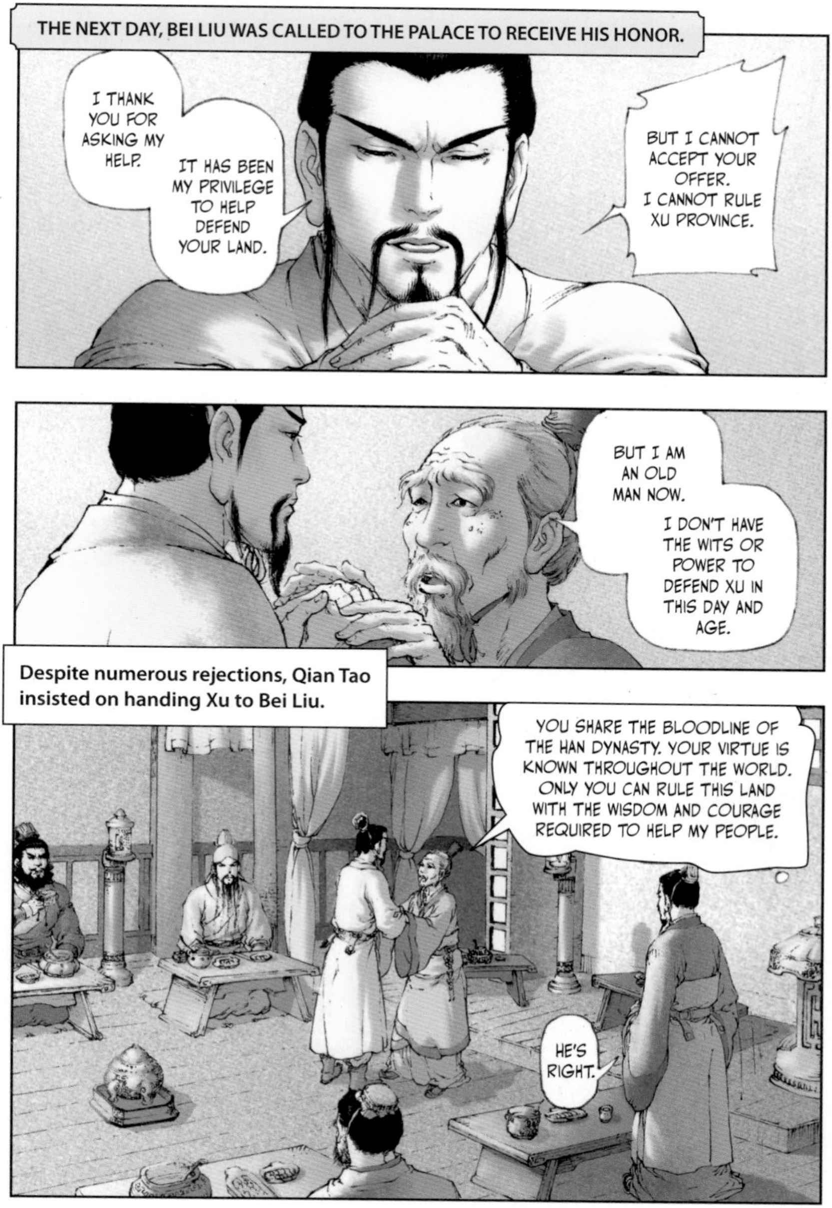
THE NEXT DAY, BEI LIU WAS CALLED TO THE PALACE TO RECEIVE HIS HONOR.
I THANK YOU FOR ASKING MY HELP.
IT HAS BEEN MY PRIVILEGE TO HELP DEFEND YOUR LAND.
BUT I CANNOT ACCEPT YOUR OFFER. I CANNOT RULE XU PROVINCE.
BUT I AM AN OLD MAN NOW.
I DON'T HAVE THE WITS OR POWER TO DEFEND XU IN THIS DAY AND AGE.
Despite numerous rejections, Qian Tao insisted on handing Xu to Bei Liu.
YOU SHARE THE BLOODLINE OF THE HAN DYNASTY. YOUR VIRTUE IS KNOWN THROUGHOUT THE WORLD. ONLY YOU CAN RULE THIS LAND WITH THE WISDOM AND COURAGE REQUIRED TO HELP MY PEOPLE.
HE'S RIGHT.

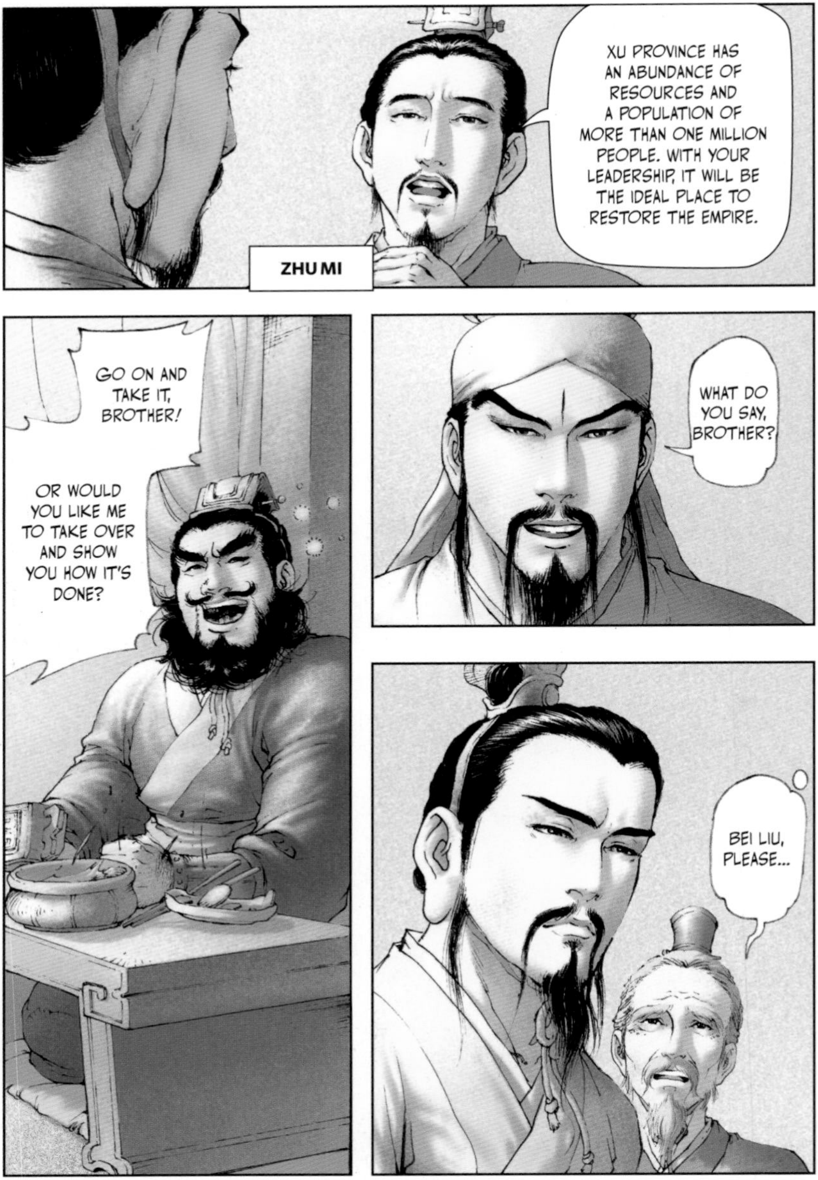
XU PROVINCE HAS AN ABUNDANCE OF RESOURCES AND A POPULATION OF MORE THAN ONE MILLION PEOPLE. WITH YOUR LEADERSHIP, IT WILL BE THE IDEAL PLACE TO RESTORE THE EMPIRE.
ZHU MI
GO ON AND TAKE IT, BROTHER!
OR WOULD YOU LIKE ME TO TAKE OVER AND SHOW YOU HOW IT'S DONE?
WHAT DO YOU SAY, BROTHER?
BEI LIU, PLEASE...

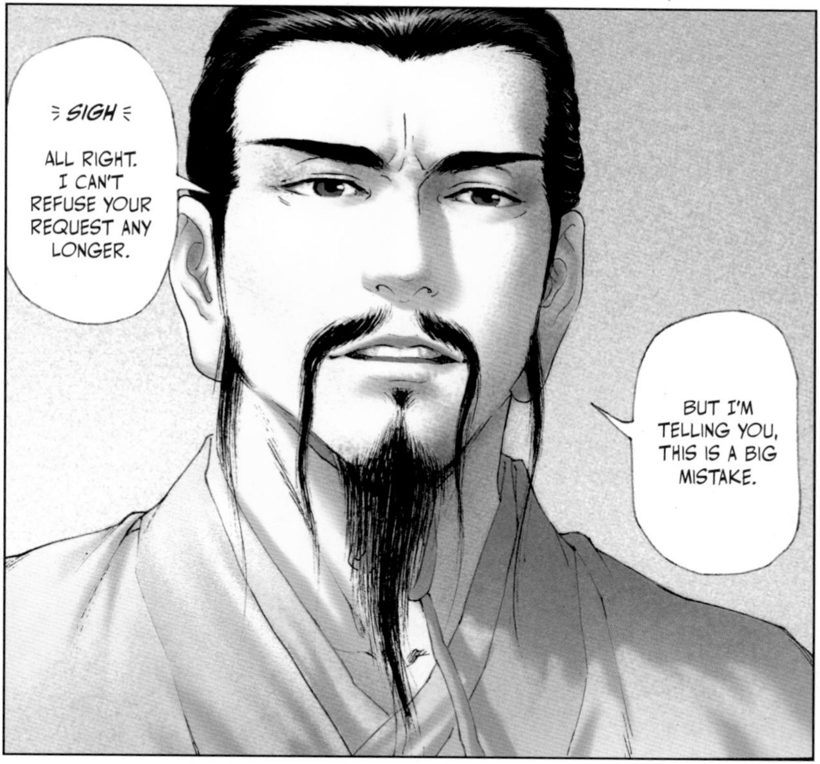
≶ SIGH ≷
ALL RIGHT. I CAN'T REFUSE YOUR REQUEST ANY LONGER.
BUT I'M TELLING YOU, THIS IS A BIG MISTAKE.

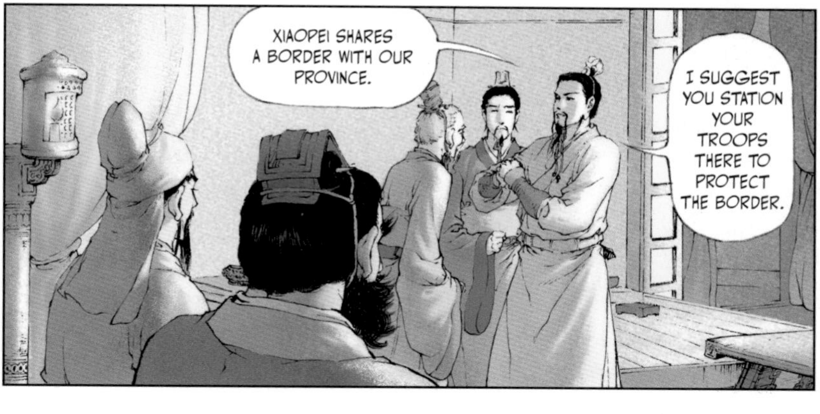
XIAOPEI SHARES A BORDER WITH OUR PROVINCE.
I SUGGEST YOU STATION YOUR TROOPS THERE TO PROTECT THE BORDER.

Chapter 2

A Soldier's Pride and the Battle of Yan Province AD 194

Summary

Bu Lu takes advantage of Cao Cao's absence and launches an attack on Yan Province. The initial battles go Bu Lu's way, but the ease with which they are won causes the general to become arrogant and complacent. Bu Lu's chief advisor, Gong Chen, warns him about the cost of his complacency, and the general accepts the advice, launching a surprise attack against Cao Cao's forces while they are on the defensive. Bu Lu then follows Gong Chen's counsel and wins a string of victories.

Cao Cao is able to fight back when one of his own advisors, Jia Guo, devises a plan to draw out Bu Lu by spreading a rumor that Cao Cao has been killed. The ensuing surprise attack severely diminishes Bu Lu's forces, while an unforeseen swarm of locusts depletes his provisions. These events force Bu Lu to retreat from Yan Province and seek sanctuary in a neighboring province.

ChangShan
BeiHai
PuYang
B
HuLuo
XiaoPei
GuanDu
C
LuoYang
A
XuZhou
ChangAn
XuDu
NanYang
ShouChun
HeFei
XiangYang

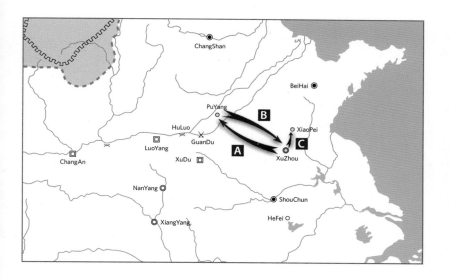

A Cao Cao returns to Yan Province and does battle with Bu Lu's forces in PuYang.

B Bu Lu's forces retreat after a string of attacks by Cao Cao's forces. He is forced to seek asylum in another province.

C Bei Liu welcomes Bu Lu into Xu Province and allows him to live in XiaoPei.

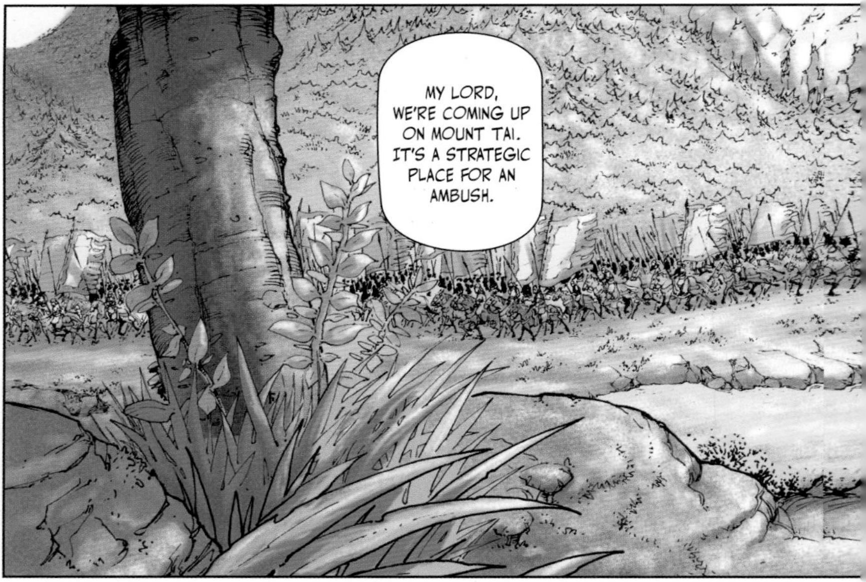
MY LORD, WE'RE COMING UP ON MOUNT TAI. IT'S A STRATEGIC PLACE FOR AN AMBUSH.

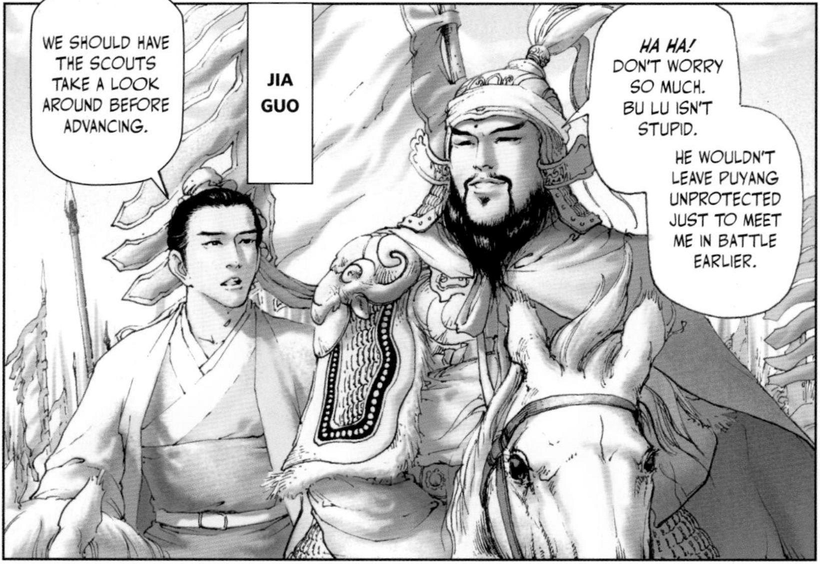
WE SHOULD HAVE THE SCOUTS TAKE A LOOK AROUND BEFORE ADVANCING.
JIA GUO
HA HA! DON'T WORRY SO MUCH. BU LU ISN'T STUPID.
HE WOULDN'T LEAVE PUYANG UNPROTECTED JUST TO MEET ME IN BATTLE EARLIER.

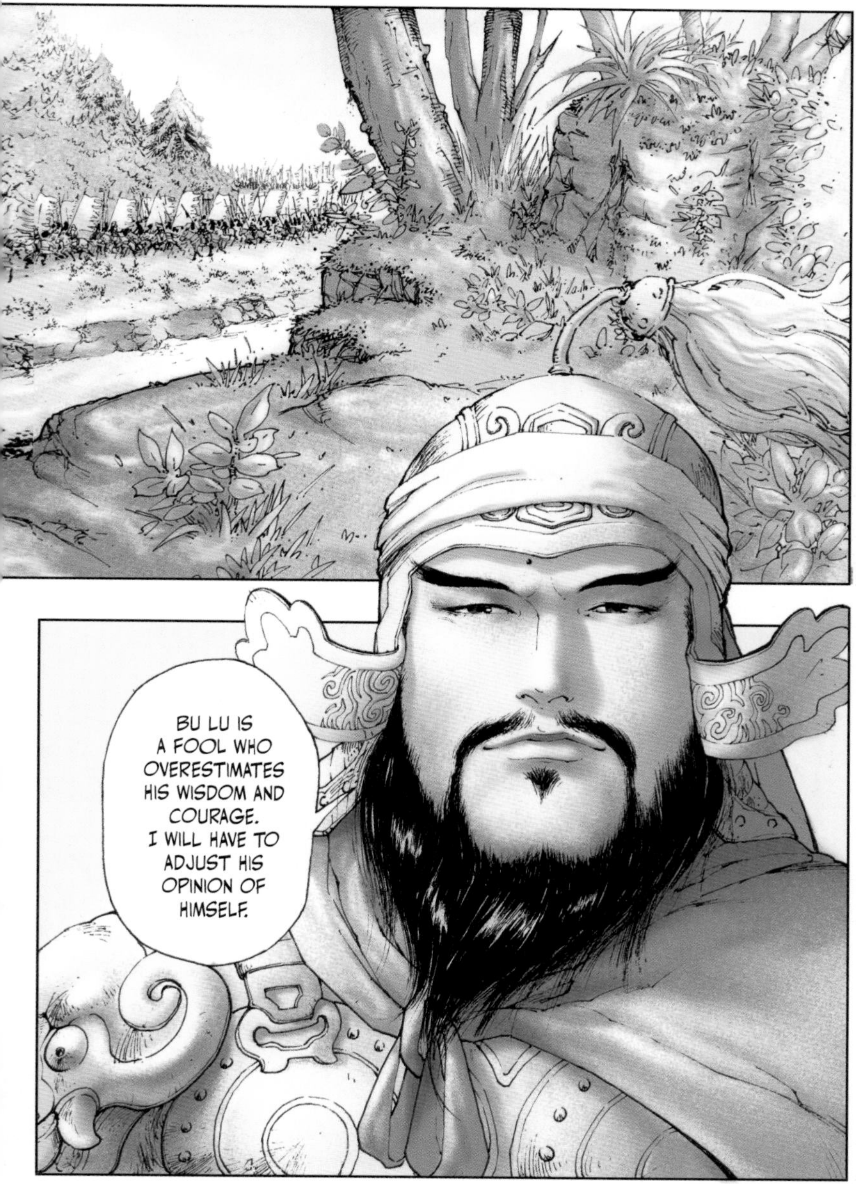
BU LU IS A FOOL WHO OVERESTIMATES HIS WISDOM AND COURAGE. I WILL HAVE TO ADJUST HIS OPINION OF HIMSELF.

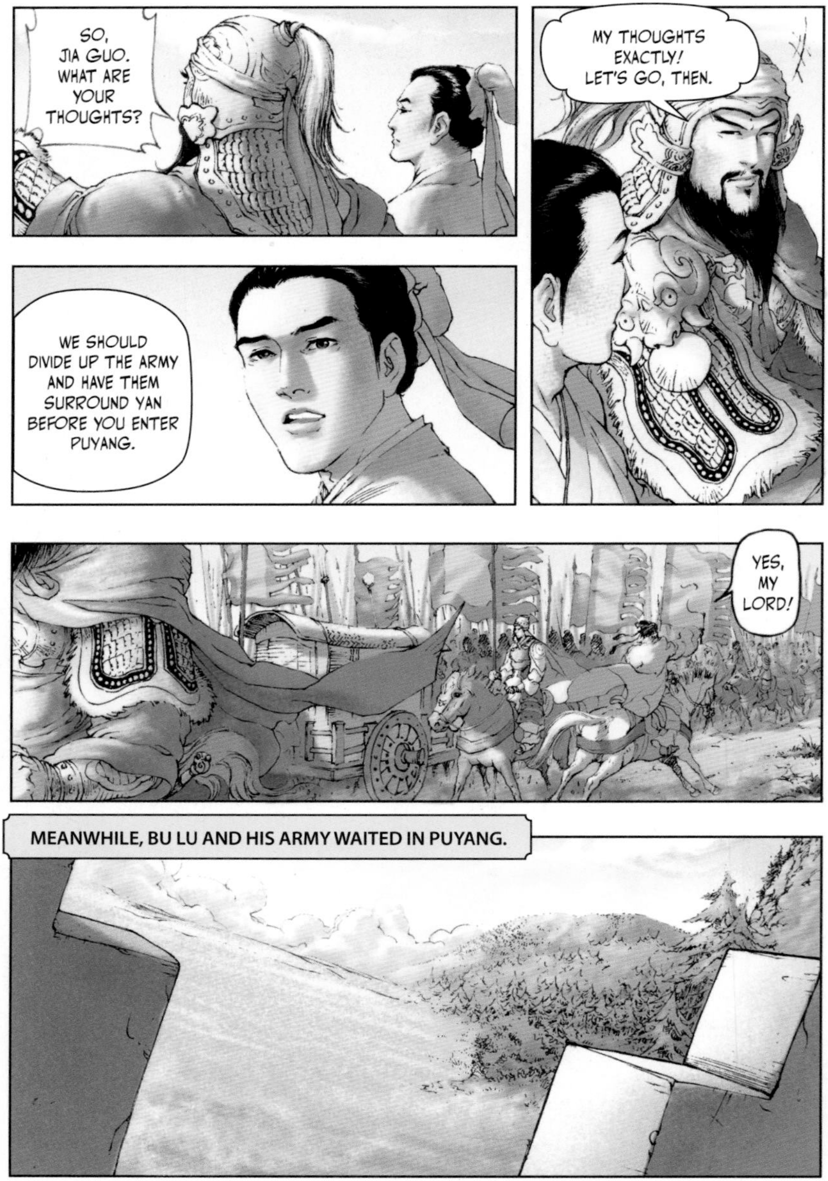
SO, JIA GUO. WHAT ARE YOUR THOUGHTS?
WE SHOULD DIVIDE UP THE ARMY AND HAVE THEM SURROUND YAN BEFORE YOU ENTER PUYANG.
MY THOUGHTS EXACTLY! LET'S GO, THEN.
YES, MY LORD!
MEANWHILE, BU LU AND HIS ARMY WAITED IN PUYANG.

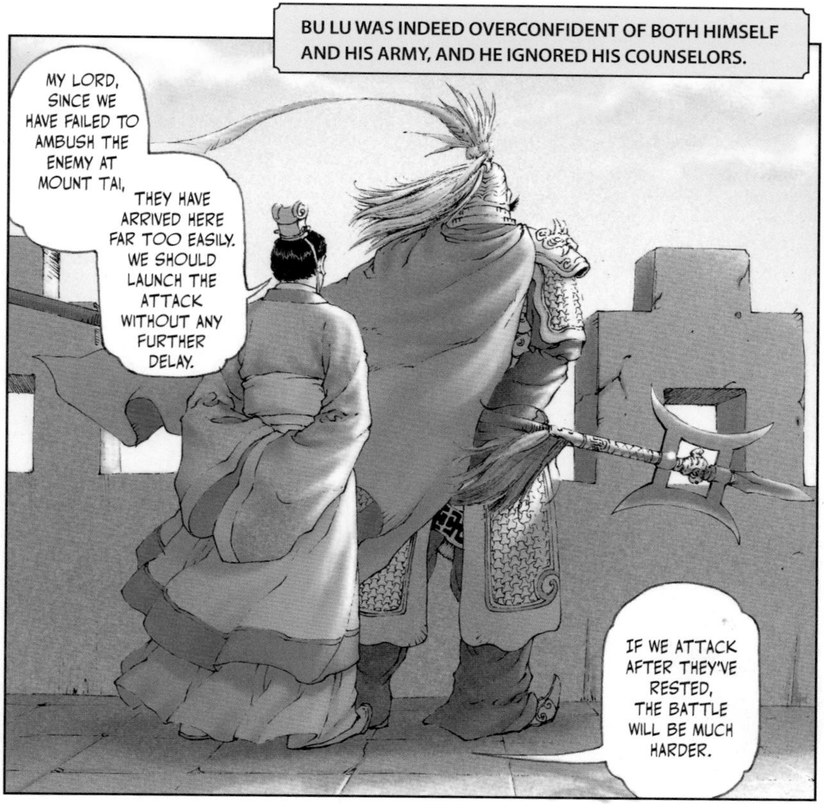
BU LU WAS INDEED OVERCONFIDENT OF BOTH HIMSELF AND HIS ARMY, AND HE IGNORED HIS COUNSELORS.
MY LORD, SINCE WE HAVE FAILED TO AMBUSH THE ENEMY AT MOUNT TAI,
THEY HAVE ARRIVED HERE FAR TOO EASILY. WE SHOULD LAUNCH THE ATTACK WITHOUT ANY FURTHER DELAY.
IF WE ATTACK AFTER THEY'VE RESTED, THE BATTLE WILL BE MUCH HARDER.

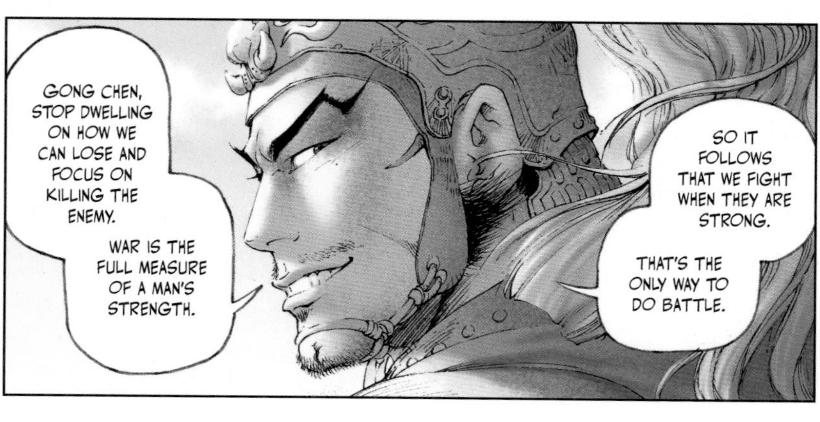
GONG CHEN, STOP DWELLING ON HOW WE CAN LOSE AND FOCUS ON KILLING THE ENEMY.
WAR IS THE FULL MEASURE OF A MAN'S STRENGTH.
SO IT FOLLOWS THAT WE FIGHT WHEN THEY ARE STRONG.
THAT'S THE ONLY WAY TO DO BATTLE.

BESIDES, I'VE FOUGHT MEN TWICE AS STRONG AS CAO CAO. HE IS NO MATCH FOR ME.

THIS BATTLE WILL BE WON BY THE ONE WITH TRUE COURAGE!

≈ SIGH ≈

GONG CHEN

AS CONFUCIUS SAID, A MAN OF COURAGE HAS NO FEAR!

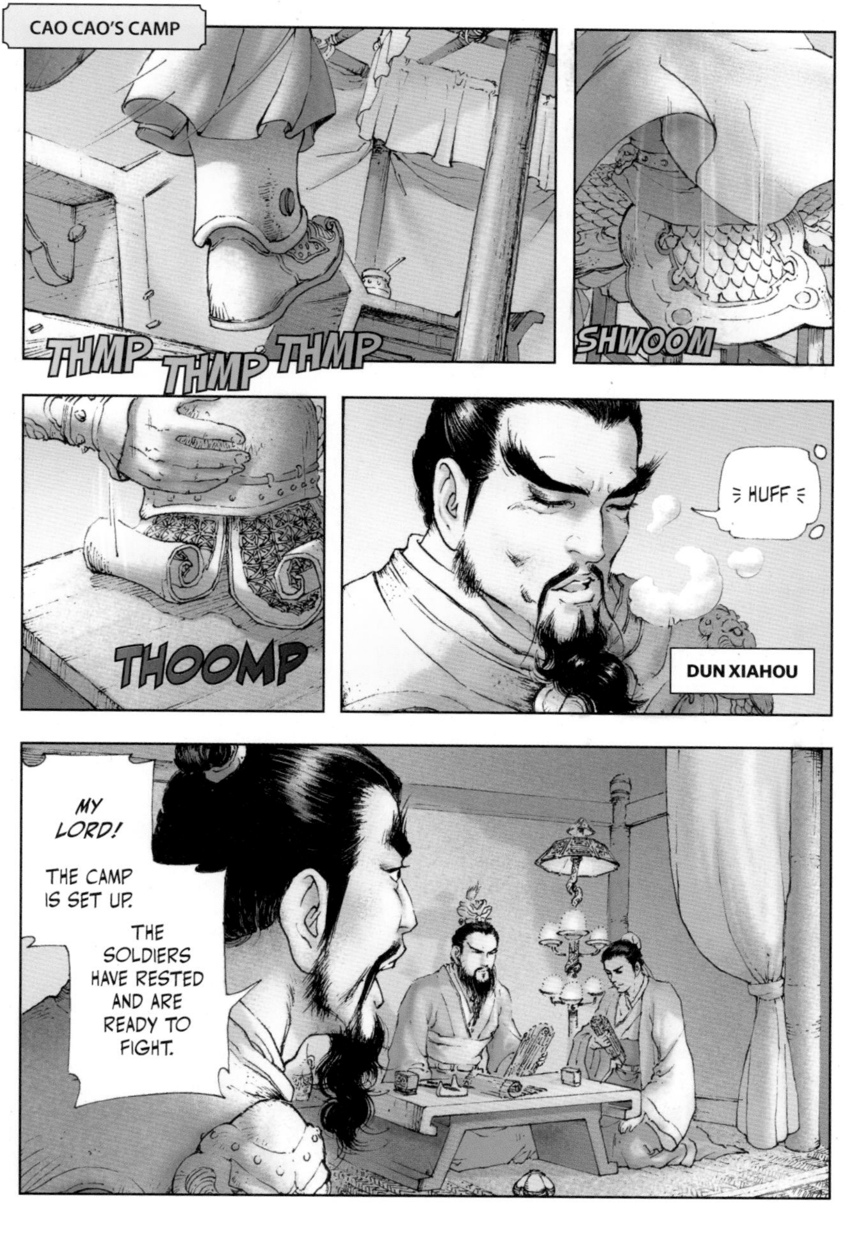
CAO CAO'S CAMP
THMP THMP THMP
SHWOOM
THOOMP
HUFF
DUN XIAHOU
MY LORD!
THE CAMP IS SET UP.
THE SOLDIERS HAVE RESTED AND ARE READY TO FIGHT.

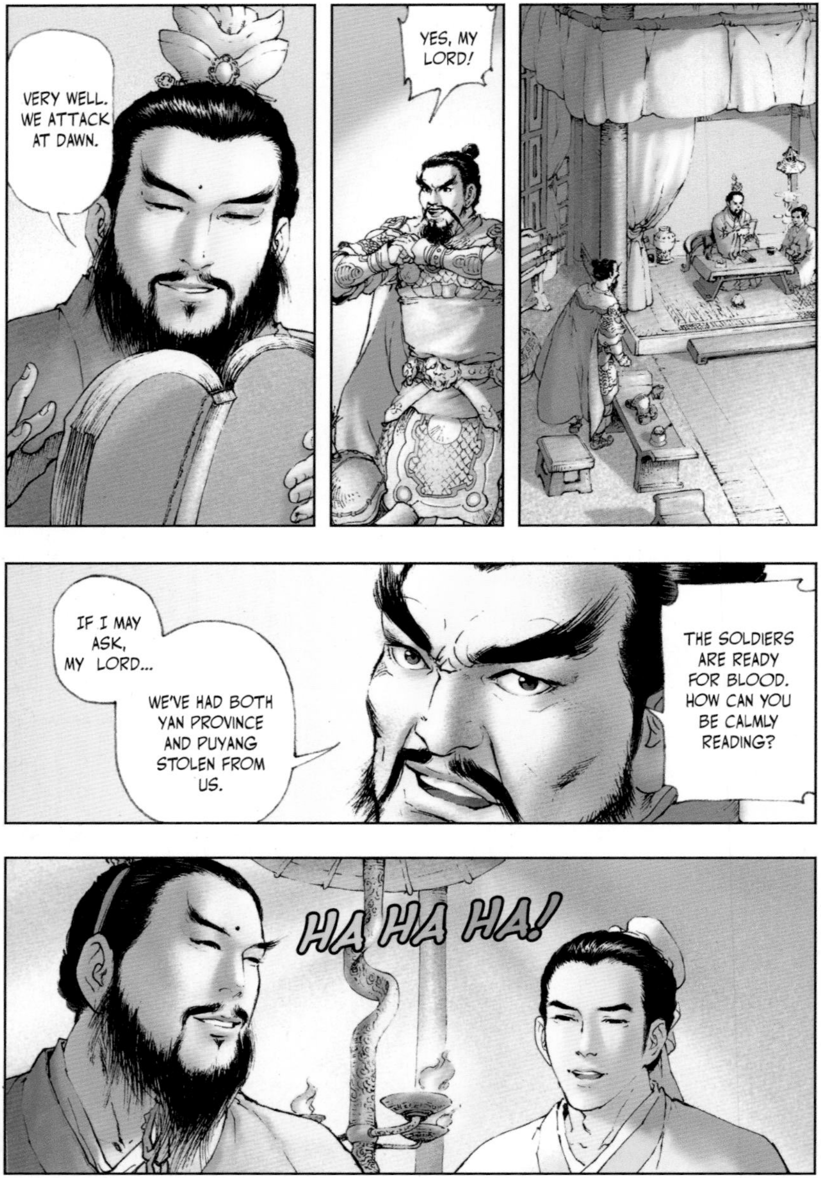
VERY WELL. WE ATTACK AT DAWN.
YES, MY LORD!
IF I MAY ASK, MY LORD...
WE'VE HAD BOTH YAN PROVINCE AND PUYANG STOLEN FROM US.
THE SOLDIERS ARE READY FOR BLOOD. HOW CAN YOU BE CALMLY READING?
HA HA HA!

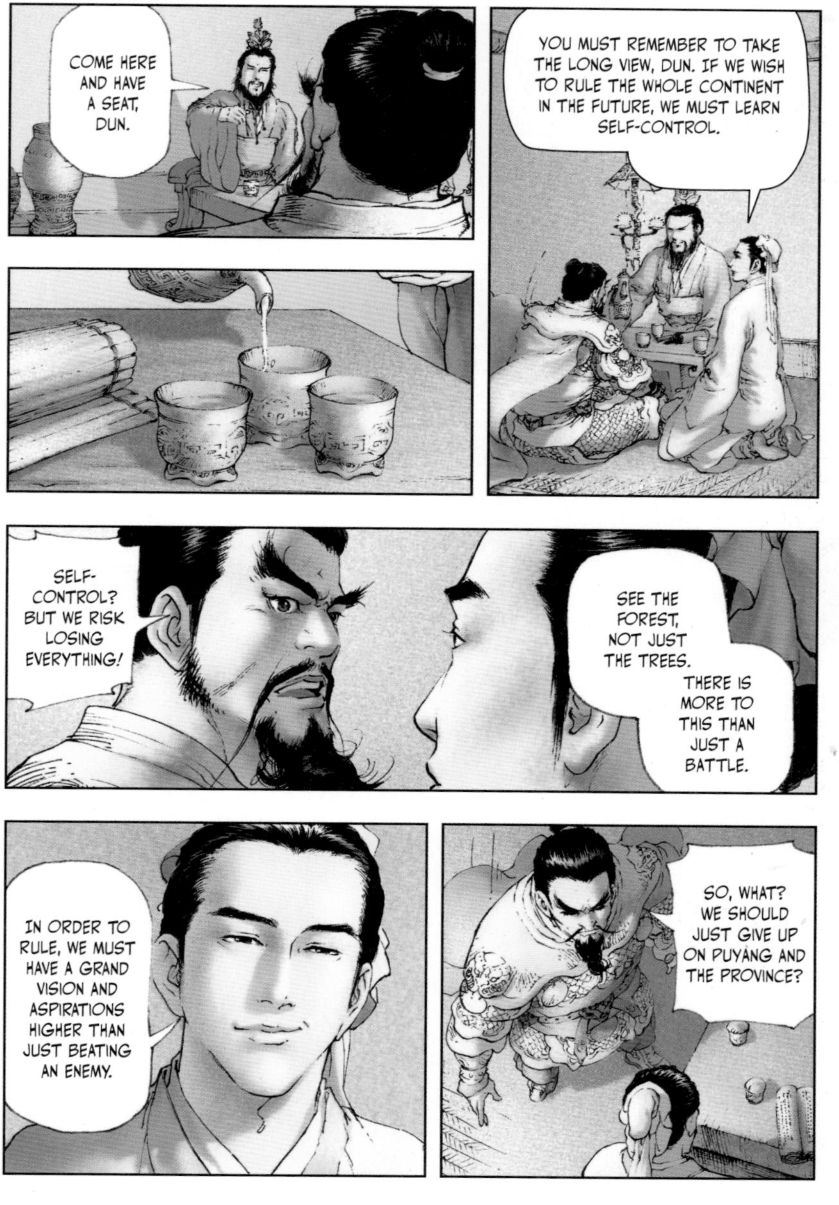
COME HERE AND HAVE A SEAT, DUN.
YOU MUST REMEMBER TO TAKE THE LONG VIEW, DUN. IF WE WISH TO RULE THE WHOLE CONTINENT IN THE FUTURE, WE MUST LEARN SELF-CONTROL.
SELF-CONTROL? BUT WE RISK LOSING EVERYTHING!
SEE THE FOREST, NOT JUST THE TREES.
THERE IS MORE TO THIS THAN JUST A BATTLE.
IN ORDER TO RULE, WE MUST HAVE A GRAND VISION AND ASPIRATIONS HIGHER THAN JUST BEATING AN ENEMY.
SO, WHAT? WE SHOULD JUST GIVE UP ON PUYANG AND THE PROVINCE?

REMEMBER, BU LU IS MARAUDING AROUND BECAUSE HE HAS NO HOME BASE.

SHAO YUAN IS IN THE NORTH, SHU YUAN THE SOUTH. JUE LI AND SI GUO ARE BASED IN CHANGAN.

EACH OF THEM ARE LIKE CAGED BEASTS WAITING TO BREAK FREE. WHAT KEEPS THEM CONTAINED IS THE FEAR OF MAKING BU LU AN ENEMY.

BESIDES, BU LU RUNNING AROUND CLAIMING PROVINCES KEEPS HIM FROM JOINING FORCES WITH SOMEONE ELSE.

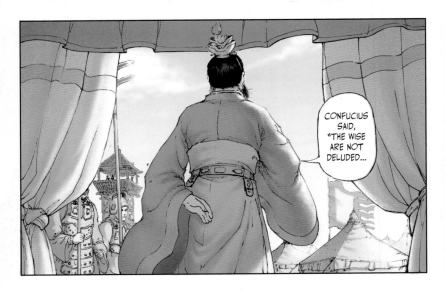

CONFUCIUS SAID, "THE WISE ARE NOT DELUDED...

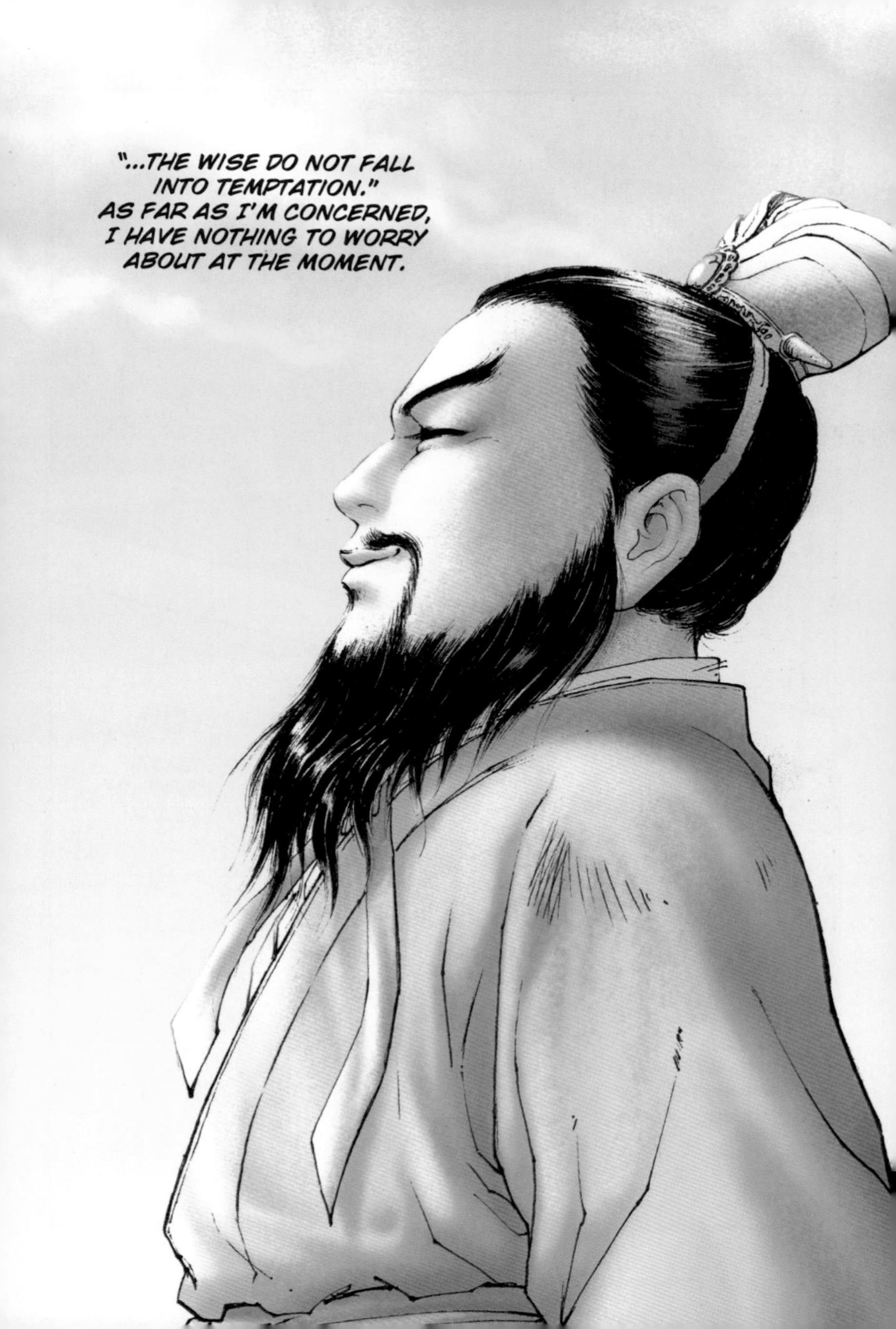
"...THE WISE DO NOT FALL INTO TEMPTATION." AS FAR AS I'M CONCERNED, I HAVE NOTHING TO WORRY ABOUT AT THE MOMENT.

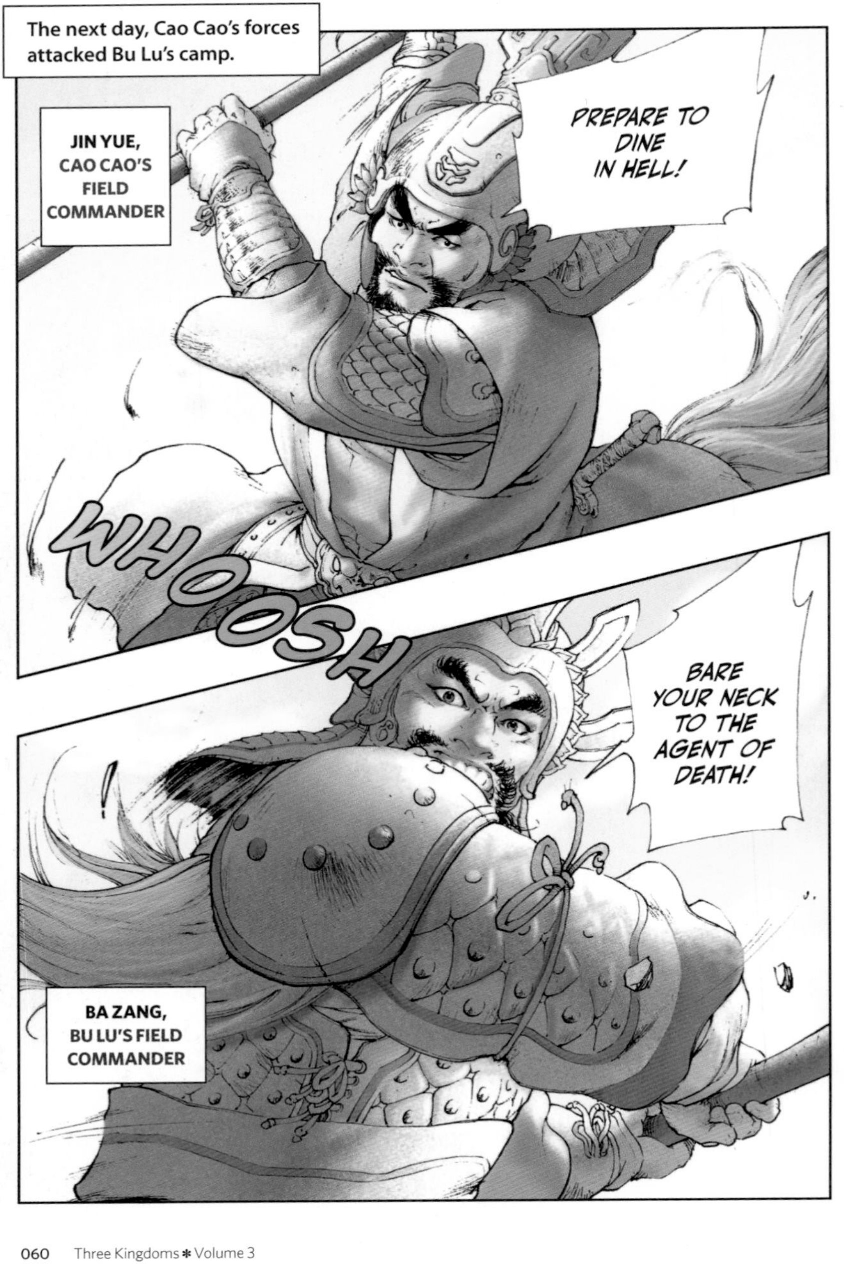
The next day, Cao Cao's forces attacked Bu Lu's camp.
JIN YUE, CAO CAO'S FIELD COMMANDER
PREPARE TO DINE IN HELL!
WHOOSH
BARE YOUR NECK TO THE AGENT OF DEATH!
BA ZANG, BU LU'S FIELD COMMANDER

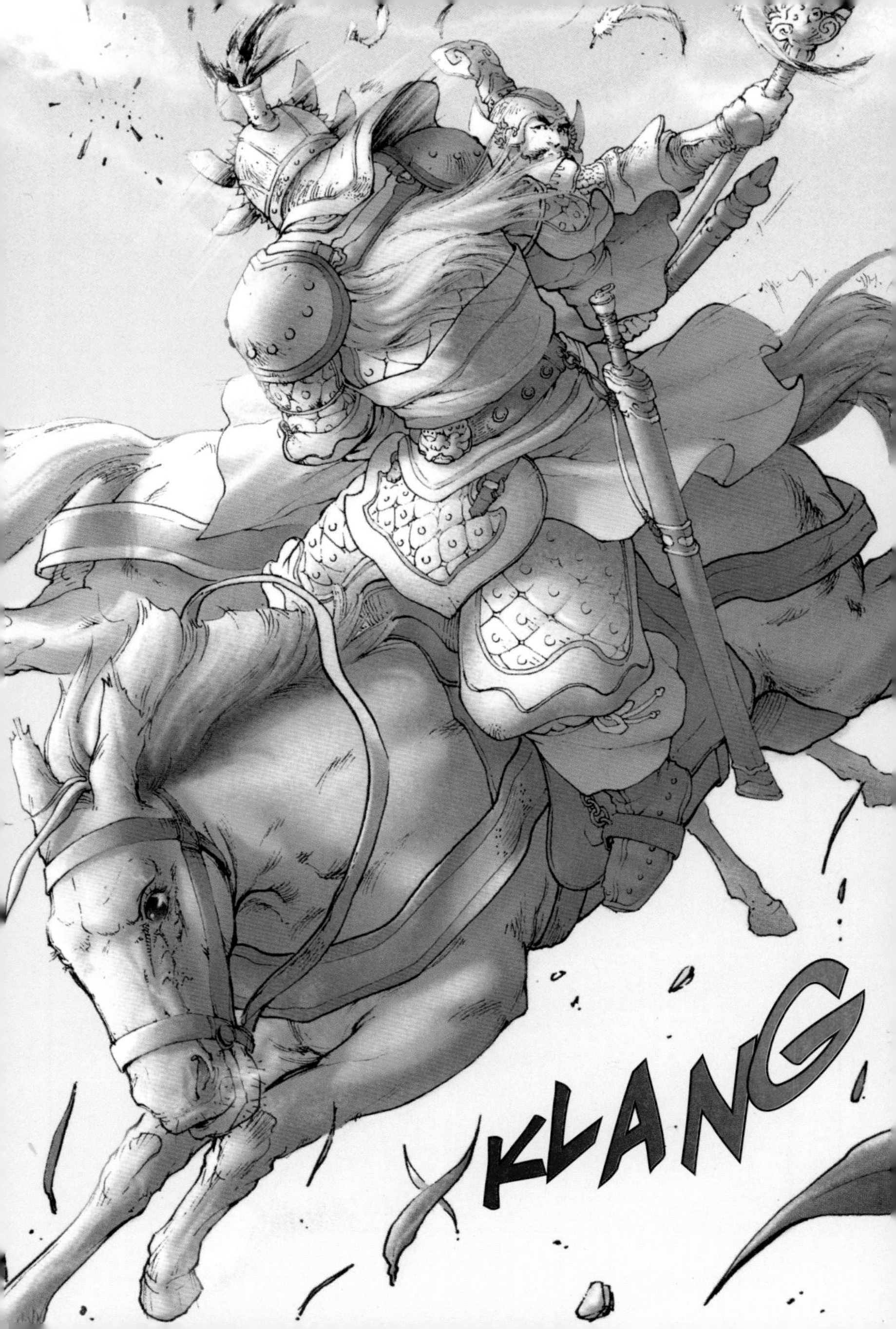
KLANG

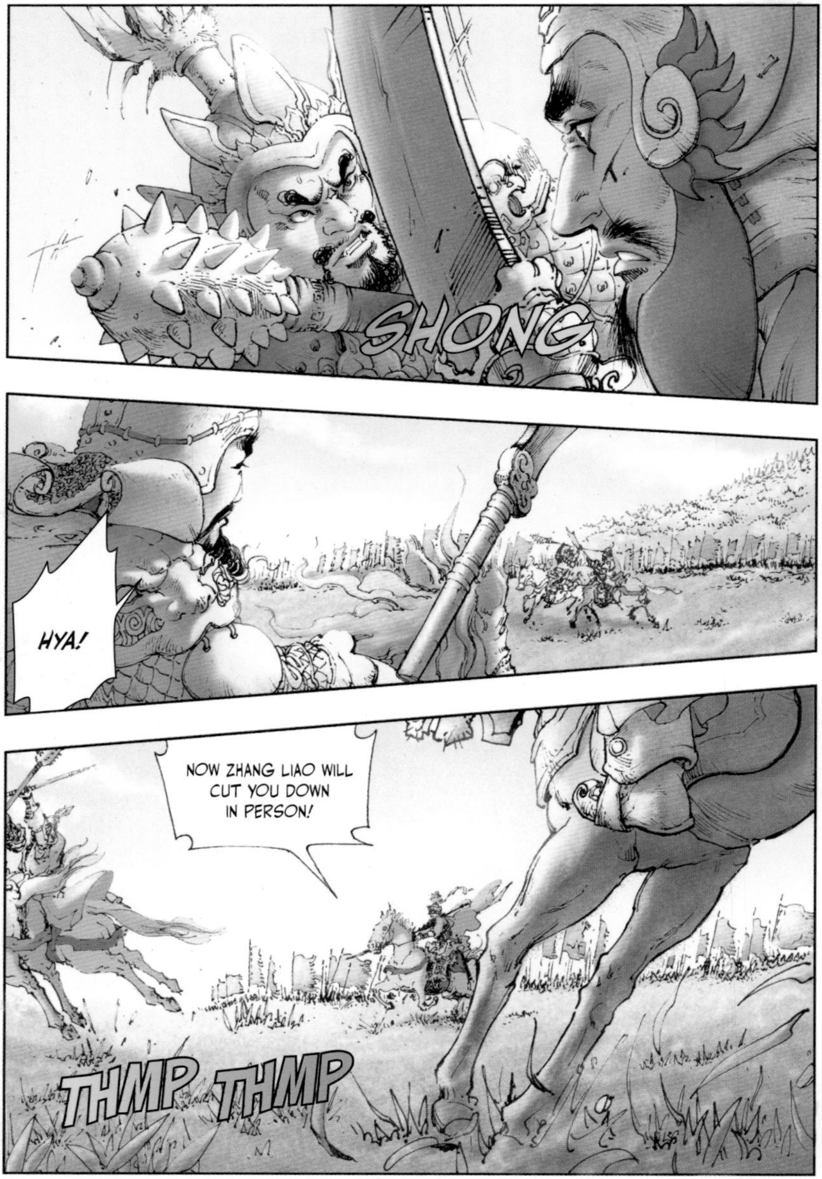
SHONG
HYA!
NOW ZHANG LIAO WILL CUT YOU DOWN IN PERSON!
THMP THMP

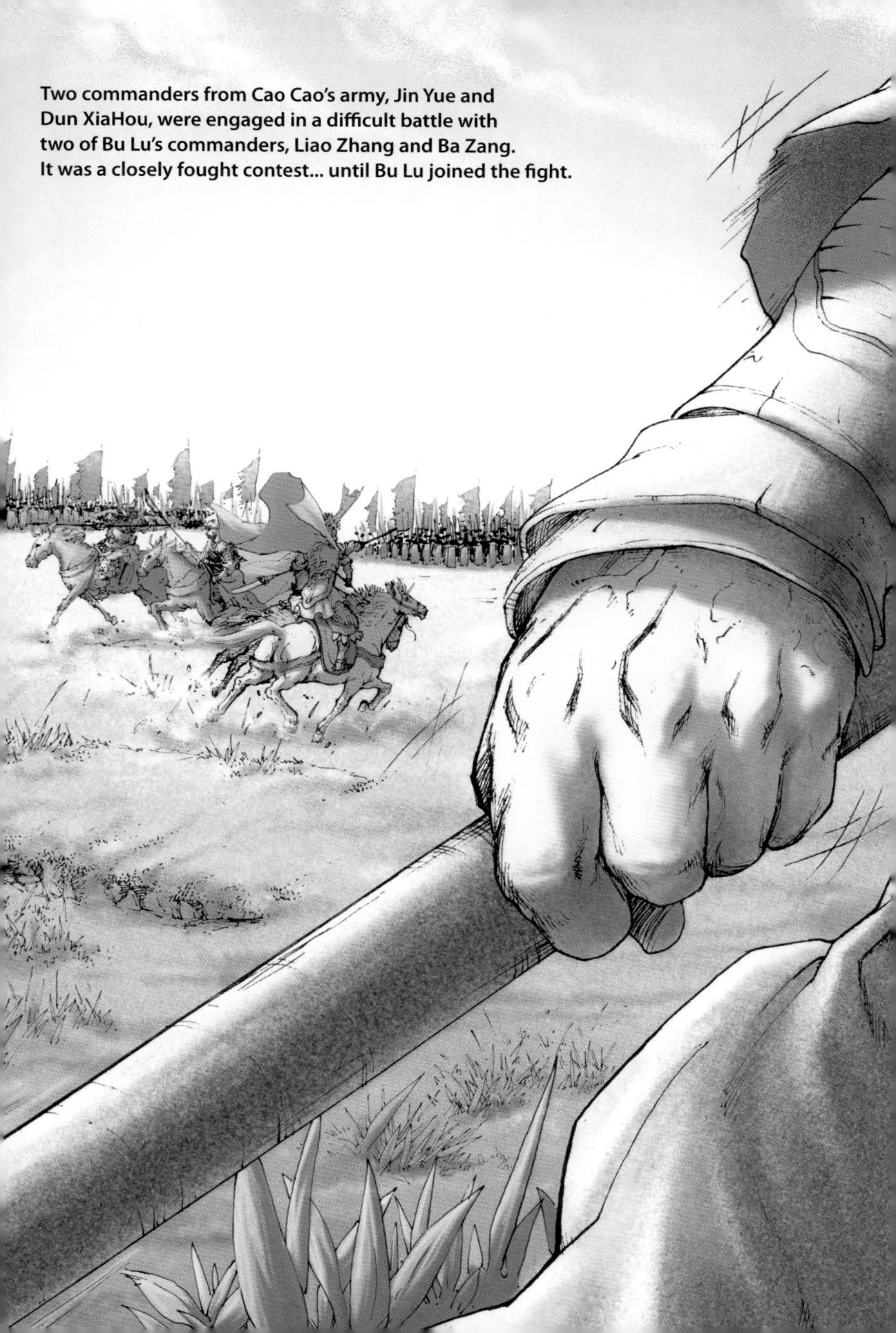
Two commanders from Cao Cao's army, Jin Yue and Dun XiaHou, were engaged in a difficult battle with two of Bu Lu's commanders, Liao Zhang and Ba Zang. It was a closely fought contest... until Bu Lu joined the fight.

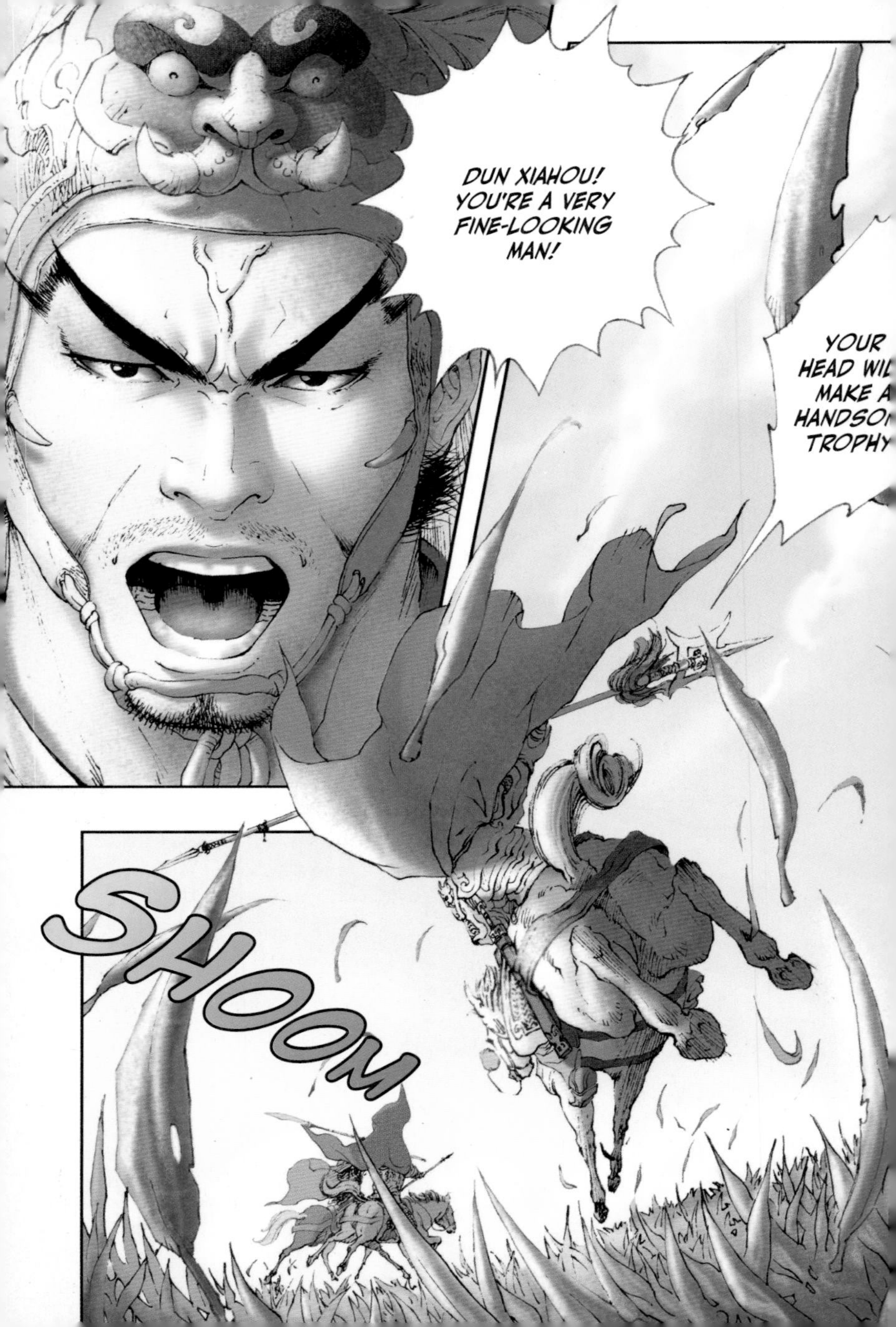
DUN XIAHOU! YOU'RE A VERY FINE-LOOKING MAN!
YOUR HEAD WIL MAKE A HANDSO TROPHY
SHOOM

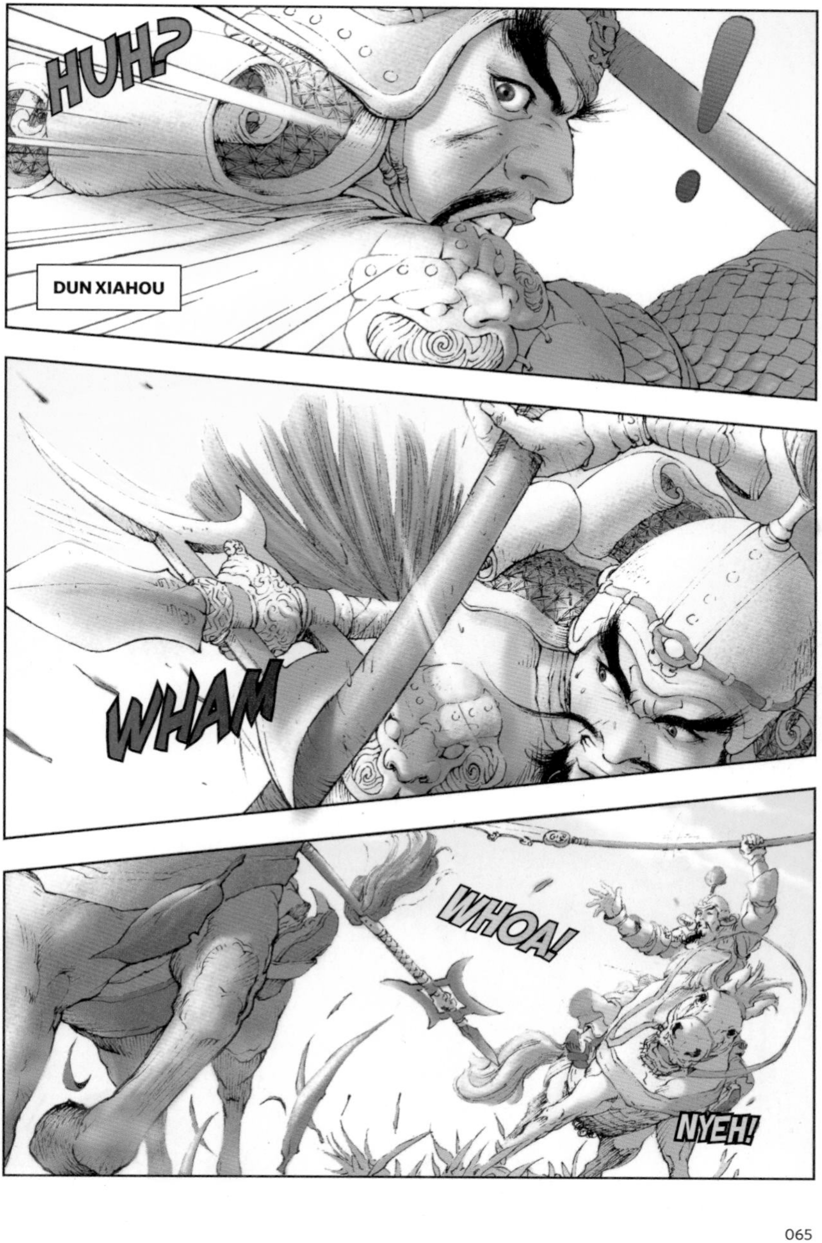
HUH?
!
DUN XIAHOU
WHAM
WHOA!
NYEH!

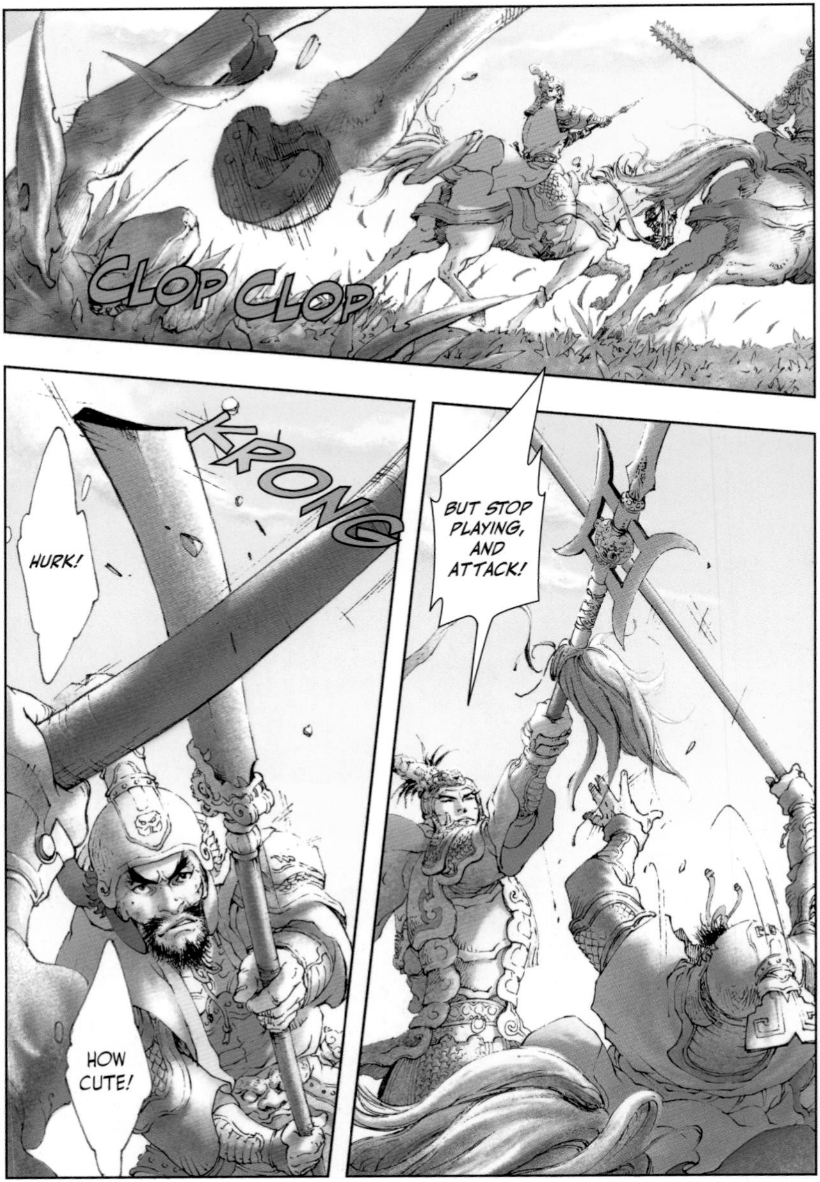
CLOP CLOP
KRONG
HURK!
HOW CUTE!
BUT STOP PLAYING, AND ATTACK!

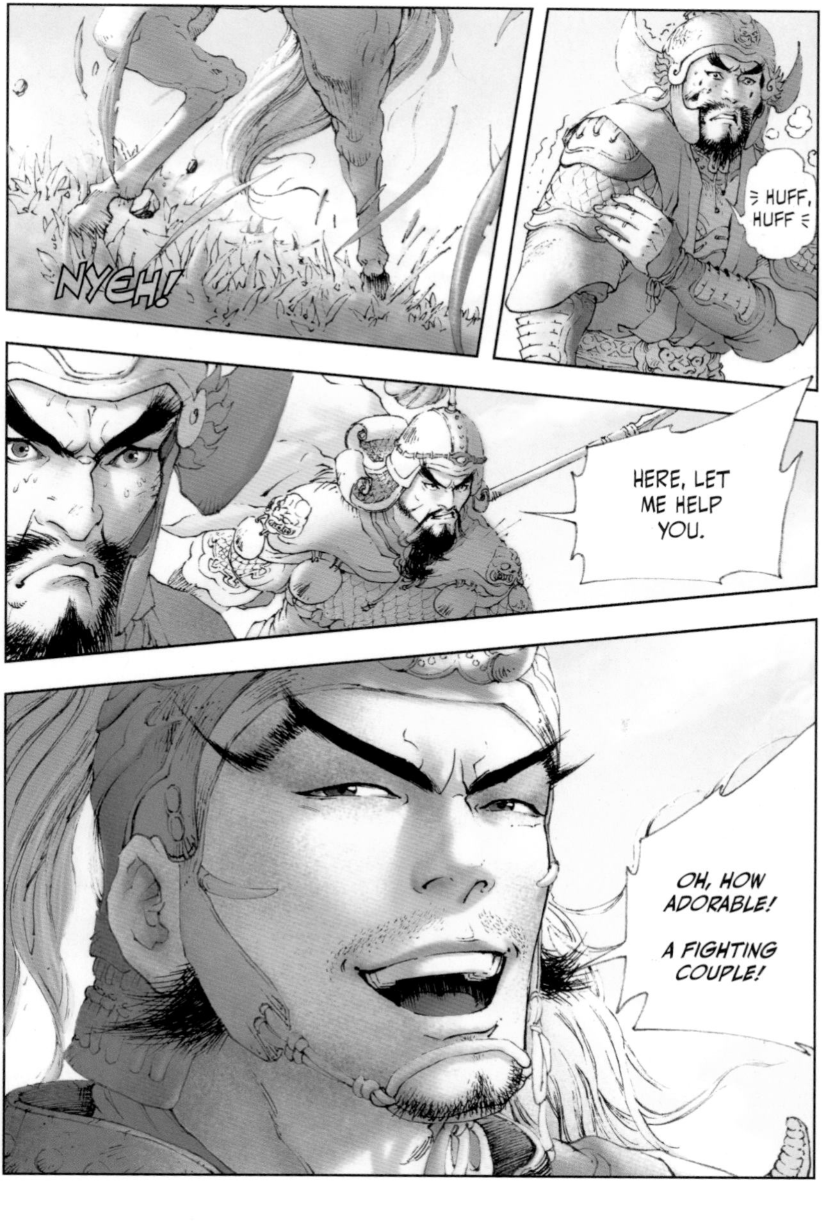
NYEH!
≡ HUFF, HUFF ≡
HERE, LET ME HELP YOU.
OH, HOW ADORABLE!
A FIGHTING COUPLE!

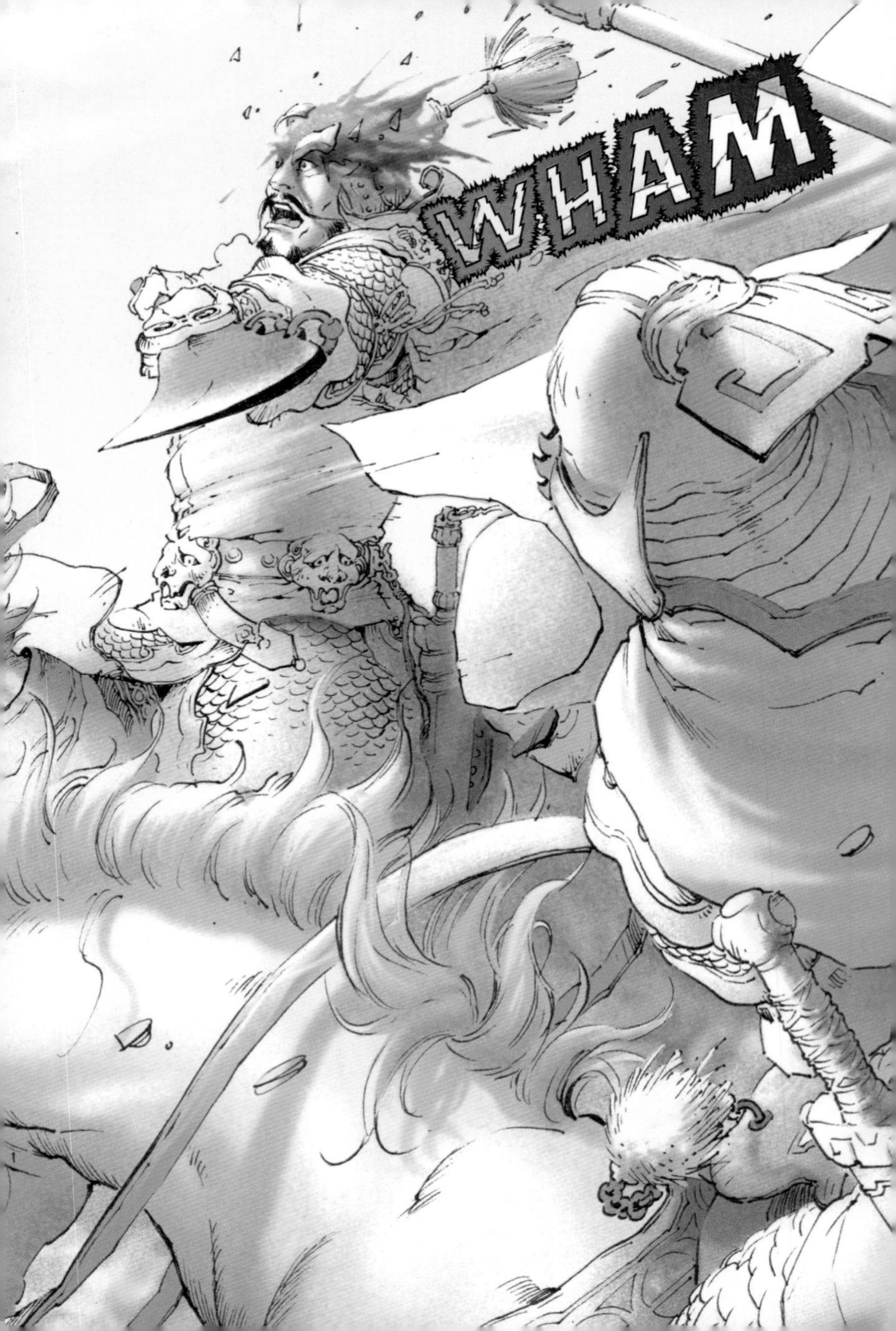
WHAM

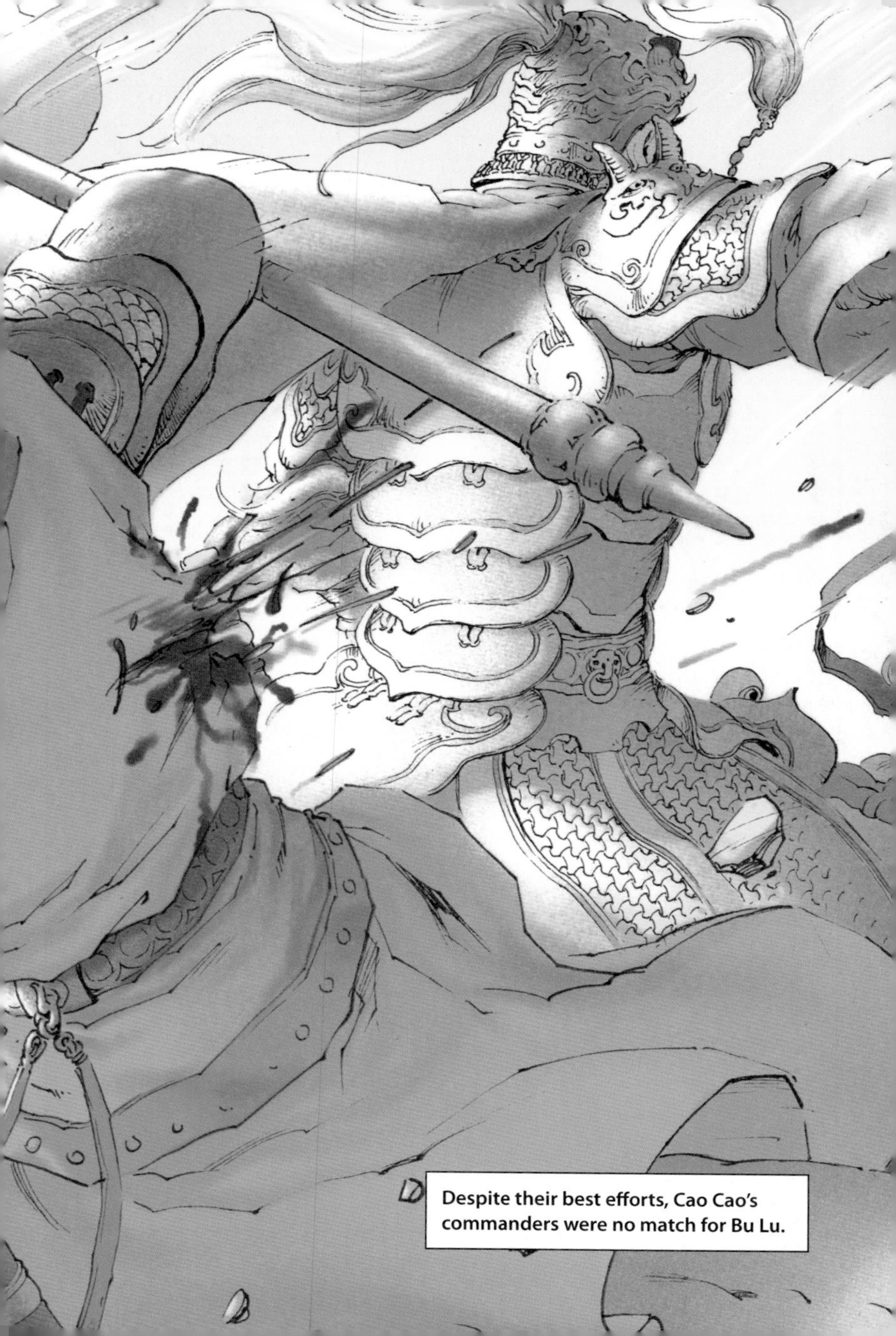
Despite their best efforts, Cao Cao's commanders were no match for Bu Lu.

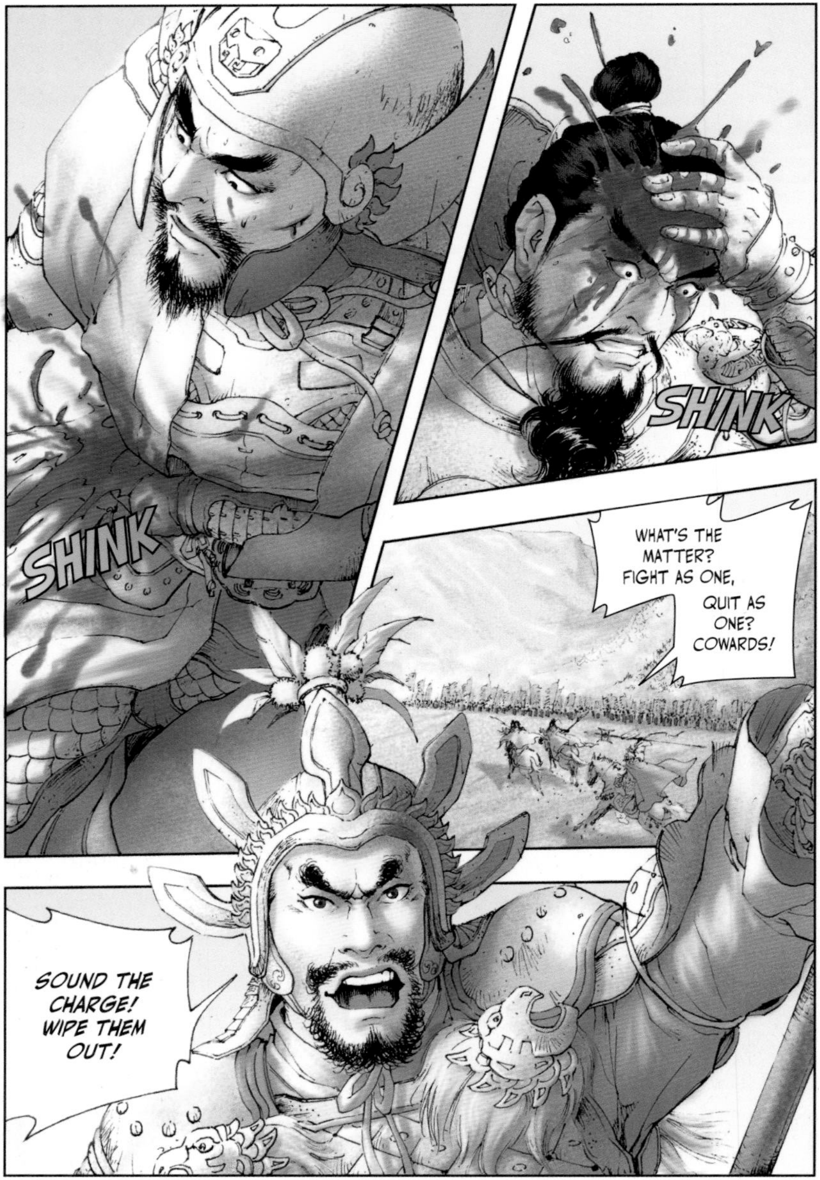
SHINK
SHINK
WHAT'S THE MATTER? FIGHT AS ONE, QUIT AS ONE? COWARDS!
SOUND THE CHARGE! WIPE THEM OUT!

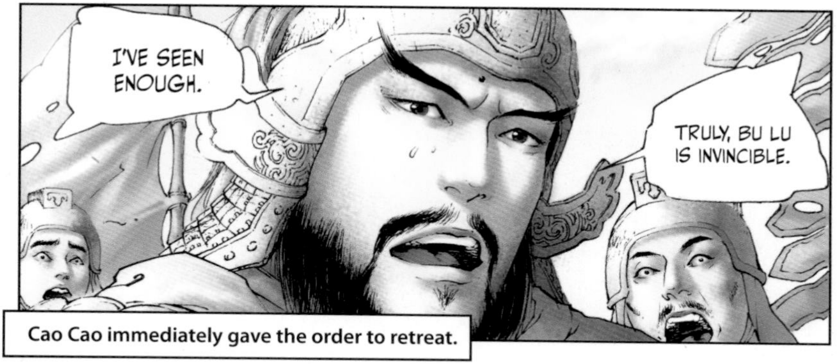
I'VE SEEN ENOUGH.
TRULY, BU LU IS INVINCIBLE.
Cao Cao immediately gave the order to retreat.

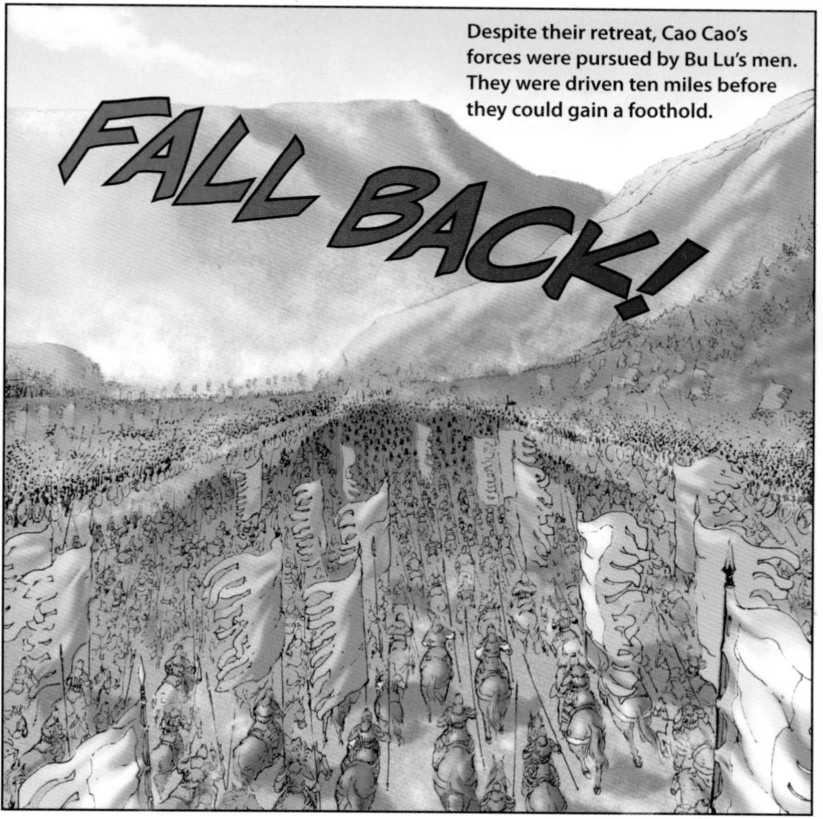
Despite their retreat, Cao Cao's forces were pursued by Bu Lu's men. They were driven ten miles before they could gain a foothold.
FALL BACK!

Later, Bu Lu celebrated his victory.

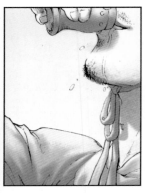

HA HA HA! GLASSES UP, EVERYONE! A TOAST TO VICTORY!

OH, GONG CHEN...

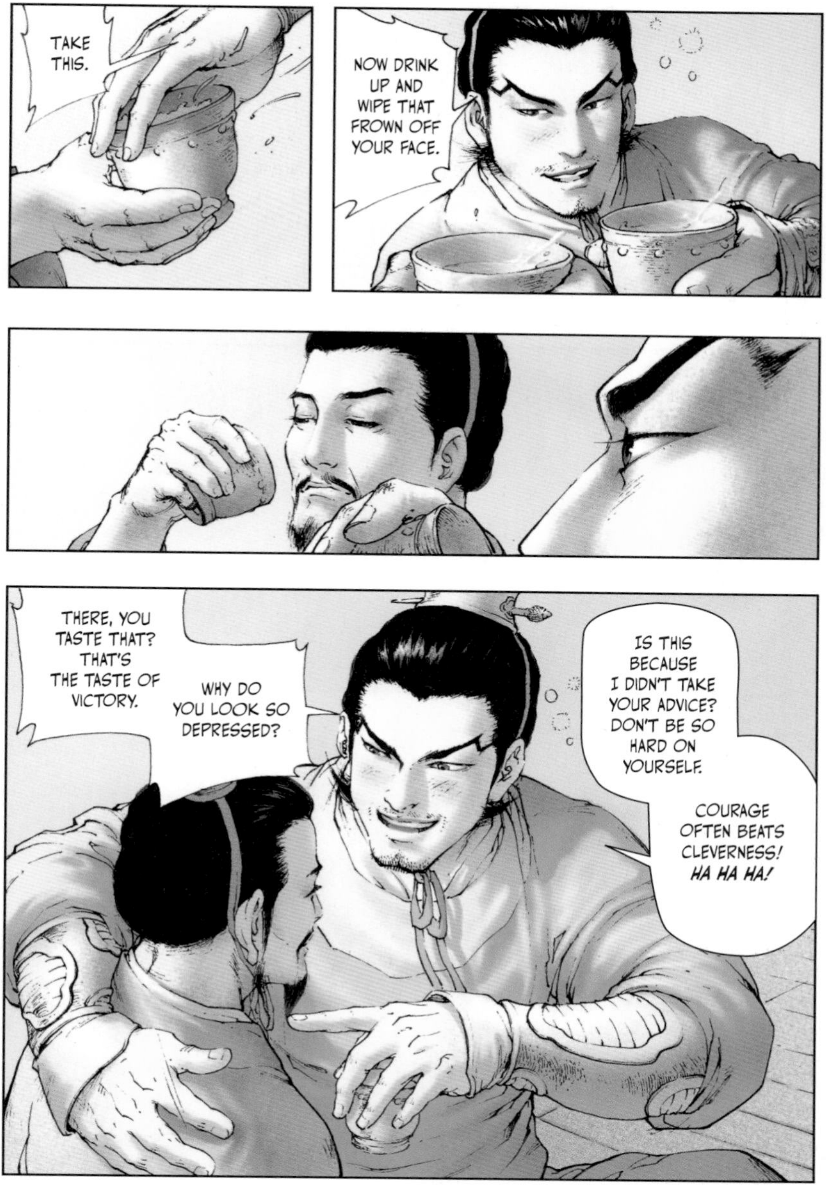
TAKE THIS.
NOW DRINK UP AND WIPE THAT FROWN OFF YOUR FACE.
THERE, YOU TASTE THAT? THAT'S THE TASTE OF VICTORY.
WHY DO YOU LOOK SO DEPRESSED?
IS THIS BECAUSE I DIDN'T TAKE YOUR ADVICE? DON'T BE SO HARD ON YOURSELF.
COURAGE OFTEN BEATS CLEVERNESS! HA HA HA!

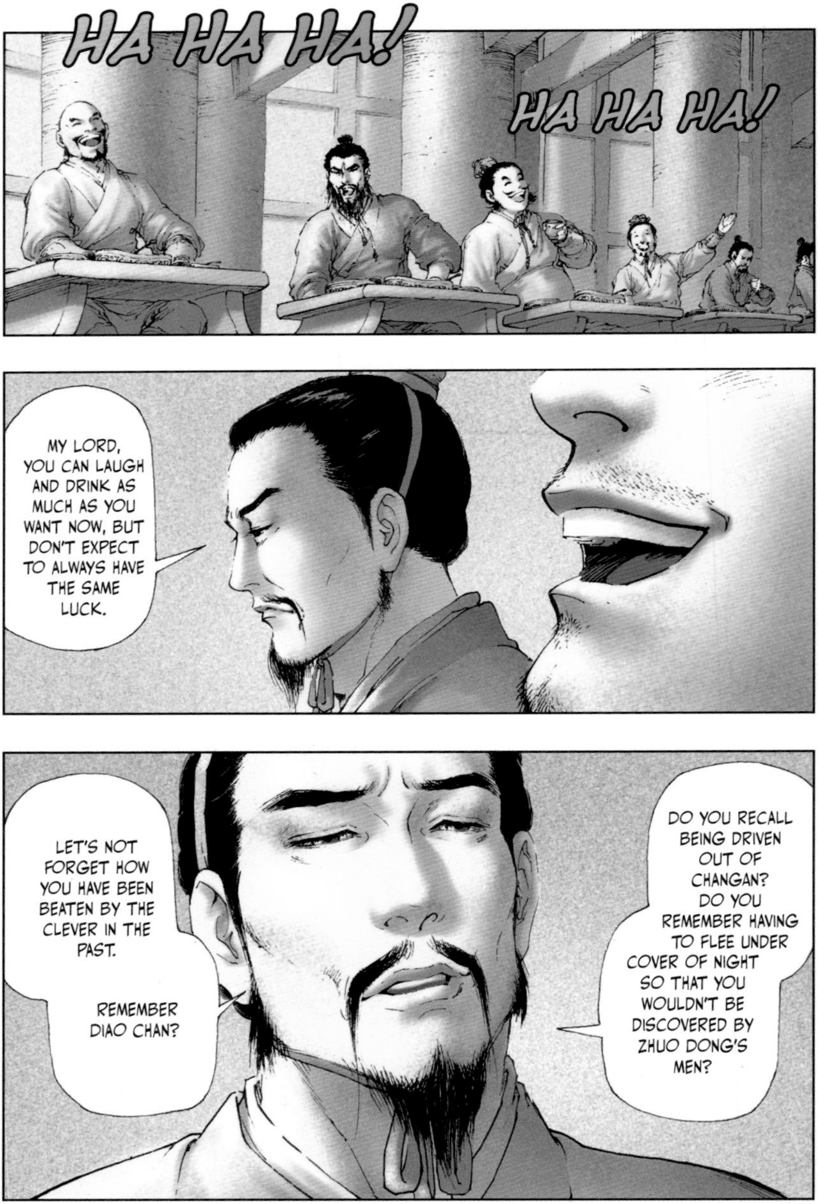
HA HA HA!
HA HA HA!
MY LORD, YOU CAN LAUGH AND DRINK AS MUCH AS YOU WANT NOW, BUT DON'T EXPECT TO ALWAYS HAVE THE SAME LUCK.
DO YOU RECALL BEING DRIVEN OUT OF CHANGAN? DO YOU REMEMBER HAVING TO FLEE UNDER COVER OF NIGHT SO THAT YOU WOULDN'T BE DISCOVERED BY ZHUO DONG'S MEN?
LET'S NOT FORGET HOW YOU HAVE BEEN BEATEN BY THE CLEVER IN THE PAST.
REMEMBER DIAO CHAN?

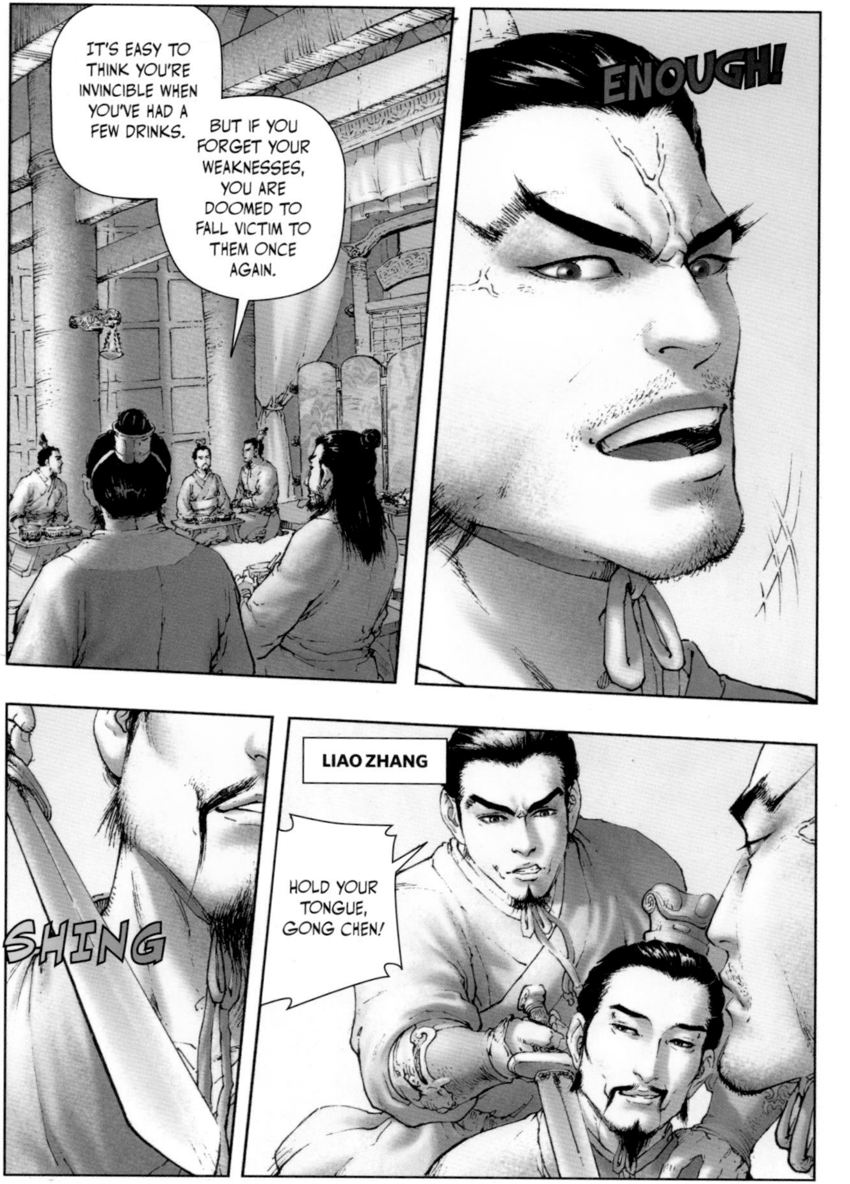
IT'S EASY TO THINK YOU'RE INVINCIBLE WHEN YOU'VE HAD A FEW DRINKS.
BUT IF YOU FORGET YOUR WEAKNESSES, YOU ARE DOOMED TO FALL VICTIM TO THEM ONCE AGAIN.
ENOUGH!
SHING
LIAO ZHANG
HOLD YOUR TONGUE, GONG CHEN!

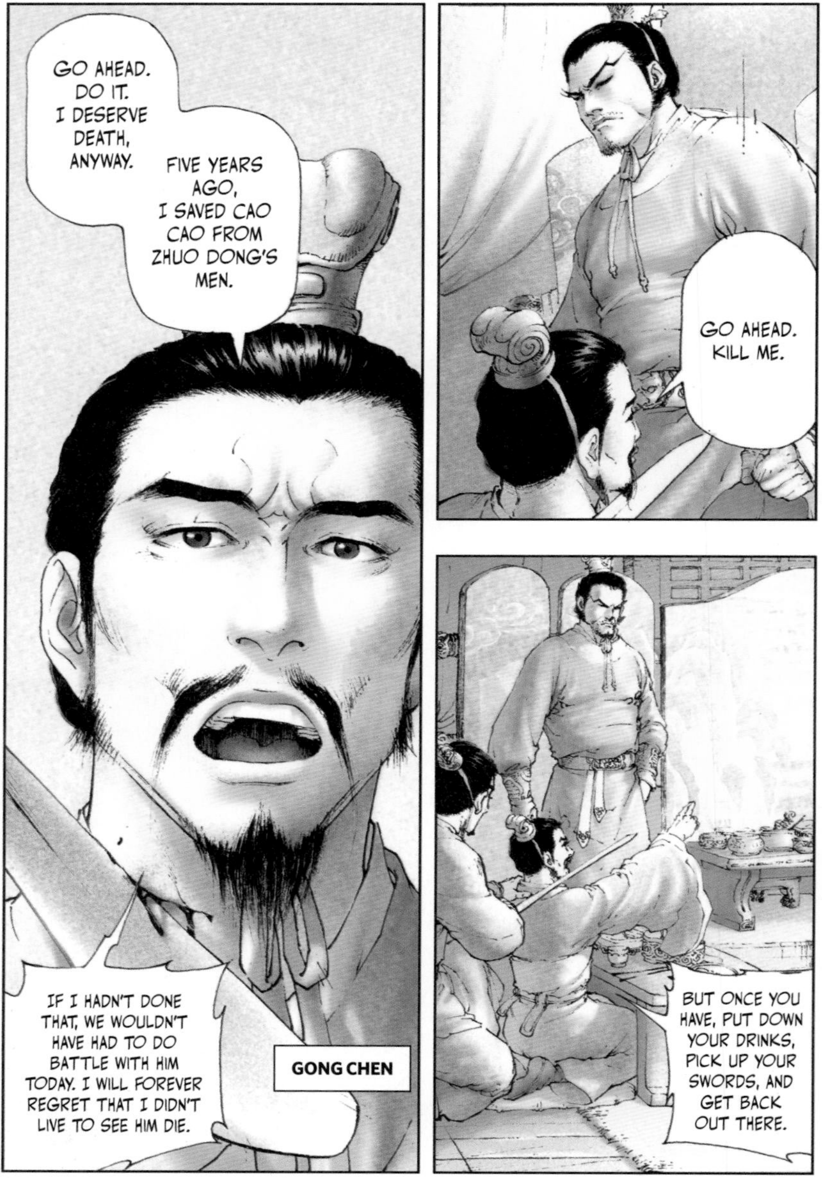
GO AHEAD. DO IT. I DESERVE DEATH, ANYWAY.
FIVE YEARS AGO, I SAVED CAO CAO FROM ZHUO DONG'S MEN.
IF I HADN'T DONE THAT, WE WOULDN'T HAVE HAD TO DO BATTLE WITH HIM TODAY. I WILL FOREVER REGRET THAT I DIDN'T LIVE TO SEE HIM DIE.
GONG CHEN
GO AHEAD. KILL ME.
BUT ONCE YOU HAVE, PUT DOWN YOUR DRINKS, PICK UP YOUR SWORDS, AND GET BACK OUT THERE.

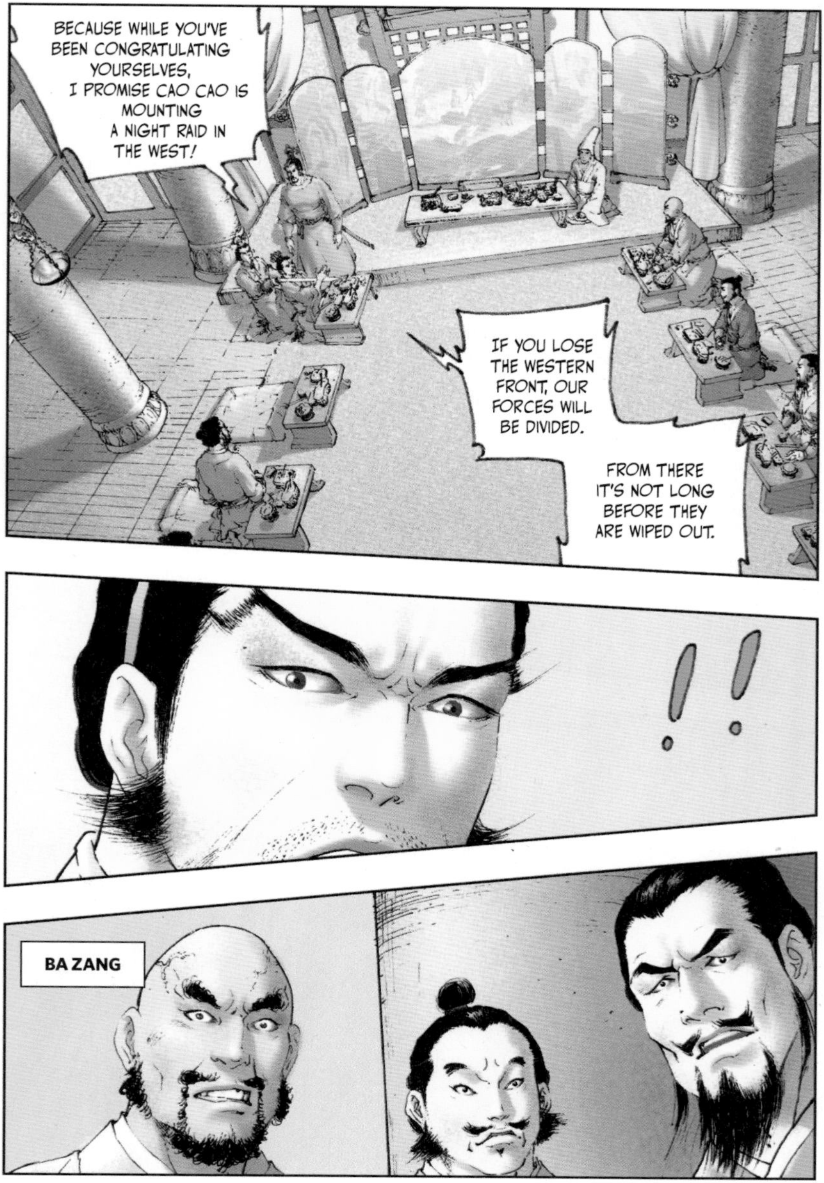
BECAUSE WHILE YOU'VE BEEN CONGRATULATING YOURSELVES, I PROMISE CAO CAO IS MOUNTING A NIGHT RAID IN THE WEST!
IF YOU LOSE THE WESTERN FRONT, OUR FORCES WILL BE DIVIDED.
FROM THERE IT'S NOT LONG BEFORE THEY ARE WIPED OUT.
!!
BA ZANG

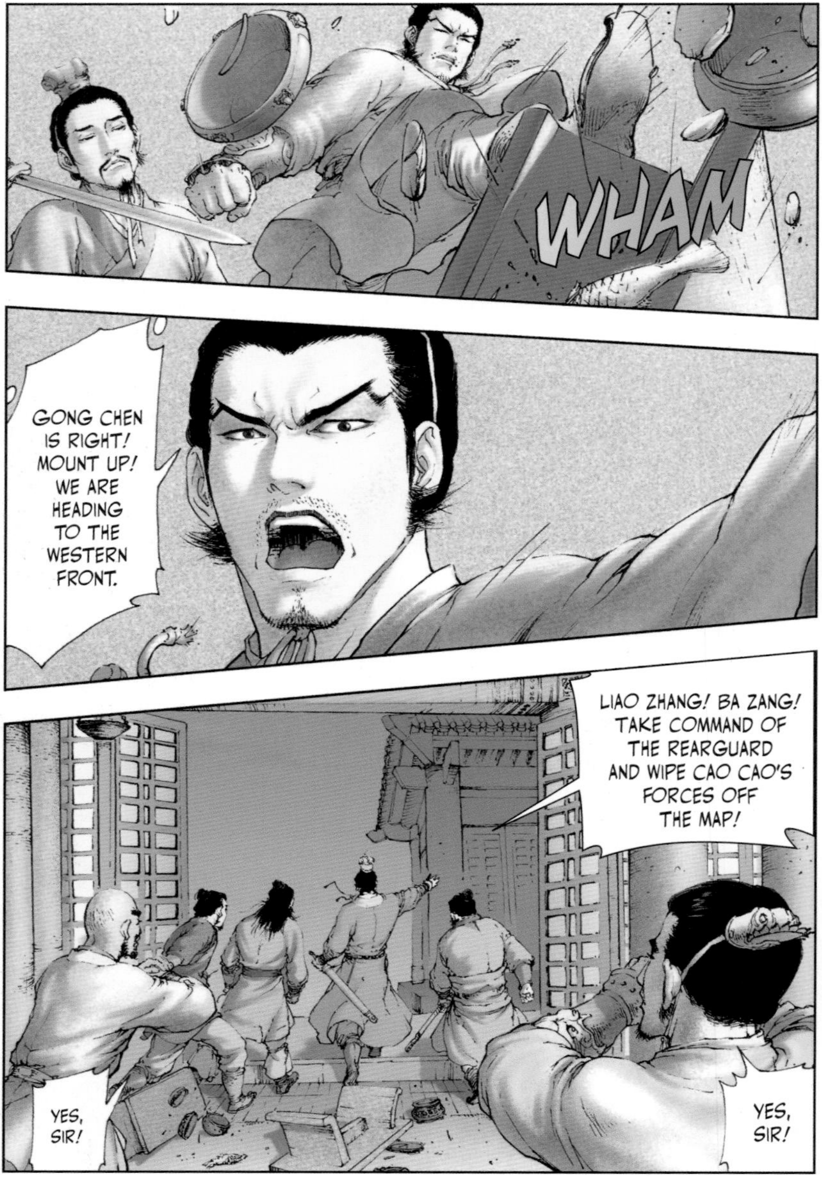
WHAM
GONG CHEN IS RIGHT! MOUNT UP! WE ARE HEADING TO THE WESTERN FRONT.
LIAO ZHANG! BA ZANG! TAKE COMMAND OF THE REARGUARD AND WIPE CAO CAO'S FORCES OFF THE MAP!
YES, SIR!
YES, SIR!

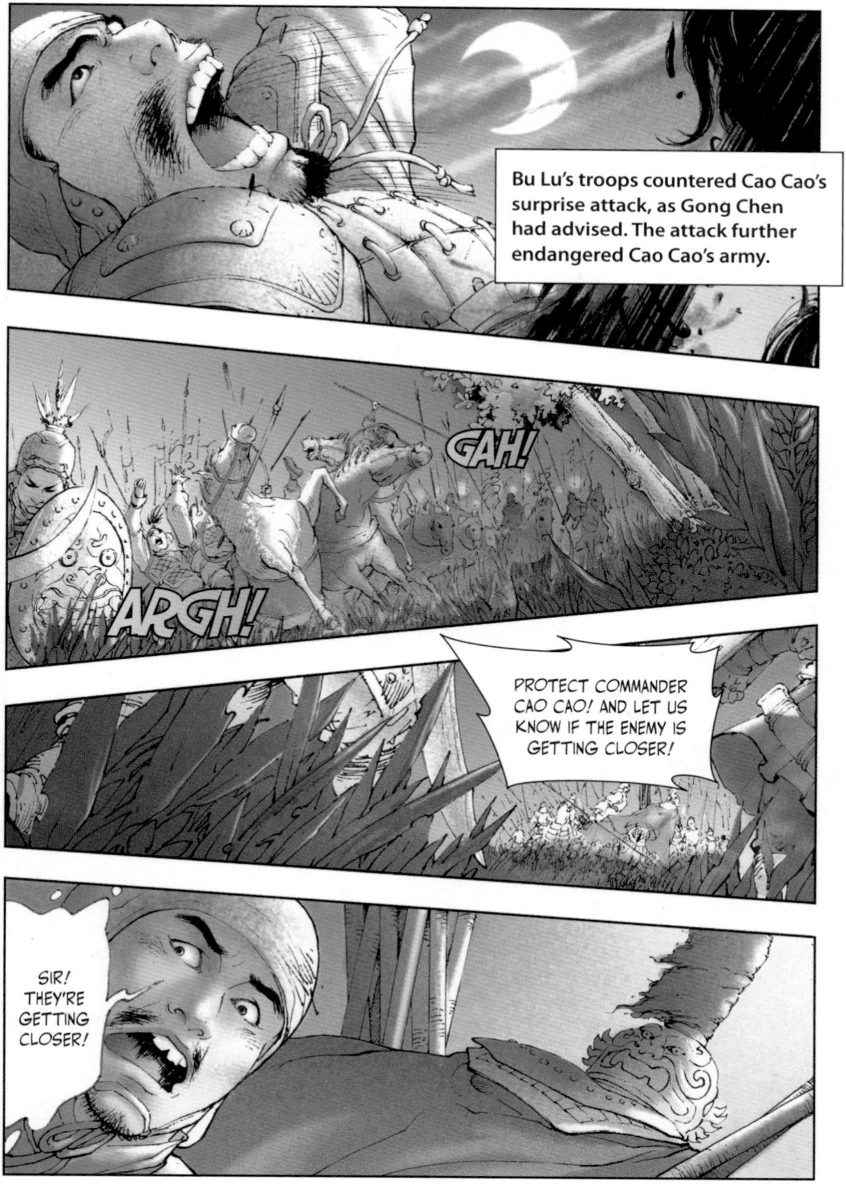
Bu Lu's troops countered Cao Cao's surprise attack, as Gong Chen had advised. The attack further endangered Cao Cao's army.
GAH!
ARGH!
PROTECT COMMANDER CAO CAO! AND LET US KNOW IF THE ENEMY IS GETTING CLOSER!
SIR! THEY'RE GETTING CLOSER!

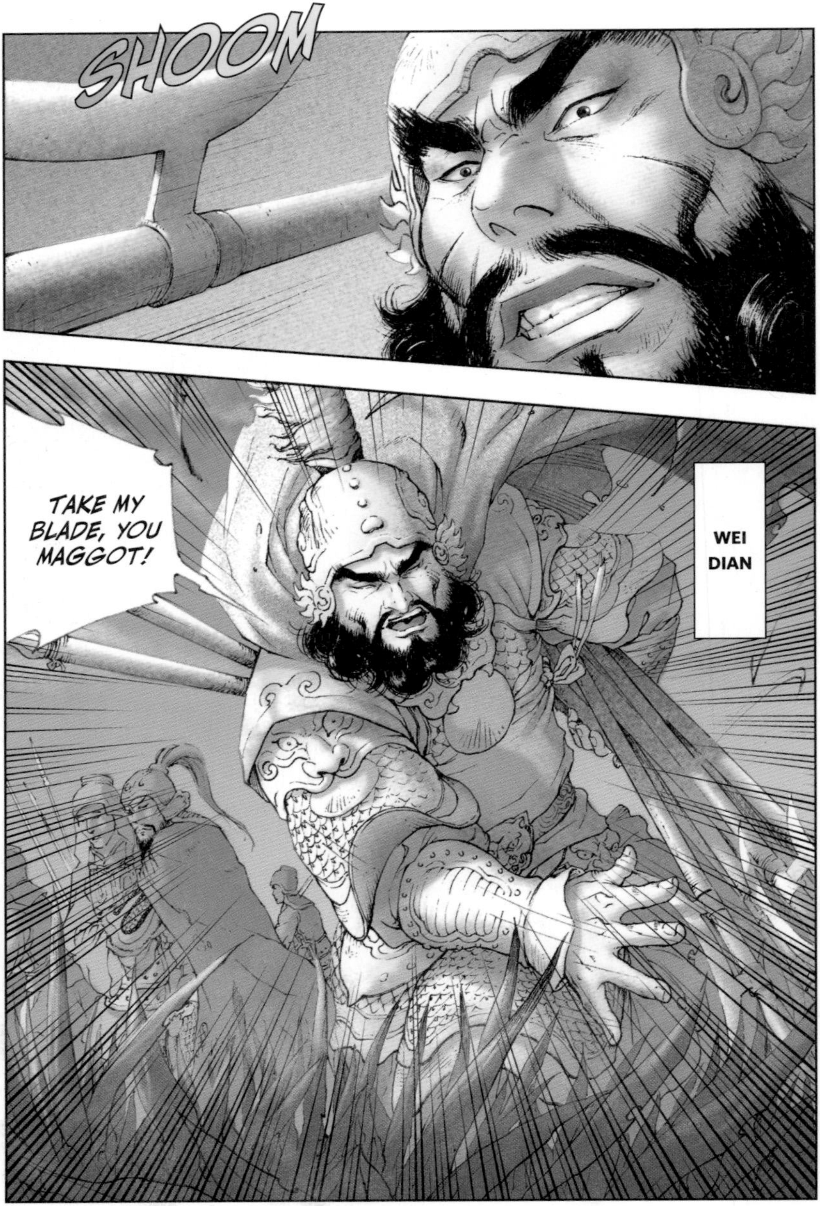
SHOOM
TAKE MY BLADE, YOU MAGGOT!
WEI DIAN

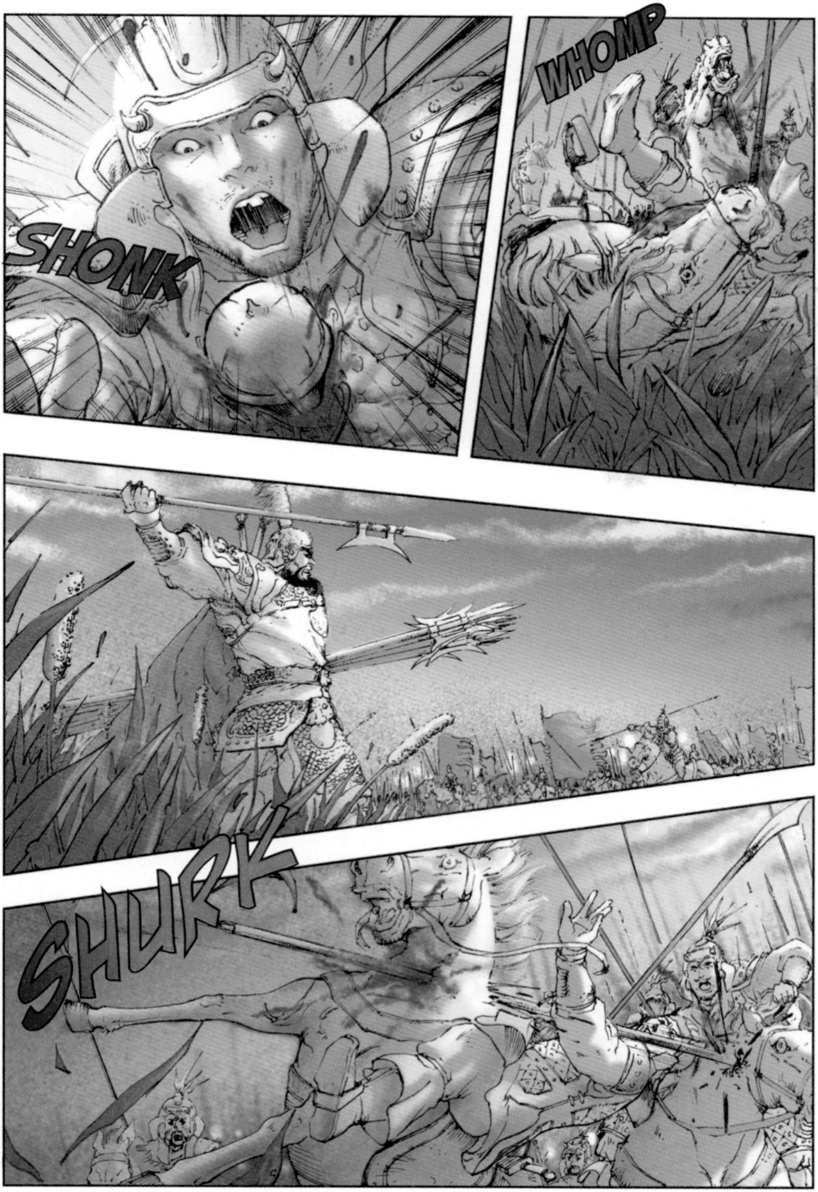
SHONK
WHOMP
SHURK

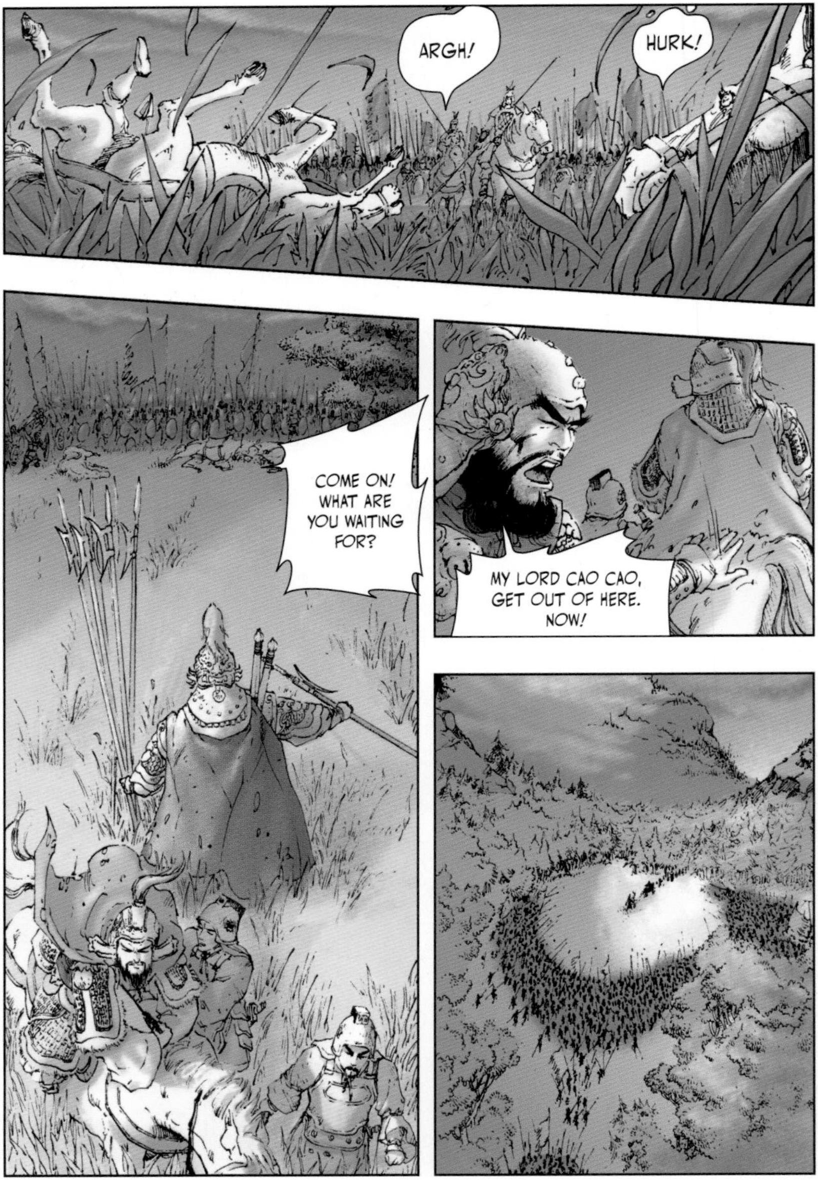
ARGH!
HURK!
COME ON! WHAT ARE YOU WAITING FOR?
MY LORD CAO CAO, GET OUT OF HERE. NOW!

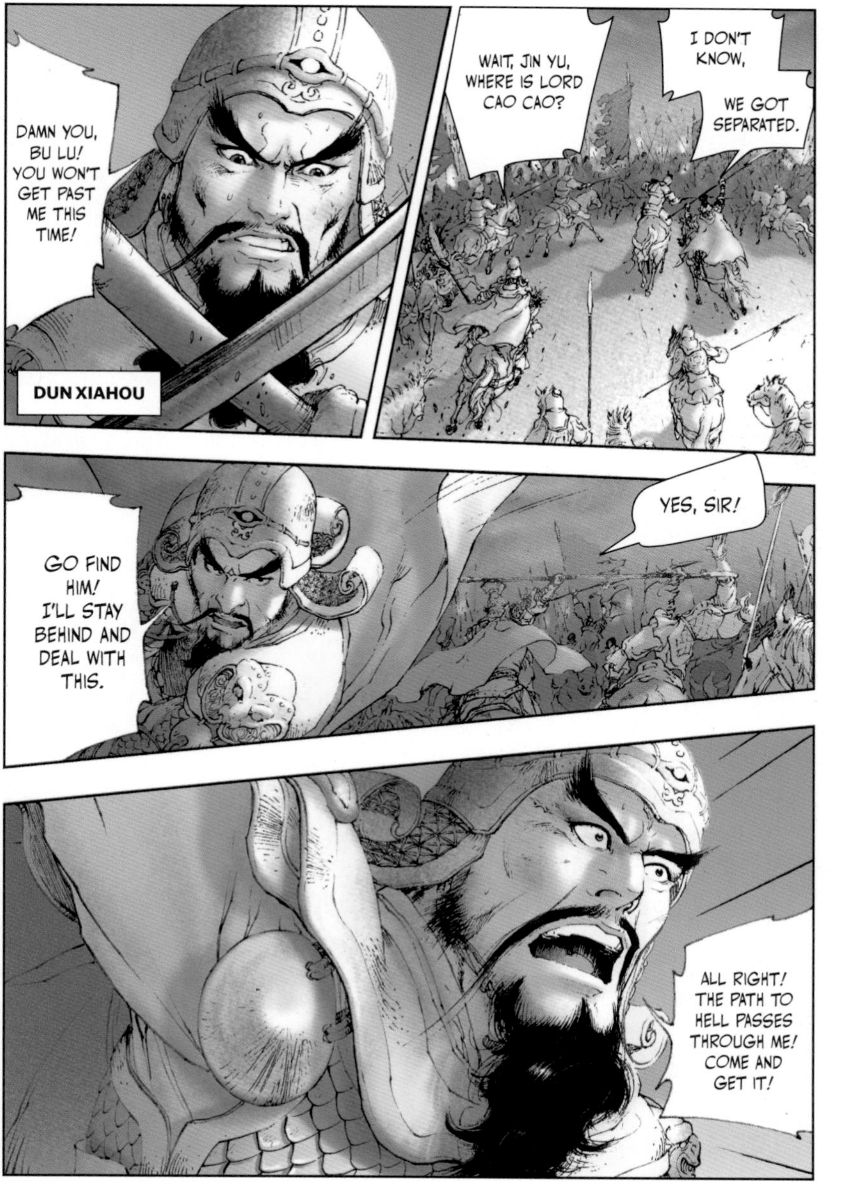
DAMN YOU, BU LU! YOU WON'T GET PAST ME THIS TIME!
DUN XIAHOU
WAIT, JIN YU, WHERE IS LORD CAO CAO?
I DON'T KNOW,
WE GOT SEPARATED.
GO FIND HIM! I'LL STAY BEHIND AND DEAL WITH THIS.
YES, SIR!
ALL RIGHT! THE PATH TO HELL PASSES THROUGH ME! COME AND GET IT!

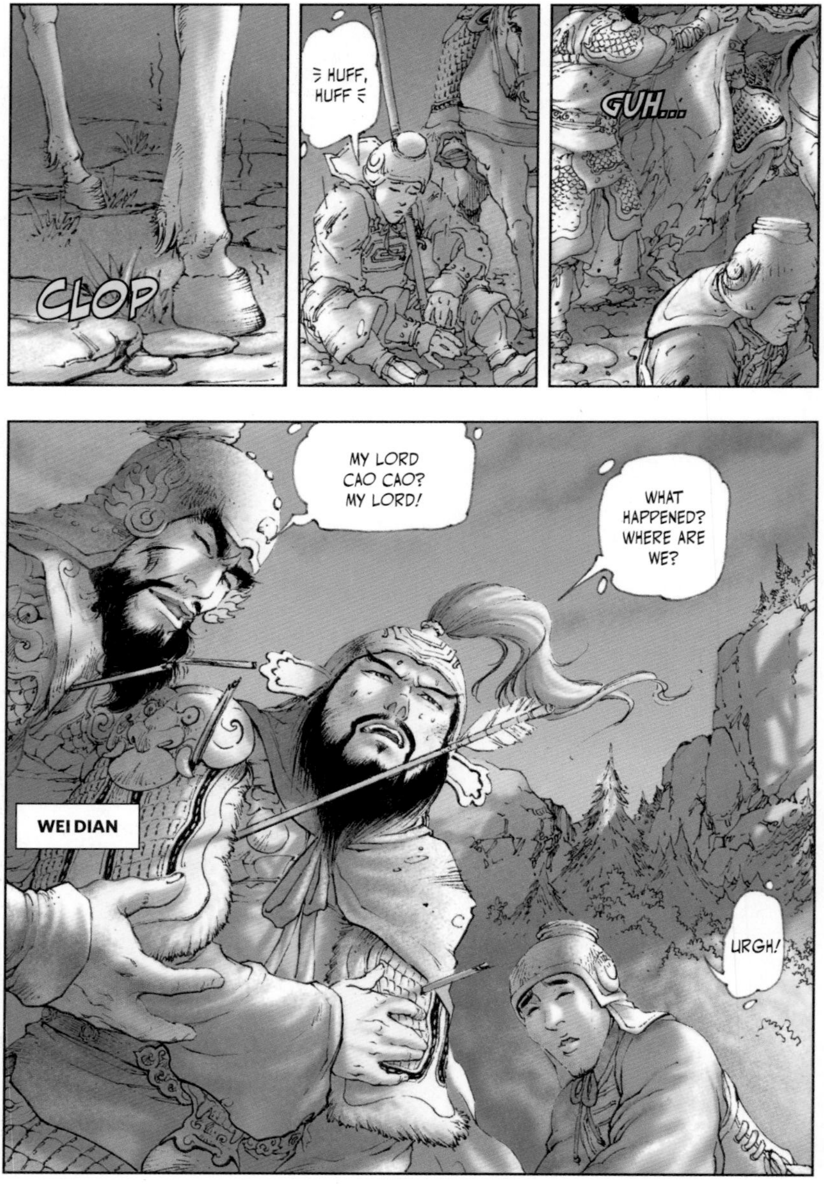
CLOP
HUFF, HUFF
GUH...
MY LORD CAO CAO? MY LORD!
WHAT HAPPENED? WHERE ARE WE?
WEI DIAN
URGH!

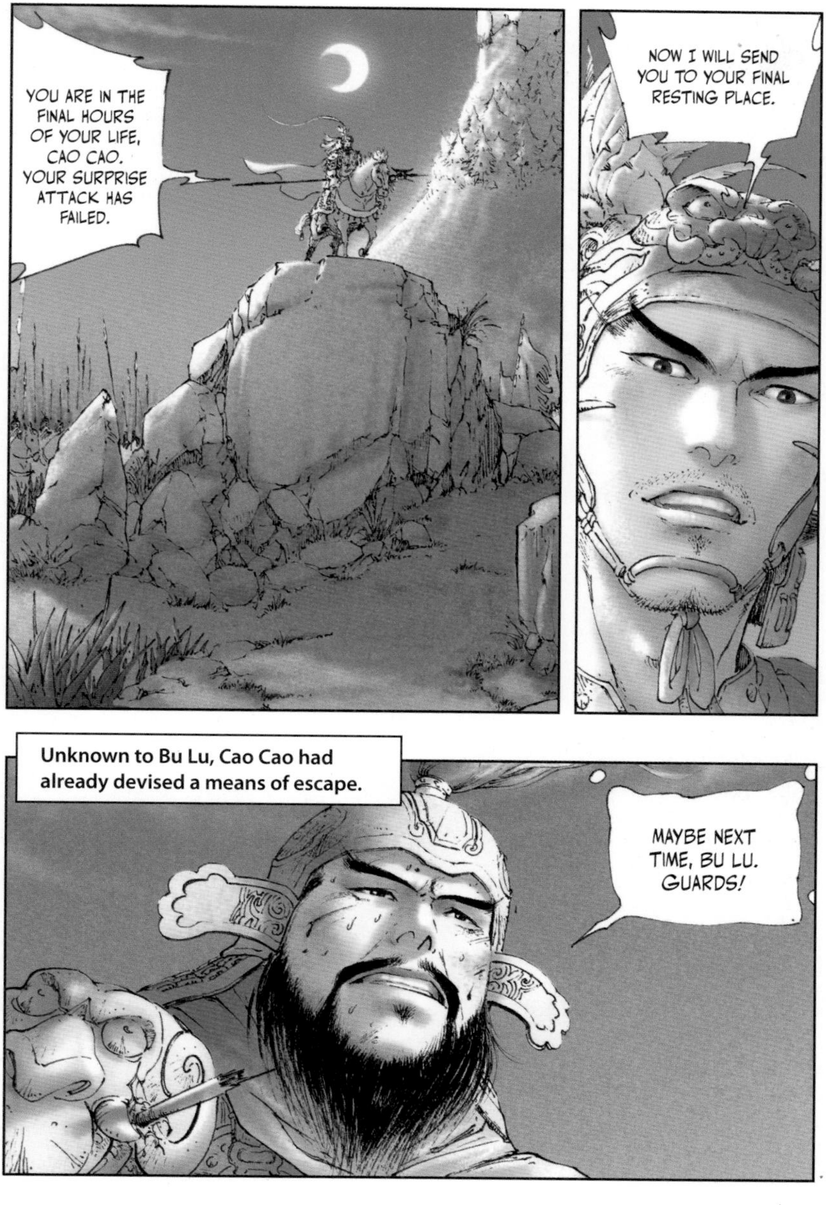
YOU ARE IN THE FINAL HOURS OF YOUR LIFE, CAO CAO. YOUR SURPRISE ATTACK HAS FAILED.
NOW I WILL SEND YOU TO YOUR FINAL RESTING PLACE.
Unknown to Bu Lu, Cao Cao had already devised a means of escape.
MAYBE NEXT TIME, BU LU. GUARDS!

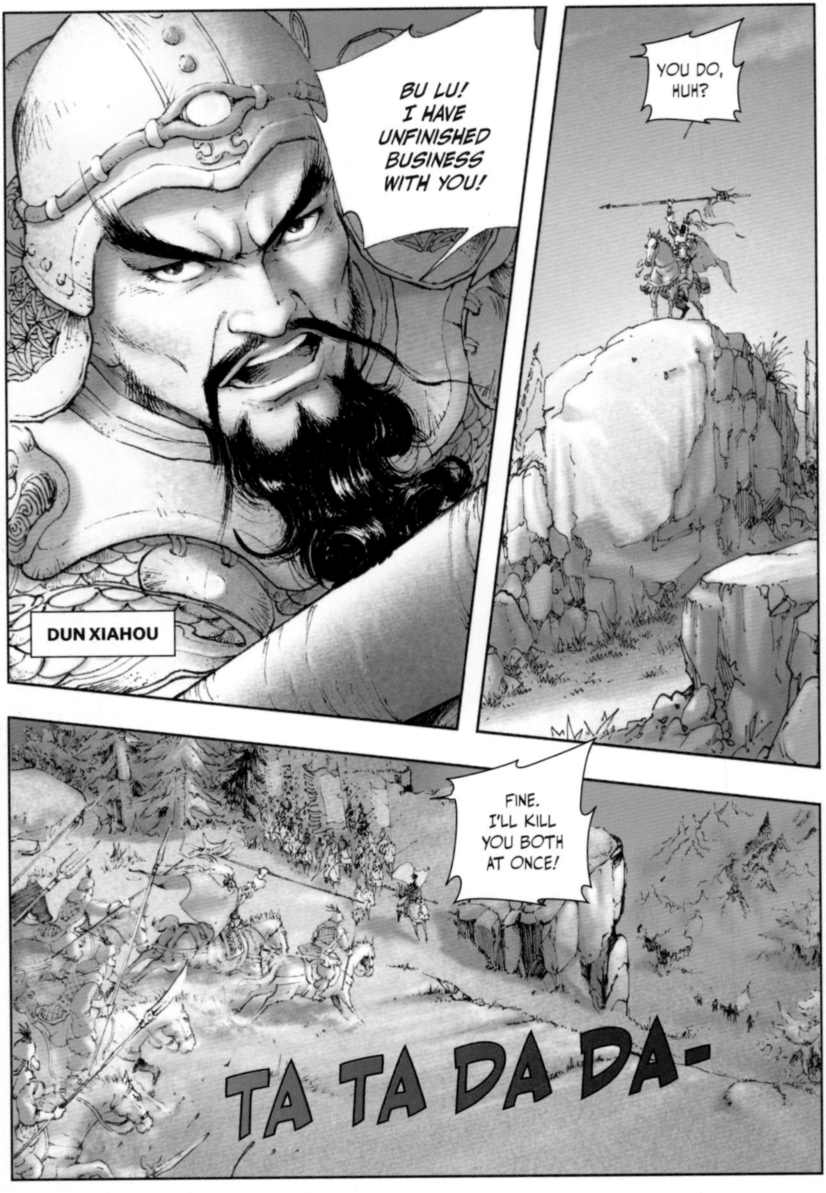
BU LU!
I HAVE
UNFINISHED
BUSINESS
WITH YOU!
DUN XIAHOU
YOU DO,
HUH?
FINE.
I'LL KILL
YOU BOTH
AT ONCE!
TA TA DA DA-

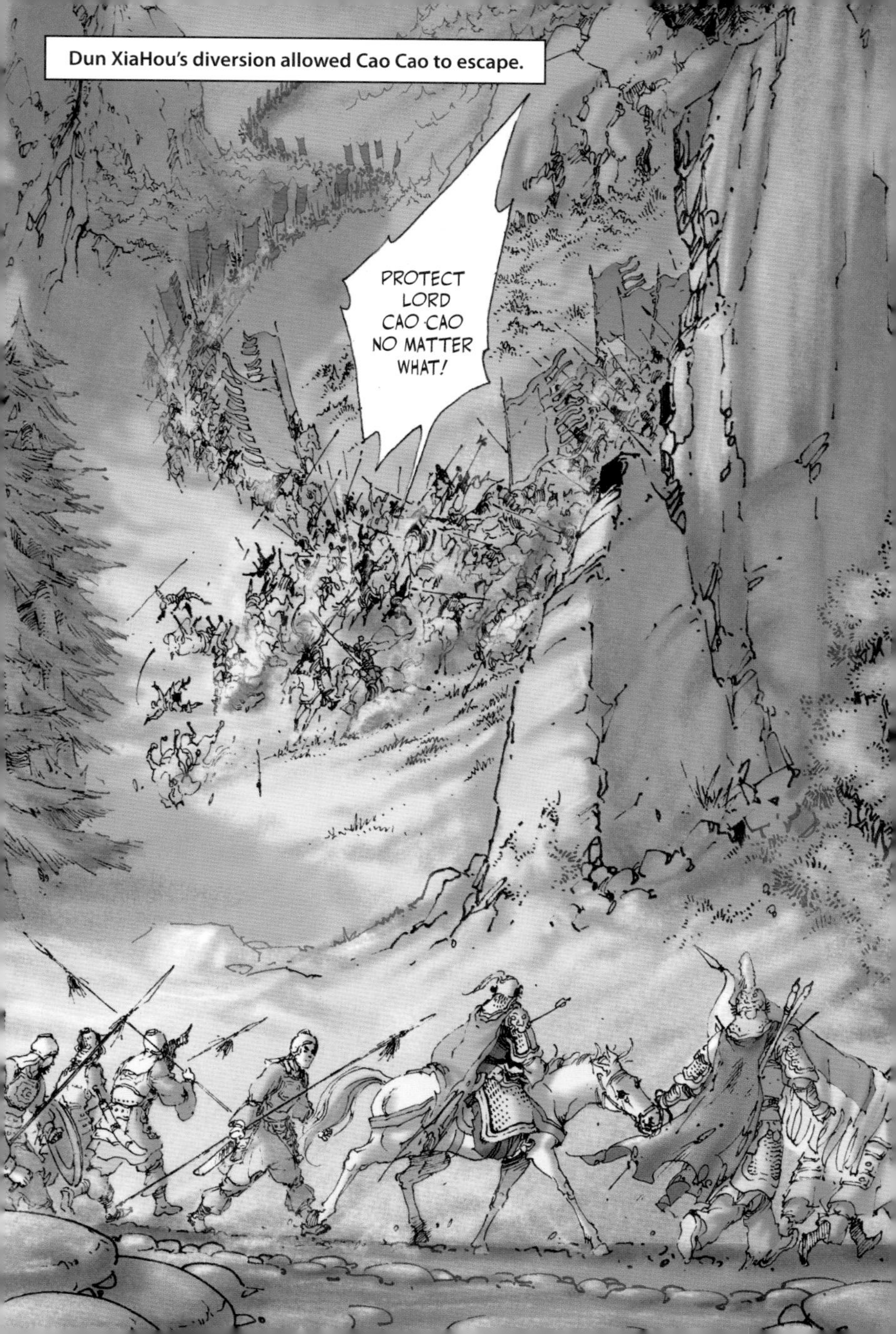
Dun XiaHou's diversion allowed Cao Cao to escape.
PROTECT LORD CAO CAO NO MATTER WHAT!

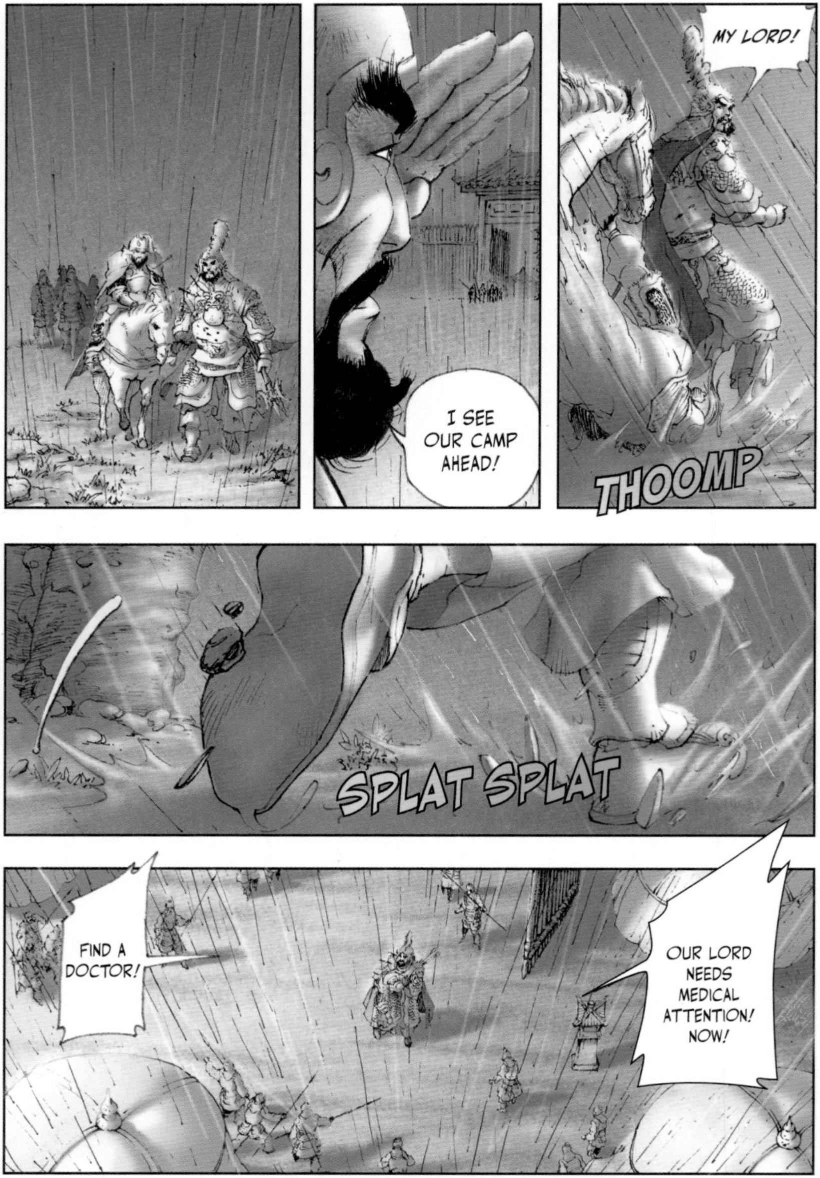
I SEE
OUR CAMP
AHEAD!
MY LORD!
THOOMP
SPLAT SPLAT
FIND A
DOCTOR!
OUR LORD
NEEDS
MEDICAL
ATTENTION!
NOW!

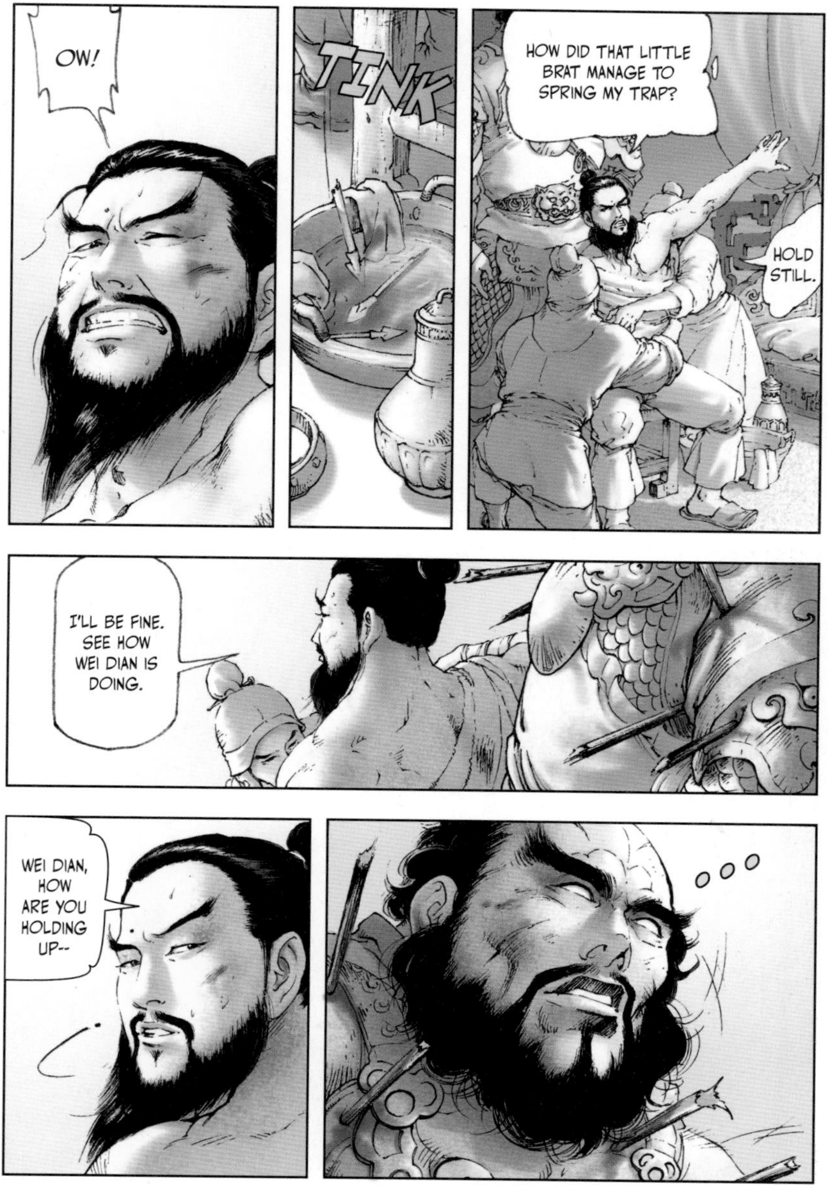
OW!
TINK
HOW DID THAT LITTLE BRAT MANAGE TO SPRING MY TRAP?
HOLD STILL.
I'LL BE FINE. SEE HOW WEI DIAN IS DOING.
WEI DIAN, HOW ARE YOU HOLDING UP--
...

HOLD STILL, COMMANDER! YOU HAVE LOST A LOT OF BLOOD.

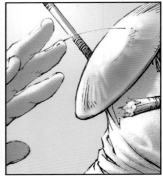

WHOMP

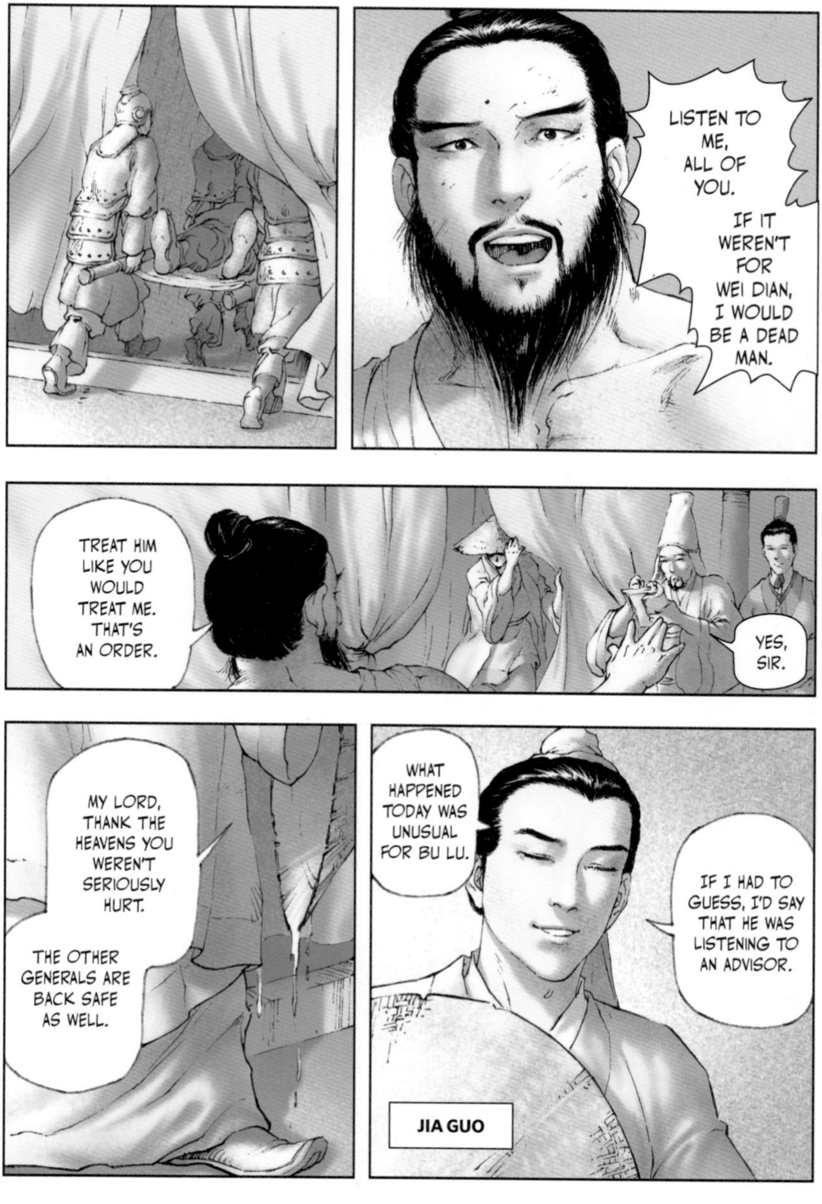

LISTEN TO ME, ALL OF YOU.
IF IT WEREN'T FOR WEI DIAN, I WOULD BE A DEAD MAN.
TREAT HIM LIKE YOU WOULD TREAT ME. THAT'S AN ORDER.
YES, SIR.
MY LORD, THANK THE HEAVENS YOU WEREN'T SERIOUSLY HURT.
THE OTHER GENERALS ARE BACK SAFE AS WELL.
WHAT HAPPENED TODAY WAS UNUSUAL FOR BU LU.
IF I HAD TO GUESS, I'D SAY THAT HE WAS LISTENING TO AN ADVISOR.
JIA GUO

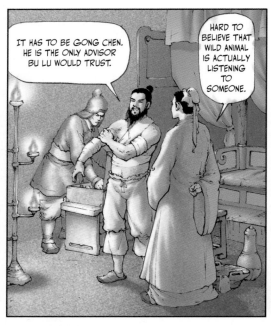

IT HAS TO BE GONG CHEN. HE IS THE ONLY ADVISOR BU LU WOULD TRUST.

HARD TO BELIEVE THAT WILD ANIMAL IS ACTUALLY LISTENING TO SOMEONE.

WHAT CHOICE DOES HE HAVE? HE CAN'T TRUST HIS OWN JUDGMENT.

EVERY TIME HE DOES, HE ENDS UP IN TROUBLE.

SO BU LU HAS BALANCED HIS IMPULSIVENESS BY ENLISTING THE HELP OF AN ADVISOR. BUT IF HE WEREN'T SO IMPULSIVE, HE WOULD HAVE REALIZED THERE ARE BETTER ADVISORS THAN GONG CHEN.

EXACTLY. GONG CHEN HAS A SIMPLE AND PREDICTABLE MIND. WE SHOULD BE ABLE TO PREDICT HIS MOVES FROM NOW ON.

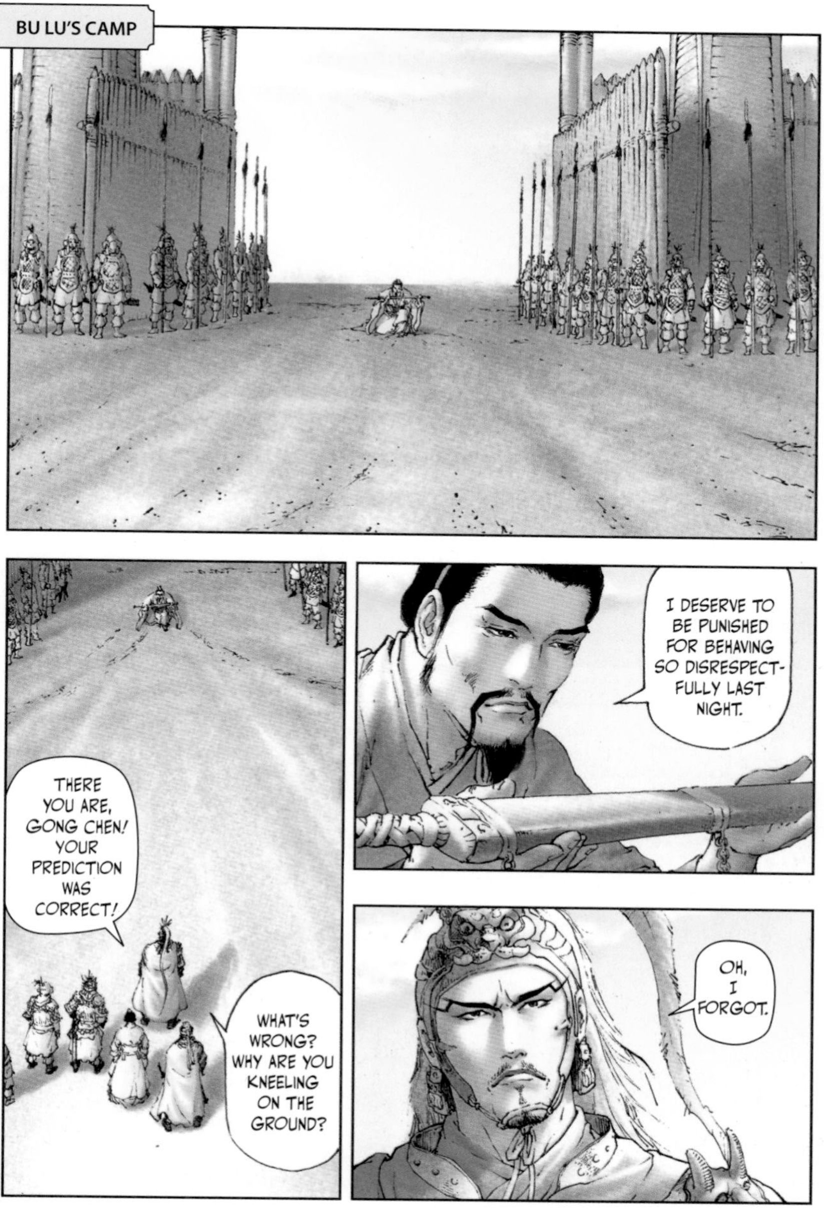
BU LU'S CAMP
THERE YOU ARE, GONG CHEN! YOUR PREDICTION WAS CORRECT!
WHAT'S WRONG? WHY ARE YOU KNEELING ON THE GROUND?
I DESERVE TO BE PUNISHED FOR BEHAVING SO DISRESPECT-FULLY LAST NIGHT.
OH, I FORGOT.

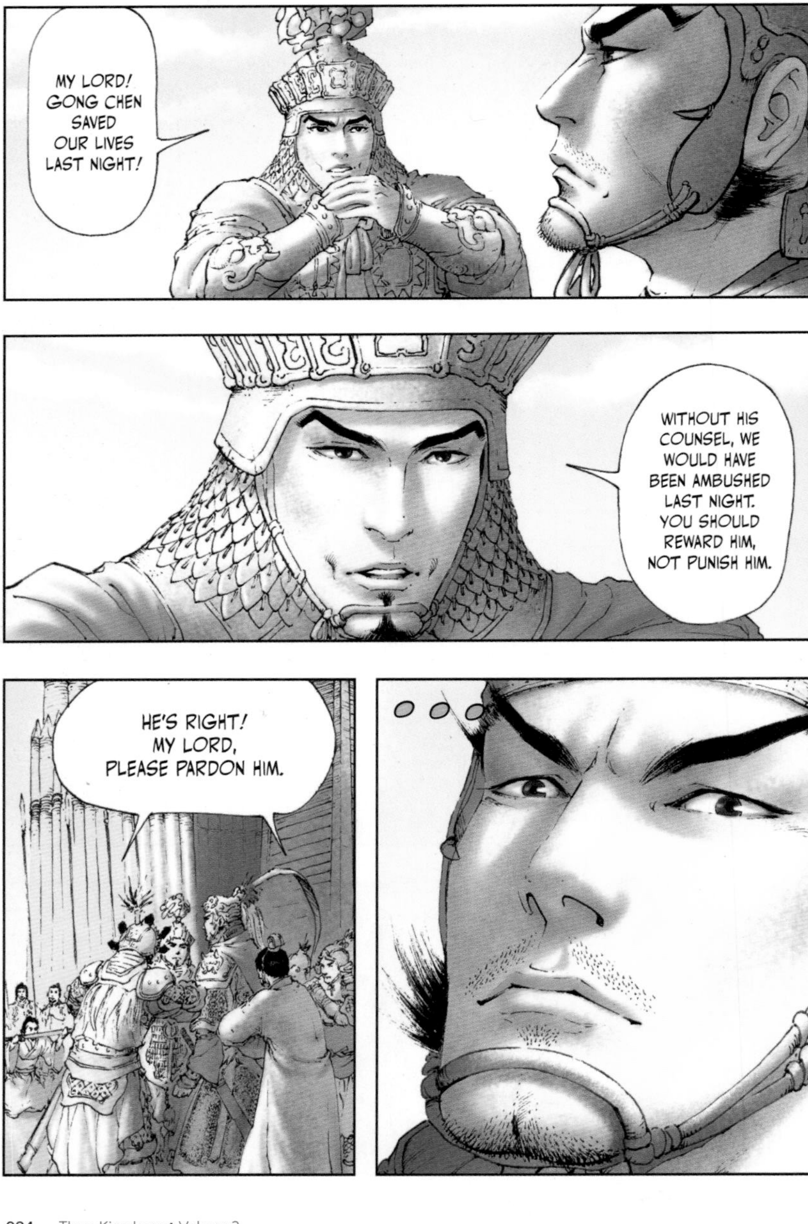
MY LORD! GONG CHEN SAVED OUR LIVES LAST NIGHT!
WITHOUT HIS COUNSEL, WE WOULD HAVE BEEN AMBUSHED LAST NIGHT. YOU SHOULD REWARD HIM, NOT PUNISH HIM.
HE'S RIGHT! MY LORD, PLEASE PARDON HIM.
...

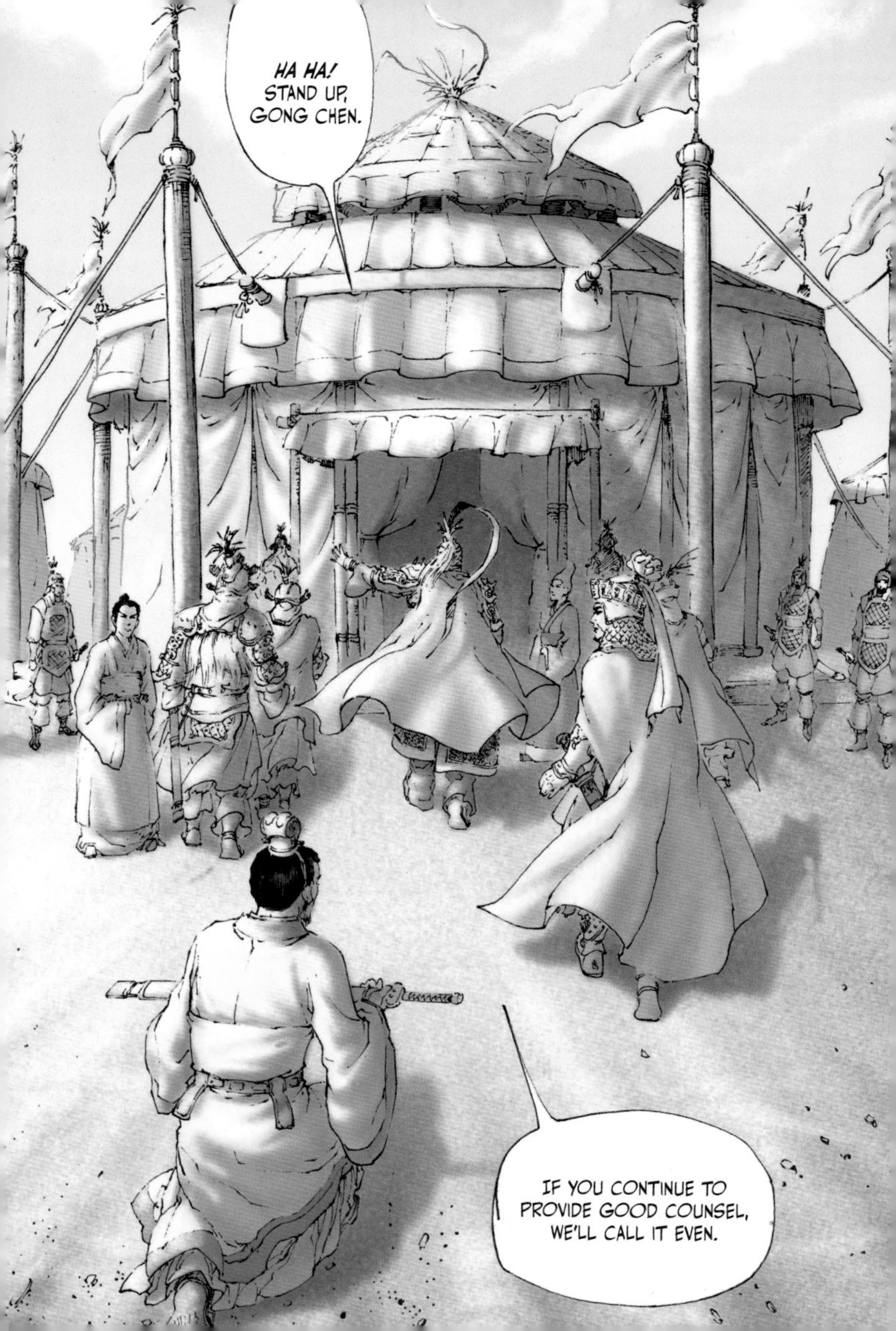
HA HA! STAND UP, GONG CHEN.
IF YOU CONTINUE TO PROVIDE GOOD COUNSEL, WE'LL CALL IT EVEN.

After earning Bu Lu's pardon and trust, Gong Chen devised another plan for defeating Cao Cao. Gong Chen sent a letter to Cao's camp, inviting him to PuYang and telling him that Bu Lu had fled the city, and it would be turned over to Cao in Bu Lu's absence.

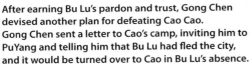

HA! THE HEAVENS SMILE ON MY QUEST FOR PUYANG.

WELL, JIA GUO. WHAT DO YOU THINK?

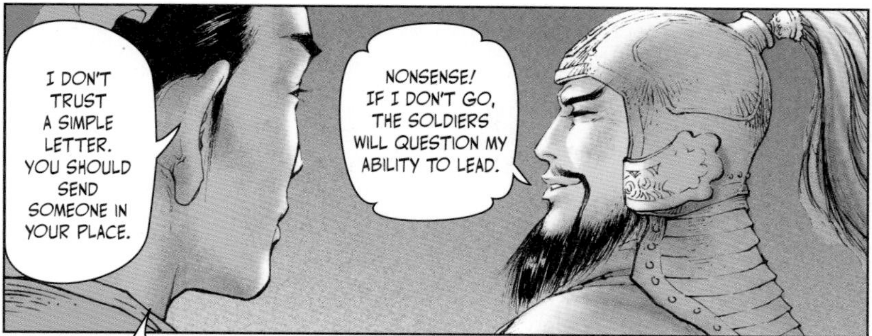
I DON'T TRUST A SIMPLE LETTER. YOU SHOULD SEND SOMEONE IN YOUR PLACE.
NONSENSE! IF I DON'T GO, THE SOLDIERS WILL QUESTION MY ABILITY TO LEAD.

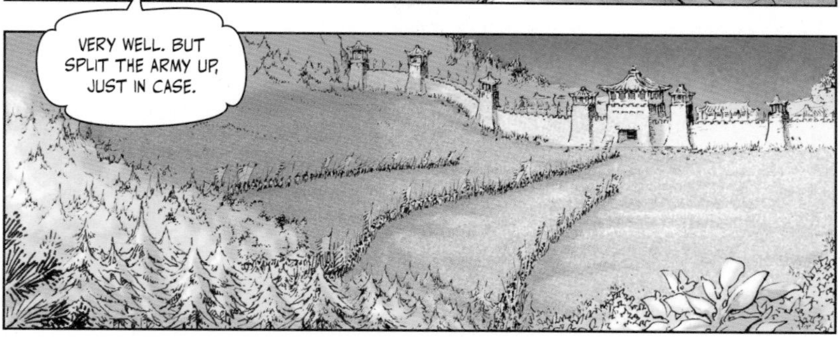
VERY WELL. BUT SPLIT THE ARMY UP, JUST IN CASE.

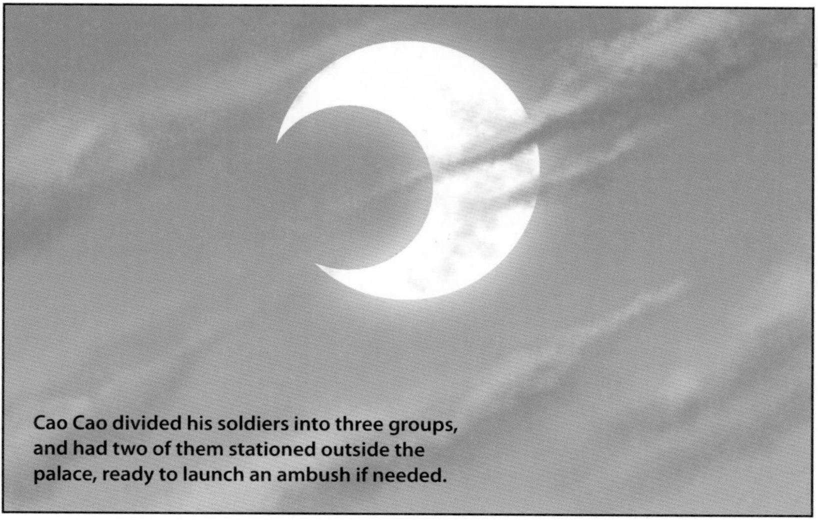
Cao Cao divided his soldiers into three groups, and had two of them stationed outside the palace, ready to launch an ambush if needed.

Inside the palace, Gong Chen awaited Cao Cao's arrival.

CAO CAO'S FORCES ARE ON THEIR WAY. EVERYONE BE READY!

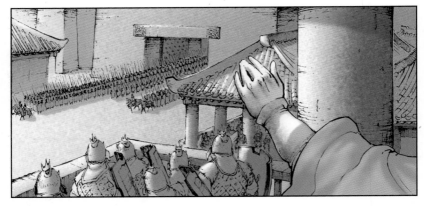

NOW! SOUND THE ATTACK!

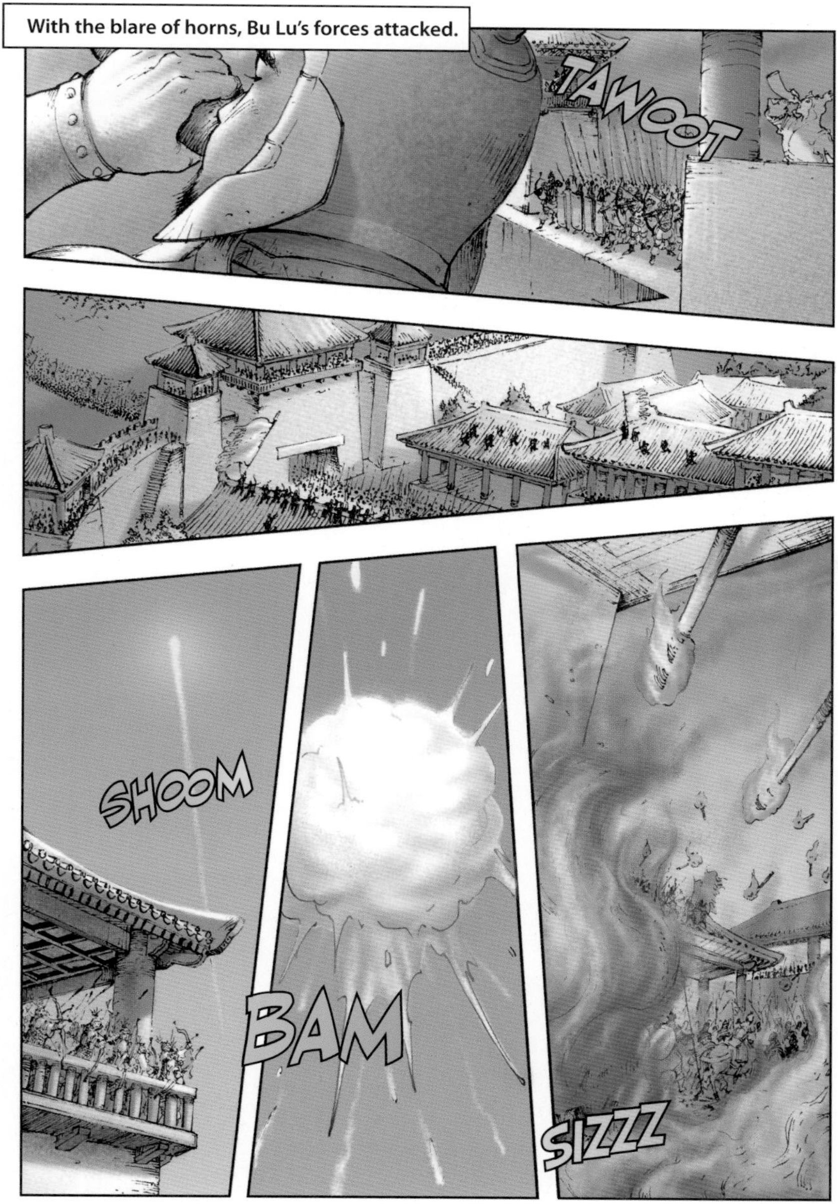
With the blare of horns, Bu Lu's forces attacked.
TAWOOT
SHOOM
BAM
SIZZZ

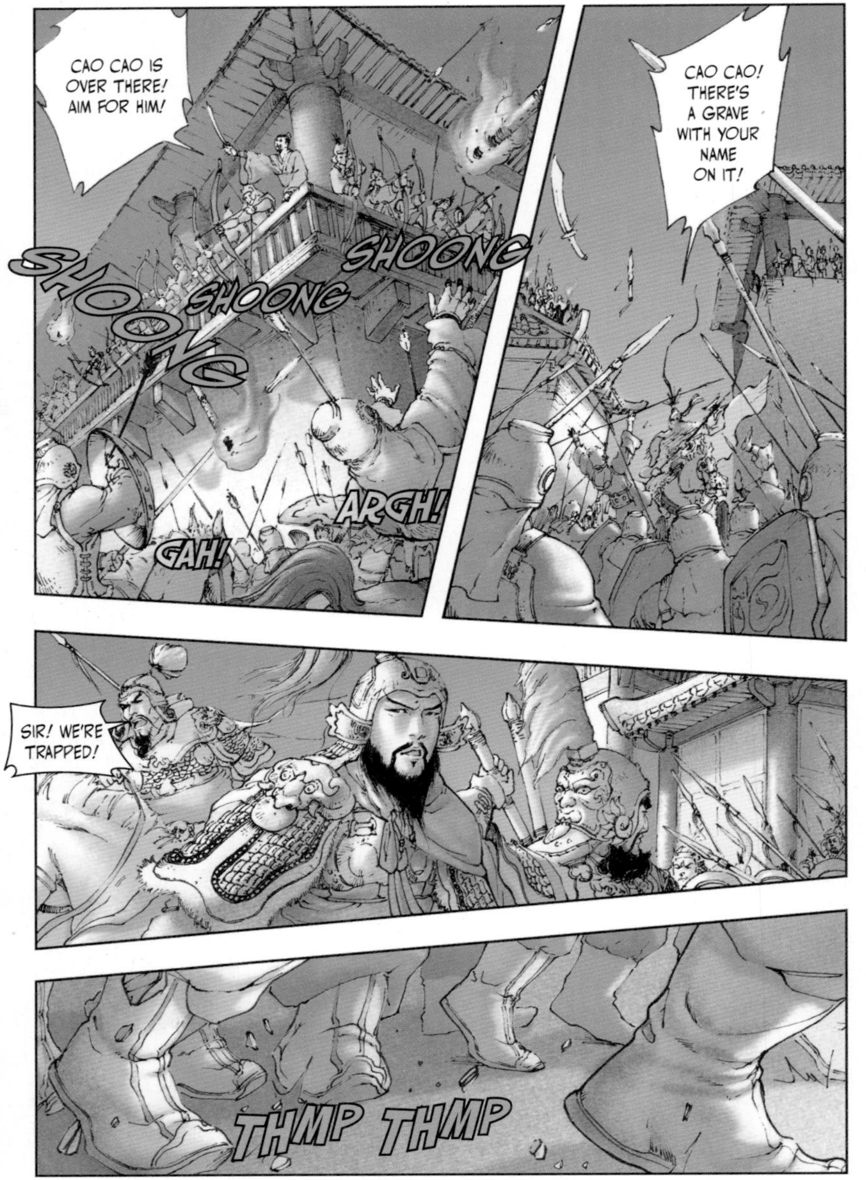
CAO CAO IS OVER THERE! AIM FOR HIM!
SHOONG
SHOONG
SHOONG
ARGH!
GAH!
CAO CAO! THERE'S A GRAVE WITH YOUR NAME ON IT!
SIR! WE'RE TRAPPED!
THMP THMP

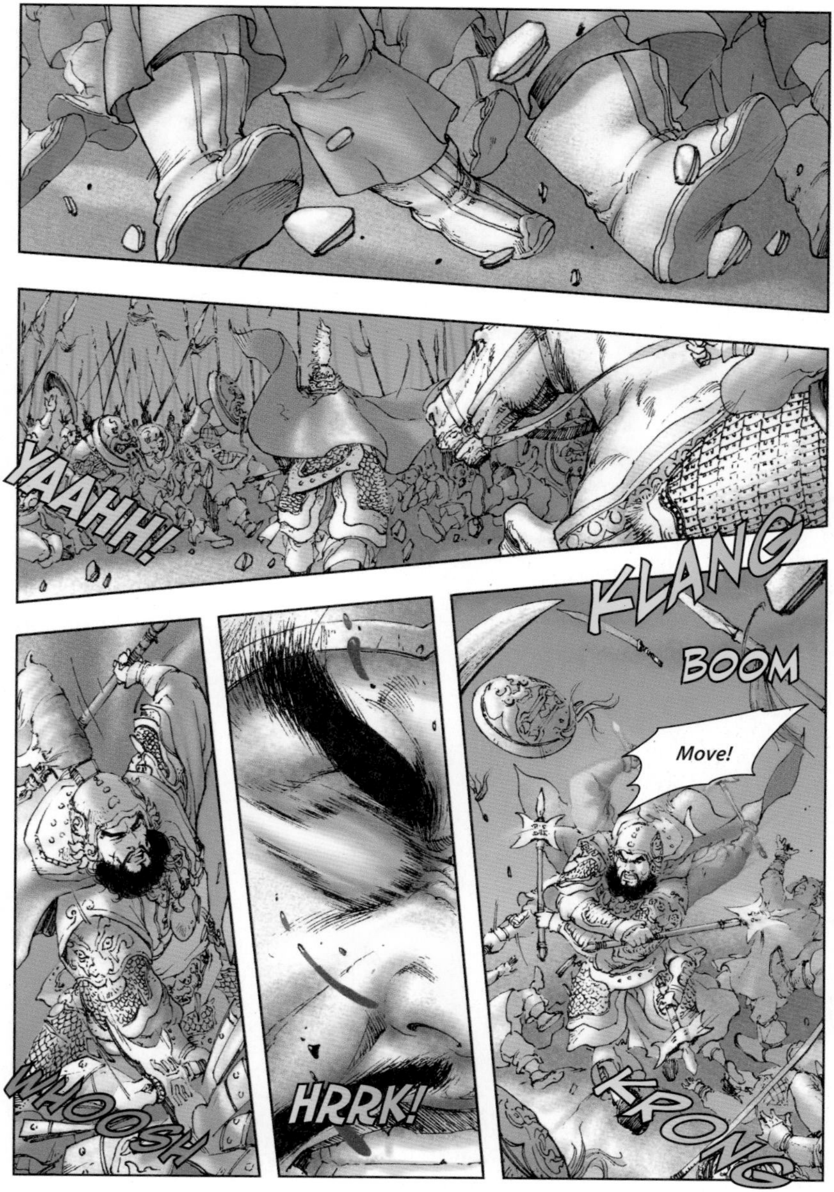
YAAHH!
KLANG
BOOM
Move!
WHOOSH
HRRK!
KRONG

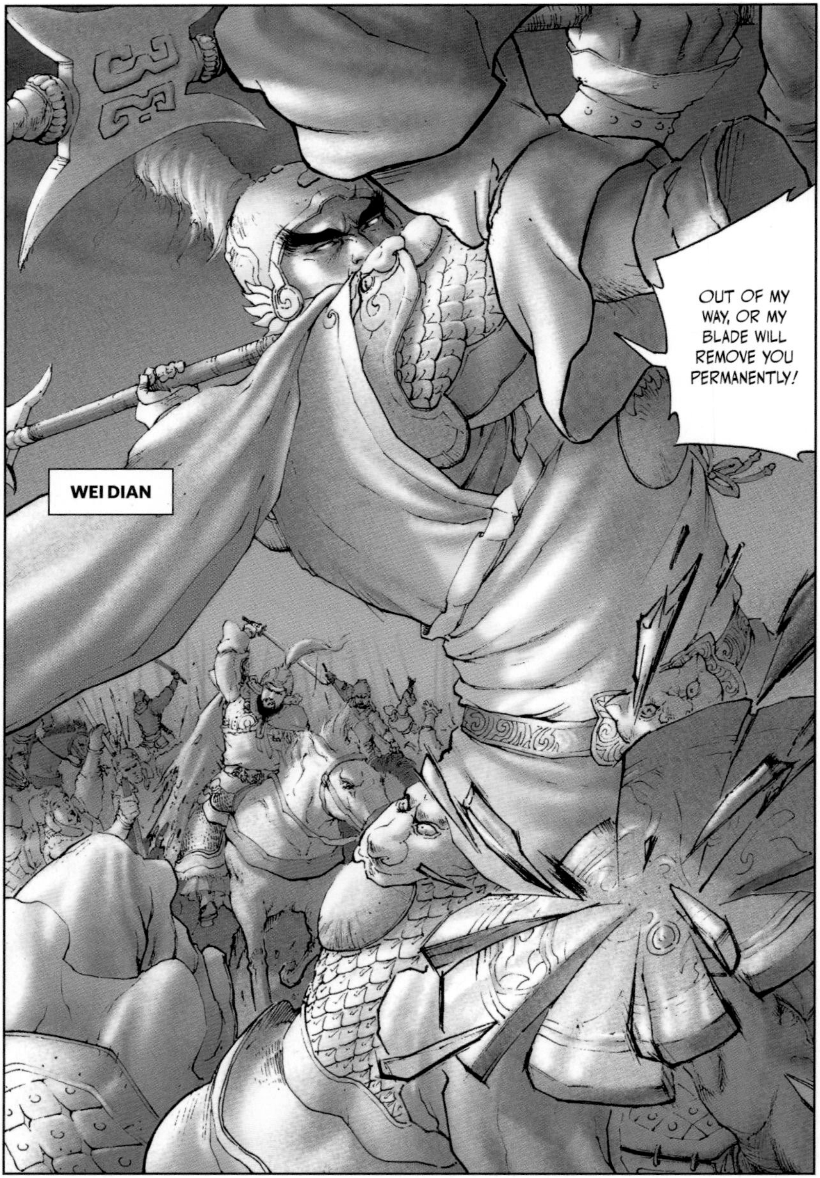
OUT OF MY WAY, OR MY BLADE WILL REMOVE YOU PERMANENTLY!
WEI DIAN

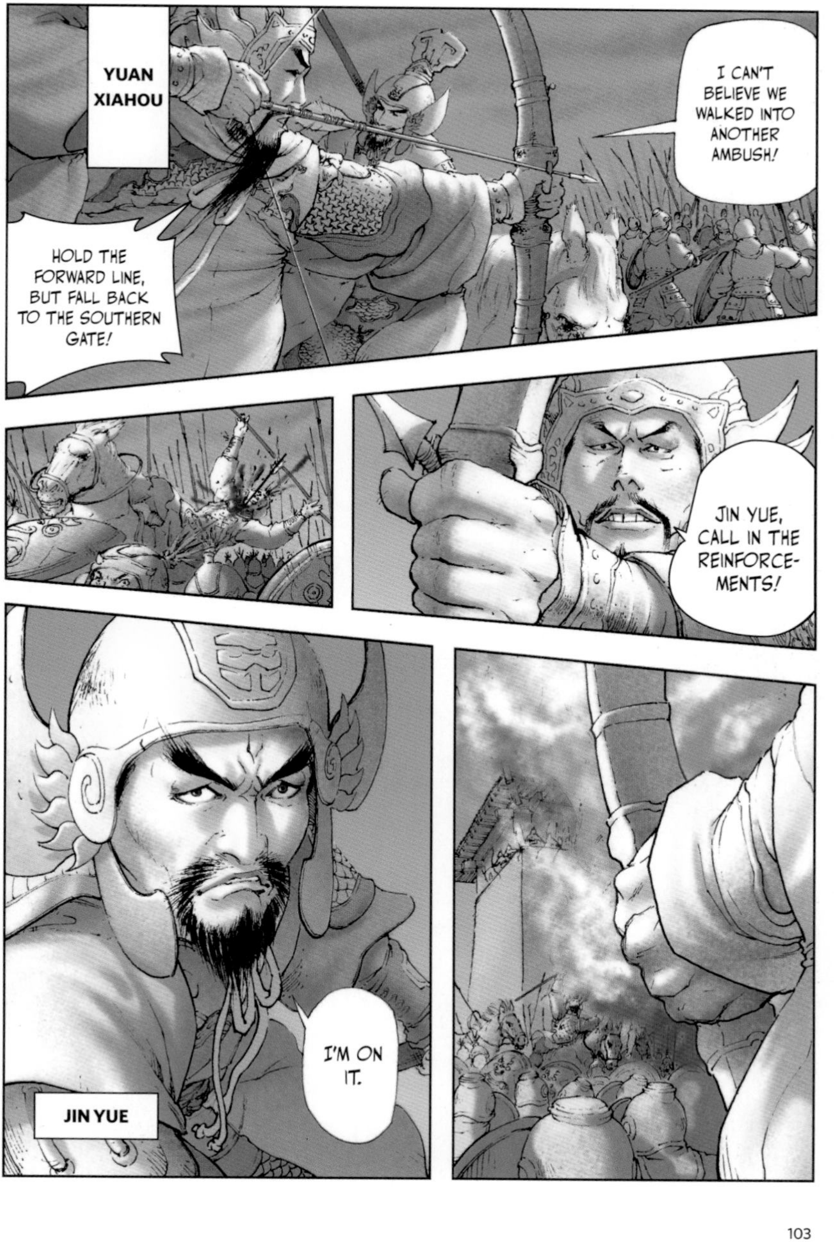
YUAN XIAHOU
I CAN'T BELIEVE WE WALKED INTO ANOTHER AMBUSH!
HOLD THE FORWARD LINE, BUT FALL BACK TO THE SOUTHERN GATE!
JIN YUE, CALL IN THE REINFORCE-MENTS!
I'M ON IT.
JIN YUE

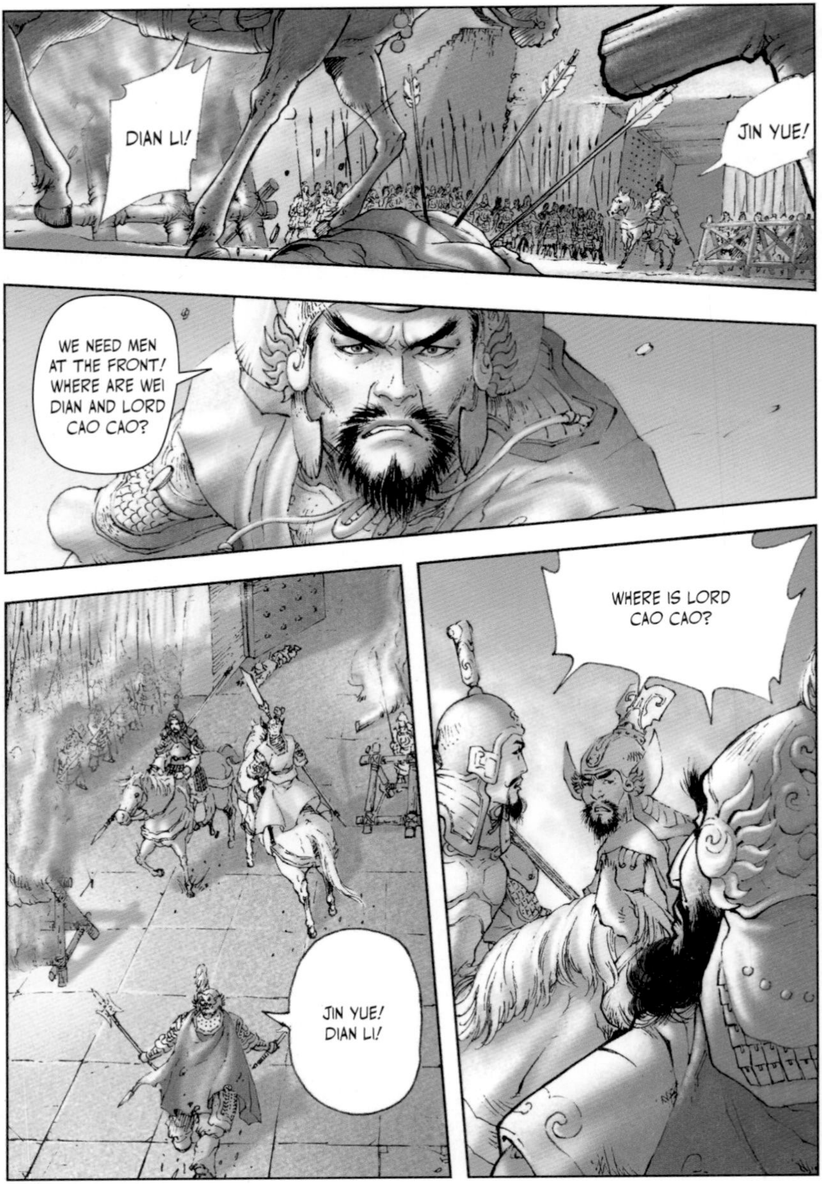

DIAN LI!
JIN YUE!
WE NEED MEN AT THE FRONT! WHERE ARE WEI DIAN AND LORD CAO CAO?
JIN YUE! DIAN LI!
WHERE IS LORD CAO CAO?

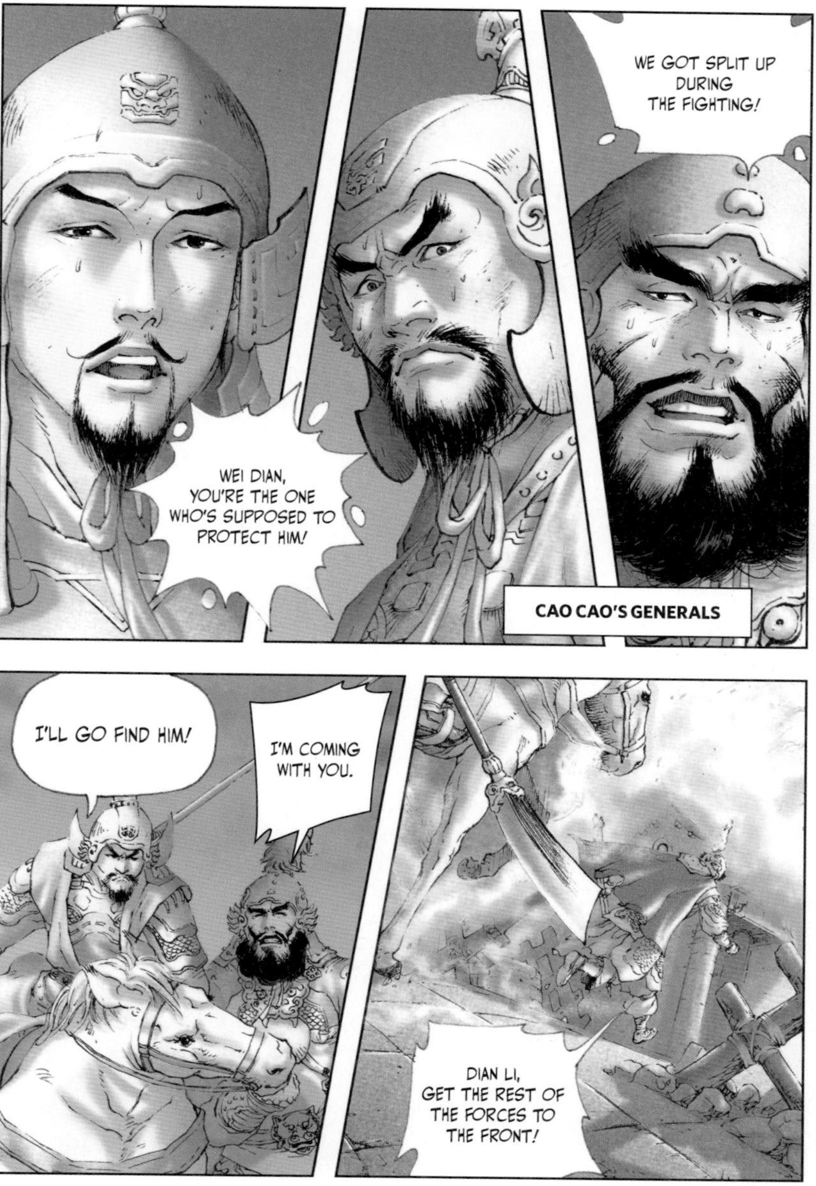
WE GOT SPLIT UP DURING THE FIGHTING!
WEI DIAN, YOU'RE THE ONE WHO'S SUPPOSED TO PROTECT HIM!
CAO CAO'S GENERALS
I'LL GO FIND HIM!
I'M COMING WITH YOU.
DIAN LI, GET THE REST OF THE FORCES TO THE FRONT!

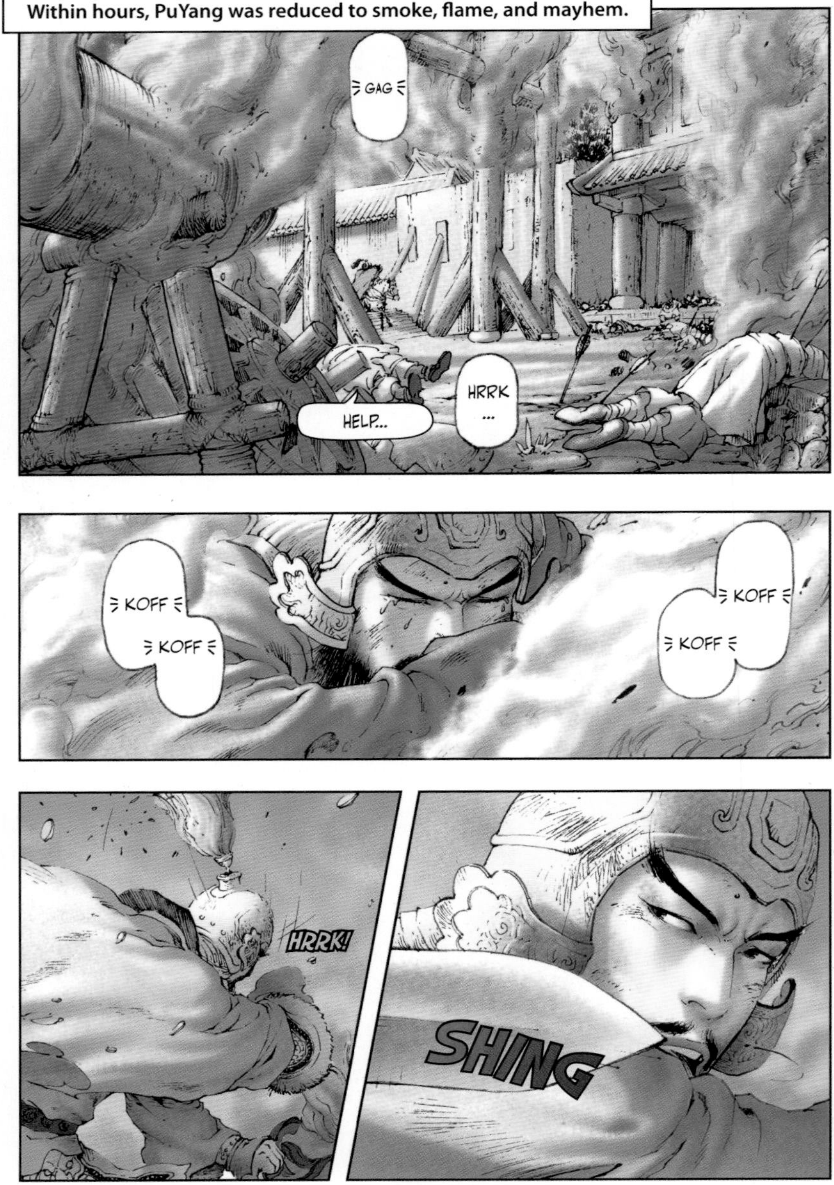
Within hours, PuYang was reduced to smoke, flame, and mayhem.
GAG
HRRK ...
HELP...
KOFF
KOFF
KOFF
KOFF
HRRK!
SHING

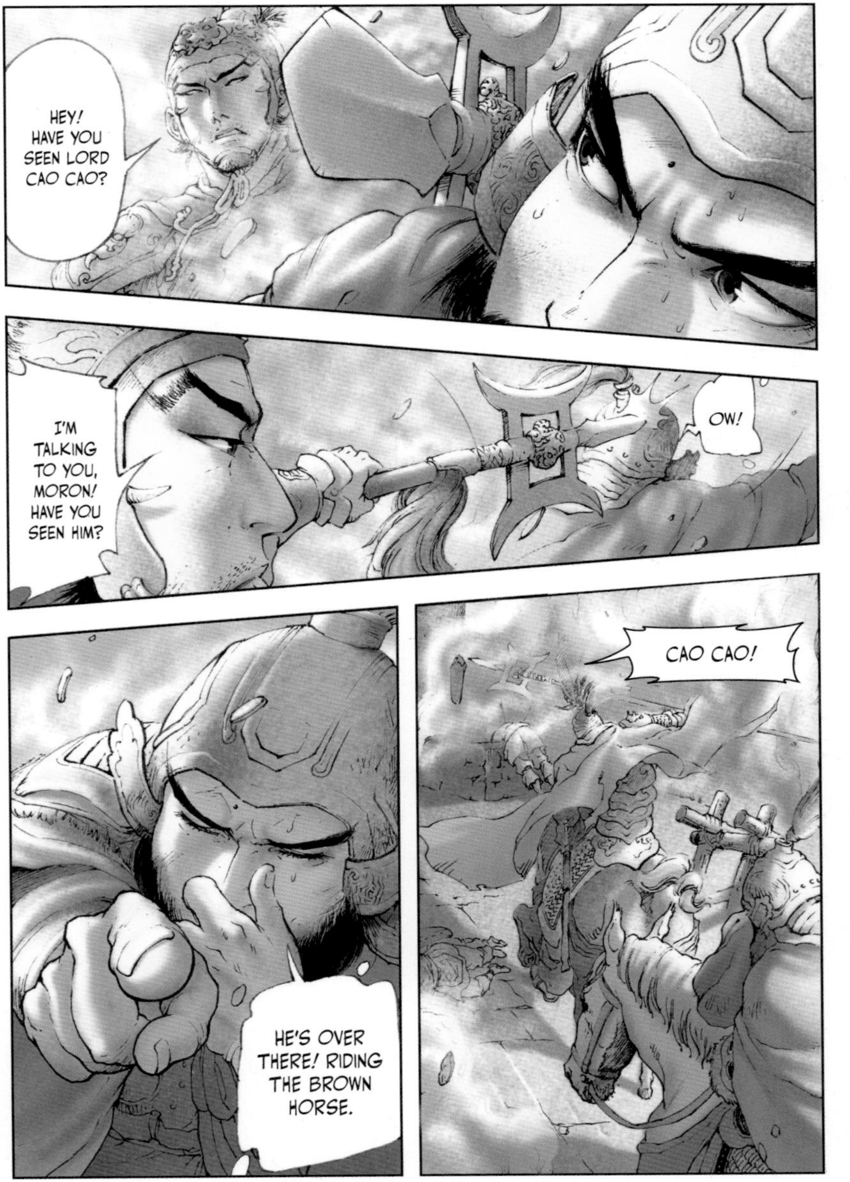
HEY! HAVE YOU SEEN LORD CAO CAO?
I'M TALKING TO YOU, MORON! HAVE YOU SEEN HIM?
OW!
HE'S OVER THERE! RIDING THE BROWN HORSE.
CAO CAO!

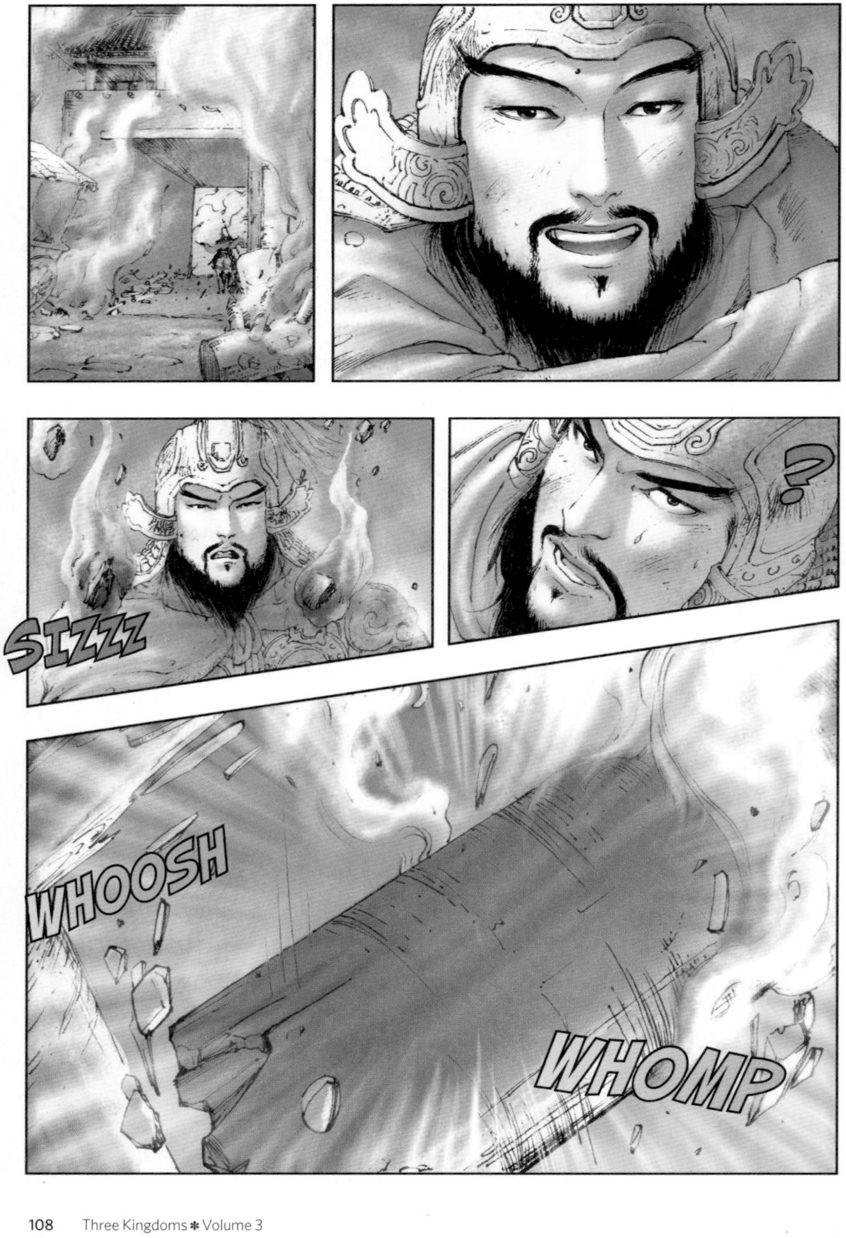
SIZZZ
?
WHOOSH
WHOMP

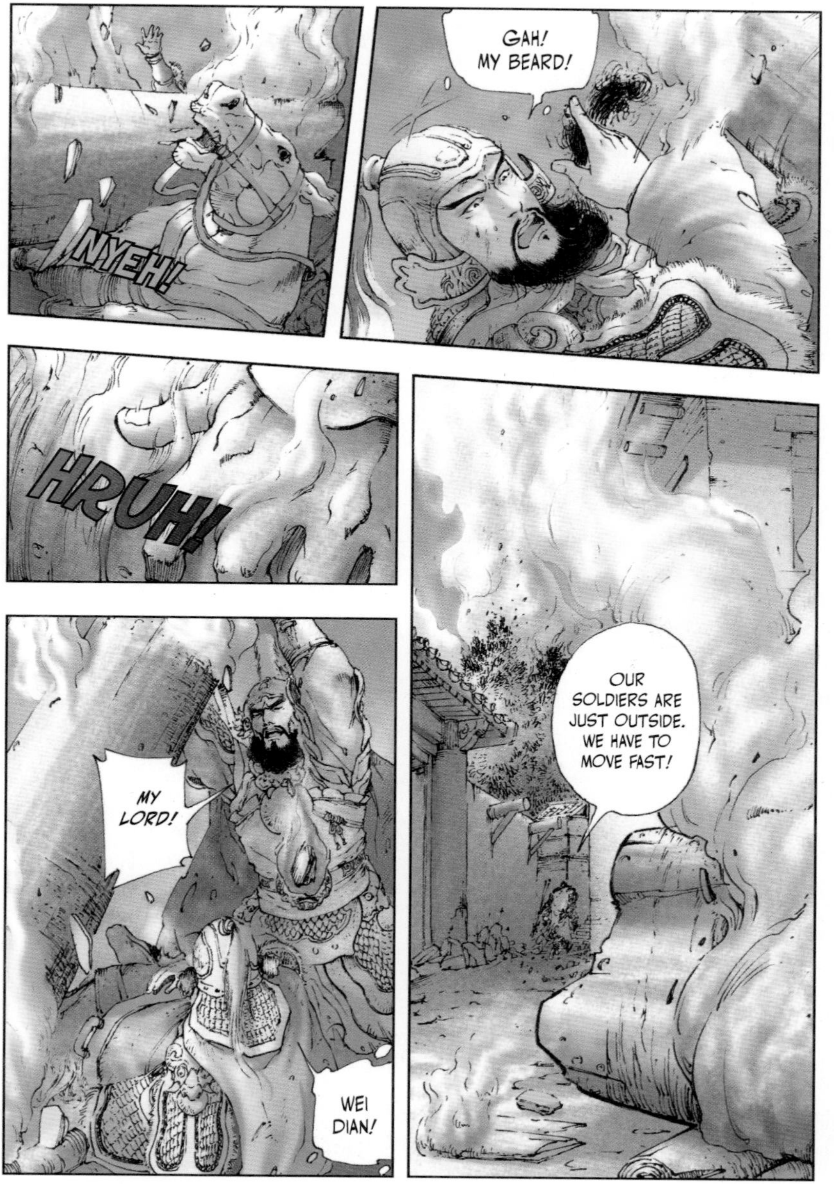
NYEH!
GAH! MY BEARD!
HRUH!
MY LORD!
WEI DIAN!
OUR SOLDIERS ARE JUST OUTSIDE. WE HAVE TO MOVE FAST!

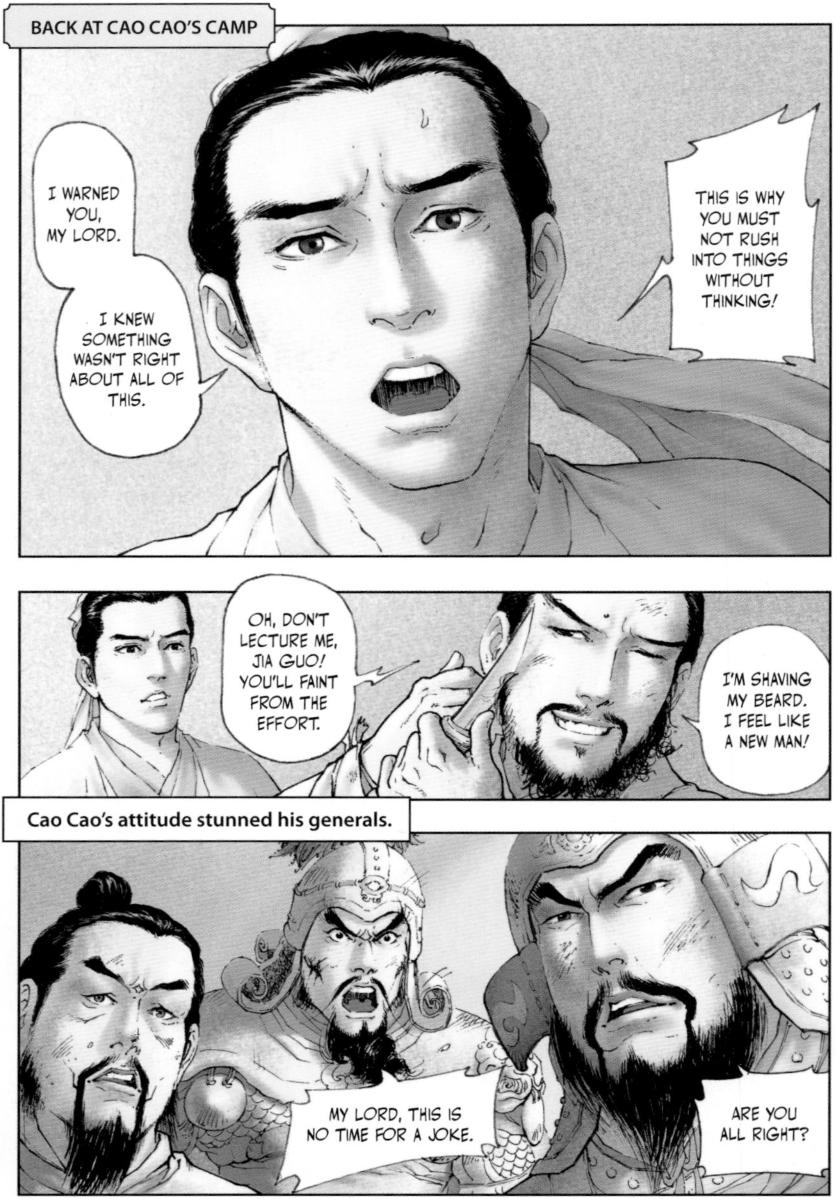
BACK AT CAO CAO'S CAMP
I WARNED YOU, MY LORD.
I KNEW SOMETHING WASN'T RIGHT ABOUT ALL OF THIS.
THIS IS WHY YOU MUST NOT RUSH INTO THINGS WITHOUT THINKING!
OH, DON'T LECTURE ME, JIA GUO! YOU'LL FAINT FROM THE EFFORT.
I'M SHAVING MY BEARD. I FEEL LIKE A NEW MAN!
Cao Cao's attitude stunned his generals.
MY LORD, THIS IS NO TIME FOR A JOKE.
ARE YOU ALL RIGHT?

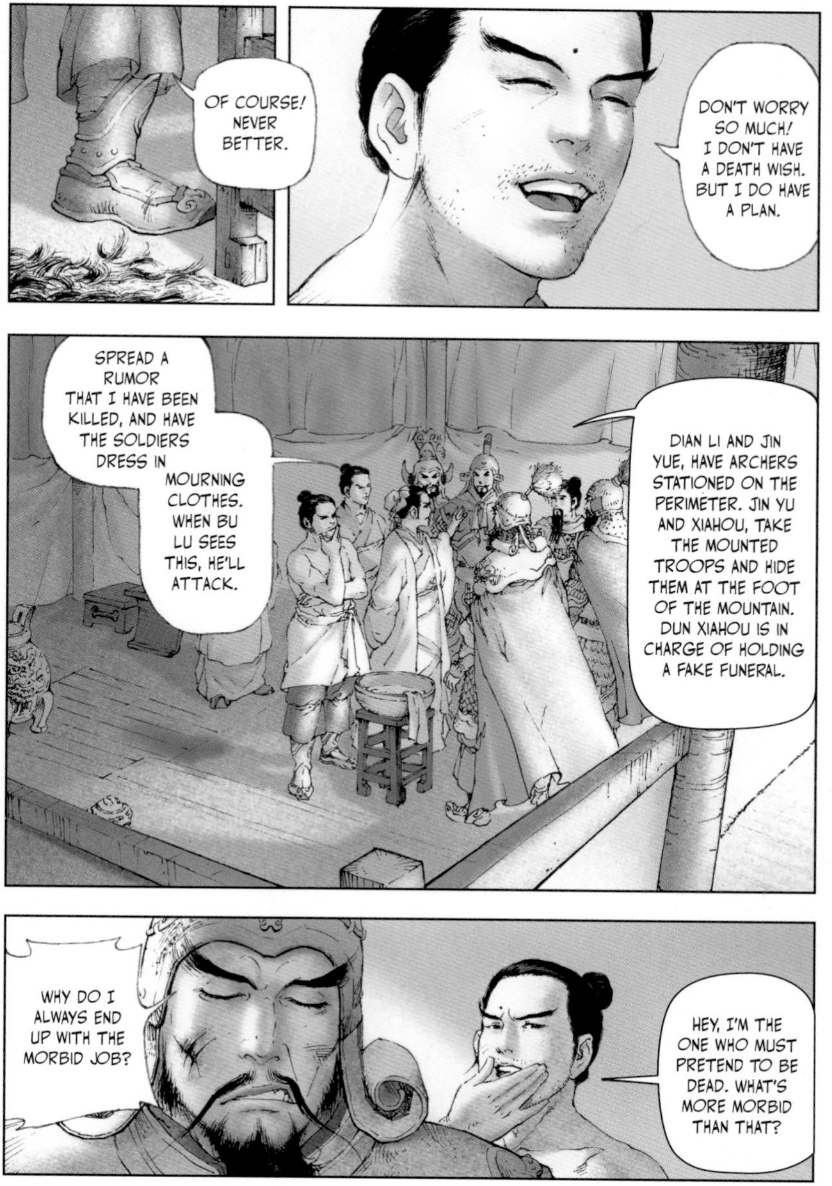
OF COURSE! NEVER BETTER.
DON'T WORRY SO MUCH! I DON'T HAVE A DEATH WISH. BUT I DO HAVE A PLAN.
SPREAD A RUMOR THAT I HAVE BEEN KILLED, AND HAVE THE SOLDIERS DRESS IN
MOURNING CLOTHES. WHEN BU LU SEES THIS, HE'LL ATTACK.
DIAN LI AND JIN YUE, HAVE ARCHERS STATIONED ON THE PERIMETER. JIN YU AND XIAHOU, TAKE THE MOUNTED TROOPS AND HIDE THEM AT THE FOOT OF THE MOUNTAIN. DUN XIAHOU IS IN CHARGE OF HOLDING A FAKE FUNERAL.
WHY DO I ALWAYS END UP WITH THE MORBID JOB?
HEY, I'M THE ONE WHO MUST PRETEND TO BE DEAD. WHAT'S MORE MORBID THAN THAT?

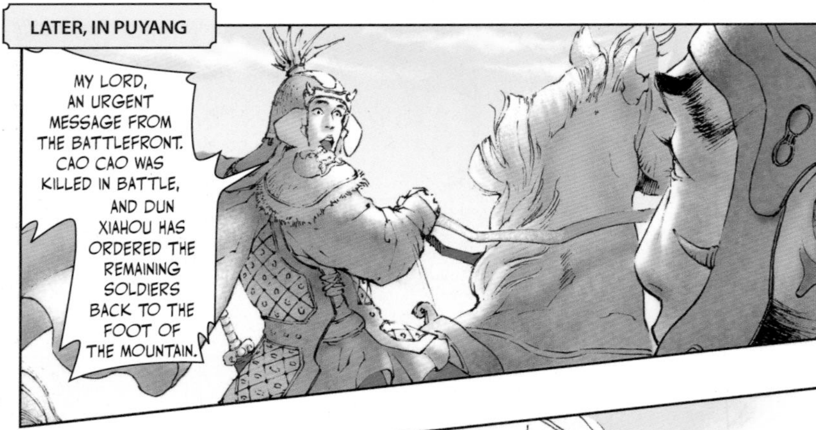
LATER, IN PUYANG
MY LORD, AN URGENT MESSAGE FROM THE BATTLEFRONT. CAO CAO WAS KILLED IN BATTLE, AND DUN XIAHOU HAS ORDERED THE REMAINING SOLDIERS BACK TO THE FOOT OF THE MOUNTAIN.

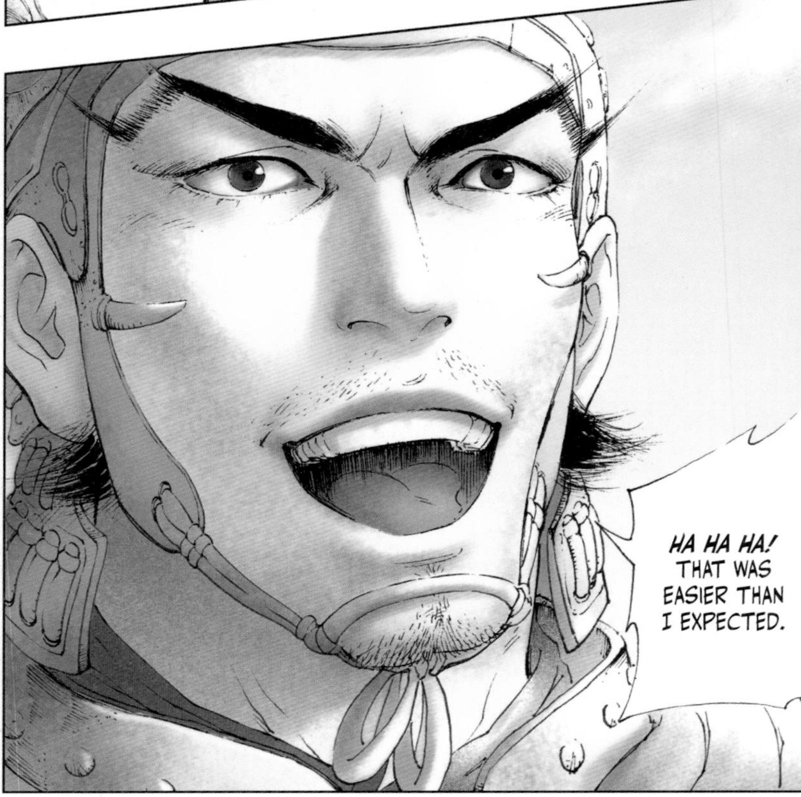
HA HA HA! THAT WAS EASIER THAN I EXPECTED.

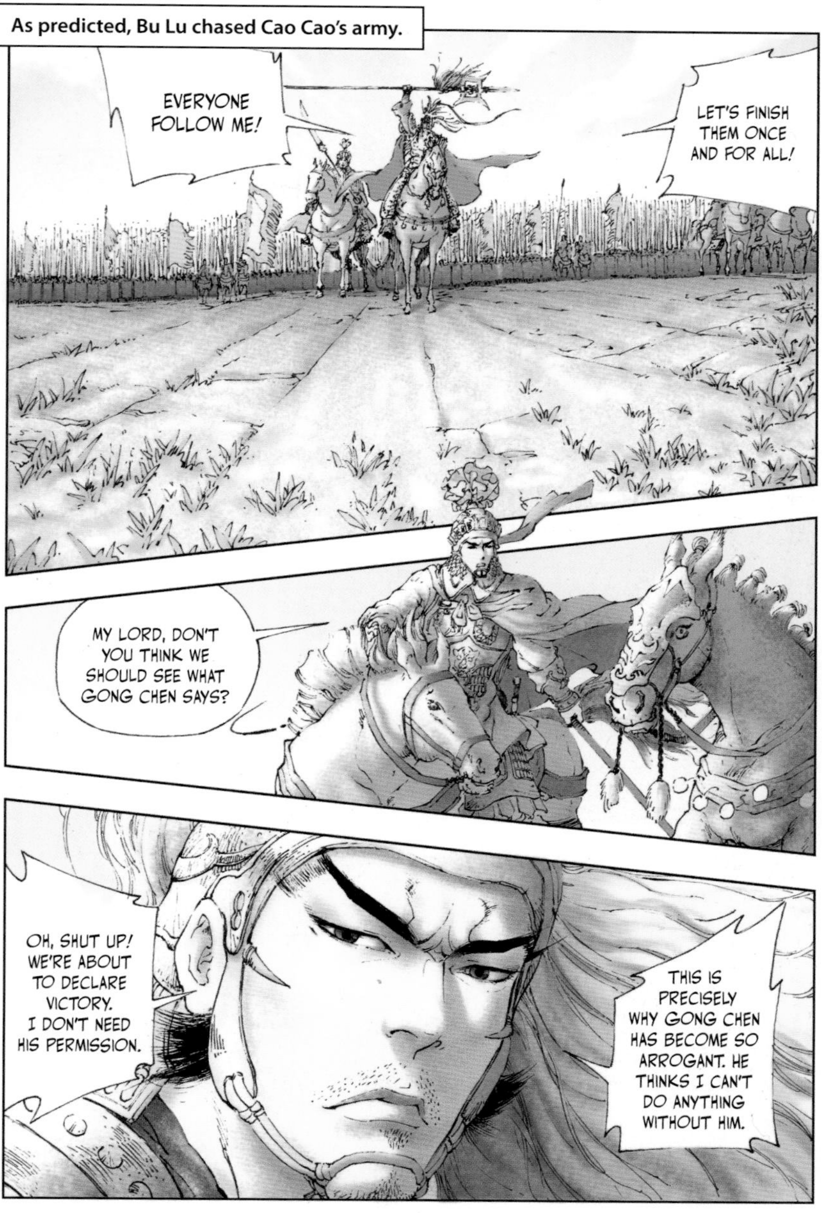
As predicted, Bu Lu chased Cao Cao's army.
EVERYONE FOLLOW ME!
LET'S FINISH THEM ONCE AND FOR ALL!
MY LORD, DON'T YOU THINK WE SHOULD SEE WHAT GONG CHEN SAYS?
OH, SHUT UP! WE'RE ABOUT TO DECLARE VICTORY. I DON'T NEED HIS PERMISSION.
THIS IS PRECISELY WHY GONG CHEN HAS BECOME SO ARROGANT. HE THINKS I CAN'T DO ANYTHING WITHOUT HIM.

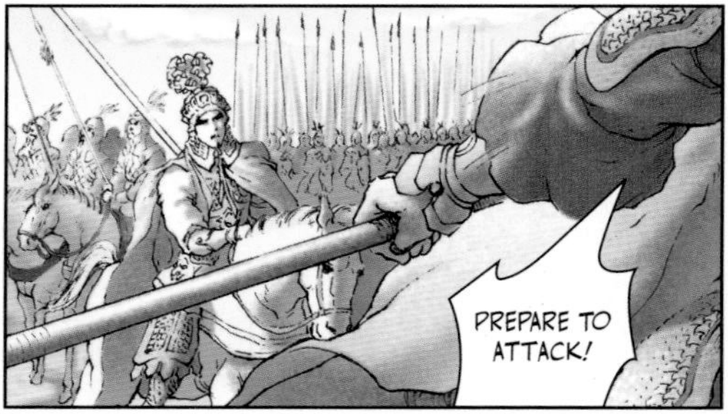
PREPARE TO
ATTACK!

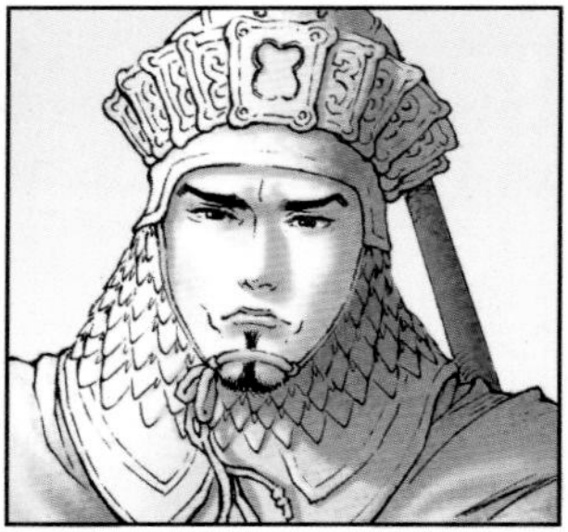

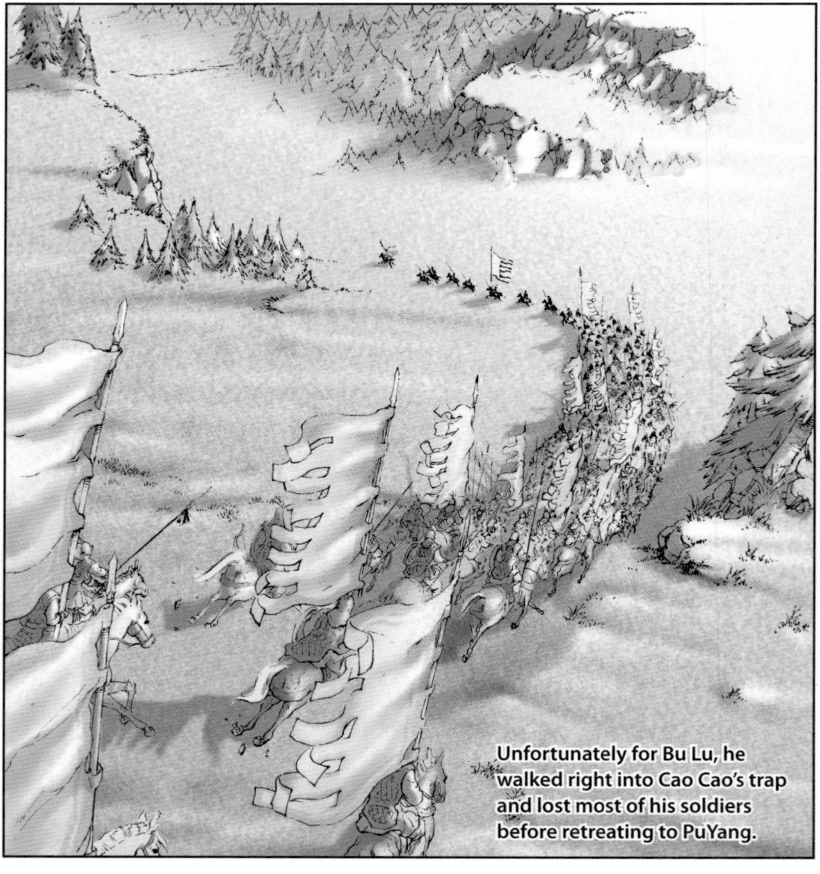
Unfortunately for Bu Lu, he
walked right into Cao Cao's trap
and lost most of his soldiers
before retreating to PuYang.

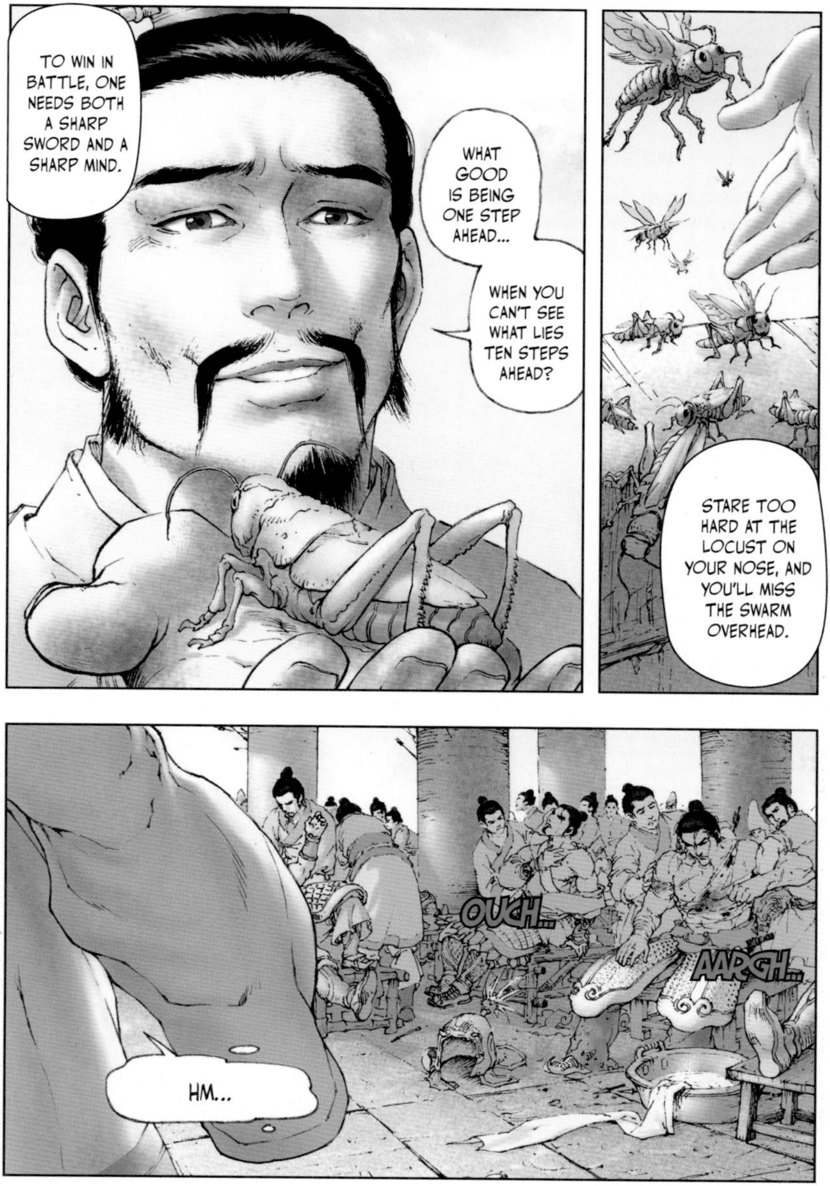
TO WIN IN BATTLE, ONE NEEDS BOTH A SHARP SWORD AND A SHARP MIND.
WHAT GOOD IS BEING ONE STEP AHEAD...
WHEN YOU CAN'T SEE WHAT LIES TEN STEPS AHEAD?
STARE TOO HARD AT THE LOCUST ON YOUR NOSE, AND YOU'LL MISS THE SWARM OVERHEAD.
OUCH...
AARGH...
HM...

Bu Lu continued to attack Cao Cao's forces, and ended up losing most of his men.

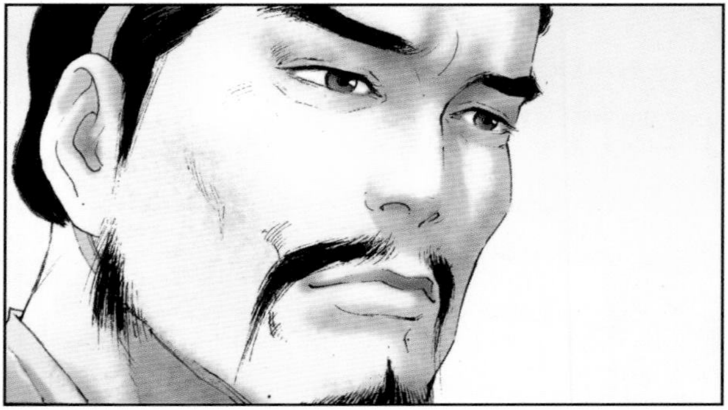

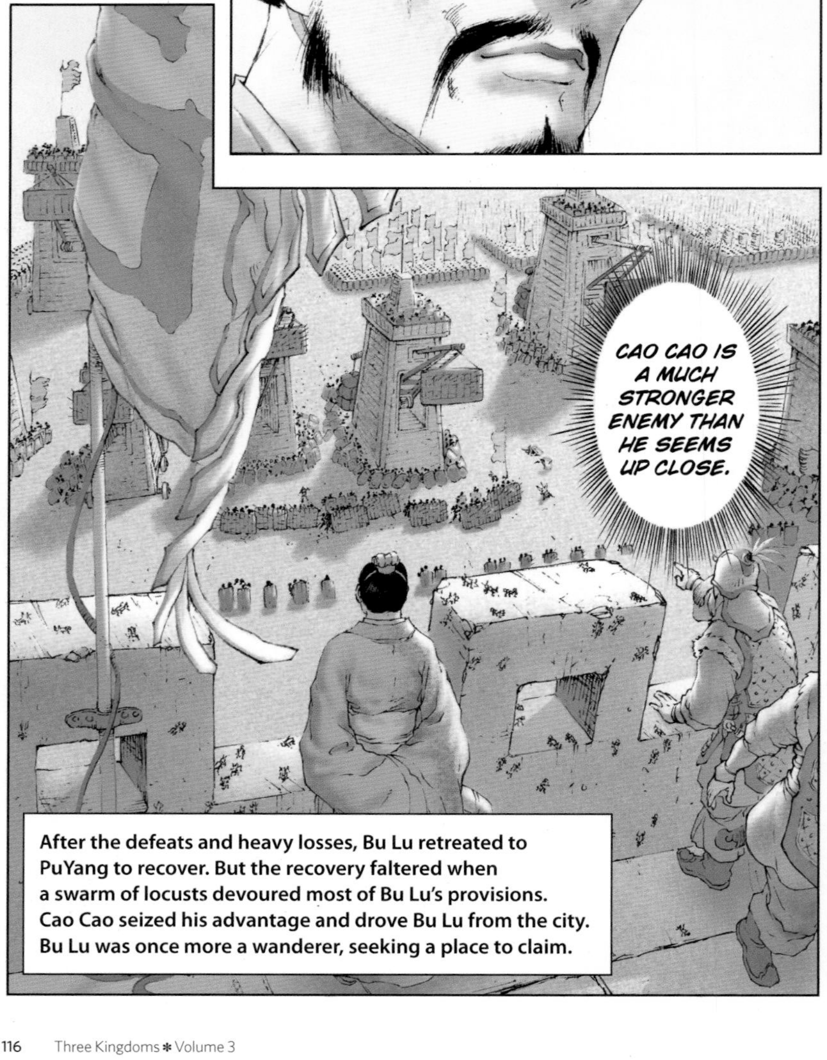
CAO CAO IS A MUCH STRONGER ENEMY THAN HE SEEMS UP CLOSE.
After the defeats and heavy losses, Bu Lu retreated to PuYang to recover. But the recovery faltered when a swarm of locusts devoured most of Bu Lu's provisions. Cao Cao seized his advantage and drove Bu Lu from the city. Bu Lu was once more a wanderer, seeking a place to claim.

IMPORTANT FEUDAL LORDS AT THE END OF THE 2ND CENTURY

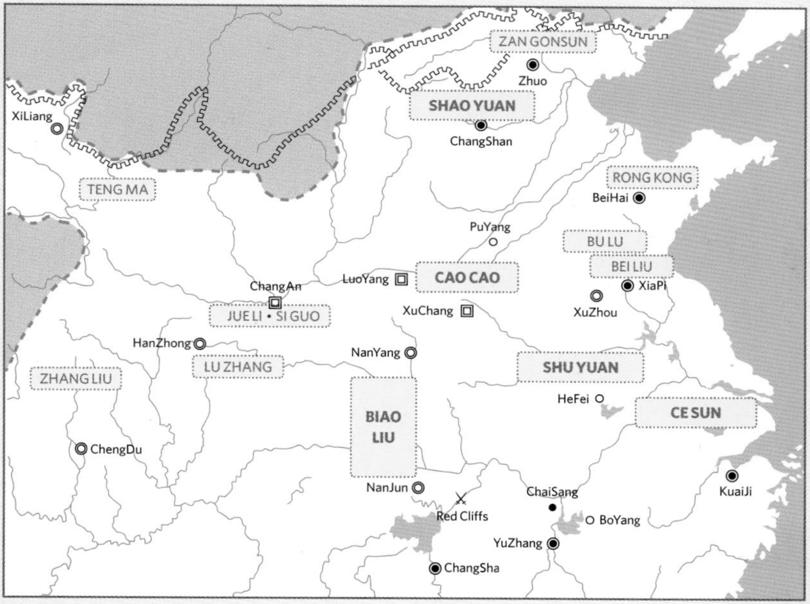

ZAN GONSUN
Zhuo
SHAO YUAN
ChangShan
XiLiang
TENG MA
RONG KONG
BeiHai
PuYang
BU LU
BEI LIU
XiaPi
LuoYang
CAO CAO
ChangAn
JUE LI • SI GUO
XuChang
XuZhou
HanZhong
NanYang
LU ZHANG
ZHANG LIU
SHU YUAN
HeFei
CE SUN
BIAO LIU
ChengDu
NanJun
ChaiSang
KuaiJi
Red Cliffs
BoYang
YuZhang
ChangSha

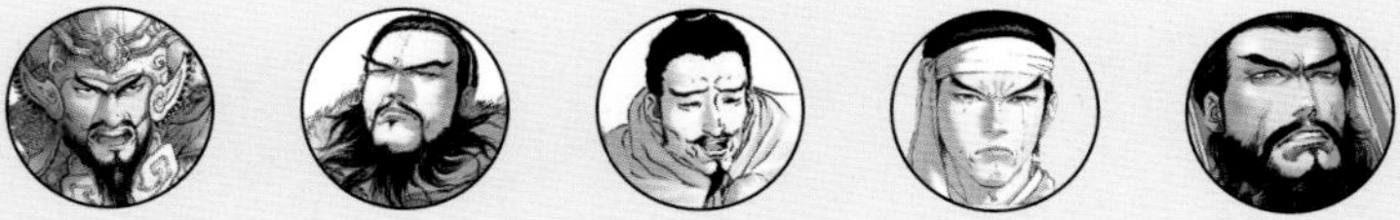

SHAO YUAN | CAO CAO | SHU YUAN | CE SUN | TENG MA

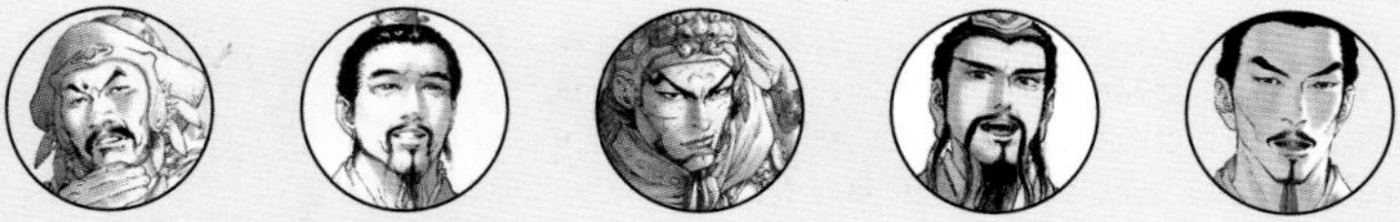

SI GUO | RONG KONG | BU LU | BEI LIU | ZAN GONSUN

Chapter 3

Cao Cao's
Unlikely Alliance AD 196

Summary

After Zhuo Dong's death a power vacuum emerges and various lords plan to take advantage. While Shao Yuan and his advisors are stuck in an endless debate, Cao Cao decides to ally himself to Emperor Xian, who has been driven out of ChangAn. It is an unlikely strategy, since the emperor is weak, but Cao Cao believes he can leverage the emperor's status as supreme ruler to coax Bu Lu and Bei Liu into fighting each other over Xu Province.

XiLiang
Zhuo
ChangShan
BeiHai
PuYang
A
HuLuo
GuanDu
XiaoPei
XiaPi
LuoYang
ChangAn
B
XuDu
XuZhou
HanZhong
NanYang
ShouChun
HeFei
XiangYang
ChengDu

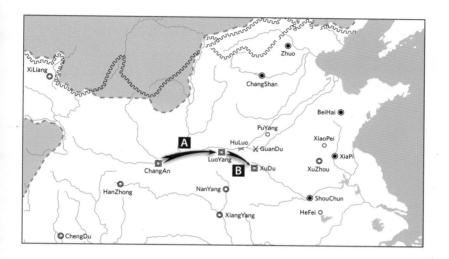

A

While Jue Li and Si Guo fight among themselves for control of ChangAn, Emperor Xian escapes to LuoYang, accompanied by a small number of loyalists.

B

Cao Cao decides to form an alliance with the emperor, and persuades him to move the capital to the city of XuDu.

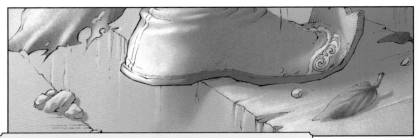

IN AD 195, EMPEROR XIAN RETURNED TO THE RUINS OF LUOYANG.

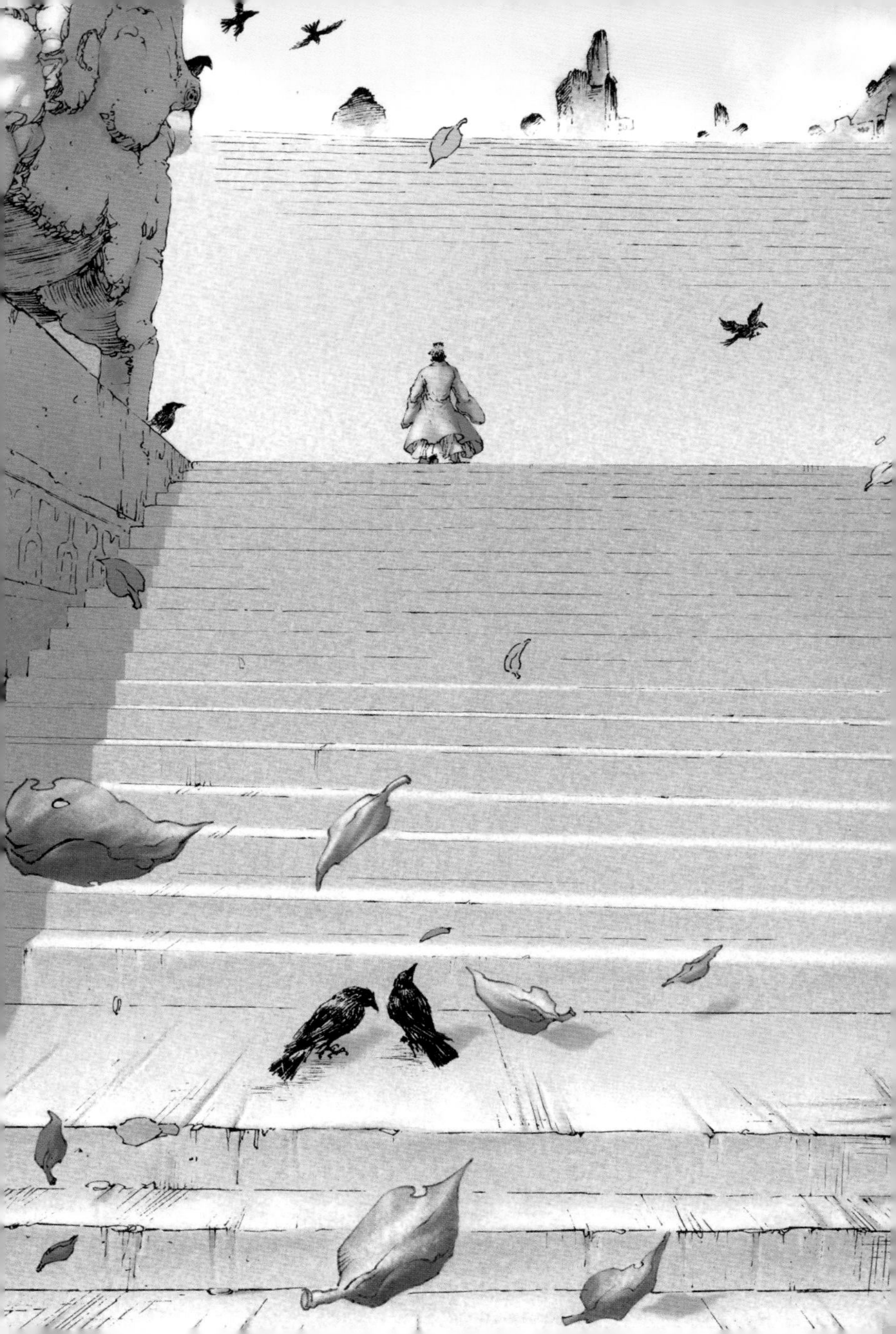

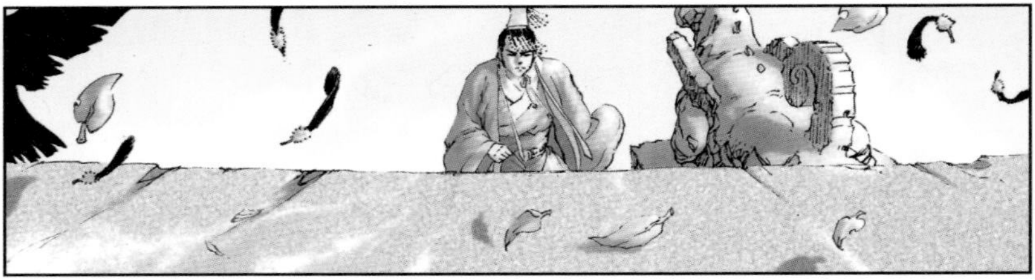

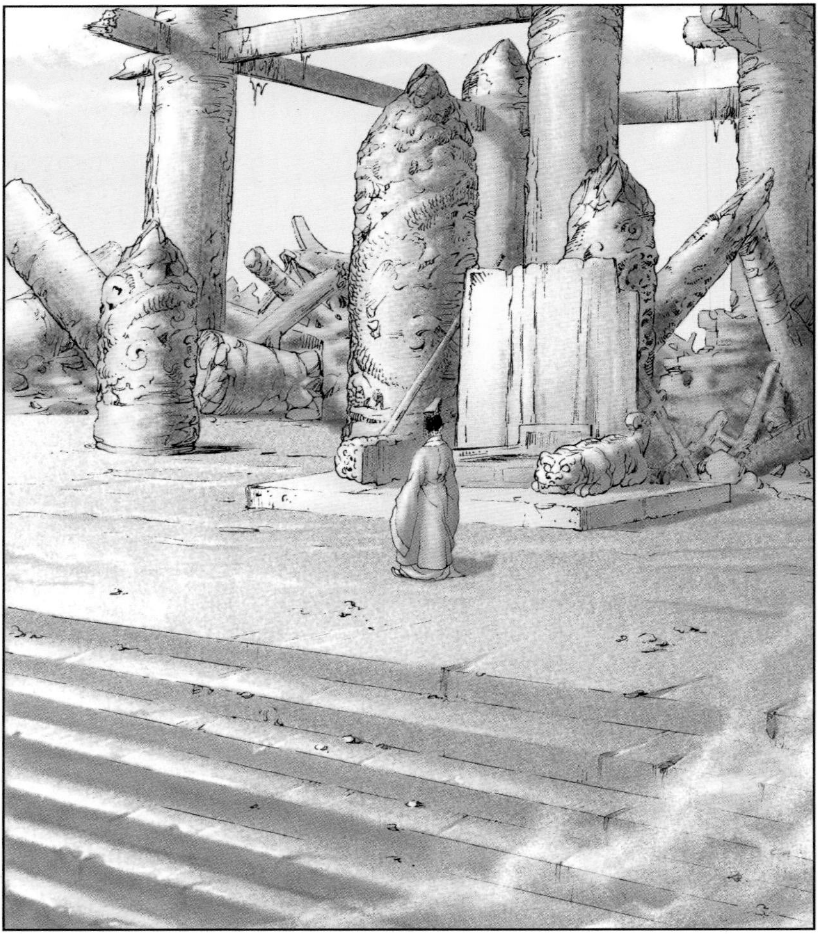

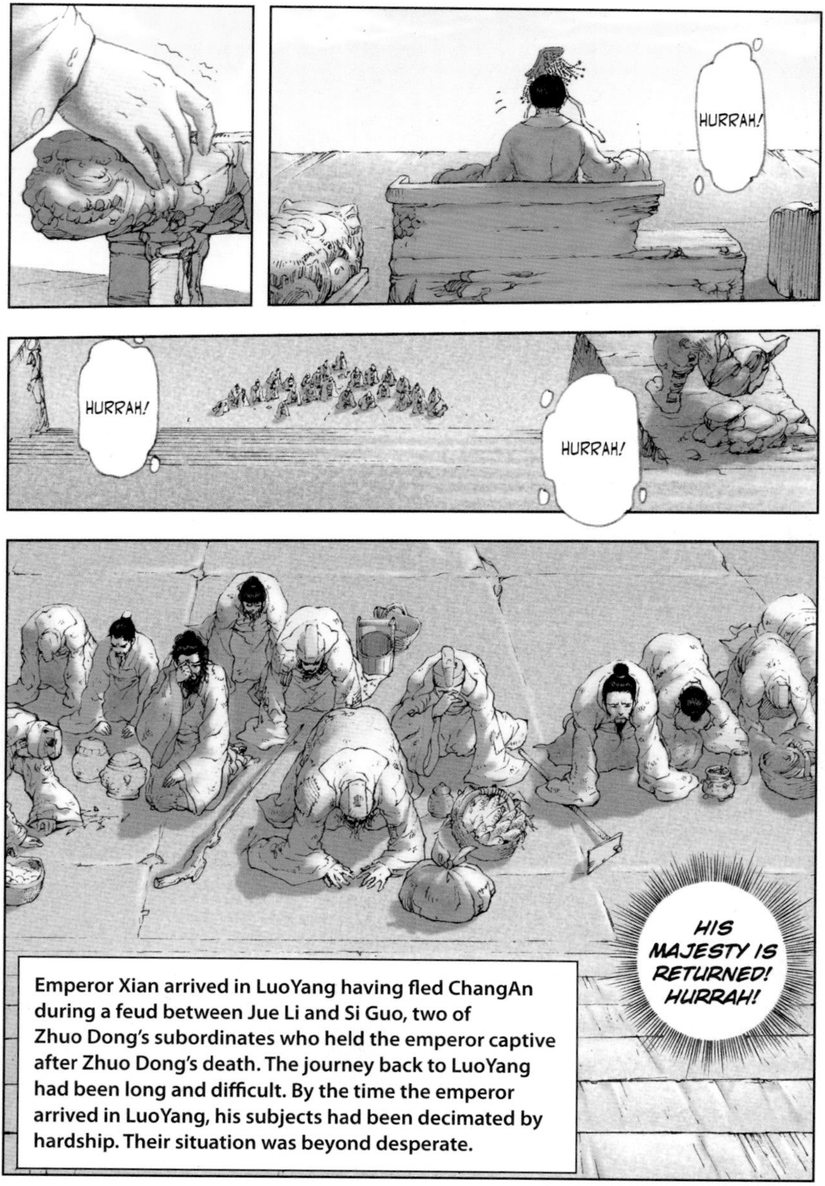
HURRAH!
HURRAH!
HURRAH!
Emperor Xian arrived in LuoYang having fled ChangAn during a feud between Jue Li and Si Guo, two of Zhuo Dong's subordinates who held the emperor captive after Zhuo Dong's death. The journey back to LuoYang had been long and difficult. By the time the emperor arrived in LuoYang, his subjects had been decimated by hardship. Their situation was beyond desperate.
HIS MAJESTY IS RETURNED! HURRAH!

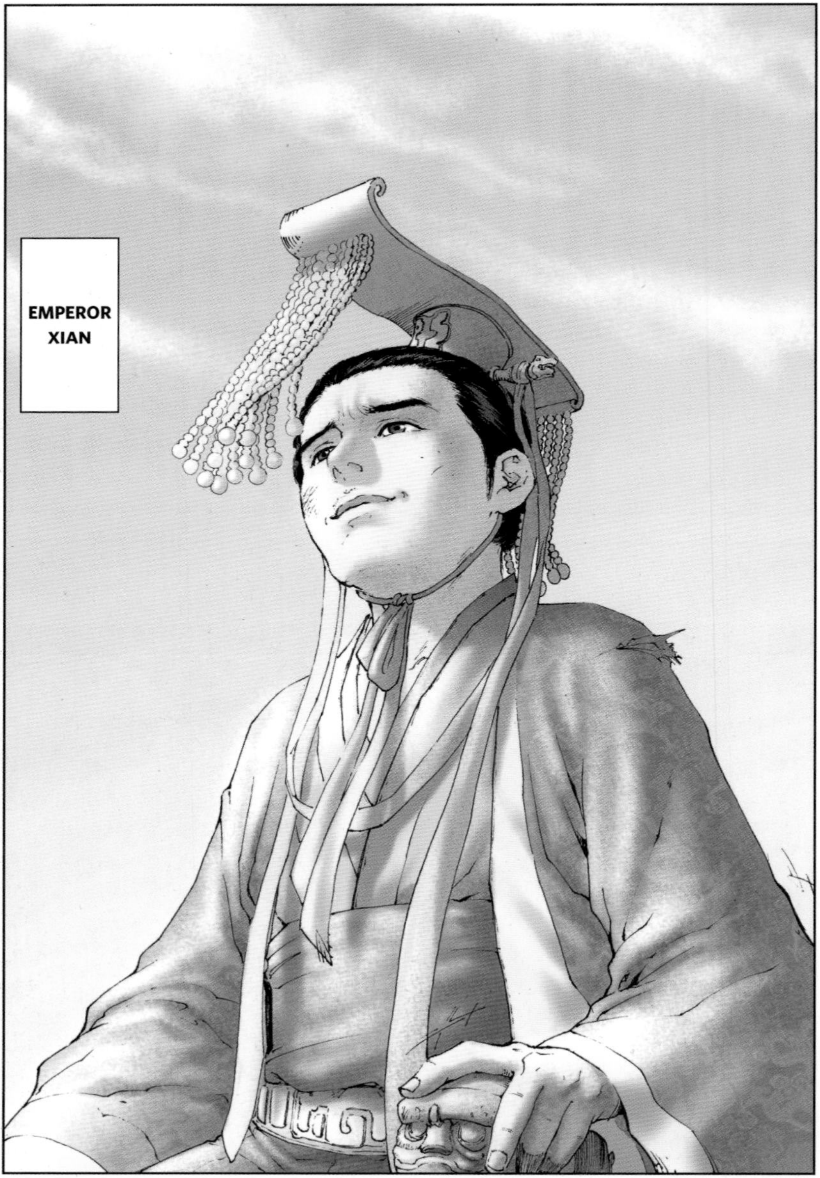
EMPEROR XIAN

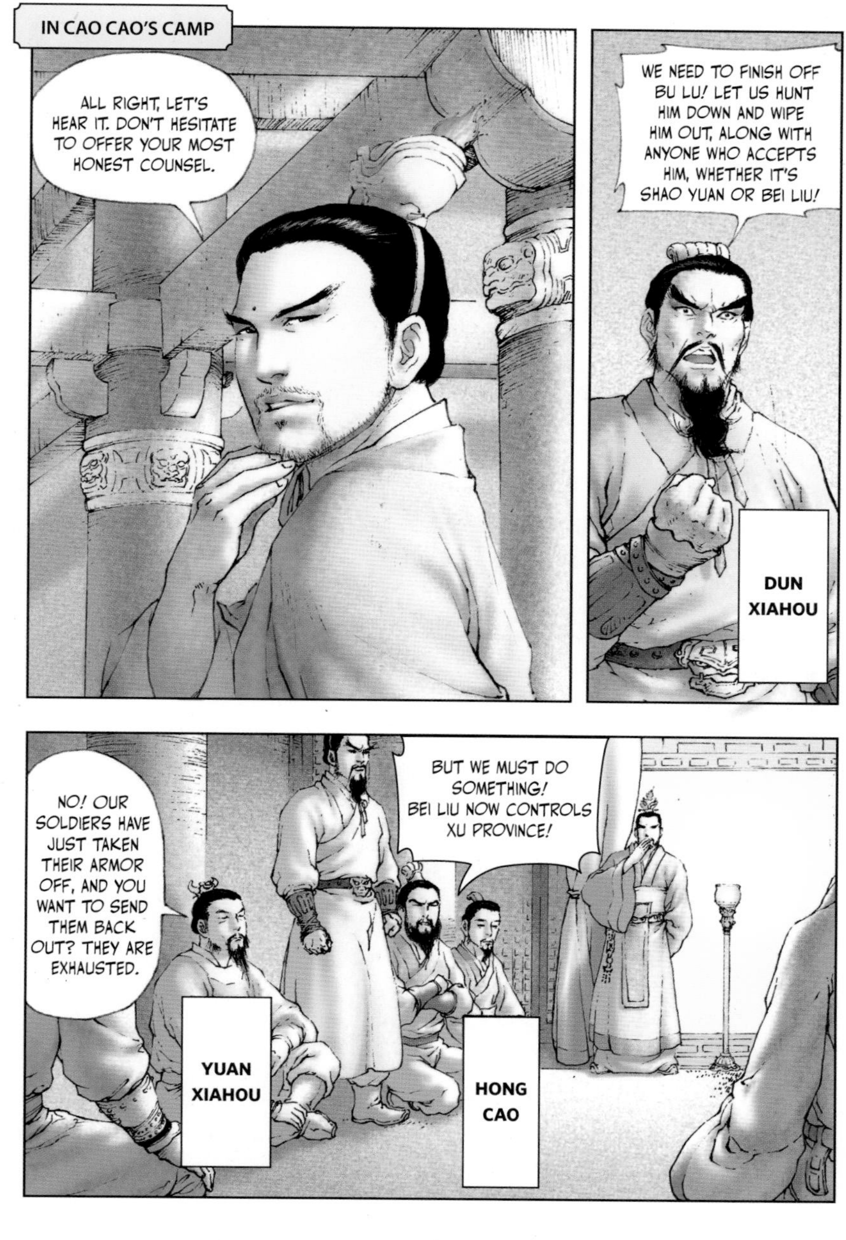
IN CAO CAO'S CAMP
ALL RIGHT, LET'S HEAR IT. DON'T HESITATE TO OFFER YOUR MOST HONEST COUNSEL.
WE NEED TO FINISH OFF BU LU! LET US HUNT HIM DOWN AND WIPE HIM OUT, ALONG WITH ANYONE WHO ACCEPTS HIM, WHETHER IT'S SHAO YUAN OR BEI LIU!
DUN XIAHOU
NO! OUR SOLDIERS HAVE JUST TAKEN THEIR ARMOR OFF, AND YOU WANT TO SEND THEM BACK OUT? THEY ARE EXHAUSTED.
YUAN XIAHOU
BUT WE MUST DO SOMETHING! BEI LIU NOW CONTROLS XU PROVINCE!
HONG CAO

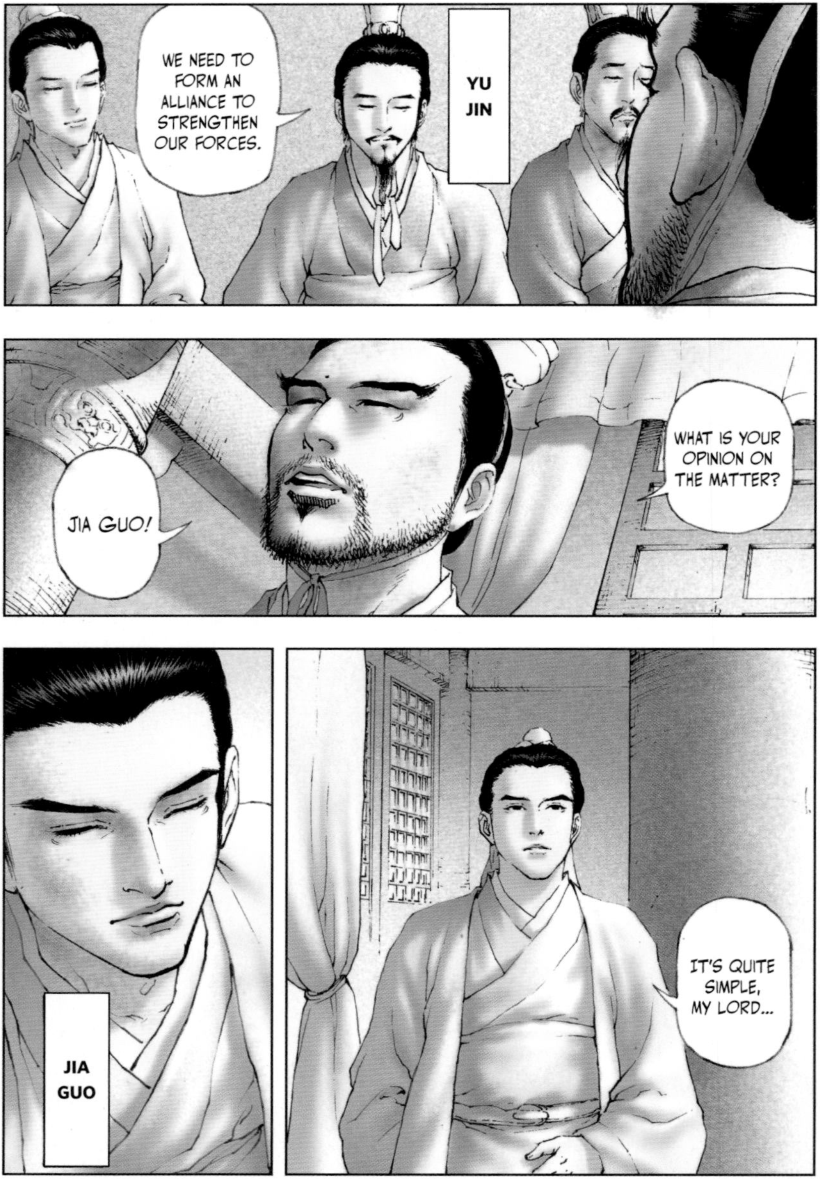
WE NEED TO FORM AN ALLIANCE TO STRENGTHEN OUR FORCES.
YU JIN
JIA GUO!
WHAT IS YOUR OPINION ON THE MATTER?
JIA GUO
IT'S QUITE SIMPLE, MY LORD...

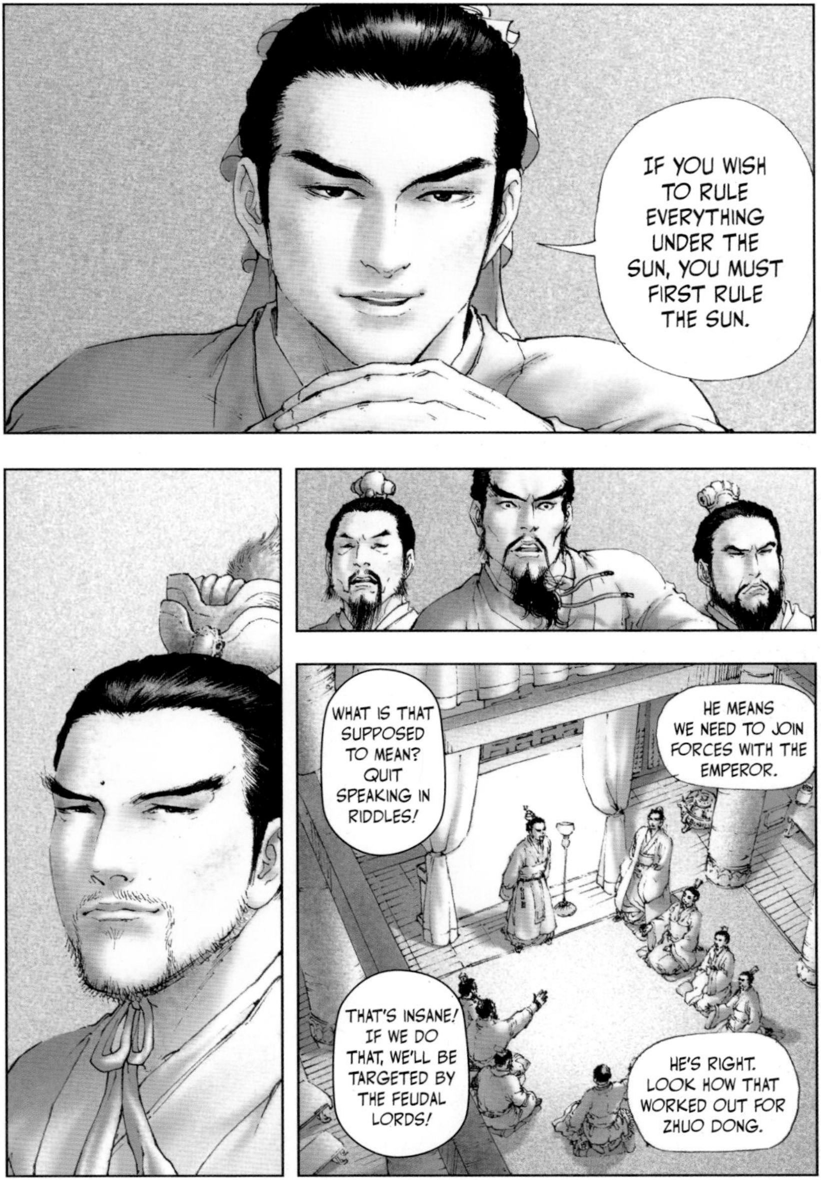
IF YOU WISH TO RULE EVERYTHING UNDER THE SUN, YOU MUST FIRST RULE THE SUN.
WHAT IS THAT SUPPOSED TO MEAN? QUIT SPEAKING IN RIDDLES!
HE MEANS WE NEED TO JOIN FORCES WITH THE EMPEROR.
THAT'S INSANE! IF WE DO THAT, WE'LL BE TARGETED BY THE FEUDAL LORDS!
HE'S RIGHT. LOOK HOW THAT WORKED OUT FOR ZHUO DONG.

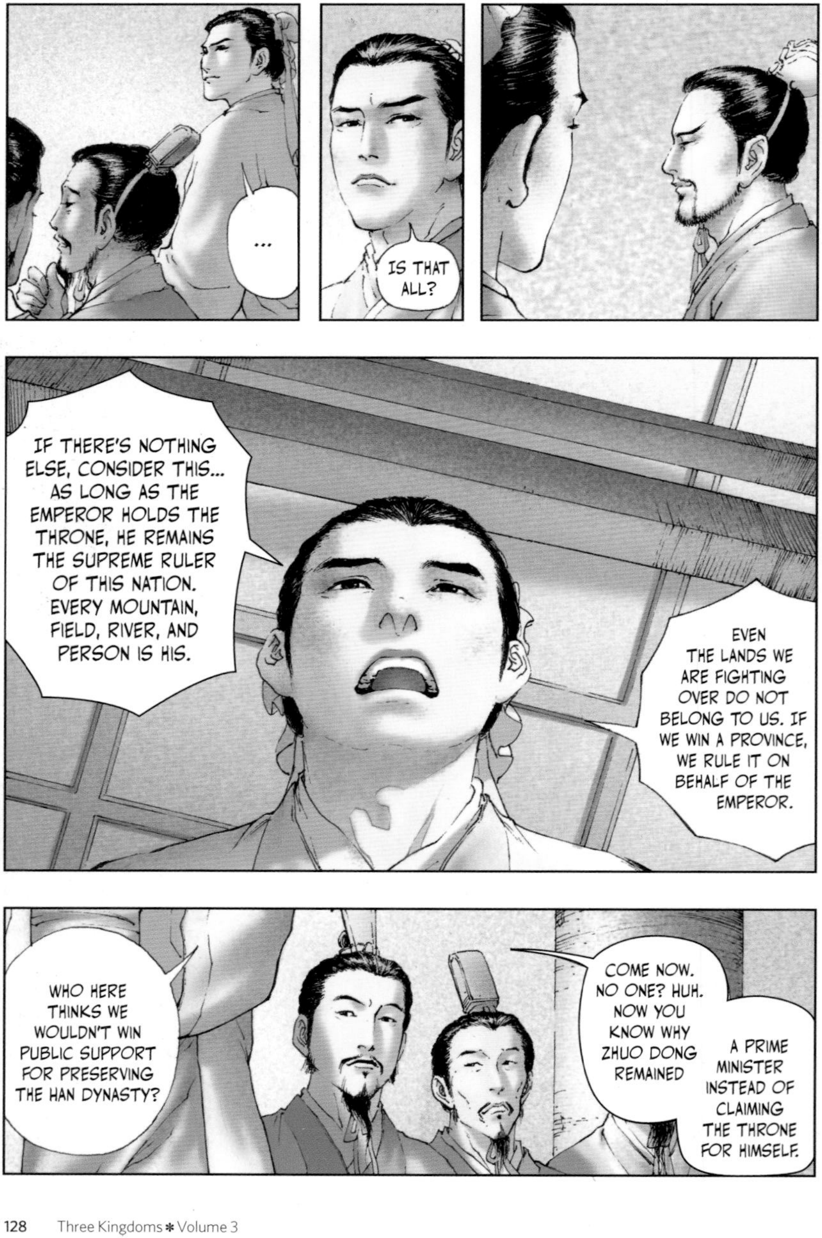
...
IS THAT ALL?
IF THERE'S NOTHING ELSE, CONSIDER THIS... AS LONG AS THE EMPEROR HOLDS THE THRONE, HE REMAINS THE SUPREME RULER OF THIS NATION. EVERY MOUNTAIN, FIELD, RIVER, AND PERSON IS HIS.
EVEN THE LANDS WE ARE FIGHTING OVER DO NOT BELONG TO US. IF WE WIN A PROVINCE, WE RULE IT ON BEHALF OF THE EMPEROR.
WHO HERE THINKS WE WOULDN'T WIN PUBLIC SUPPORT FOR PRESERVING THE HAN DYNASTY?
COME NOW. NO ONE? HUH. NOW YOU KNOW WHY ZHUO DONG REMAINED
A PRIME MINISTER INSTEAD OF CLAIMING THE THRONE FOR HIMSELF.

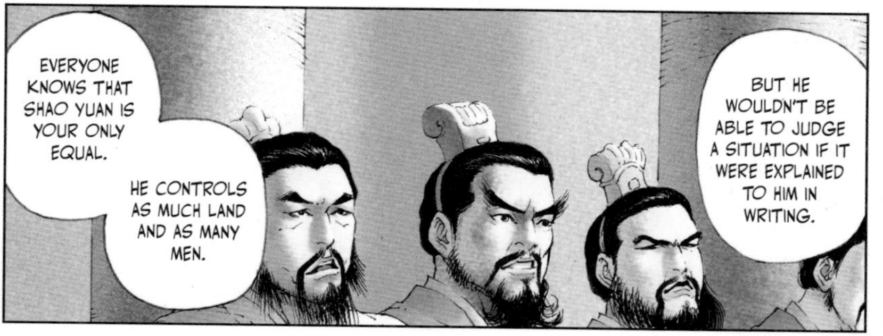
EVERYONE KNOWS THAT SHAO YUAN IS YOUR ONLY EQUAL.
HE CONTROLS AS MUCH LAND AND AS MANY MEN.
BUT HE WOULDN'T BE ABLE TO JUDGE A SITUATION IF IT WERE EXPLAINED TO HIM IN WRITING.

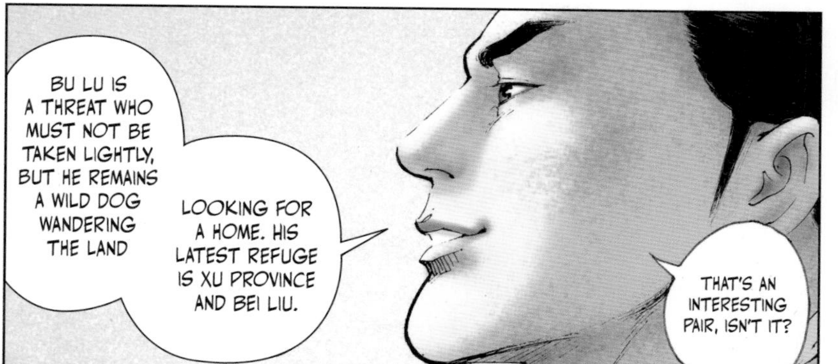
BU LU IS A THREAT WHO MUST NOT BE TAKEN LIGHTLY, BUT HE REMAINS A WILD DOG WANDERING THE LAND
LOOKING FOR A HOME. HIS LATEST REFUGE IS XU PROVINCE AND BEI LIU.
THAT'S AN INTERESTING PAIR, ISN'T IT?

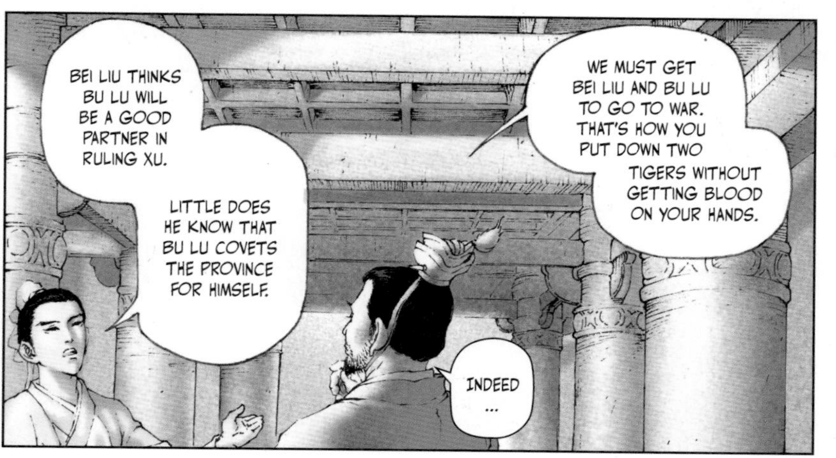
BEI LIU THINKS BU LU WILL BE A GOOD PARTNER IN RULING XU.
LITTLE DOES HE KNOW THAT BU LU COVETS THE PROVINCE FOR HIMSELF.
WE MUST GET BEI LIU AND BU LU TO GO TO WAR. THAT'S HOW YOU PUT DOWN TWO
TIGERS WITHOUT GETTING BLOOD ON YOUR HANDS.
INDEED ...

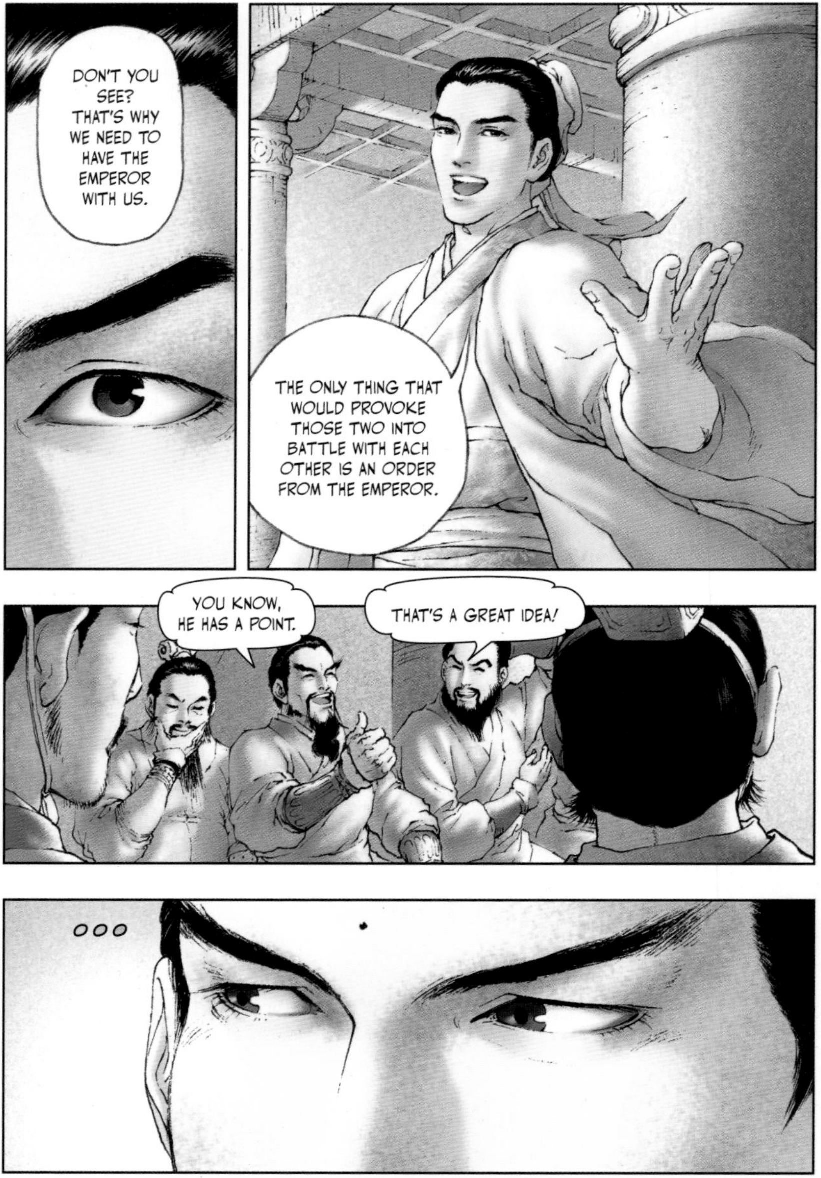
DON'T YOU SEE? THAT'S WHY WE NEED TO HAVE THE EMPEROR WITH US.
THE ONLY THING THAT WOULD PROVOKE THOSE TWO INTO BATTLE WITH EACH OTHER IS AN ORDER FROM THE EMPEROR.
YOU KNOW, HE HAS A POINT.
THAT'S A GREAT IDEA!
OOO

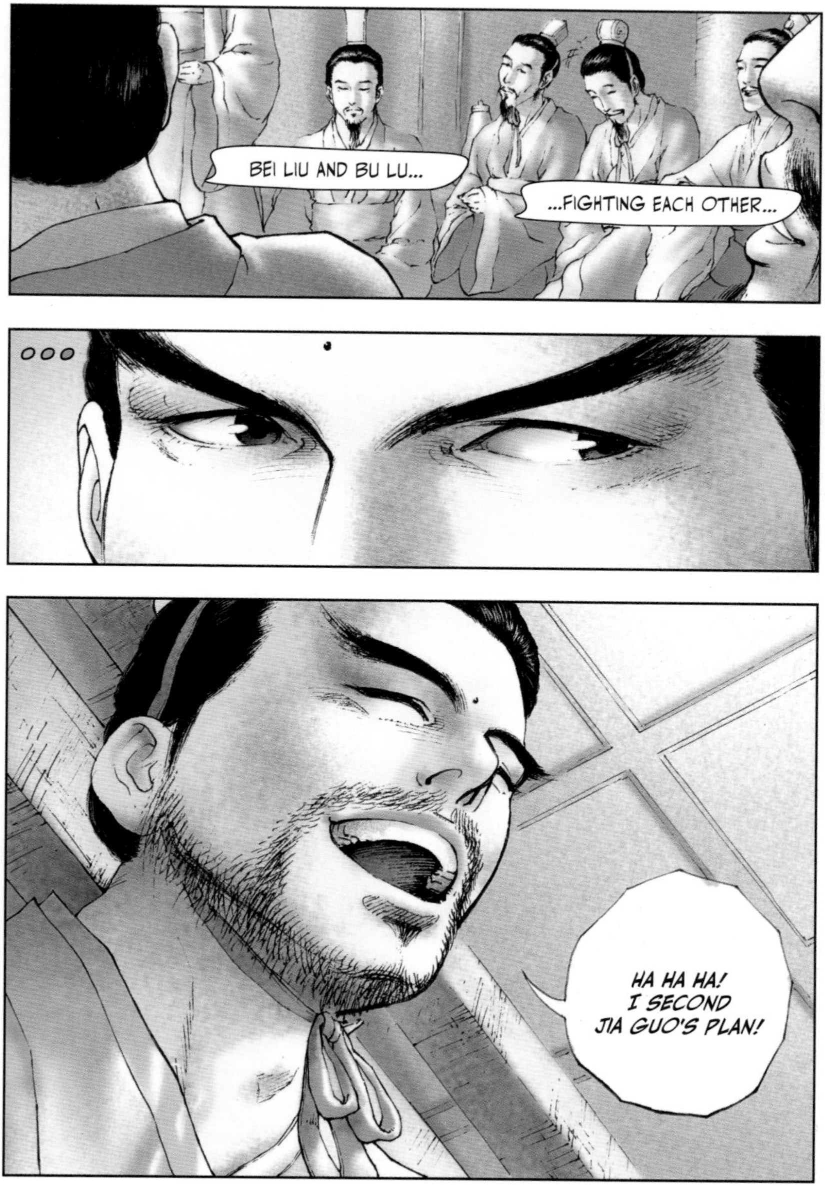
BEI LIU AND BU LU...
...FIGHTING EACH OTHER...
HA HA HA!
I SECOND
JIA GUO'S PLAN!

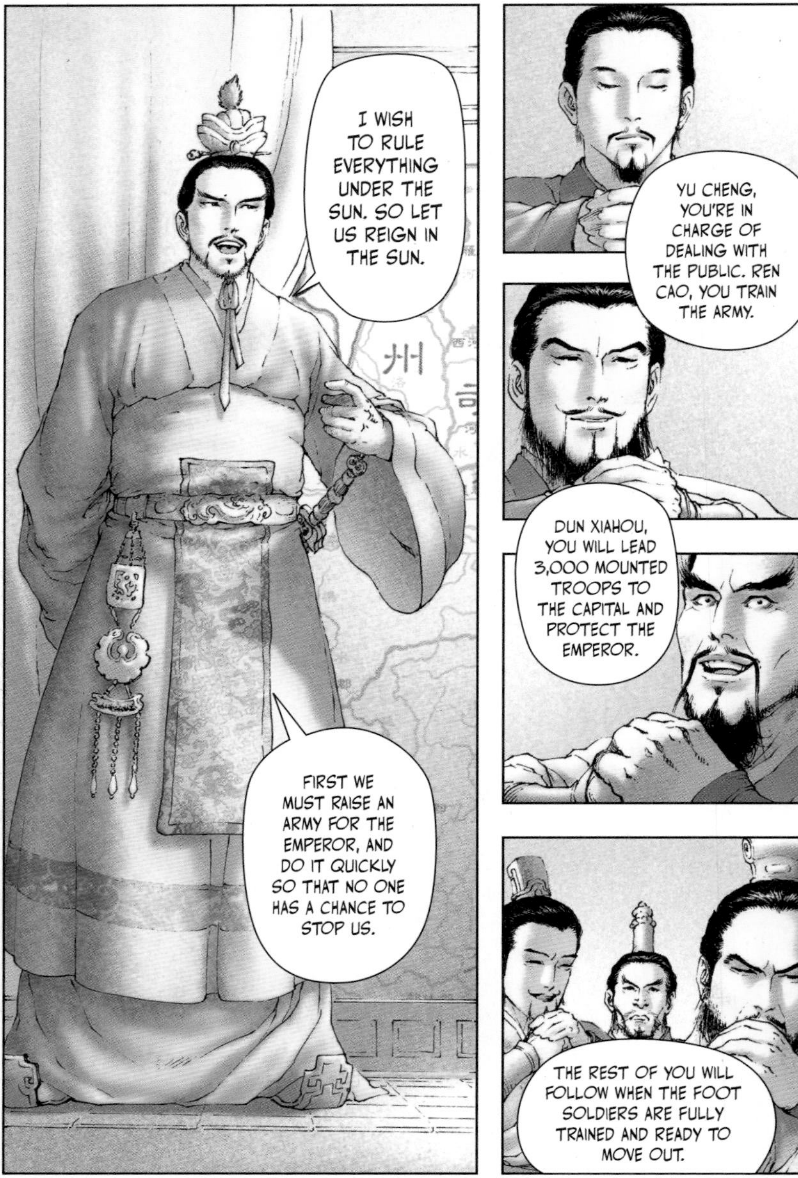
I WISH TO RULE EVERYTHING UNDER THE SUN. SO LET US REIGN IN THE SUN.
FIRST WE MUST RAISE AN ARMY FOR THE EMPEROR, AND DO IT QUICKLY SO THAT NO ONE HAS A CHANCE TO STOP US.
YU CHENG, YOU'RE IN CHARGE OF DEALING WITH THE PUBLIC. REN CAO, YOU TRAIN THE ARMY.
DUN XIAHOU, YOU WILL LEAD 3,000 MOUNTED TROOPS TO THE CAPITAL AND PROTECT THE EMPEROR.
THE REST OF YOU WILL FOLLOW WHEN THE FOOT SOLDIERS ARE FULLY TRAINED AND READY TO MOVE OUT.

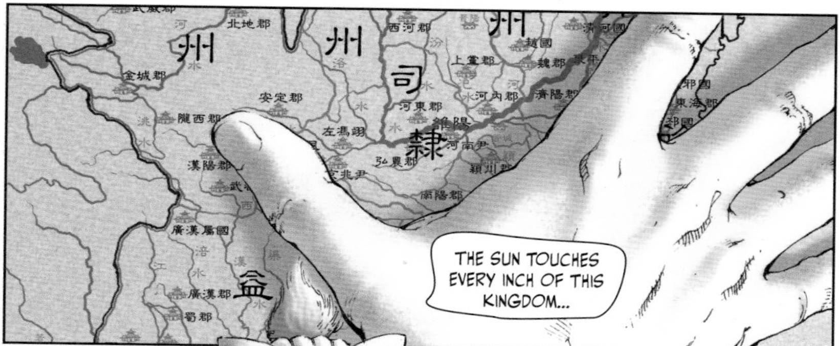
THE SUN TOUCHES EVERY INCH OF THIS KINGDOM...

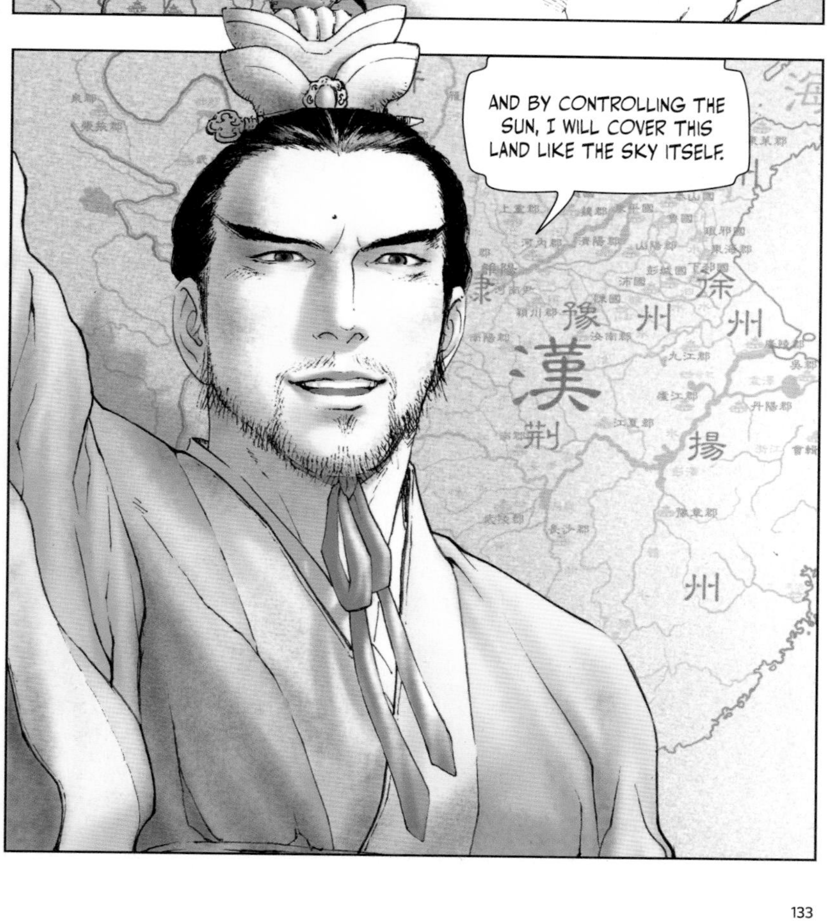
AND BY CONTROLLING THE SUN, I WILL COVER THIS LAND LIKE THE SKY ITSELF.

CAO CAO'S ARMY ENTERS LUOYANG.

Once Cao Cao had raised his desired army, he set out for LuoYang and defeated the remaining forces of Jue Li and Si Guo, two men who controlled the emperor after Zhuo Dong's downfall. The emperor thanked Cao Cao by appointing him to a high-ranking position in the government. Cao Cao recommended the emperor transfer the capital to XuDu, and the emperor agreed.

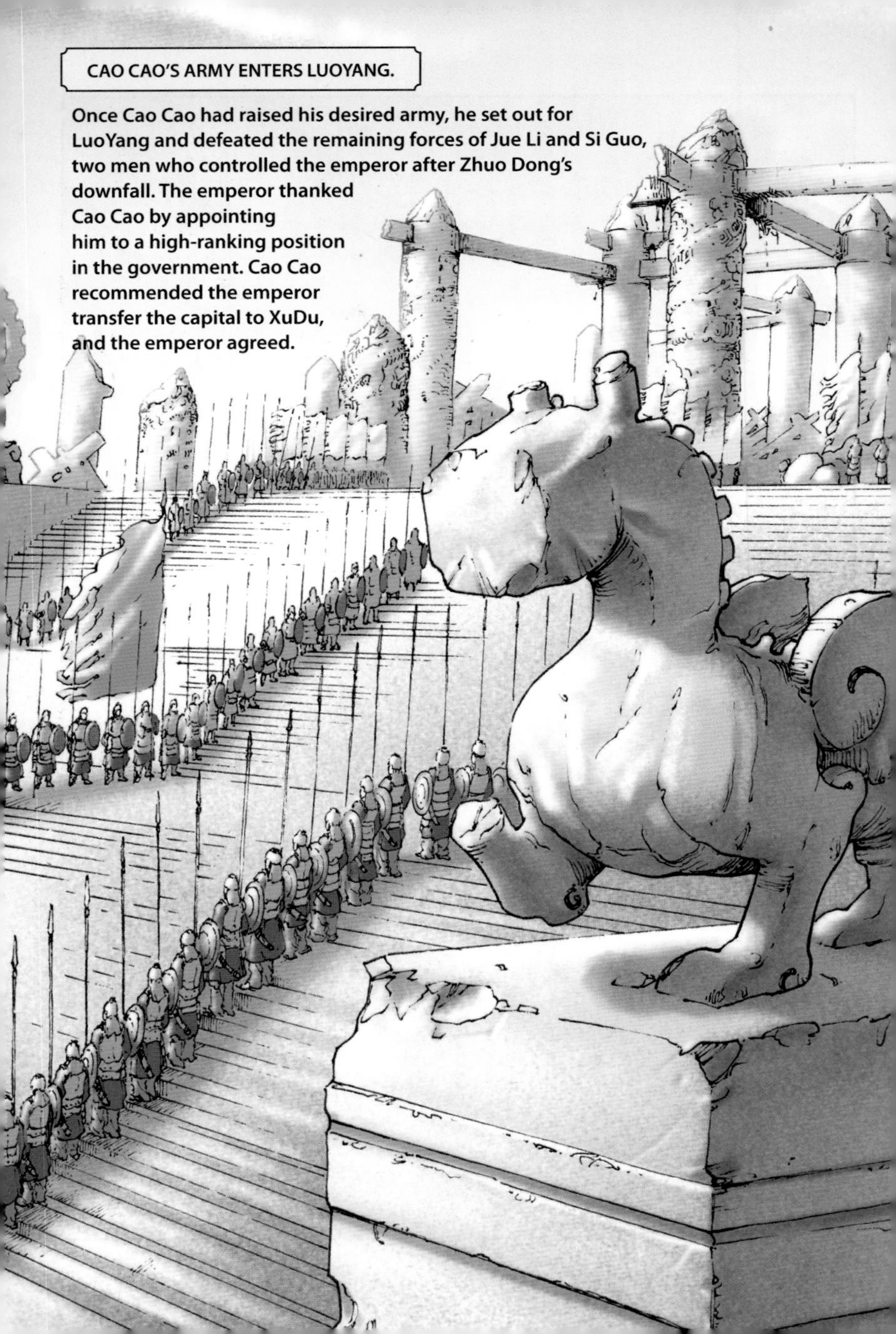

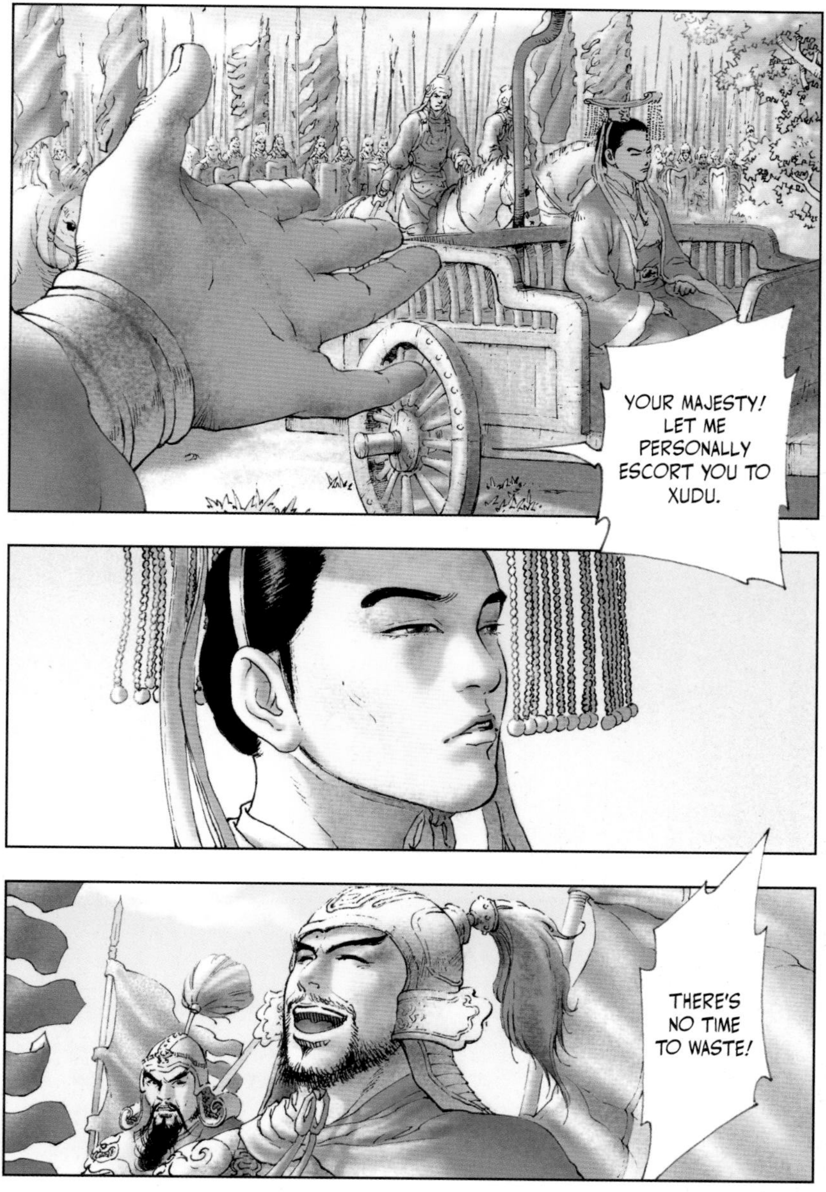
YOUR MAJESTY! LET ME PERSONALLY ESCORT YOU TO XUDU.
THERE'S NO TIME TO WASTE!

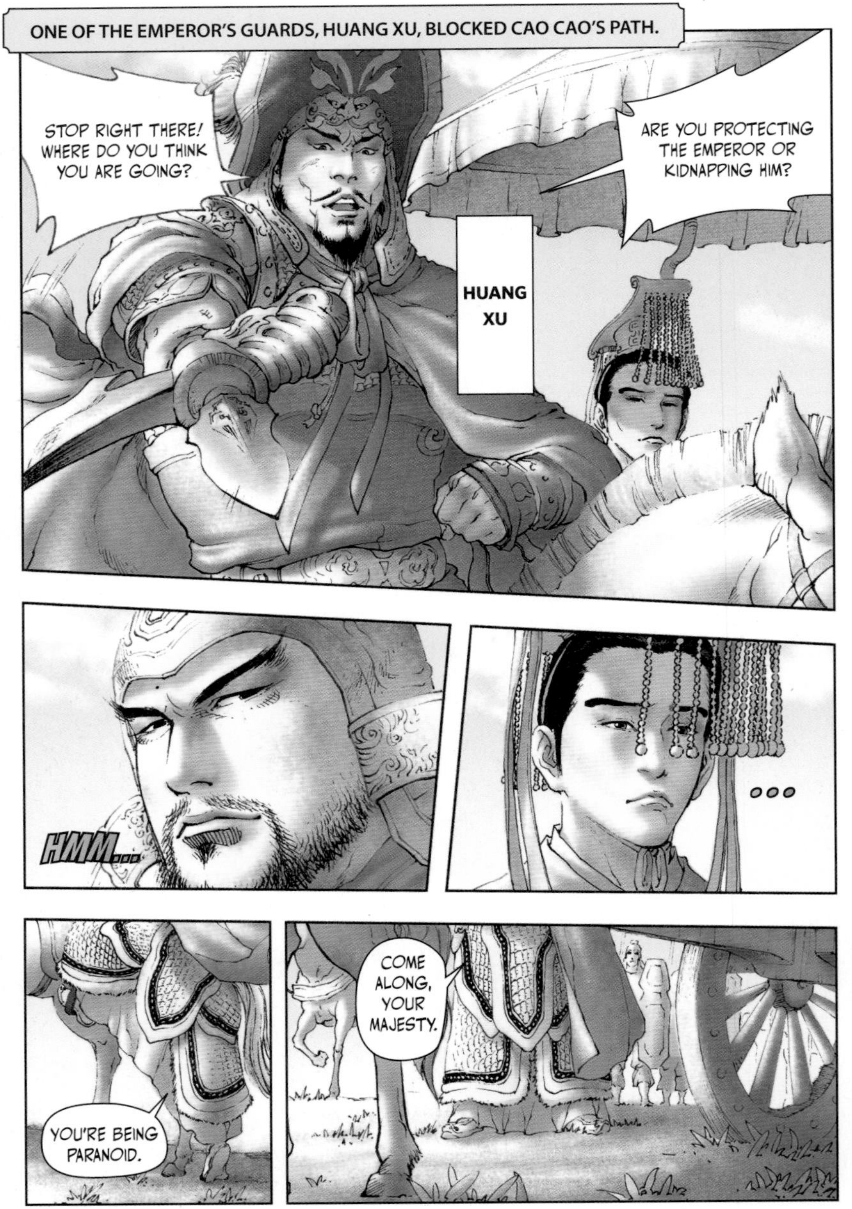
ONE OF THE EMPEROR'S GUARDS, HUANG XU, BLOCKED CAO CAO'S PATH.
STOP RIGHT THERE! WHERE DO YOU THINK YOU ARE GOING?
ARE YOU PROTECTING THE EMPEROR OR KIDNAPPING HIM?
HUANG XU
HMM...
...
YOU'RE BEING PARANOID.
COME ALONG, YOUR MAJESTY.

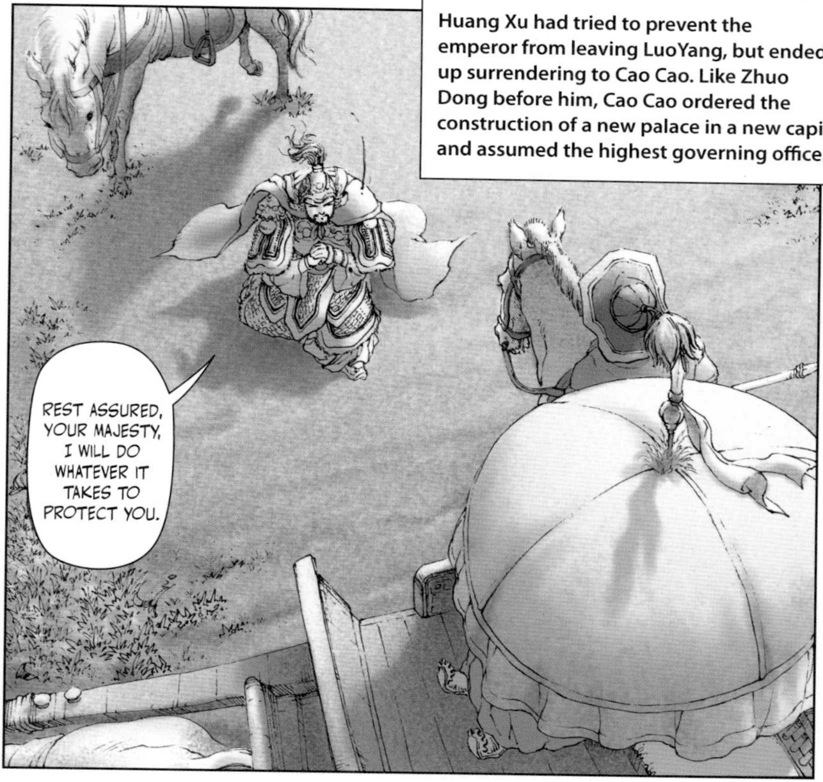
Huang Xu had tried to prevent the emperor from leaving LuoYang, but ended up surrendering to Cao Cao. Like Zhuo Dong before him, Cao Cao ordered the construction of a new palace in a new capital and assumed the highest governing office.
REST ASSURED, YOUR MAJESTY, I WILL DO WHATEVER IT TAKES TO PROTECT YOU.

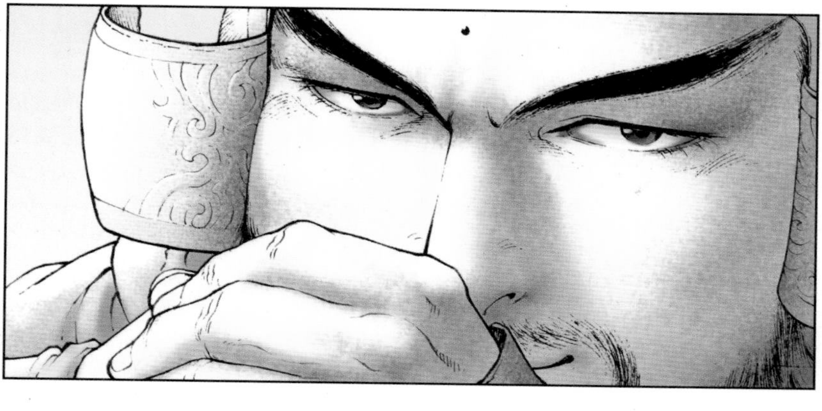

Chapter 4

Cao Cao Breaks Up the Xu Alliance AD 196

Summary

Bu Lu, having been driven out of Yan by Cao Cao's forces, has taken up residence in the Xu Province, at the behest of Bei Liu. This act of generosity does not go unpunished, as Cao Cao had expected Bu Lu to end up in Xu, and he convinces Bu Lu, using the persuasive power of his new alliance with Emperor Xian, to launch a takeover of Xu while Bei Liu's forces are preoccupied in battle against Shu Yuan. Bu Lu recognizes that Cao Cao is deliberately pitting him against Bei Liu. However, he also recognizes that Bei Liu is a legitimate potential adversary, and must therefore be overthrown. Although Bei Liu has left Fei Zhang in charge of Xu while he is away, Bu Lu captures the province with little incident.

Surprisingly, when Bei Liu returns from battle he is eager to make peace with Bu Lu. It turns out that Bei Liu has anticipated these moves by Cao Cao and Bu Lu, and has decided to surrender Xu to Bu Lu, as he expects there will be several more people who attempt to conquer the province...

ChangShan
BeiHai
PuYang
HuLuo
XiaoPei
LuoYang
GuanDu
B
XuZhou
C
ChangAn
XuDu
A
NanYang
ShouChun
HeFei
XiangYang

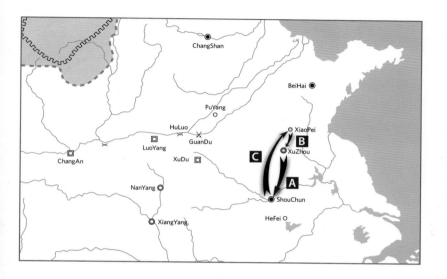

A Bei Liu, in response to a royal request, attacks Shu Yuan, leaving Fei Zhang to defend XuZhuo.

B Once Bei Liu is gone, Cao Cao sends a royal message to Bu Lu urging him to take over Xu Province in Bei Liu's absence. He overthrows Fei Zhang and conquers the territory easily.

C Bei Liu accepts the new reality, and returns to Xu to make peace with Bu Lu and continue living in XiaoPei.

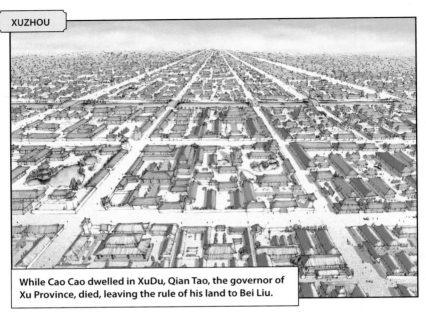

XUZHOU

While Cao Cao dwelled in XuDu, Qian Tao, the governor of Xu Province, died, leaving the rule of his land to Bei Liu.

GOVERNOR BEI LIU! I'D LIKE TO INTRODUCE YOU TO A COUPLE OF PEOPLE.

COME ON IN.

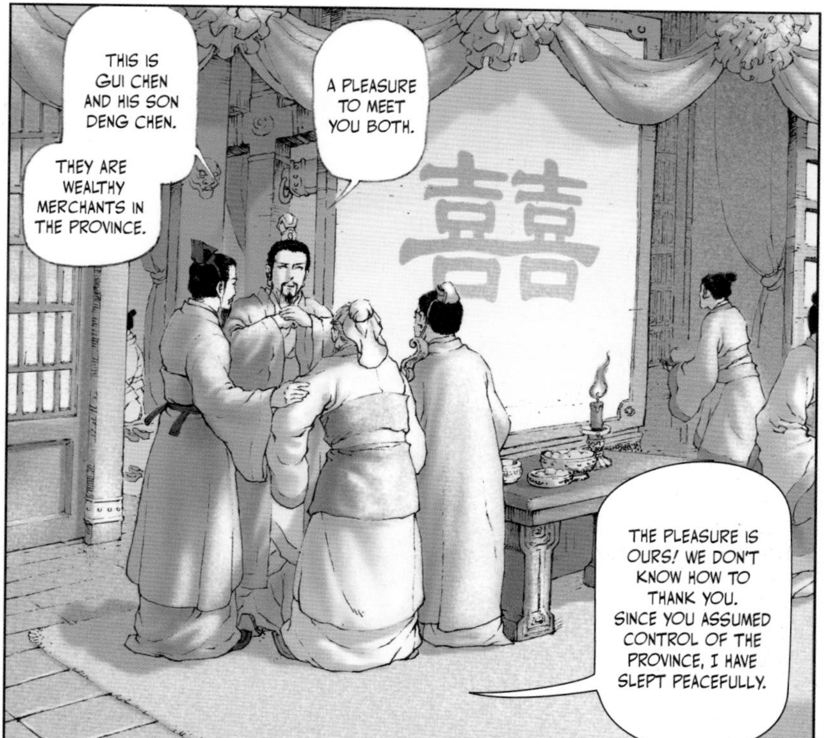
THIS IS GUI CHEN AND HIS SON DENG CHEN.
THEY ARE WEALTHY MERCHANTS IN THE PROVINCE.
A PLEASURE TO MEET YOU BOTH.
THE PLEASURE IS OURS! WE DON'T KNOW HOW TO THANK YOU. SINCE YOU ASSUMED CONTROL OF THE PROVINCE, I HAVE SLEPT PEACEFULLY.

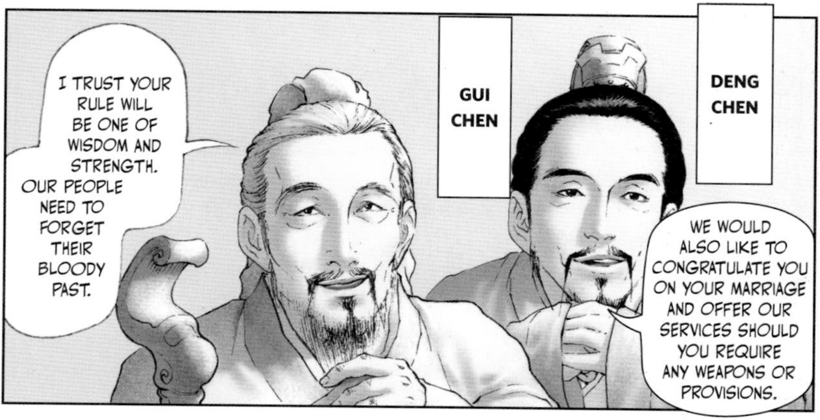
GUI CHEN
DENG CHEN
I TRUST YOUR RULE WILL BE ONE OF WISDOM AND STRENGTH. OUR PEOPLE NEED TO FORGET THEIR BLOODY PAST.
WE WOULD ALSO LIKE TO CONGRATULATE YOU ON YOUR MARRIAGE AND OFFER OUR SERVICES SHOULD YOU REQUIRE ANY WEAPONS OR PROVISIONS.

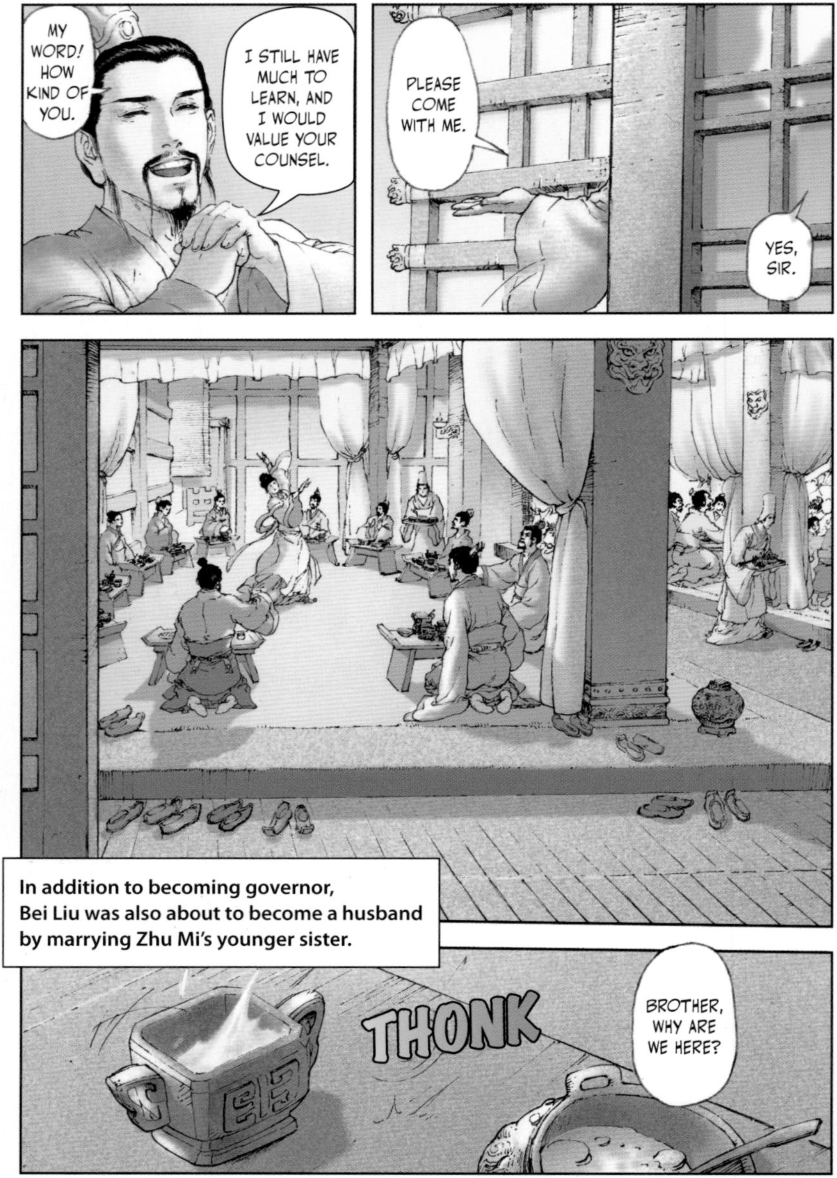

MY WORD! HOW KIND OF YOU.
I STILL HAVE MUCH TO LEARN, AND I WOULD VALUE YOUR COUNSEL.
PLEASE COME WITH ME.
YES, SIR.
In addition to becoming governor, Bei Liu was also about to become a husband by marrying Zhu Mi's younger sister.
THONK
BROTHER, WHY ARE WE HERE?

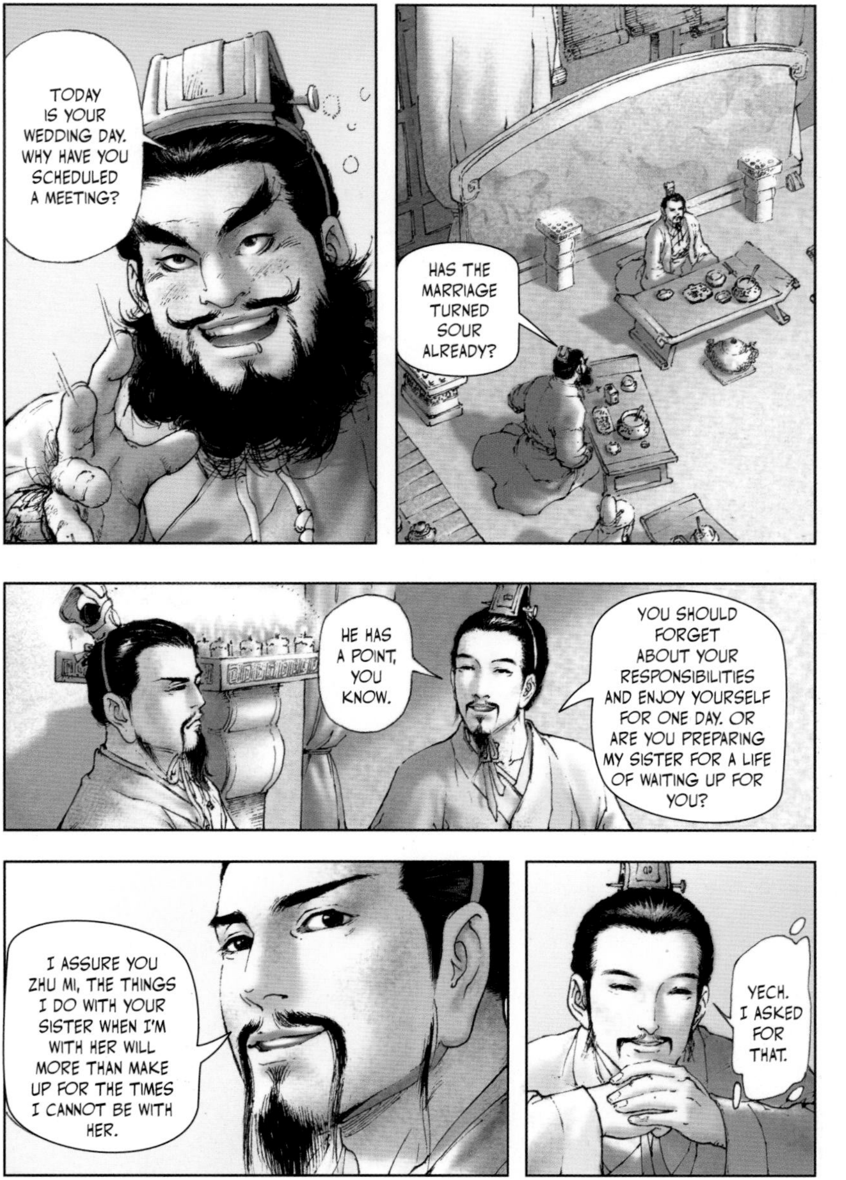
TODAY IS YOUR WEDDING DAY. WHY HAVE YOU SCHEDULED A MEETING?
HAS THE MARRIAGE TURNED SOUR ALREADY?
HE HAS A POINT, YOU KNOW.
YOU SHOULD FORGET ABOUT YOUR RESPONSIBILITIES AND ENJOY YOURSELF FOR ONE DAY. OR ARE YOU PREPARING MY SISTER FOR A LIFE OF WAITING UP FOR YOU?
I ASSURE YOU ZHU MI, THE THINGS I DO WITH YOUR SISTER WHEN I'M WITH HER WILL MORE THAN MAKE UP FOR THE TIMES I CANNOT BE WITH HER.
YECH. I ASKED FOR THAT.

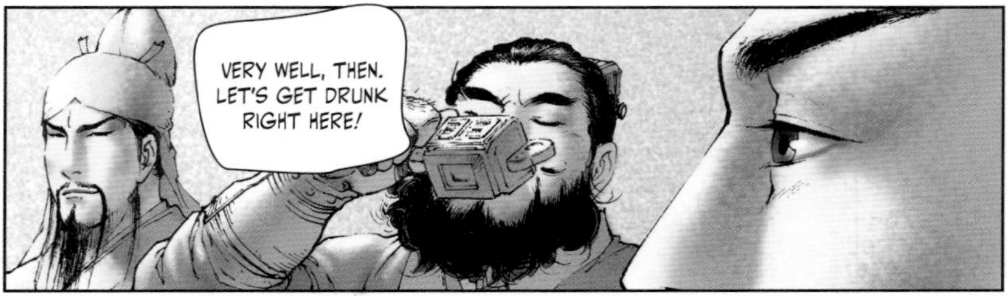
VERY WELL, THEN. LET'S GET DRUNK RIGHT HERE!

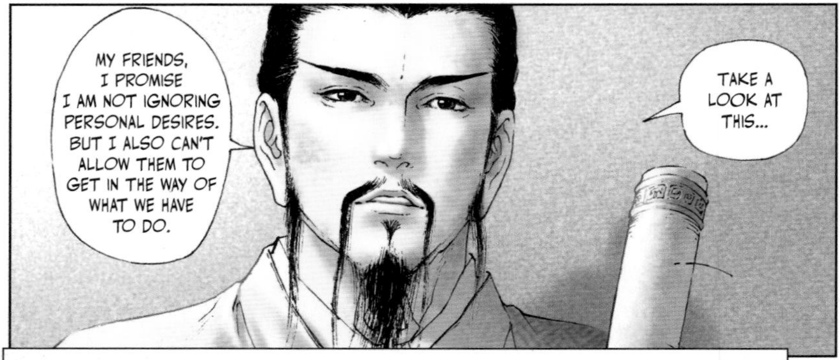
MY FRIENDS, I PROMISE I AM NOT IGNORING PERSONAL DESIRES. BUT I ALSO CAN'T ALLOW THEM TO GET IN THE WAY OF WHAT WE HAVE TO DO.
TAKE A LOOK AT THIS...

Bu Lu, who had been wandering the countryside following his defeat to Cao Cao, had sent a letter to Bei Liu. It contained an unexpected request.

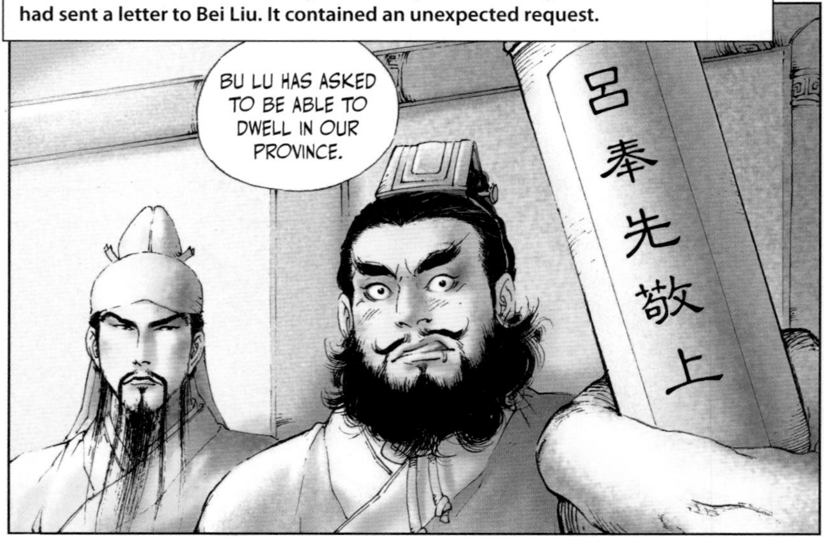
BU LU HAS ASKED TO BE ABLE TO DWELL IN OUR PROVINCE.
呂奉先敬上

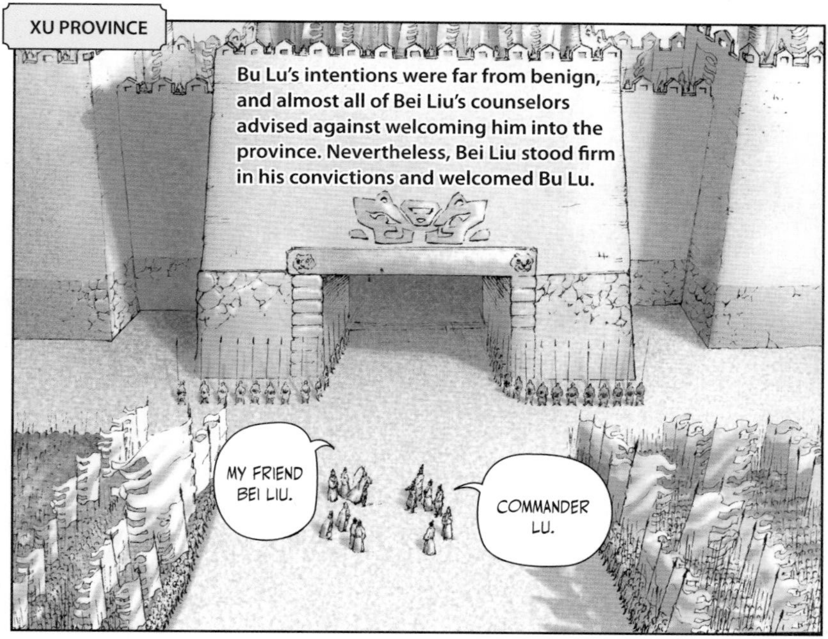
XU PROVINCE
Bu Lu's intentions were far from benign, and almost all of Bei Liu's counselors advised against welcoming him into the province. Nevertheless, Bei Liu stood firm in his convictions and welcomed Bu Lu.
MY FRIEND BEI LIU.
COMMANDER LU.

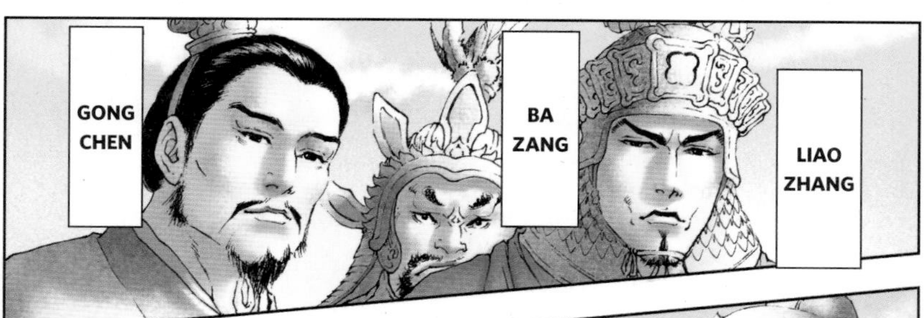
GONG CHEN
BA ZANG
LIAO ZHANG

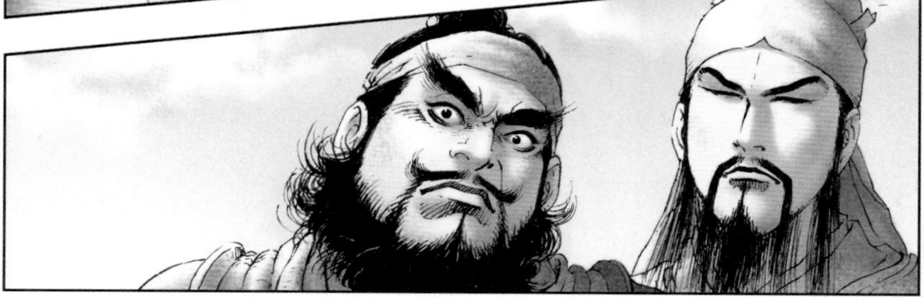

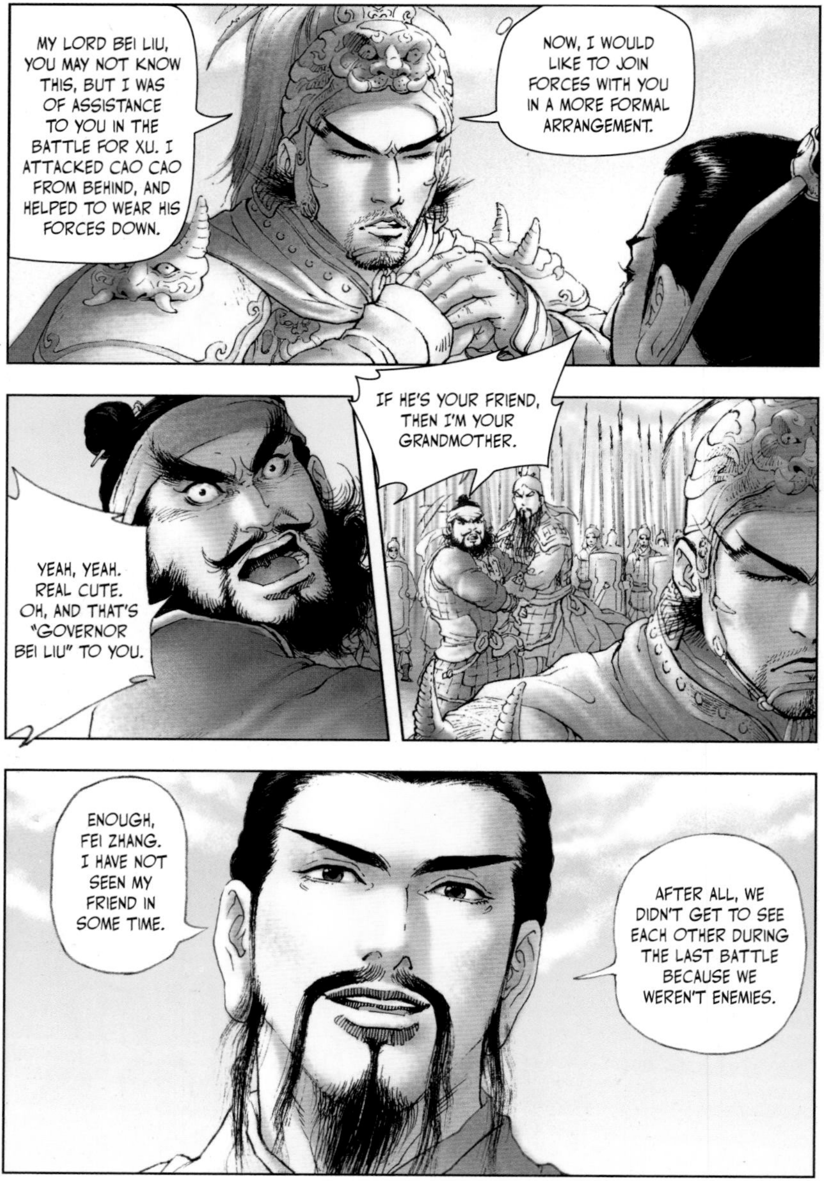
MY LORD BEI LIU, YOU MAY NOT KNOW THIS, BUT I WAS OF ASSISTANCE TO YOU IN THE BATTLE FOR XU. I ATTACKED CAO CAO FROM BEHIND, AND HELPED TO WEAR HIS FORCES DOWN.
NOW, I WOULD LIKE TO JOIN FORCES WITH YOU IN A MORE FORMAL ARRANGEMENT.
IF HE'S YOUR FRIEND, THEN I'M YOUR GRANDMOTHER.
YEAH, YEAH. REAL CUTE. OH, AND THAT'S "GOVERNOR BEI LIU" TO YOU.
ENOUGH, FEI ZHANG. I HAVE NOT SEEN MY FRIEND IN SOME TIME.
AFTER ALL, WE DIDN'T GET TO SEE EACH OTHER DURING THE LAST BATTLE BECAUSE WE WEREN'T ENEMIES.

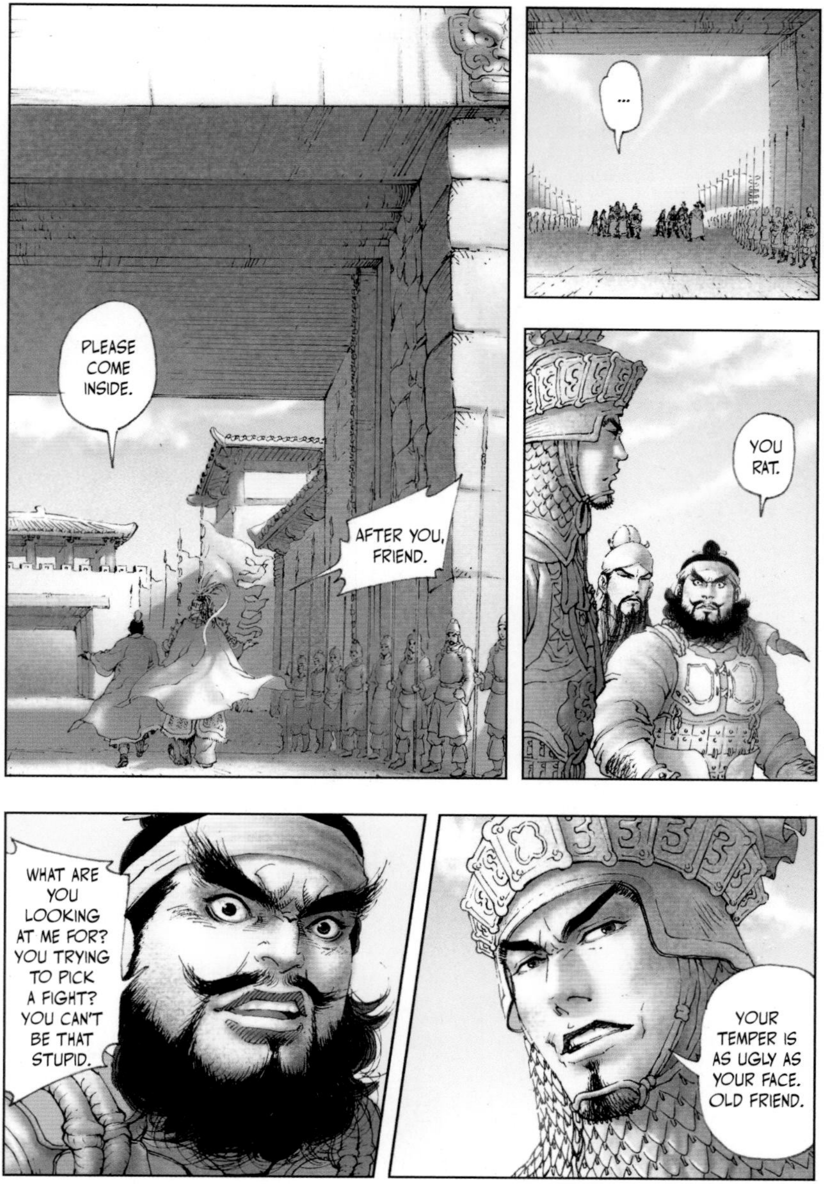
PLEASE COME INSIDE.
AFTER YOU, FRIEND.
...
YOU RAT.
WHAT ARE YOU LOOKING AT ME FOR? YOU TRYING TO PICK A FIGHT? YOU CAN'T BE THAT STUPID.
YOUR TEMPER IS AS UGLY AS YOUR FACE. OLD FRIEND.

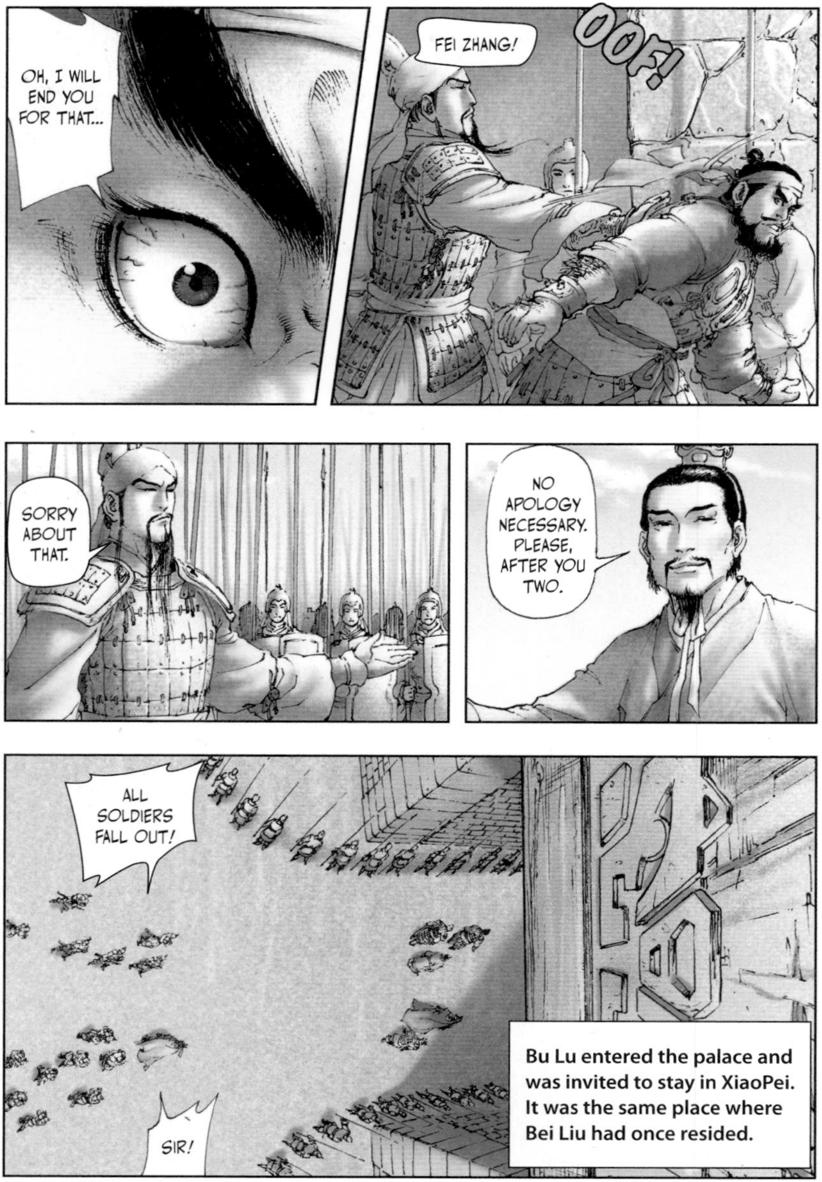
OH, I WILL END YOU FOR THAT...
FEI ZHANG!
OOF!
SORRY ABOUT THAT.
NO APOLOGY NECESSARY. PLEASE, AFTER YOU TWO.
ALL SOLDIERS FALL OUT!
SIR!
Bu Lu entered the palace and was invited to stay in XiaoPei. It was the same place where Bei Liu had once resided.

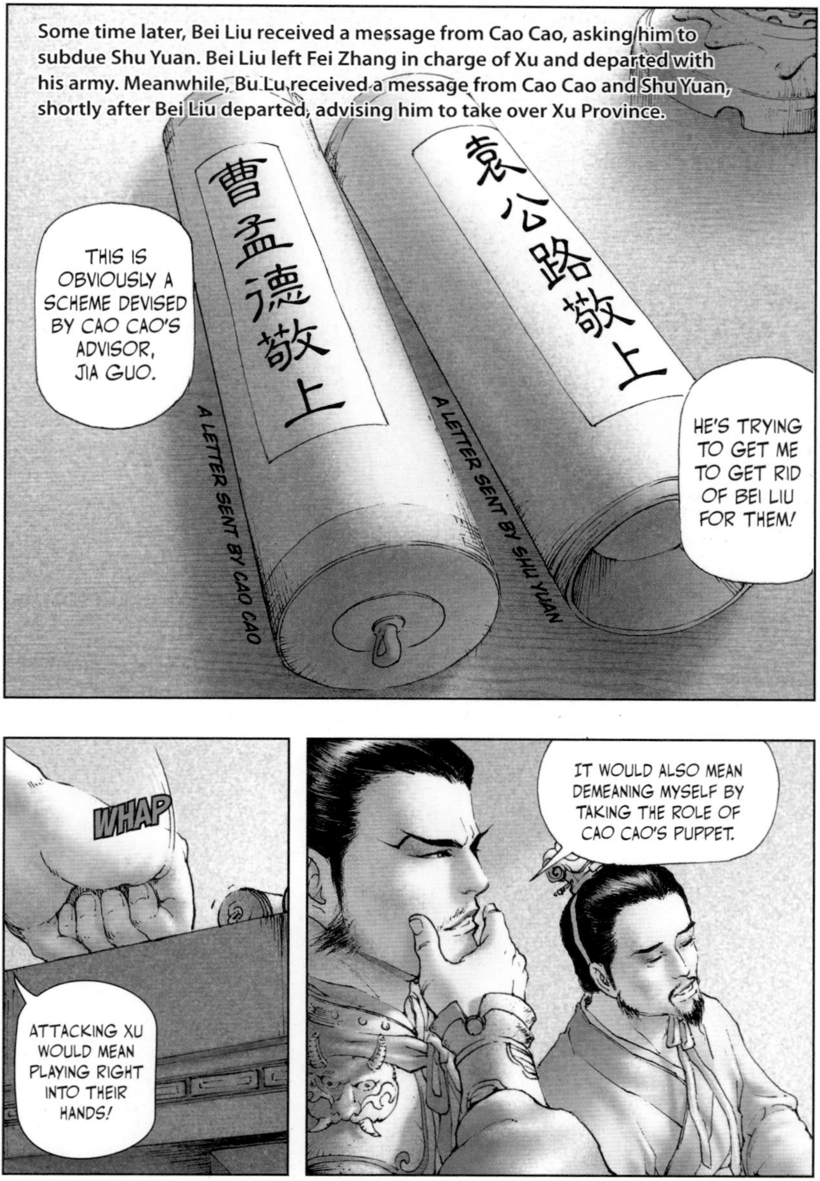
Some time later, Bei Liu received a message from Cao Cao, asking him to subdue Shu Yuan. Bei Liu left Fei Zhang in charge of Xu and departed with his army. Meanwhile, Bu Lu received a message from Cao Cao and Shu Yuan, shortly after Bei Liu departed, advising him to take over Xu Province.
曹孟德敬上
袁公路敬上
A LETTER SENT BY CAO CAO
A LETTER SENT BY SHU YUAN
THIS IS OBVIOUSLY A SCHEME DEVISED BY CAO CAO'S ADVISOR, JIA GUO.
HE'S TRYING TO GET ME TO GET RID OF BEI LIU FOR THEM!
WHAP
ATTACKING XU WOULD MEAN PLAYING RIGHT INTO THEIR HANDS!
IT WOULD ALSO MEAN DEMEANING MYSELF BY TAKING THE ROLE OF CAO CAO'S PUPPET.

YES, BUT CAO CAO HAS DEVISED A WAY OF GETTING RID OF BEI LIU.

HE BELIEVES BEI LIU WILL MAKE A PLAY FOR RULE OF THE NATION, WITH XU AS HIS BASE.

HM... SO GETTING RID OF BEI LIU ELIMINATES A FUTURE THREAT. WE HAVE NOTHING TO LOSE, DO WE?

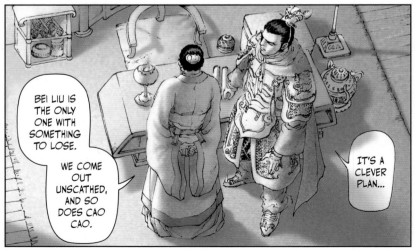

BEI LIU IS THE ONLY ONE WITH SOMETHING TO LOSE.

WE COME OUT UNSCATHED, AND SO DOES CAO CAO.

IT'S A CLEVER PLAN...

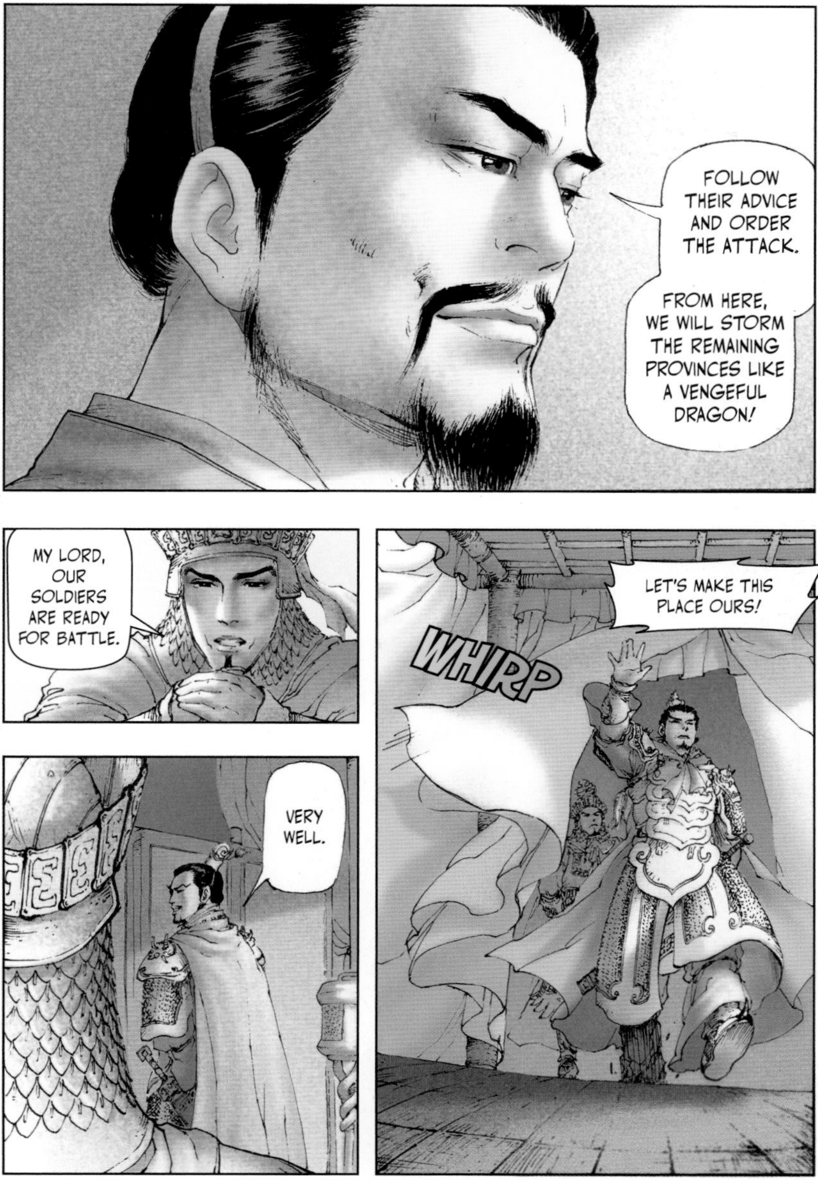
FOLLOW THEIR ADVICE AND ORDER THE ATTACK.
FROM HERE, WE WILL STORM THE REMAINING PROVINCES LIKE A VENGEFUL DRAGON!
MY LORD, OUR SOLDIERS ARE READY FOR BATTLE.
VERY WELL.
LET'S MAKE THIS PLACE OURS!
WHIRP

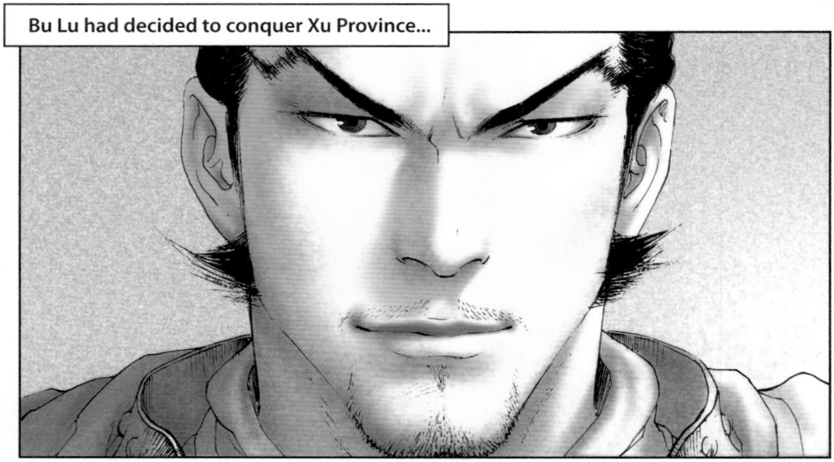
Bu Lu had decided to conquer Xu Province...

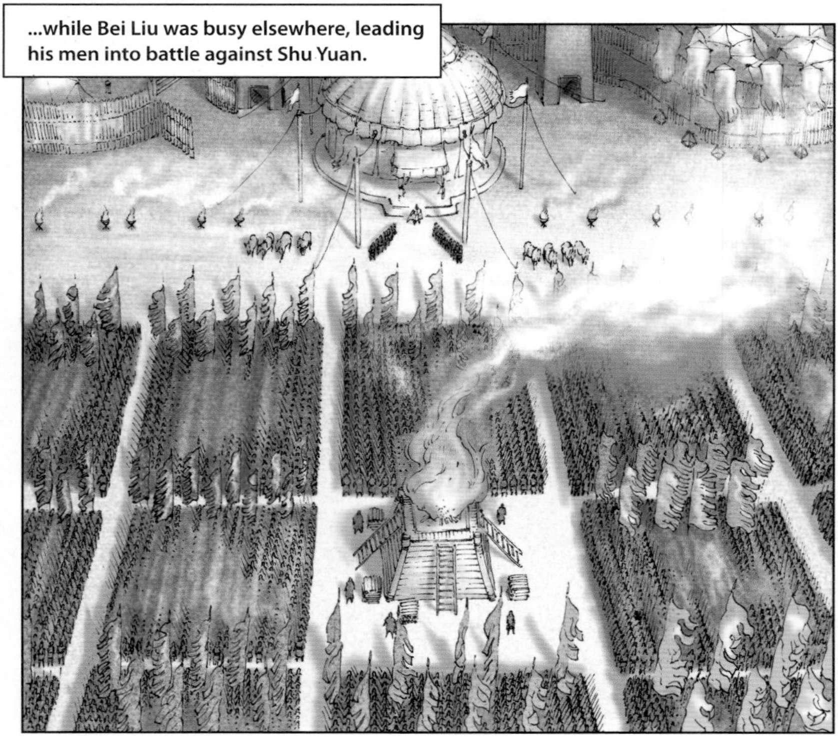
...while Bei Liu was busy elsewhere, leading his men into battle against Shu Yuan.

EMPEROR XIAN

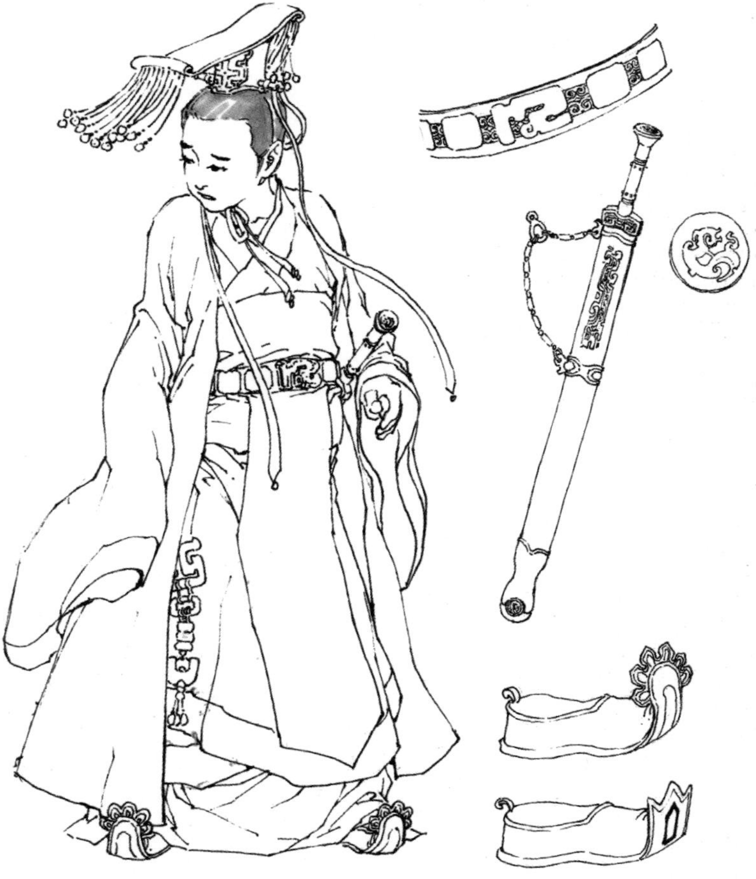

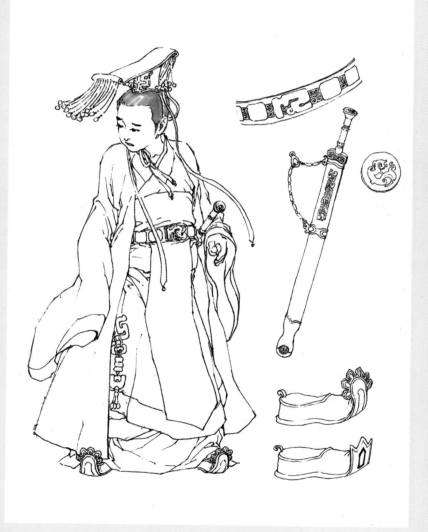

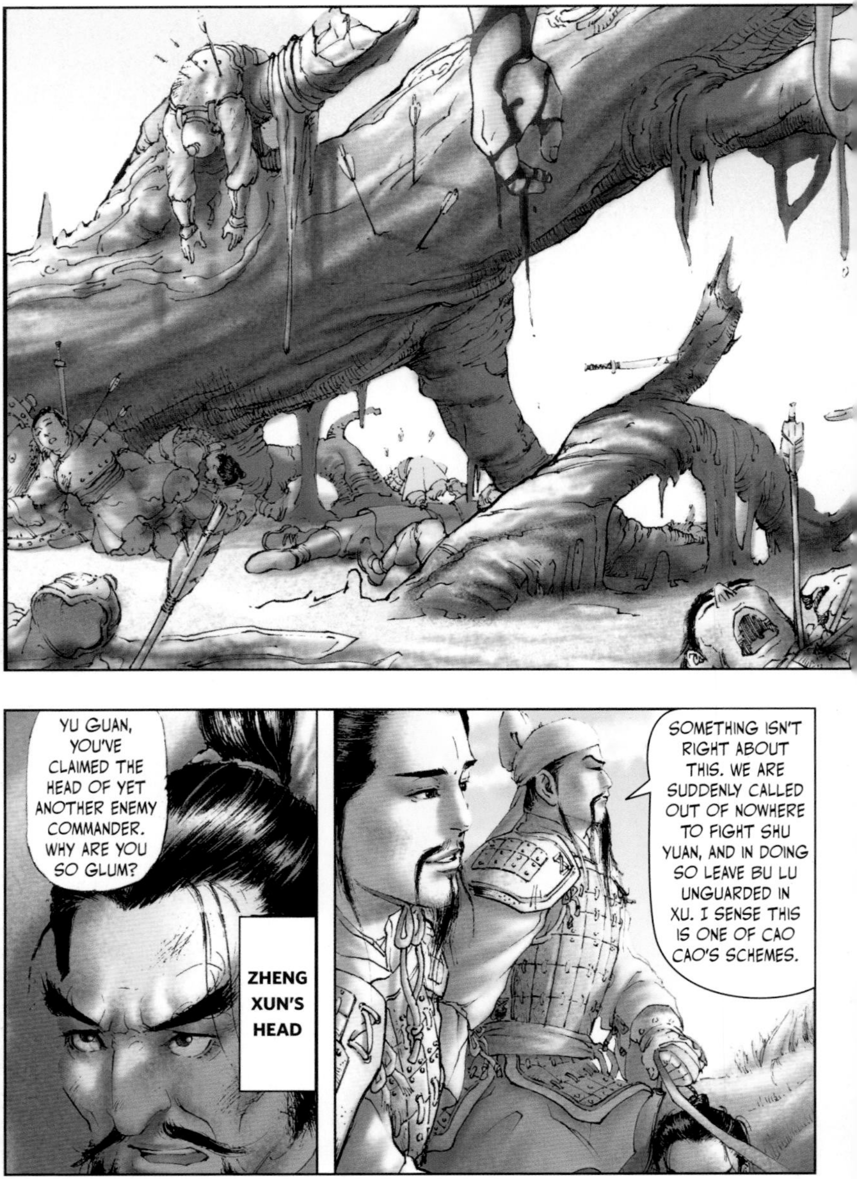
YU GUAN, YOU'VE CLAIMED THE HEAD OF YET ANOTHER ENEMY COMMANDER. WHY ARE YOU SO GLUM?
ZHENG XUN'S HEAD
SOMETHING ISN'T RIGHT ABOUT THIS. WE ARE SUDDENLY CALLED OUT OF NOWHERE TO FIGHT SHU YUAN, AND IN DOING SO LEAVE BU LU UNGUARDED IN XU. I SENSE THIS IS ONE OF CAO CAO'S SCHEMES.

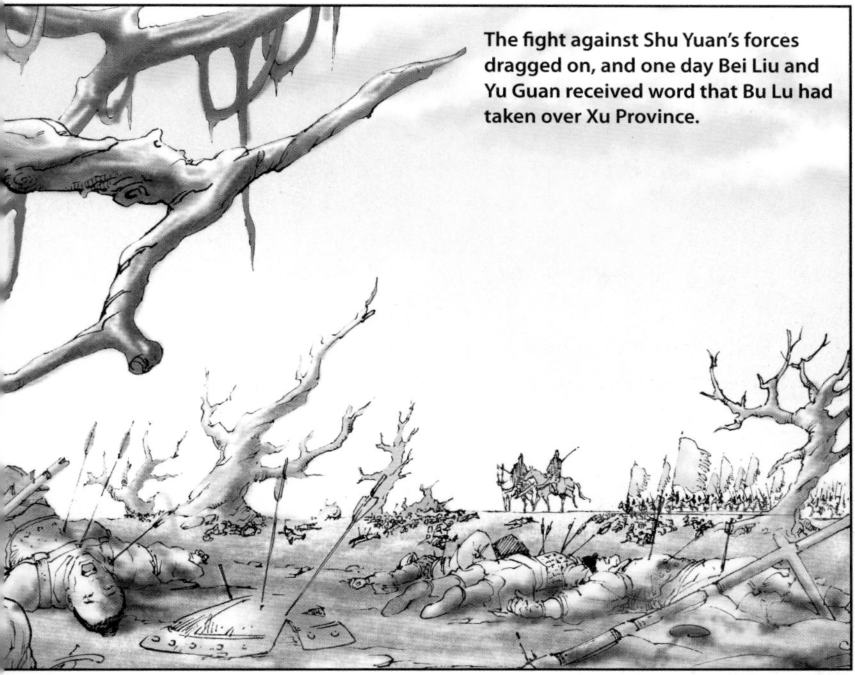
The fight against Shu Yuan's forces dragged on, and one day Bei Liu and Yu Guan received word that Bu Lu had taken over Xu Province.

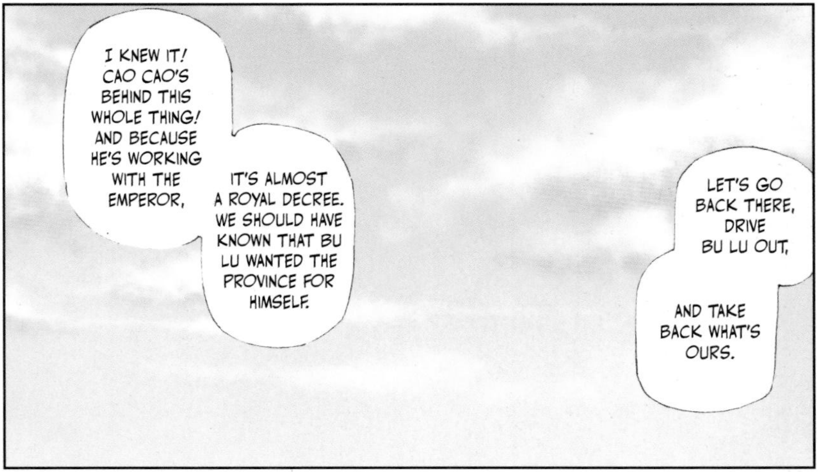
I KNEW IT! CAO CAO'S BEHIND THIS WHOLE THING! AND BECAUSE HE'S WORKING WITH THE EMPEROR,
IT'S ALMOST A ROYAL DECREE. WE SHOULD HAVE KNOWN THAT BU LU WANTED THE PROVINCE FOR HIMSELF.
LET'S GO BACK THERE, DRIVE BU LU OUT,
AND TAKE BACK WHAT'S OURS.

COME HERE, YU GUAN.

THE CIRCLE IS XU PROVINCE. YES?

NOW, UP HERE...

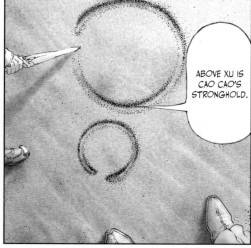

ABOVE XU IS CAO CAO'S STRONGHOLD.

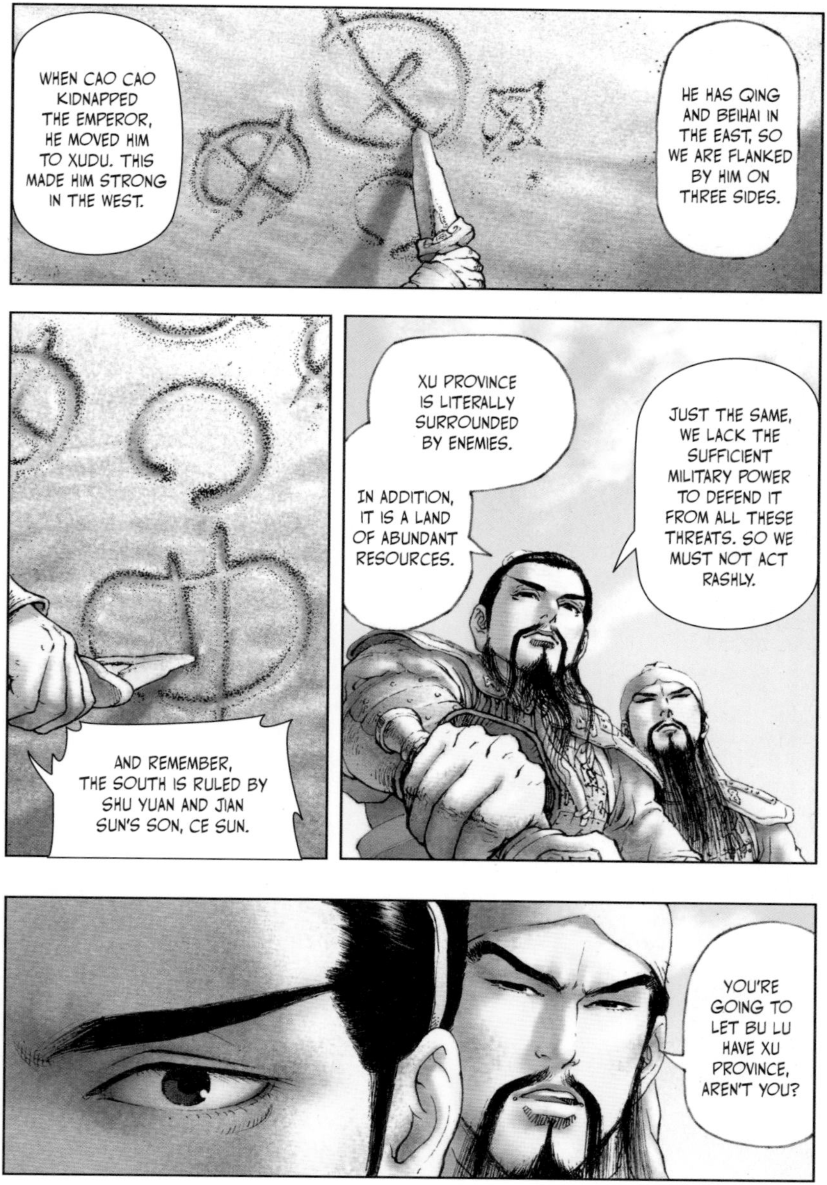

WHEN CAO CAO KIDNAPPED THE EMPEROR, HE MOVED HIM TO XUDU. THIS MADE HIM STRONG IN THE WEST.
HE HAS QING AND BEIHAI IN THE EAST, SO WE ARE FLANKED BY HIM ON THREE SIDES.
AND REMEMBER, THE SOUTH IS RULED BY SHU YUAN AND JIAN SUN'S SON, CE SUN.
XU PROVINCE IS LITERALLY SURROUNDED BY ENEMIES.
IN ADDITION, IT IS A LAND OF ABUNDANT RESOURCES.
JUST THE SAME, WE LACK THE SUFFICIENT MILITARY POWER TO DEFEND IT FROM ALL THESE THREATS. SO WE MUST NOT ACT RASHLY.
YOU'RE GOING TO LET BU LU HAVE XU PROVINCE, AREN'T YOU?

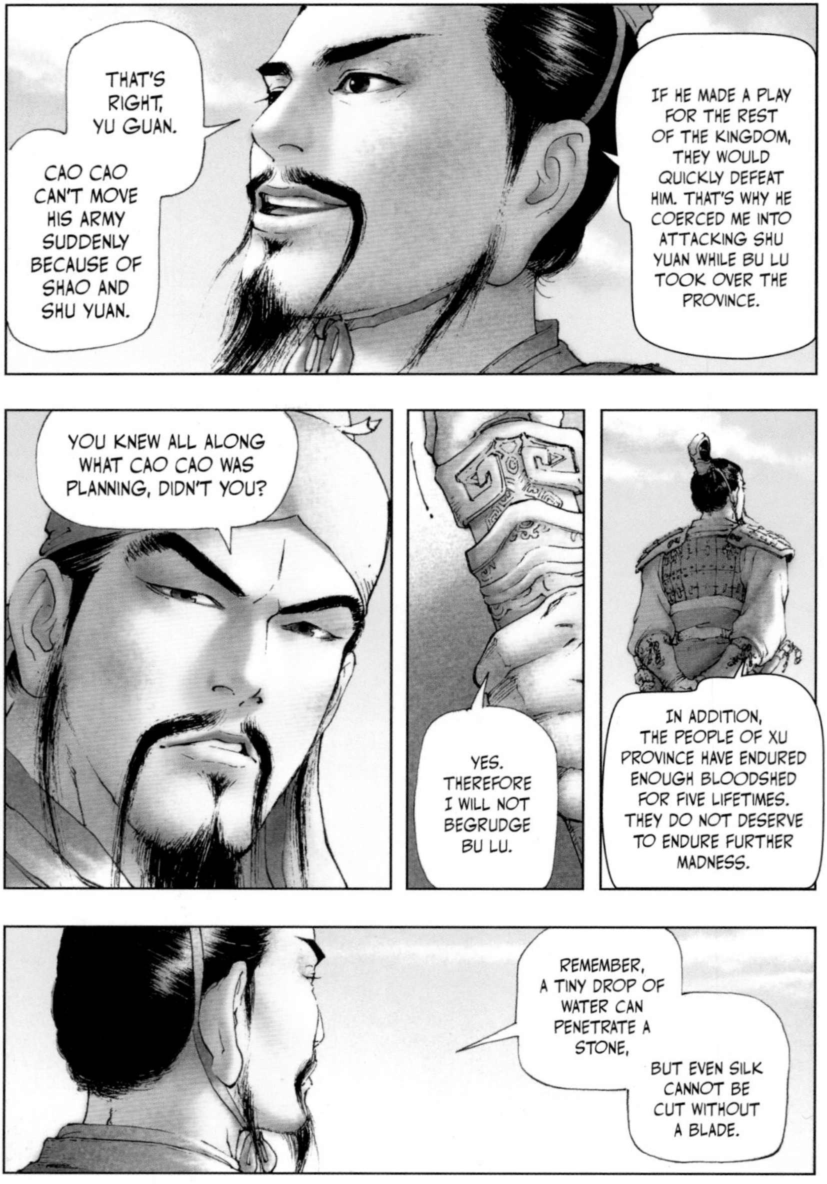
THAT'S RIGHT, YU GUAN.
CAO CAO CAN'T MOVE HIS ARMY SUDDENLY BECAUSE OF SHAO AND SHU YUAN.
IF HE MADE A PLAY FOR THE REST OF THE KINGDOM, THEY WOULD QUICKLY DEFEAT HIM. THAT'S WHY HE COERCED ME INTO ATTACKING SHU YUAN WHILE BU LU TOOK OVER THE PROVINCE.
YOU KNEW ALL ALONG WHAT CAO CAO WAS PLANNING, DIDN'T YOU?
YES. THEREFORE I WILL NOT BEGRUDGE BU LU.
IN ADDITION, THE PEOPLE OF XU PROVINCE HAVE ENDURED ENOUGH BLOODSHED FOR FIVE LIFETIMES. THEY DO NOT DESERVE TO ENDURE FURTHER MADNESS.
REMEMBER, A TINY DROP OF WATER CAN PENETRATE A STONE,
BUT EVEN SILK CANNOT BE CUT WITHOUT A BLADE.

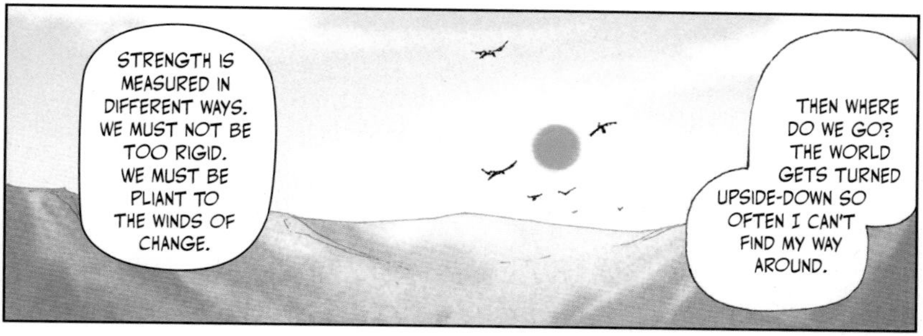
STRENGTH IS MEASURED IN DIFFERENT WAYS. WE MUST NOT BE TOO RIGID. WE MUST BE PLIANT TO THE WINDS OF CHANGE.
THEN WHERE DO WE GO? THE WORLD GETS TURNED UPSIDE-DOWN SO OFTEN I CAN'T FIND MY WAY AROUND.

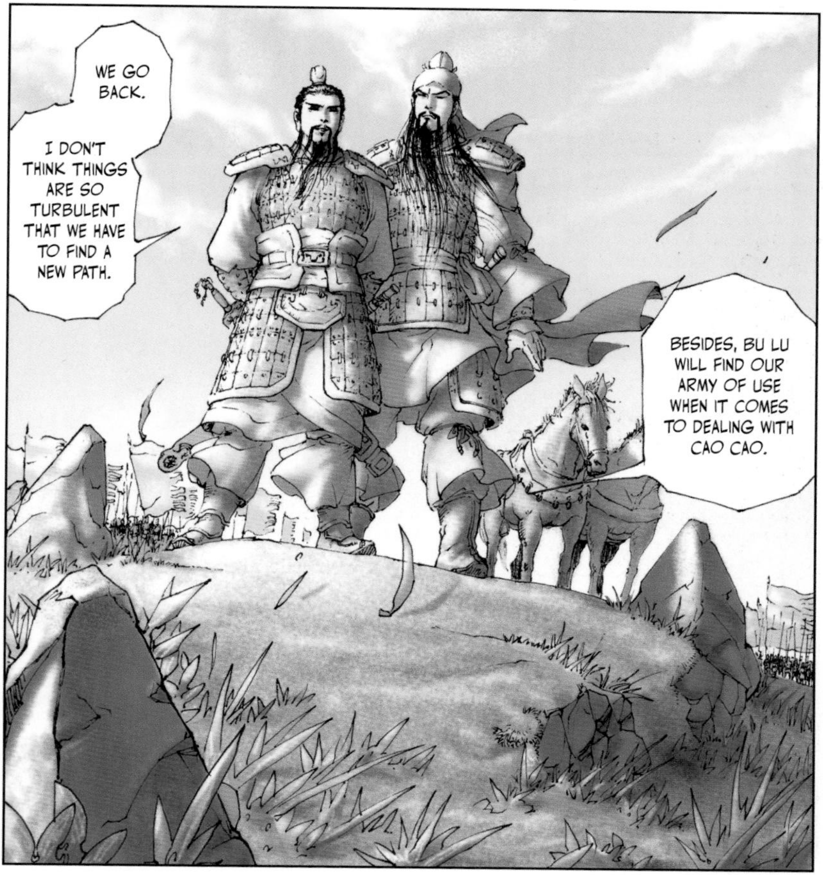
WE GO BACK.
I DON'T THINK THINGS ARE SO TURBULENT THAT WE HAVE TO FIND A NEW PATH.
BESIDES, BU LU WILL FIND OUR ARMY OF USE WHEN IT COMES TO DEALING WITH CAO CAO.

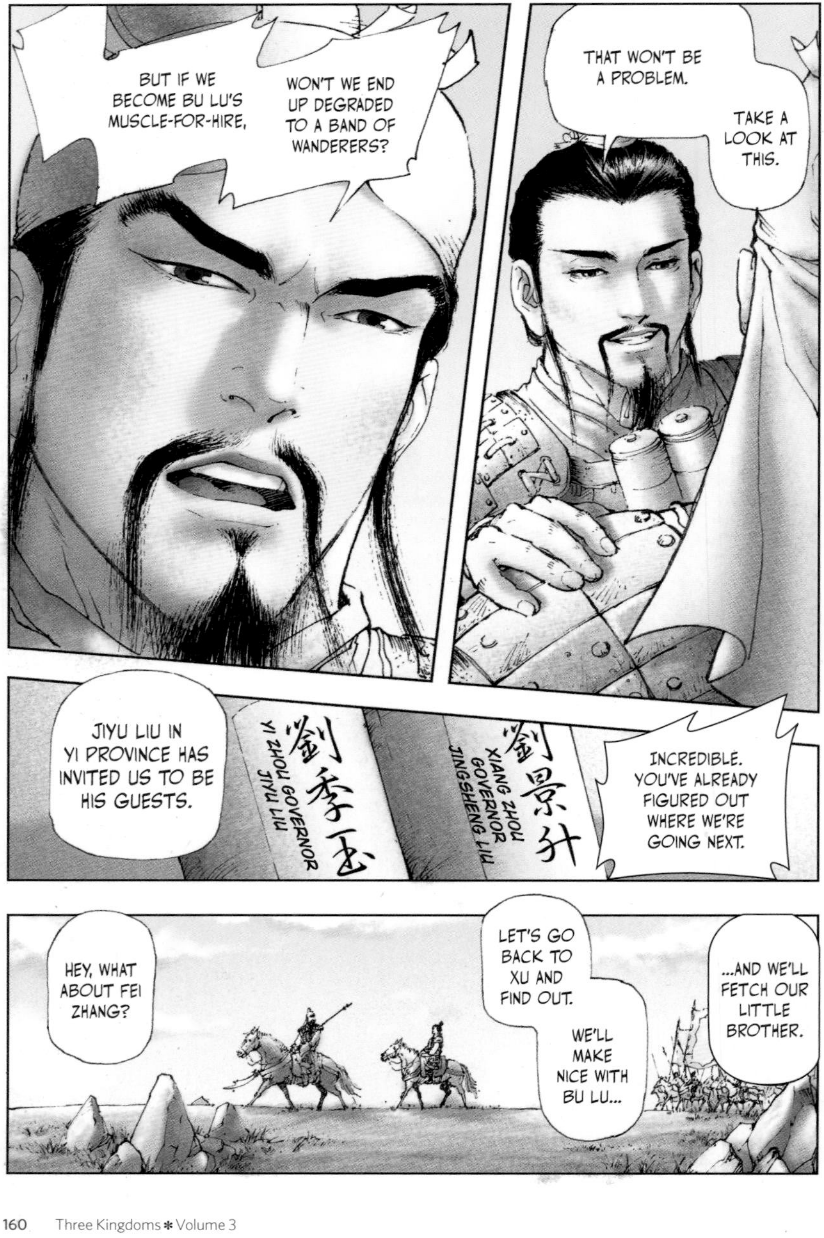
BUT IF WE BECOME BU LU'S MUSCLE-FOR-HIRE,
WON'T WE END UP DEGRADED TO A BAND OF WANDERERS?
THAT WON'T BE A PROBLEM.
TAKE A LOOK AT THIS.
JIYU LIU IN YI PROVINCE HAS INVITED US TO BE HIS GUESTS.
劉季玉
YI ZHOU GOVERNOR JIYU LIU
劉景升
XIANG ZHOU GOVERNOR JINGSHENG LIU
INCREDIBLE. YOU'VE ALREADY FIGURED OUT WHERE WE'RE GOING NEXT.
HEY, WHAT ABOUT FEI ZHANG?
LET'S GO BACK TO XU AND FIND OUT.
WE'LL MAKE NICE WITH BU LU...
...AND WE'LL FETCH OUR LITTLE BROTHER.

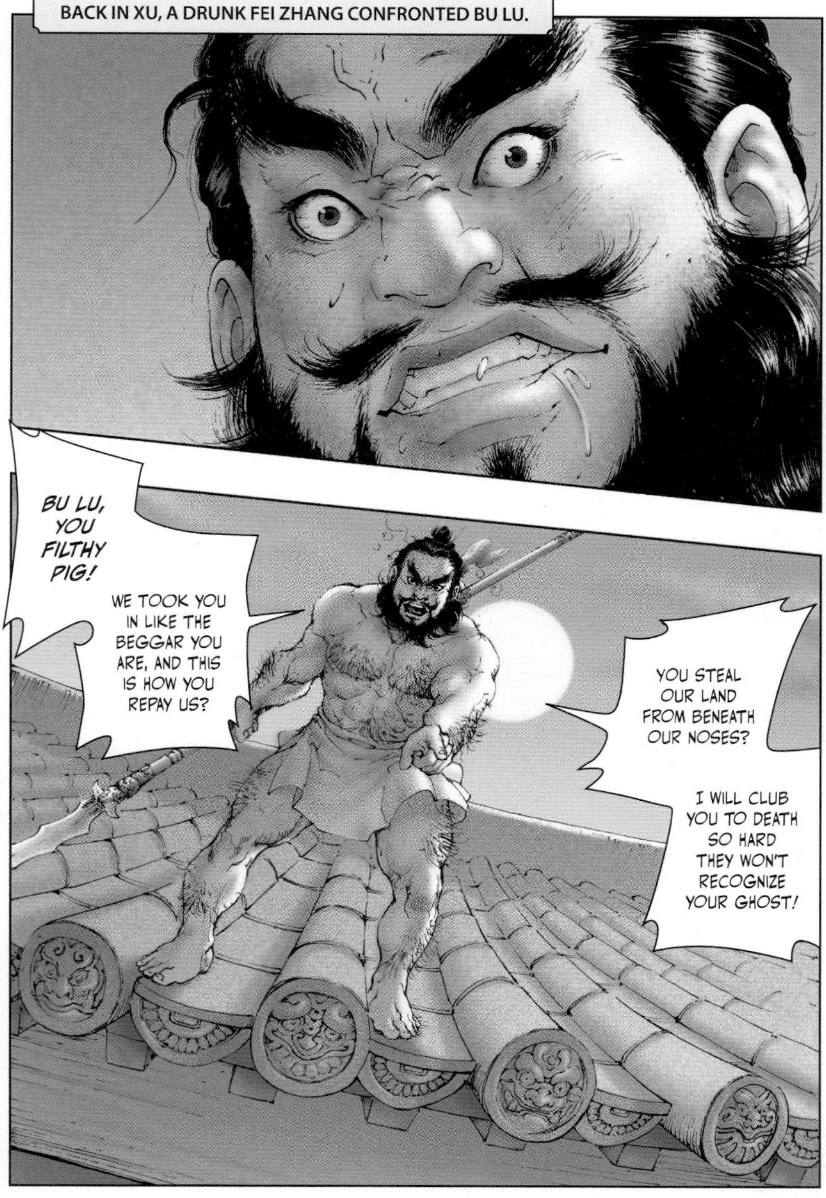
BACK IN XU, A DRUNK FEI ZHANG CONFRONTED BU LU.
BU LU, YOU FILTHY PIG!
WE TOOK YOU IN LIKE THE BEGGAR YOU ARE, AND THIS IS HOW YOU REPAY US?
YOU STEAL OUR LAND FROM BENEATH OUR NOSES?
I WILL CLUB YOU TO DEATH SO HARD THEY WON'T RECOGNIZE YOUR GHOST!

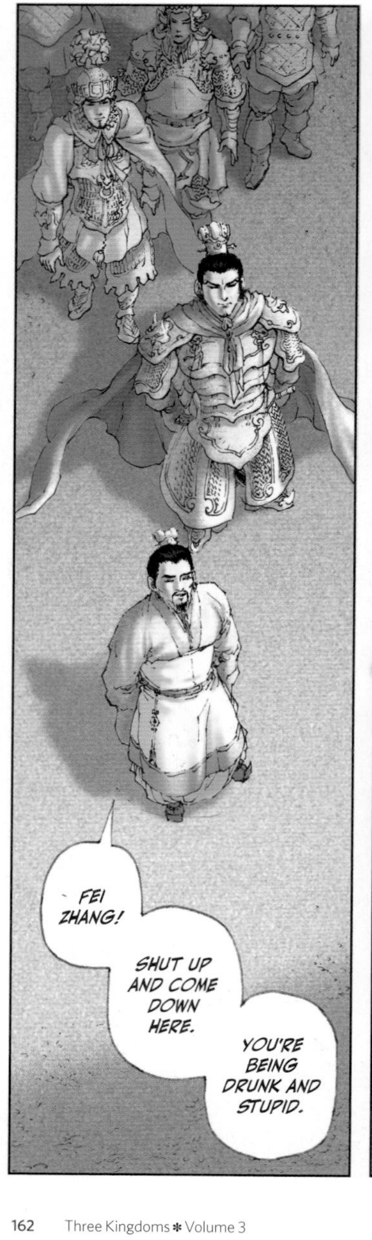
FEI ZHANG!
SHUT UP AND COME DOWN HERE.
YOU'RE BEING DRUNK AND STUPID.

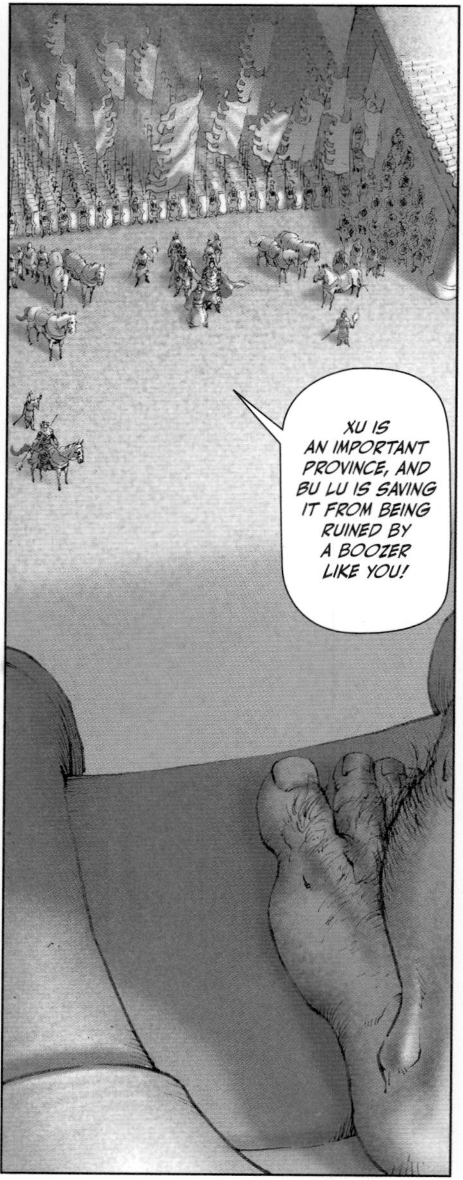
XU IS AN IMPORTANT PROVINCE, AND BU LU IS SAVING IT FROM BEING RUINED BY A BOOZER LIKE YOU!

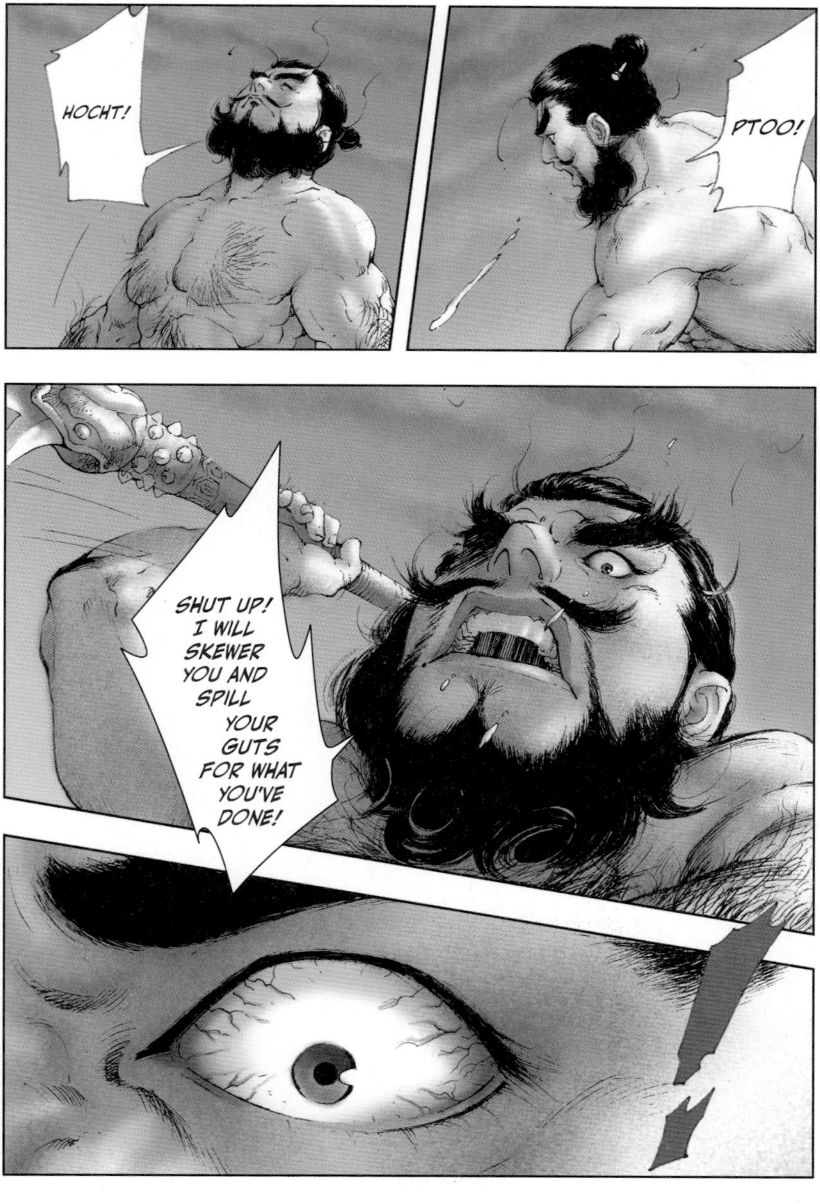
HOCHT!
PTOO!
SHUT UP! I WILL SKEWER YOU AND SPILL YOUR GUTS FOR WHAT YOU'VE DONE!

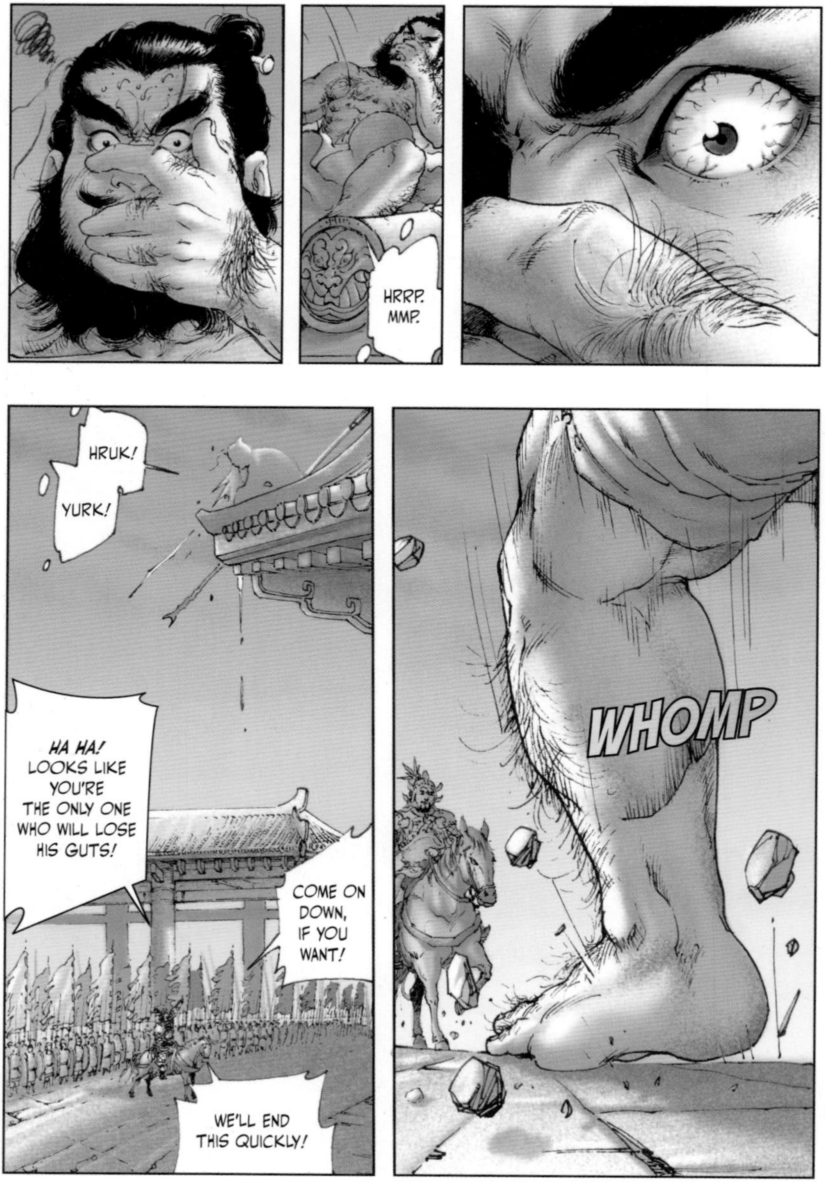
HRRP. MMP.
HRUK!
YURK!
HA HA! LOOKS LIKE YOU'RE THE ONLY ONE WHO WILL LOSE HIS GUTS!
COME ON DOWN, IF YOU WANT!
WE'LL END THIS QUICKLY!
WHOMP

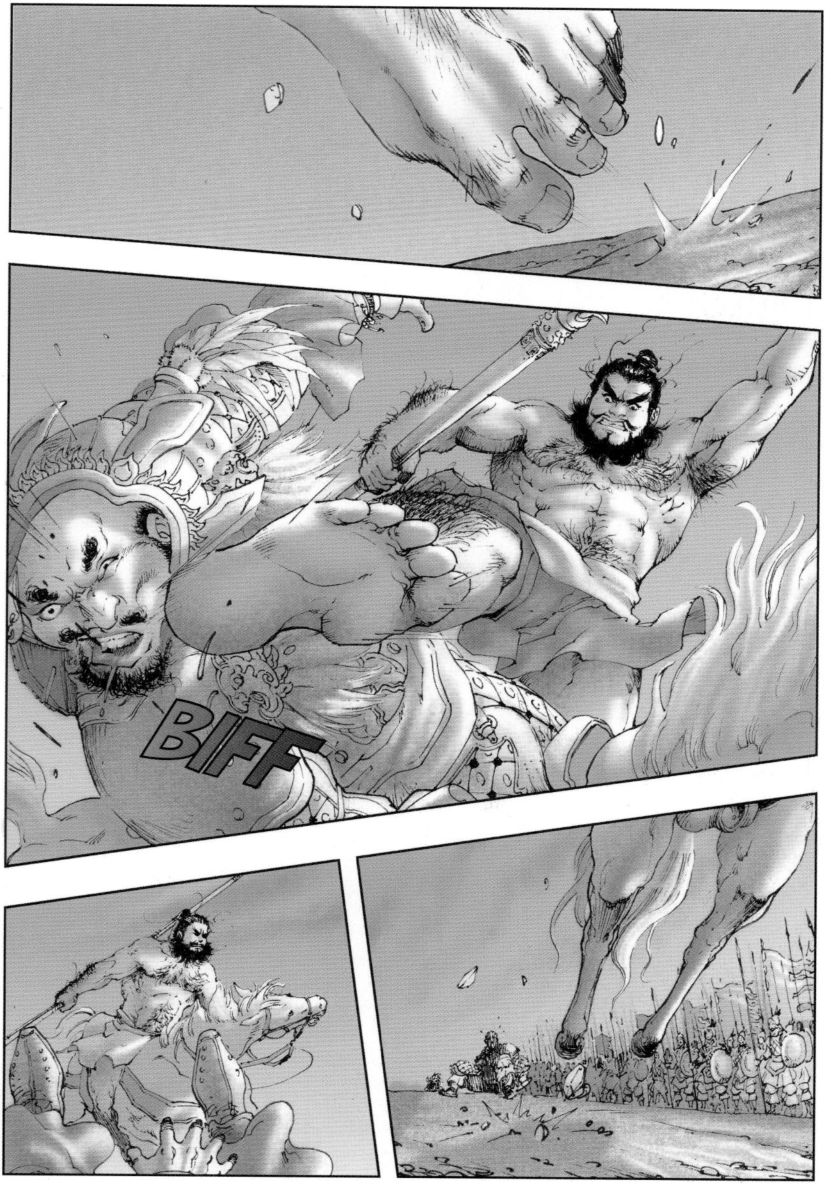
BIFF

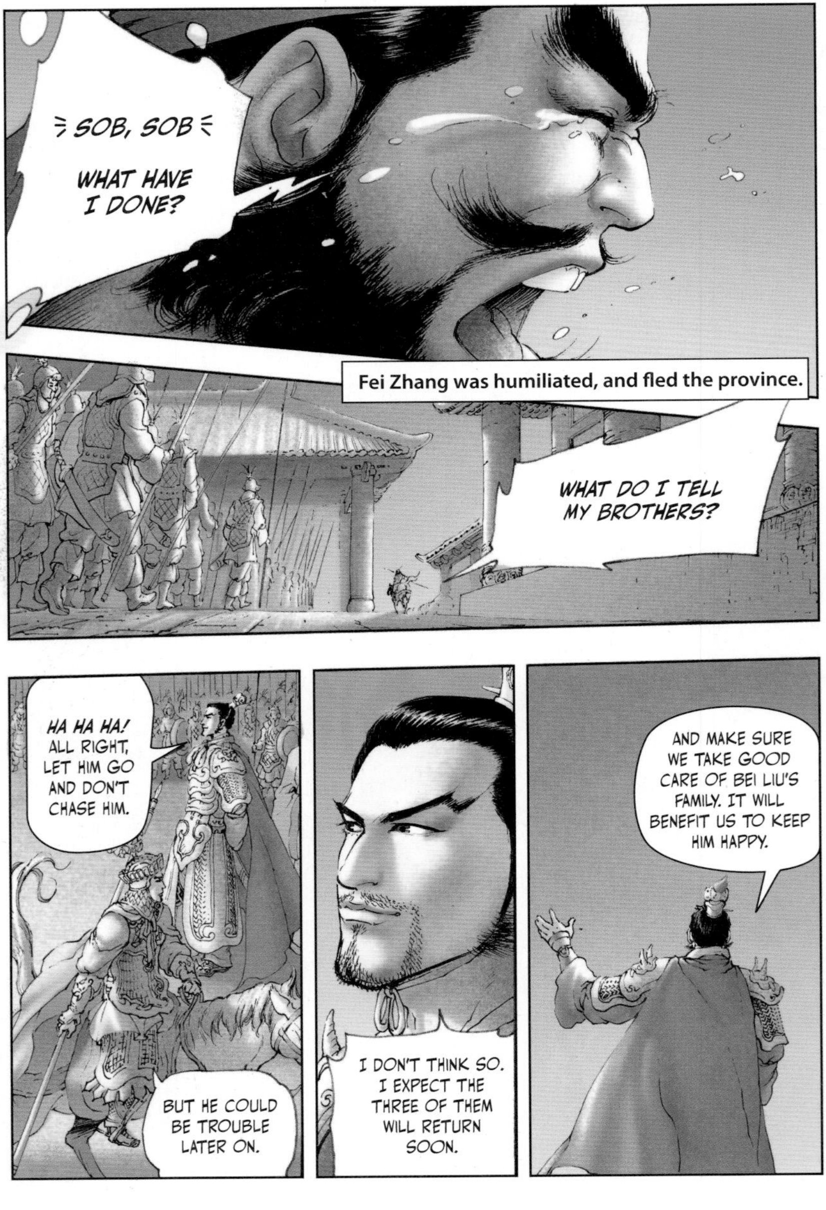

≡ SOB, SOB ≡
WHAT HAVE I DONE?
Fei Zhang was humiliated, and fled the province.
WHAT DO I TELL MY BROTHERS?
HA HA HA! ALL RIGHT, LET HIM GO AND DON'T CHASE HIM.
BUT HE COULD BE TROUBLE LATER ON.
I DON'T THINK SO. I EXPECT THE THREE OF THEM WILL RETURN SOON.
AND MAKE SURE WE TAKE GOOD CARE OF BEI LIU'S FAMILY. IT WILL BENEFIT US TO KEEP HIM HAPPY.

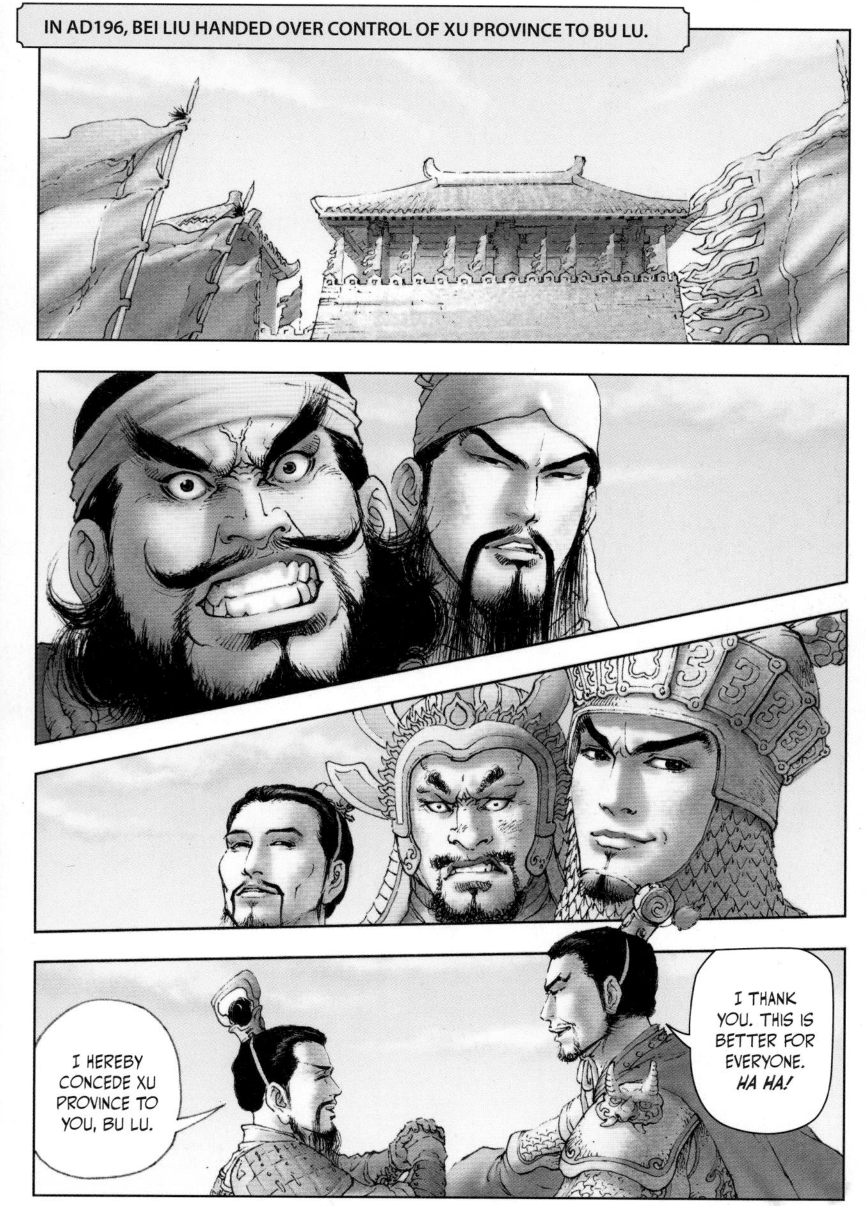
IN AD196, BEI LIU HANDED OVER CONTROL OF XU PROVINCE TO BU LU.
I HEREBY CONCEDE XU PROVINCE TO YOU, BU LU.
I THANK YOU. THIS IS BETTER FOR EVERYONE. HA HA!

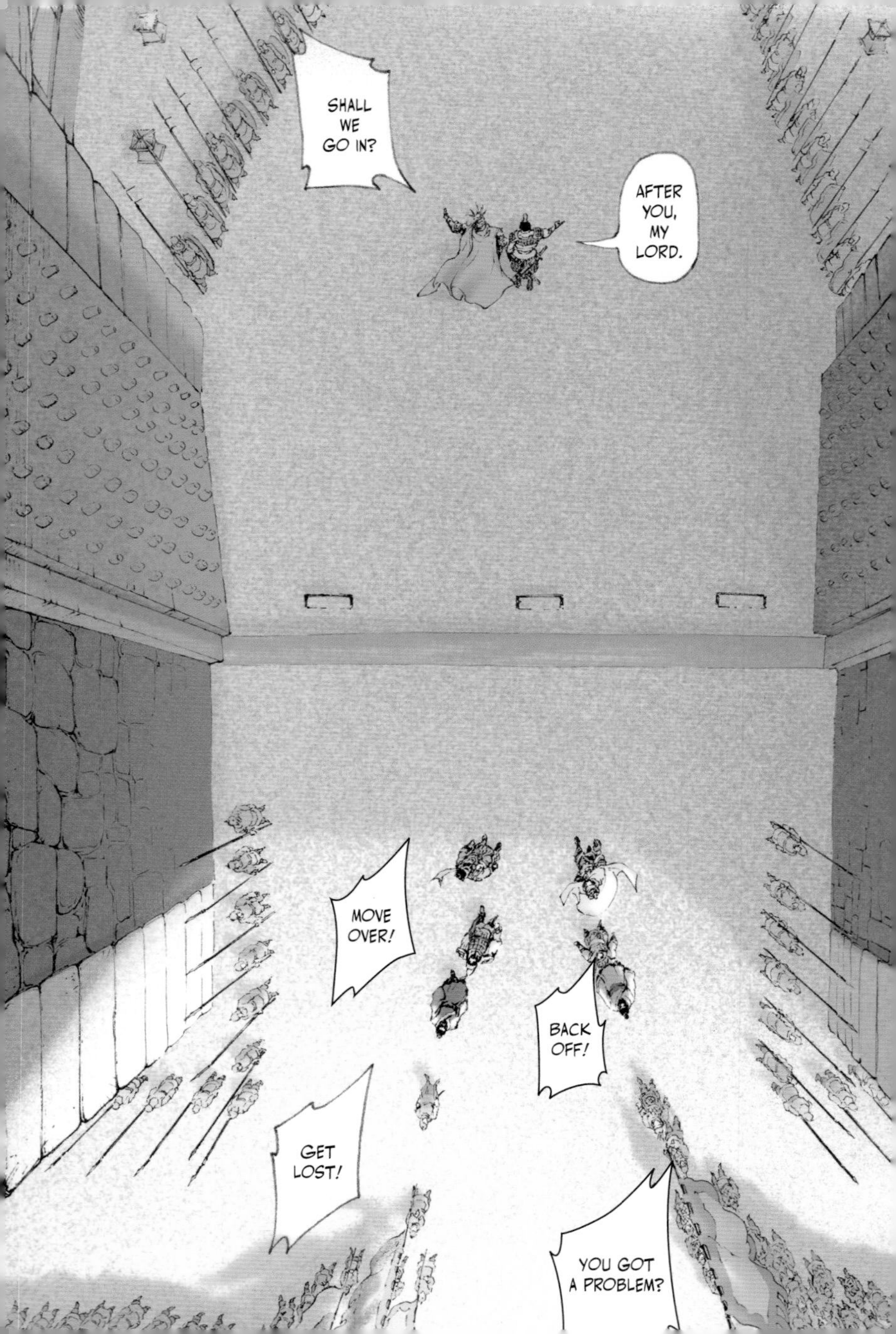
SHALL WE GO IN?
AFTER YOU, MY LORD.
MOVE OVER!
BACK OFF!
GET LOST!
YOU GOT A PROBLEM?

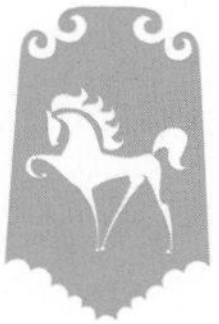

THE POWER OF PERCEPTION

The death of Zhuo Dong has created a vacuum of power in the Han Dynasty. Emperor Xian, who was installed by Zhuo Dong precisely because he was a weak emperor, has fled the capital city, while Zhuo Dong's lieutenants fight each other over what remains of his power. Bu Lu, Zhuo Dong's most senior commander and eventual murderer, has also fled the capital and now roams the countryside looking for a place to call home. Meanwhile, various feudal lords engage in an endless string of regional disputes, attempting to position themselves favorably for an eventual campaign to win the throne.

But the reason these regional skirmishes seem to have no end is because it's difficult to wield power when there is no centralized way of determining authority. That's why allies become enemies so easily, and why land changes hands almost like a game of musical chairs: because there is no single authority that can control the various lords and their ambitions. China may still be under the rule of the Han Dynasty, but its strength has been waning since the Yellow Scarves Rebellion. Despite this, Cao Cao understands something that the others fail to grasp: Even though the Han Dynasty has little real power, the perception of imperial power among the people remains very strong, because at the end of the day everyone understands that they are subjects of the dynasty. That's why Jian Sun claimed the Emperor's Hereditary Seal, because even that small token can create a sense of authority around the one who holds it. That's also what drives Cao Cao's decision to come to the aid of the exiled emperor: now that Cao Cao has amassed tremendous power and an enormous army, all he needs to become the most powerful man in China is the perception of authority. Allying himself with the emperor will not only endear him to the people, it will make it easier for him to manipulate the other lords into fighting one another, thus ridding Cao Cao of enemies and clearing the way for him to eventually inherit the throne.

The power of perception is something visible even today: think about royal weddings in Europe, most especially those in Great Britain. The Queen of England, while still technically the supreme ruler, has little in the way of real power to make or enforce laws. However, when a royal wedding occurs, the whole of the United Kingdom (and most of the rest of the world) turns its attention to a display of almost unimaginable opulence that demands reverence and awe. The royal family may not have any real power, but they remain incredibly powerful.

ZAN GONGSUN

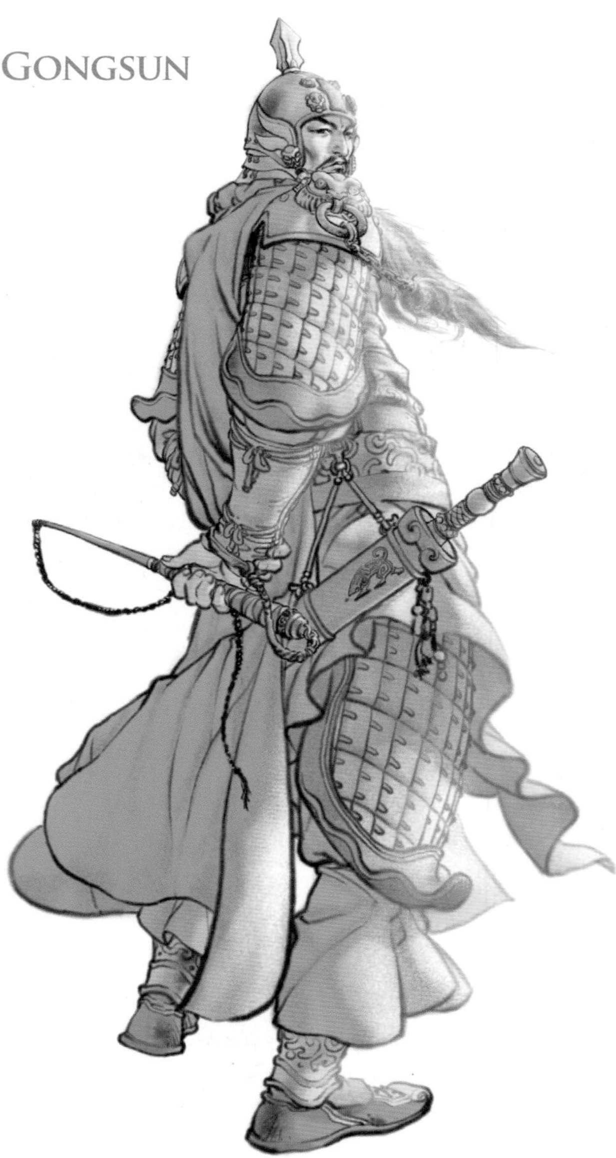

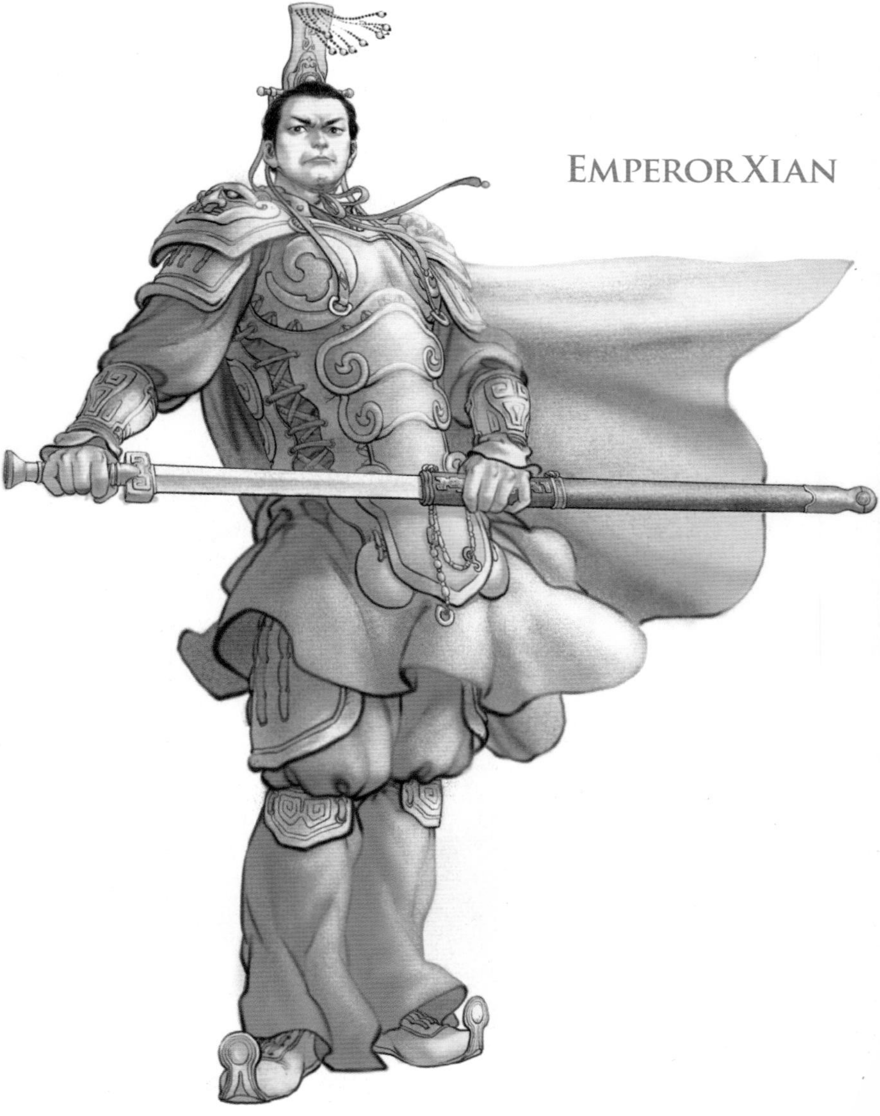

EMPEROR XIAN

Wei Dian

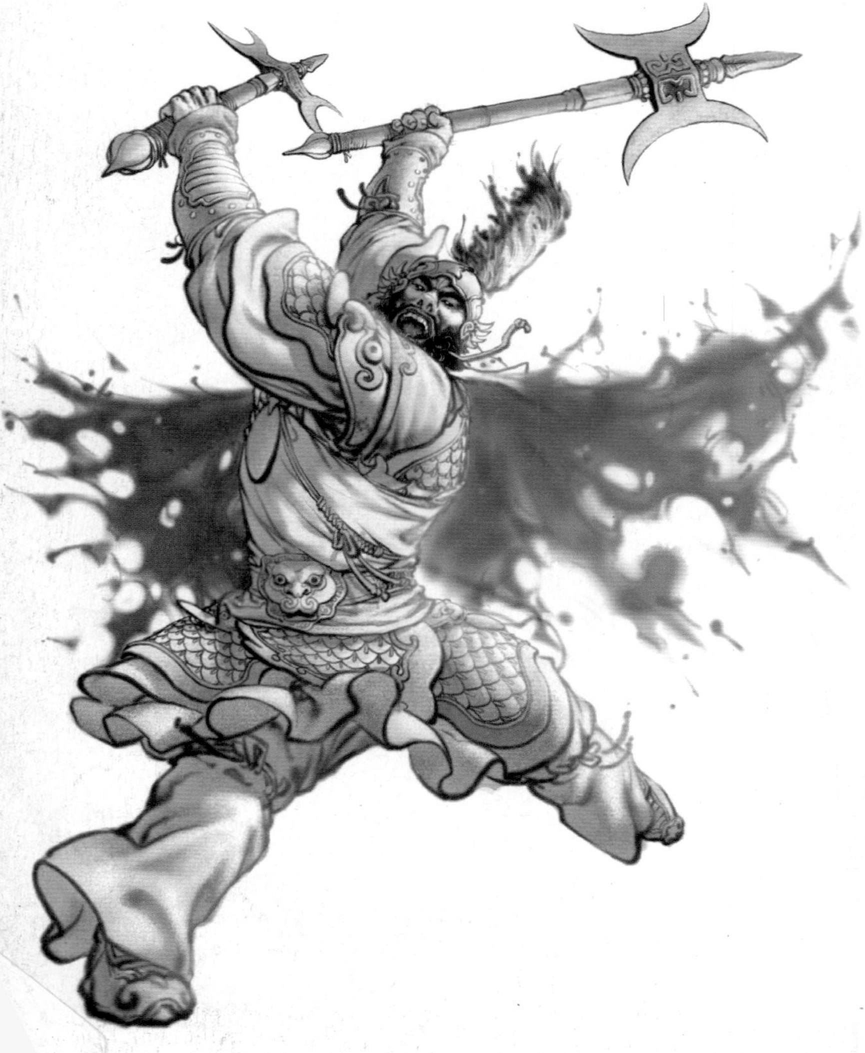

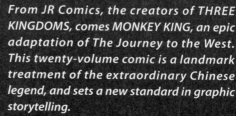

Legends from China THREE KINGDOMS

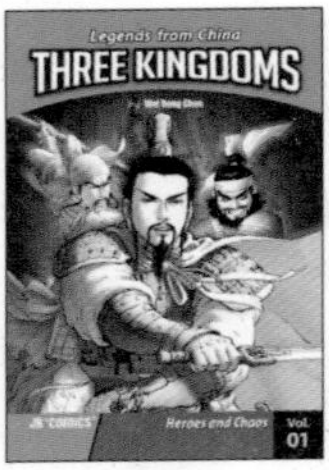
Legends from China
THREE KINGDOMS
Heroes and Chaos
Vol. 01
Vol. 01

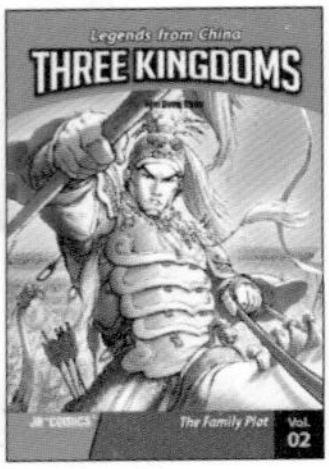
Legends from China
THREE KINGDOMS
The Family Plot
Vol. 02
Vol. 02

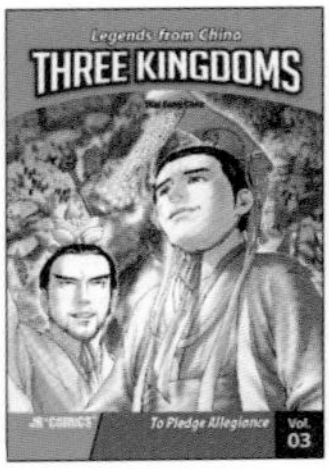
Legends from China
THREE KINGDOMS
To Pledge Allegiance
Vol. 03
Vol. 03

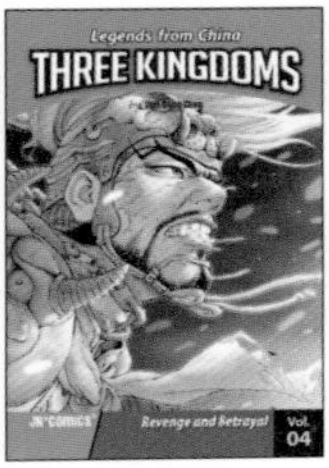
Legends from China
THREE KINGDOMS
Revenge and Betrayal
Vol. 04
Vol. 04

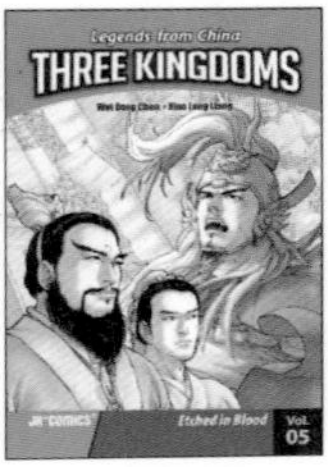
Legends from China
THREE KINGDOMS
Etched in Blood
Vol. 05
Vol. 05

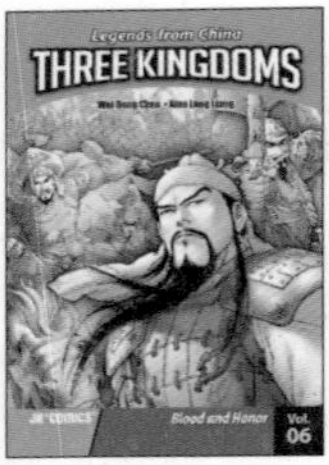
Legends from China
THREE KINGDOMS
Blood and Honor
Vol. 06
Vol. 06

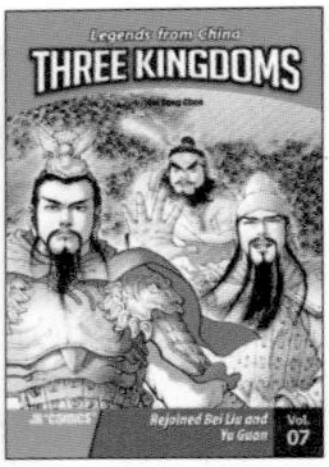
Legends from China
THREE KINGDOMS
Rejoined Bei Liu and Yu Guan
Vol. 07
Vol. 07

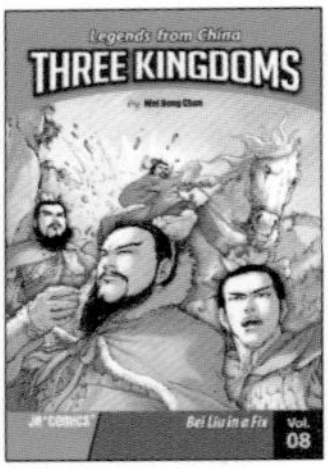
Legends from China
THREE KINGDOMS
Bei Liu in a Fix
Vol. 08
Vol. 08

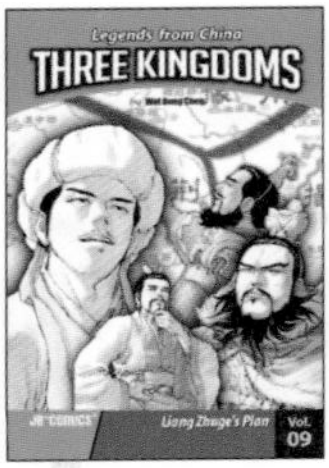
Legends from China
THREE KINGDOMS
Liang Zhuge's Plan
Vol. 09
Vol. 09

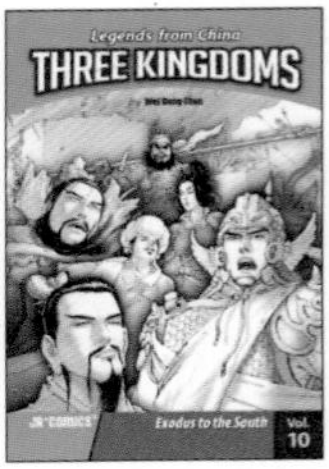
Legends from China
THREE KINGDOMS
Exodus to the South
Vol. 10
Vol. 10

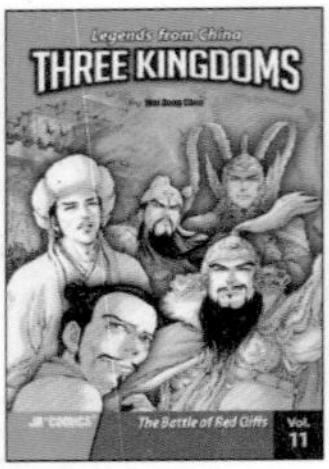
Legends from China
THREE KINGDOMS
The Battle of Red Cliffs
Vol. 11
Vol. 11

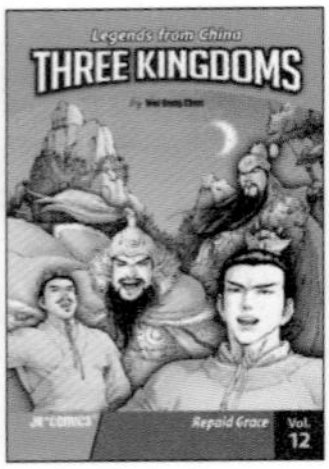
Legends from China
THREE KINGDOMS
Repaid Grace
Vol. 12
Vol. 12

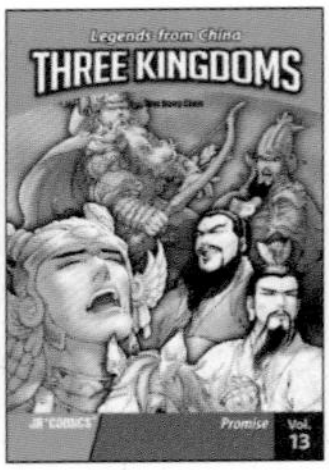
Legends from China
THREE KINGDOMS
Promise
Vol. 13
Vol. 13

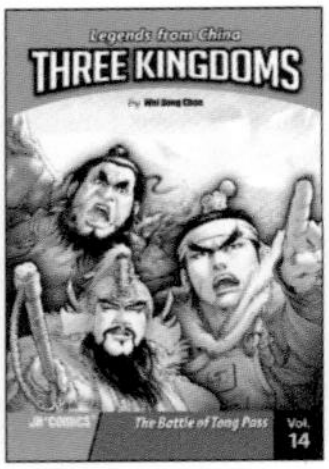
Legends from China
THREE KINGDOMS
The Battle of Tong Pass
Vol. 14
Vol. 14

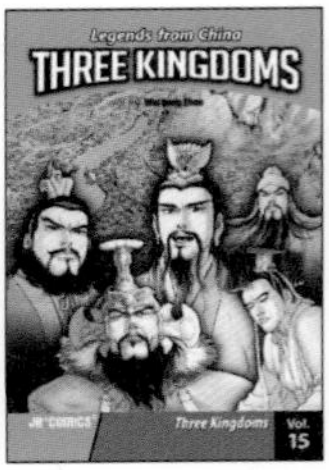
Legends from China
THREE KINGDOMS
Three Kingdoms
Vol. 15
Vol. 15

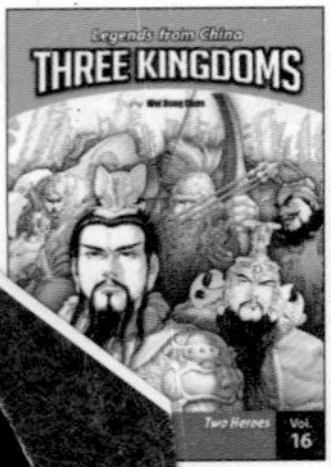
Legends from China
THREE KINGDOMS
Two Heroes
Vol. 16
6

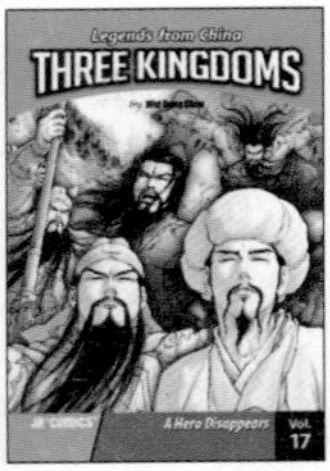
Legends from China
THREE KINGDOMS
A Hero Disappears
Vol. 17
Vol. 17

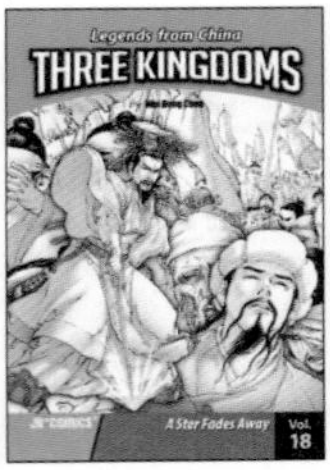
Legends from China
THREE KINGDOMS
A Star Fades Away
Vol. 18
Vol. 18

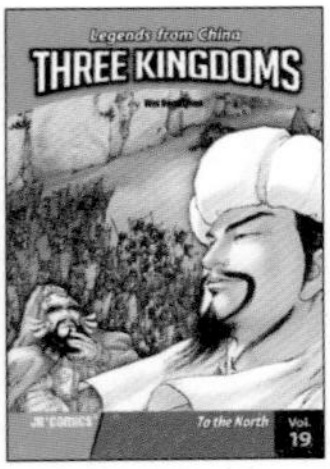
Legends from China
THREE KINGDOMS
To the North
Vol. 19
Vol. 19

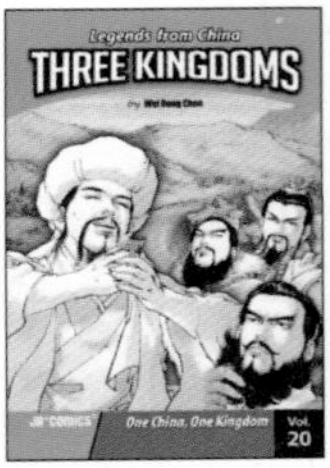
Legends from China
THREE KINGDOMS
One China, One Kingdom
Vol. 20
Vol. 20